FURY

BOOK TWO ECHO

J.L. KELLY

BY J.L. KELLY

The Glory Series

The Psalm of the Offended

The Stripped

The Choice

The Honor Series

The Secret

FURY SERIES

Book one Eros

Book two Echo

FURY

BOOK TWO ECHO

J.L. Kelly

WIDE BLUE sky
long shadow
PUBLISHERS

Fort Worth, Texas

WIDE BLUE sky *long shadow* publishing LLC
Fort Worth, Texas
www.JLKellybooks.com www.4jlkelly.com

Edited by J. Scott Wilson of Piedmont Copy Desk

Cover Design by Danielle De Shane.

FURY book two ECHO/ J.L. Kelly - 1st ed.
ISBN 978-0-9897745-4-3
Library of Congress control number 2014919334

Dedication

To You Love
For repeating lessons
Even the easy ones
So we *remember*
Your grace is amazing
Your presence our peace
Your Spirit our victorious resurrection power
JLK

AUTHOR'S NOTE

PLEASE NOTE: Reviewers agree that my stories are raw, real, sometimes intense and might not be for readers who are looking for the classic "sweet" Christian story where characters do everything right and the story world is heavenly. Unapologetically I was not called to write that way. My style is to write it real—meaning closer to real life, exploring issues of universal importance in a God honoring way by telling the truth in love—so that story may be a tool to inspire spiritual transformation, discover the love of God and His grace & peace in Jesus Christ. My characters will never be perfect but they will proclaim to you the love, grace and mercy of a perfect God.- JLK

I began writing this series of stories about twenty years ago.

A novel started with three adopted sisters, Stephanie, Samantha and Blair. From these characters others characters were born and stories began to spin off.

These character-driven books became interrelated, sharing supporting characters but each with their own stand-alone unique story and theme.

I share this so that you don't get frustrated, thinking there is a **linear time line developing** from one book to the next. In fact, if you started The Glory Series with *The Psalm of the Offended*-Cheyenne & Bennett's story-you have found you've back tracked in time as you begin to read *The Stripped* or *The Choice*, or *The Secret*-a real tangled tale that includes a wide ensemble cast from the family. *The Glory* will take you back even further with the advent of one of the founding sisters, the story of Samantha & Honey. As the *FURY* series will take you forward into the future with Jaxson Cooper's daughter, Jaclyn.

The FURY series builds upon its self; five books involved in one epic tale.

The other stories stand alone, moving back or forth in time to focus on one character's story.

Confused? I hope not. And if you are, refer to this character chart or the glossary.

Character Chart

The Cooper Family

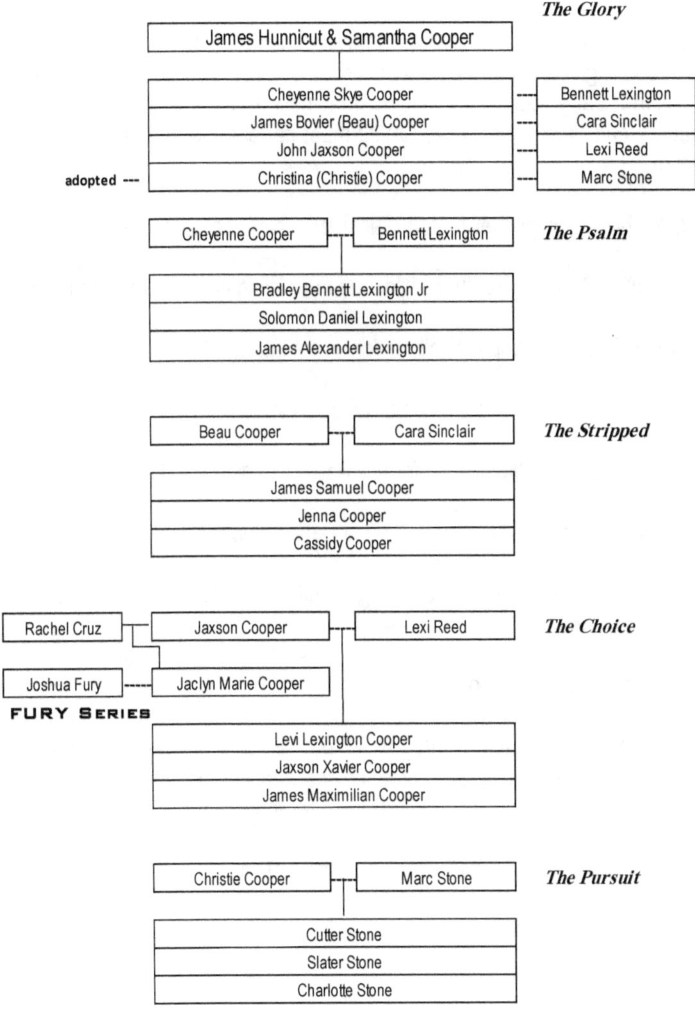

Glossary of Terms and Proper Names

Ares – a depressant drug used to slow or control the intensity of the drug Eros.

Babel – Located in the center of the International Inner Port City, it is the world's tallest building. The tower is the meeting place of the powerful and the world's court of culture. Babel claims to inspire imagination and be the heralded spring of creativity and unity although you must meet certain criteria to be allowed inside its system.

Brett Webb – Ace pitcher for the Washington National's baseball team.

Caleb Fury – Younger brother of Joshua Fury killed in action in Damascus.

Chevaux Ranch – Cooper family ranch in the Texas hill country.

CX Ranch – Jaxson Cooper's horse ranch in North Texas.

Czenky the Bear of Moscow – former Czar of Russia killed by the Viper.

Dr. Herschel Duchovny – medical doctor at *Stratia.*

Dr. Ida DePaul – Eros expert that consults with *Stratia* from the Heatherwood treatment center.

Dr. Lucas – Chief Doctor of *Stratia.*

Eros – a hormone derivative drug used to chemically stimulate a woman's body to lust that was invented by the elite Sheikhs and now is being reproduced by the Russians in a weaker pill form called Cupid for the mass market.

Haifa – daughter of Sheikh Khaeel bin Kalfin Al-Thani.

Harry Olstrom – English born bastard of the Viper.

Heatherwood – Eros treatment center in Virginia.

International Inner Port City - IIPC is the heart of the new world and globally governed. Created from the ashes of the economic global failure and the needs to resurrect a struggling Europe with the oil-rich Middle East. The city is the size of Manhattan. The IIPC claims to be the global seat of power, peace and culture.

Jaxson Cooper – father of Jaclyn Cooper and NFL Hall Of Fame Tight End who now owns the CX Ranch and is married to Lexi Cooper.

Jenna Cooper – Cousin of Jaclyn Cooper and fashion designer.

LaRue – French born bastard of the Viper.

Lexi Cooper – Wife of Jaxson Cooper, stepmother of Jaclyn Cooper and partner at Lexington Law Firm.

Nathan and Denise Oliver – Foster parents of Joshua and Caleb Fury.

Ned Neuville - International law professor at Georgetown Law School.

Rachel Cruz – Famous Singer and birth mother of Jaclyn Cooper.

Red Remmi- Interpol officer at Babel.

Samuel Cooper (Cletus) – Cousin of Jaclyn Cooper and heir of the Chevaux Ranch.

Sheikh Khaeel bin Kalfin Al-Thani- Arab King of vast power, and nobility.

***Stratia*-** the name comes from the Greek *strategos*—a captain or principal, a translation of the Hebrew *Asaramel*—a prince in the court of the people of God. Luke explains them in the New Testament as the Temple wardens, the boundary keepers, a sanctuary security force who historically protected the ignorant, innocent and intentional from touching what was holy and having God's holiness break out against them from the Holy of Holies in His Tabernacle when Israel traveled in the wilderness. They also guarded what was holy from the enemies of God who wished to take it. They were both protector and predator. *Stratia* members are a global group of Saints, chosen for specific purposes and called out from many sectors to contend against evil with a sole allegiance to God as they protect the apostolate—with its arduous duties and functions, and contend against the enemies of the Lord Jesus Christ and His church.

The Bull - Marc Stone is the leader of the support branch of *Stratia* who oversees training of the warriors, supplies, communications, and mission tactics.

The Eagle - Curtis Lexington is the leader of the intelligence branch of *Stratia* who is tasked with gathering, processing and analyzing global information. The Eagle has liaisons with Pearce Harrison at the CIA and Red Remmi at Interpol.

The Lion – Joshua Fury is the lead warrior who carries out the duties of *Stratia*.

The Man - Wisdom- is the unnamed centenarian who administrates *Stratia*.

The Peregrine - Christie Cooper Stone works in partnership with the Bull of *Stratia*.

The Termite – Dr. Lisette Frances is a profiler, military psychiatrist and evaluator for *Stratia*.

The Viper - Yrasrevda Tsilevich A Russian Prince, now the Czar of Russia. Fourth generation *Vor V Zakone*, thief in law. Family originally from the Baltic region of Old Latvia. Often resides at Babel in the IIPC.

Victor Vdmar - skilled Russian tattoo artist that resides in the United States.

Warriors of *Stratia* - Seth Ruthledge (the Kid), Petra, Eli, Pax, Slim and Vin.

Pain Echoes

Things we don't want to remember we can't forget.
Abuse. Failure. Rejection. Betrayal. Death.
We rehearse the hurt- making present the pain-yet to learn
To remember is to "make present" God
Hear the echo of the blows into His glorious cross
evil's wounds now victory's scars.
Love extends the offer
Take the cup and break the bread. Make present my death.
See. Me. Here.
The very worst.
And you, wounded and unable to forget,
Will you not bear scars?
Heal. How.
Make present His promises.
God says I AM WHO I AM, my name forever
Remember me.
I AM Emmanuel. With you God.
With you in the unholy blast
and through the painful echo.
Overcoming. Unable to forget. To stop.
To separate myself from My love for you.
I wait. Until the perfection of time.
To remember. I act.
Despite your blindness. I AM. Despite your understanding. I AM.
Despite the unholiness of the detonation. I AM.
God with you. Always.
Working good. Overcoming the unforgettable evil.
In the worst. I make evil's wounds victory's scars.
Now, you remember. Make present. Believe. Act.
I AM was there. Furious in His jealous love for you.
Remember. Make present. Believe. Act
Collect your stones. Build an altar. Record your story.
Telling 'this was really about that.'
Shout your praise until the unforgettable worst moment
Echoes of His love. His. Love. His Love.

MURDER IS AN ACT OF HATRED TOWARD GOD
FOR MAKING OR ACCEPTING ANOTHER
WHO OFFENDS US OR TROUBLES US
OR IS FAVORED WITH GIFTS AND HONORS
WE DO NOT HAVE OR STANDS IN OUR WAY.
DIETRICH BONHOEFFER

PROLOGUE

Sibling rivalry. He coined the phrase.

The first-born son of Adam was happiest when he was an only child. The delight of his beautiful mother. The pride of his hard-working father. Named "Another Man". He was the second man. The heir of the couple, now a family, Cain was doted upon. He was carried with his parents everywhere. Kept upon his mother's lap, nestled to sleep at her breast, cocooned between the couple. Loved. Like no other child was ever loved. Until "Vanity" was born.

His brother's name a sigh of two sounds. Abel. Crowded him out of his mother's lap. Cain was no longer held. He could walk. For a while he held his father's hand. But Adam's hands were too busy working the earth and there beside his father Cain was trained how to till and weed and plant. How to cut the briars and scourge out the weeds from taking over the crops. He learned to wipe the sweat off his brow from the brutal back-breaking labor. He'd been given no choice for his occupation. He was to be a farmer.

Abel was given a staff to be a shepherd. He walked the fields instead of crouching over them. He sang with the wind at his back as he herded his flocks over the green valleys near the river. The sweat never ran down into his eyes. And the animals were simple to tend, easy to count as they reproduced. None of them were cursed like the ground that Cain tilled. The animals multiplied so easily. All a man had to do was sit and watch them in the shade.

Cain never sat. He squatted in the scorching sun until muscles bulged from his strong back and thighs and arms. He squinted until lines had formed into his darkened face. Every night he came home to the circle of his growing family tired and a little bit more resentful as he handed over what the ground had produced. With each new sibling there was another mouth to feed and more responsibility on his elder shoulders. More separation from his parents. And there were times when he would look towards the Garden of Eden and the flaming guardian at its gate and wonder how his parents could have eaten from the tree of the knowledge of good and evil. Why their God had not put the guardian with its mighty sword before the tree to protect them from the fate of the fall.

His father, Adam, named the choice to rebel sin. And each time they repeated that choice, to choose their own way, to let *self* usurp the place of God, death occurred. His father would kill an innocent of the flock as a sacrifice to cover the offense. And his mother still wept. With her head bowed and her mouth covered, she'd sink at times to the dust of the earth and be inconsolable with grief.

During the sacrifice when he was very young was the first time he remembered seeing Elohim. The Creator had appeared at his mother's side and lifted her face, wiped her tears, set her hand into his father's and given the simple command. They were to *be fruitful, increase in number, fill the earth and subdue it.*

The command was stated again today. His father often repeating what was required, teaching his family the Creator's charge. Resentment gathered in Cain's belly as the girl beside him took his hand. They were to be fruitful, increase in number, fill the earth. Cain shifted away, broke contact with her. He didn't want her, children, more mouths to feed when it was impossible to subdue this cursed earth, make things grow. He swept his family. Looked at Eve, taken from his father's side and formed. That's what he wanted, a woman made for him, from him. God could do that again. He would ask Him at the sacrifice tonight. He would bring his best to Him tonight and when he was blessed, he would ask Him to make him a wife and let them live in the Garden.

Cain hadn't disobeyed and eaten of the tree of the knowledge of good and evil. It was unfair that he was being punished for what Adam and Eve did. It was unfair what was required to bring to the altar. A man should bring the work of his hands to offer as sacrifice. His best grain should be acceptable and received as an offering as the Creator himself had cursed the ground and made them toil to produce it. Cain had to barter for what took three cycles of the moon to grow for the young lamb of his brother's flock. Abel always gave him his pick with a smile. But wouldn't any man smile when he was handed over enough grain to feed his belly and he never had to humble himself and come to barter for what he did not have?

So this time Cain refused to give of his best for what he thought was his brother's less than best. Cain came to the sacrifice with the works of his hands. He had poured the weight of a lamb upon the altar in pure grain. He'd separated it carefully, prepared it kernel by kernel. A field of harvest, a storehouse of seed, blessing of their nourishment to give as the price of his sacrifice. On top of the seed he placed fruit of the vine and the trees, ripe figs and spices, showcasing all the things he had worked so hard to produce. Cain had proudly laid out the bounty of harvest on the altar for God.

And Elohim came among them. He spoke to Adam and Eve blessing them. Then he looked with favor on Abel. His wife was pregnant with their first, fruitful, they were pleasing the Creator, meeting his commands.

Alone, Cain waited patiently to be acknowledged. His work spoke for itself. The fragrance still filled the air with spice and sweetness and would soon have his father calling for them to share the cup of blessing and drink the wine Cain had generously brought to share.

“What did your father teach you about the first sacrifice?” the Creator’s question was asked to Abel but it was clearly heard by the entire family.

“In the garden, you killed an animal and its mate to cover my parents after they had eaten from the tree of the knowledge of good and evil. They knew they were naked and the fig leaves they had worked together to cover them were replaced by a substitute that died in their place.”

“Is that fig you brought to the altar?” Elohim had turned to Cain now to ask the next question.

“Yes,” he answered.

“Were the fig leaves an adequate covering for your parents' nakedness?”

Cain looked into his Creator's eyes and thought about that, then he spoke, "The leaves covered them."

"Was their sin covered from me?"

"You know all things," Adam answered.

Elohim still looked into Cain's eyes. He answered, "I don't understand sometimes. Why it has to be this way."

"My way?" Elohim asked.

"Yes," he answered softly even as his father began to speak loudly.

"We do things God's way. The best works of our hands don't cover our sins, my son."

But Cain had stopped listening. He wanted things his way. Hated God's way. He looked down and away from the bright light of the Creator’s glory. His presence did not bring him joy but shame. His ways did not bring him peace but resentment. His commands did not bring him fulfillment but frustration. He felt her beside him. This eldest sister they were pushing on him to take as a wife. He didn’t want a sister for a wife. He wanted a woman like Eve, taken from his own body, part of him, perfect in beauty. A woman more like Abel’s young tender wife. And Cain deserved the best. He worked harder than anyone else. Was smarter than any of them. Stronger. More generous. More giving. Hadn't he sacrificed enough to all of them? And he'd always be second best. Adam the first man, Cain the second. Cain would never be the leader. And so much was expected of him. Really what difference did it really make anyway? Fig leaves or fur coat? Barbeque or bread?

Cain frowned. He wanted to live in the garden. Return. To a time when it was perfect. God could have stopped the fall from happening. But He didn't. God could make it all perfect again. Now. Start it all over. For them. He had that power. The Creator could do anything yet He let man choose.

Elohim said clearly, "Bring a lamb to my altar, Cain."

Yahweh-Elohim wanted him to go barter with his brother for an animal to sacrifice because the work of his hands wasn't adequate. Cain clenched his fists.

"*Why are you so angry? Why is your face downcast? If you do what is right you will be accepted? But if you do not do what is right, sin is crouching at your door; it desires to have you, but you must master it.*"

"Abel," Cain said softly. "Let us go out to your field."

1

In days not so distant from ours...

The Fury of *Stratia* gripped the hilt of a dagger formed for his palm and slit the throat of his enemy. The body struggled. Death, a horrid sound, the blood warm as it ran onto his hands. He placed the man down gently. Moved forward quickly. Silent. He wiped his face, smelled the metal of blood, his gaze scanning, seeing. Doorways in an alley lined with passages. A small sedan zipped out. He melted into the shadows. A hand signal moved two men. He stepped over the dead. Moved on. Up ahead was the house that served as the barracks of an enemy that murdered the innocent by the hundreds with their sophisticated bombs. They were to attack. Put everyone to the sword in silence. After the point man took out the guard, they slipped over the wall. He met resistance. Three this time. Fast. Messy. Blood was in his mouth, metallic and bitter. He moved on, wiping his blade against his pants, his death grip secure, steady. His gaze seeing, a signal leading others. Inside the house they ambushed. Knives a silent testimony. Then a gun blasted, sounding out an alarm, striking a man on their flank.

The Mission changing as it often did. Silence no longer a privilege and guns were drawn. Fired. It was survival and duty. Kill everyone. Now by any means. They went at it with a vengeance. The dead were everywhere. He was searching for the living. He scanned the room. Saw the man. A turban of black. The mark of a jihadist general. A gunshot. Then an odd sound. The man fell.

Instinct had him shouting. His body flying, taking two of his men to the floor. The three came down hard as a blast rang out. The bomb screeched into his ears. The heat like a tidal wave. Then the metal. It ripped into him like a thousand bullets. Next the blast wind struck, sucking back toward the detonation. Unmercifully the force drawing like a vacuum into a hungry belly. There was overwhelming pain.

Even in the simulator there was overwhelming pain in the bomb's echo as his ears began to scream from the ringing ricochet.

Eli erupted first. It was his nature. His reaction time so acute. It made him a lethal warrior. His passion the hot inner core of his *Stratia* team. He dragged in air like he'd sprinted a mile uphill as he tore off his sim gear and stated with horror, "I shot the general and he blew up! Killed us all. What happened?"

Silence was the answer.

From another warrior there was an agitated snarl. Muscles rolling up as the warrior stood to a neck-bending height. Like a pit bull, Pax was showing teeth. His scarred face terrifying. The lightning bolt of silver that crossed over his nose from brow to lip was a stark contrast upon his tense black skin. "Someone better answer him. You feel me?" There was silence as he rubbed his chest, griped his Virtual Reality headgear with a tight fist in the hologram simulator room. They knew better than to throw it down. The penalty was steeper than the payoff for a moment of temper. The equipment was to be as respected as their weapons.

"They'll tell us at debrief," Petra's female voice was controlled and calm. Her rapier body stood Amazon tall. Her only sign of discomfort a quick rotating of a shoulder. Self-control as steel as her ice blue eyes were sharp with intelligence. She looked at him. "Are we cleared, Fury?"

He gave a decisive nod. She led the team out of the vid chamber, Vin and Slim following. The veteran partners were always in sync like harmony. Whether spear heading or flanking, the pair got the job done. Their silent glances a certain communication. Neither smiled as the Kid gasped, "I can't breathe." His strong young body was still bent over. Face white with pain, striped with red where the mask's tension had married with his sweat. "Something is wrong. Am I bleeding?"

"No." Eli heaved him up, pushed him forward, shielded him from the view window. "Don't give the IT team anything to crow over. Let's go, Kid."

As they stored their gear, Fury processed the drill on the way to the evaluation room. They had failed. He'd fought a dozen. Taken three wounds before the blast. The Kid showing uncommon courage jumping armed men. Taking out their weapons. They'd systematically worked the room, from the center to the perimeter with synchronized teamwork. Done everything right. Keeping to the plan, following orders, going with instinct. He could still taste the blood in his mouth, feel its sticky heat on his skin. Hear the shocking blast ringing in his ears. The bite of shrapnel a mortal wound in his back. The power of the echo, sucking everything up. Since the integration of the holograms, the training vids were getting just a little too real. The IT team had explained the pain kept the drills as close to reality as possible and pushed you past the VR game world to simulated life and death decision making. His body believed it. The adrenaline making it hard to unwind for the evaluation. Fury put his focus on his breathing, took deep long, slow breaths as the mission critique began just thirty minutes from game over.

It was disturbing to watch this part of himself as the action replayed. The ugly brutality of the warrior engaged in war. The violence of the disagreement between good and evil. Whether in preparation or participation, as predator or protector, yielding shields or swords, war was the repulsive rage of sin—often against itself, always against the wrath of holiness. When you put God's people into the devils' world, hatred was going to break out against you.

Seeing the enemy, the warrior felt the energy manifest yet again in him. In the early days the power had come like a gale. A burst of wind filling his sails to a tension, propelling him in the ordained direction. His body had known what to do with the power before he'd been taught. Reacting to evil with alarming responses and lethal accuracy. Innately he killed like a predator. Hands and feet and strength submitting with subconscious precision. His mind categorizing the chilling deeds to black and white, knowing instinctually evil's disguise to look gray and its power to destroy all that was good. The sword was his duty, the strength to wield it his gift. His name a calling of lineage.

He was the Lion of *Stratia.* A vicious and deadly opponent, a leader of mighty men sworn to protect and defend, guarding what is holy and contending with the evil forces against it. His creator had put this foreign hurricane force inside of him. The calm eye, surrounded by the volatile nature of the storm. It was humbling. And Fury found it always an odd aftertaste to witness his own deeds on a training vid as his team debriefed.

That dark menacing zealot was him. That violent offensive force was unknown and mysteriously unrecognized by the familiar core of who he imagined himself to be. A thinker. The need to process and use his genius cerebral muscle too often his thorn in the flesh. At peace he was turtle slow. Aroused, he was lethally reactive, driven, consumed, passionate. At heart, he was a quiet man. A doctor. Who found solace in music, solitude. And often an uncomfortable purpose in his God's calling to a community of warriors.

As the screen went black he looked at his boss across the table. Marc Stone was his commander. *Stratia's* face of strength, they called him the

Bull. It fit his stubborn, hard-headed force of character. He'd once been where Fury was, in the field, the lead warrior. Now he was the voice of Command, and as Marc's thundercloud metal-blue eyes connected with his gaze, he answered their question with his Scottish burr.

"That was a body bomb, lads. It deploys at loss of life. The Zealots are using them in their top leaders. Implanting a stable chemical in a small pod by the heart. When the blood fails to circulate another chemical is injected into the pod. It becomes unstable and boom. You've got a suicide bomb that has the potential to take out everything in fifteen meters with the blast wave." Marc cued the weapons expert. "Give them a refresher course on explosives."

"When a bomb explodes, the area around the explosion becomes over pressurized. Highly compressed air particles traveling faster than the speed of sound dissipate over time and distance for a matter of milliseconds. The initial blast wave inflicts the most damage, and following it comes the high-velocity shockwaves that travel at supersonic strength through organs and tissues transporting energy. This energy knocks you down.

"As the bomb explodes, the bomb casing and shrapnel of nails, screws or components that made up the bomb will be violently thrown outward and away from the explosion. As they strike flesh or structures there can be secondary fragmentation that causes even more damage.

"With the shrapnel comes a fireball of high temperatures, resulting in burns. This heat can ignite fuel sources or flammable materials near the blast as well.

"Finally, at the explosion site a vacuum is created by the rapid outward movement of the blast. This vacuum will almost immediately refill itself with the surrounding atmosphere, creating a strong pull on any nearby person or structural surface after the initial push effect of the blast is delivered. As this vacuum is refilled, it creates a high-intensity blast wind that causes fragmented objects like glass and debris to be drawn back in toward the source of the explosion. A one-two punch. Since a human body is the source, and his death detonates the explosion, the shrapnel can be jewelry, weapons, bones or even teeth."

"So what can we wear to protect ourselves?" Eli broke in.

"In some cases, protective measures may amplify the destructive effects."

A trainer advised, "Being forewarned and prepared is best."

"So you've got us a sensory weapon. To forewarn us, true?" Pax asked.

"Not yet."

The Kid was rubbing his chest. "Honestly, I split in two thousand pieces from that hit."

"You were four meters from the source."

"You blew me up in VR style," he told the lab tech. "I don't know how you did it, but sir, you really blew me apart in there."

"Sorry, Kid. The new magnetic sensory system is powerful."

"Maybe you need to strap on and check it out. At four meters from the source," Eli plucked his tooth pick out and pointed it at the IT man. "My heart jerked around before you had me flat-line, Techy. How many of us went KIA."

"Only Petra survived." Marc answered.

"Thanks to the Fury."

"He shielded us both," Pax praised. "Took us down as he warned of the incoming fire."

"I thought it was a launched missile. Heard a click."

"A click?"

"Yes, sir." He told the trainer. "I heard a click."

"Your instincts are notoriously acute, Fury."

"You mean Divine," Fury corrected. "Let's give the credit where it's due."

"*Soli Deo Gloria*," his team said together. "We take no credit."

"There was no click." The IT tech crossed his arms.

"There was. Fury don't bear false witness." Pax was in a protective snarl.

There was a debate. Facts and Intel discussed. They knew enough to simulate. To give them a horrible taste of evil's new trick. He wasn't afraid. *Stratia* would work the problem. Prepare them for the worst. Train them to be the best. God would take care of the rest. He was faithful to arm the warrior with strength. He listened to the recap. Agreed with the trainers' assessment. Until they suggested they report to Lucas for a medical evaluation.

"I'm feeling better, sir." The Kid popped to attention. "Totally, recuperated. All those thousand pieces put back together again. I'm fine. Just fine, sir. Right as rain. It was only the aftertaste of adrenalin, sir."

"Report to Dr. Lucas." It was a command not a suggestion. "All of you." The Bull growled. He led the procession into the granite carved hall of the Command center deep underground. Carved from rock, with stainless walls, the place was like a sublevel fortress. They passed the amphitheater-style control room. Its semi circles of video screens showed the world in real time as operators spoke to those in the field. Elevators took them up, to offices and the private hospital wing as Eli blistered the Kid. Advised him to keep his simulated wounds to himself.

"Insult to injury," Eli clamped down on the toothpick. "They knew that was coming. The mission was 'game over' the minute the Sheikh was dead. Now you got us with our pants down, Kid. They get the opportunity to sweep out the corners and dust for cobwebs. I hate those docs."

"Let us not forget they save lives, Elijah." Petra was looking up at the elevator numbers.

"No one is wounded, Sis."

The bickering began. It was part of the chemistry of his team being a family. He endured it. Just as he stepped out first and led the team to follow orders. He was trained as a doctor, hated to be a patient. The poking and prodding. The tests and the small talk.

"Have you heard from Jaclyn?" Dr. Herschel Duchovny was bold enough to begin the minute the door shut them inside for the private examine.

"Her father."

"It's been two weeks since she left."

He only nodded. The doctor's gaze held his. Confused. He glanced at the glass wall to ensure their privacy then he leaned closer, whispered, "But she's your wife."

He was silent.

"You told me. In Hebrew. Remember? The marriage is between you and her father. Not to be revealed yet. Especially to her. A sacred covenant. Because of the Eros. That drug is wickedness. The lust the two of you fought through on your secret wedding night—

He made a sound. It was a warning, low and dire. Duchovny only raised his manicured brows over ridiculously stylish eyeglasses. Fury spoke. "Are. You. Done."

"Almost." Immediately he got busy. A pin light to his eyes. Checked the pupils' reactions. "Headache?"

"Absolutely." The word had a sharp edge, a tight T.

"You added to your tattoo." With his stethoscope he touched the new extension of the artwork. It came from the sacred symbol of his position, that roaring symbol of wind and lion that banded his right bicep and shoulder, marked him as the Fury of *Stratia*. The new ink curled like a wingtip brushing over his heart. Hidden in the markings was a name. In Hebrew. His name for her. Sacred. Duchovny pressed the instrument there, listening to his heart. "Maybe I should get a tat. What do you think?"

"Curious George?" he suggested.

"The monkey." He laughed. "That's good. He dressed like a doctor once, I think." He used his PDA, thumbs tapping keys. "Yes. See." He showed him a picture of the monkey.

The Fury's electric blue eyes glanced up with impatience. "I was kidding."

The doctor pocketed the phone, then asked, "Has Jaclyn's skin healed from her tattoo removal?"

"Her father tells me, yes."

"We did a good job with that." He smiled like it was a favorite memory. "Working together. That high-tech laser is remarkable. To take off those heinous Russian markings. Who would have known they would booby trap their art with poison and we'd almost kill her," he cleared his throat. Their gazes connecting, the doctor wise enough to be very afraid to continue any further with a discussion on their enemy's mark. "Any side effects from the poison?"

His nonverbal negative only had Duchovny asking more. "Any symptoms of lingering serum sickness from the anti-venom we gave her?"

He exhaled the no this time.

"Any nightmares? You know post-traumatic stress disorder usually shows up in re-experiencing symptoms—flashbacks, nightmares, frightening thoughts. Words, objects or situations can trigger re-experiencing from the subconscious. She could have very serious symptoms that go away in a few weeks or she might not show any symptoms for weeks or months. Then wham! Like a bomb. Detonated with a word. She's freaking out over the rape."

Fury lifted his gaze to Herschel and felt his flesh ignite in his impatience. He had his own PTSD flashback. Jaclyn dying from the poison. Him searching for the source. Cornering Duchovny in a supply closet. His flesh roaring with temper, slammed Duchovny into the wall, stripped him, searching for Russian tattoos. The man had been clean, except for the scars from a whip across his back. The brutal torture leaving the marks of persecution for his faith. Earning Fury's immediate respect and repentance.

He'd sinned. Stepped outside of God's direction. Used his own wisdom trying to save his wife. Fallen under the impatient drilling of a righteous man who had no control of his tongue or awareness of social graces or personal boundaries. He'd not fall again into the trap just because the man was slow to sanctify himself. Fury clenched the examining table, so he wouldn't use his hands to shut him up and thought about Duchovny's scars of persecution to widen his mercy.

"People with PTSD can feel emotionally numb, especially with people they were once close to. You should warn her father. And yourself. She might try to stay on the down low as she deals. Close you off. Avoid intimacy. That's why she hasn't called you. You should contact her."

His muscles clenched.

"And watch for avoidance symptoms. Hiding out. Feeling guilt, shame, worry, depression. Losing interest in things she's always enjoyed. Having trouble sleeping or remembering the event at all. That's common. Or she could go hyper-aroused. Startle easy. Be on edge. Angry outbursts. These symptoms will stay constant instead of being triggered. Tough to deal with and make it hard to do daily task or even concentrate. She'll probably need psychotherapy or a round of antidepressants could help."

"Ida is treating her."

"Then I'll discuss it with her—

"No." He made a distinct boundary. "She's not *Stratia.*"

"She took the job. Didn't you hear? Ida's consulting for us now on the growing threat of Eros. That drug of violation is the worst evil. The very worst evil to possess a woman's hormones and make her go into heat like an animal."

"Miss Cooper is a civilian and not your concern."

"*Mrs. Fury* is a priority to me. I care—

"Mr. Cooper is caring right now. She's to be with her father to heal. That's the covenant. The priority, Duchovny."

"And your priority?" he questioned.

"Keeping her safe."

"Any Intel on the Viper?"

Fury growled. His whole body going hot.

"Sorry! Sorry, I forgot, we don't say their names. Him, I meant, lower case h-i-m, lower form of life, slithering evil, spawn of a snake, him. I meant him. I'm still learning not to call them by a name. Give them any glory. him."

He clenched down on the energy, said with much control, "She's safe."

"You doing okay?"

He just rubbed his head.

"I can give you something for the headache. The heartache . . . well." He gave a smile that knew too much.

Fury stood. He was finished with tests. Finished with this discussion. Done with the patience drill. Sometimes you just needed to run before you killed someone.

He yanked the black shirt over his head, slid his shoulders through the tension of the high tech material, making his way to the door and wondering at his moment of insanity when he'd allowed Duchovny to overhear the sacred. That's what conviction did. Conviction had made him speak the Hebrew words out loud in his hearing, knowing the completed Jew knew what he was saying. Conviction had extended the trust to create the necessary unity he'd broken in his sin with the doctor of *Stratia* in his rage to save Jaclyn from the venom.

Now he was *convicted* it had been a huge mistake. How could this man with a mouth on constant flow keep any kind of sacred secret…

"If you need to talk."

Now he growled. Low and lethal. "You need to stop. Talking."

The rebuke only made the young doctor cock his chin and grin.

A broken jaw would have to be wired shut. Fury escaped before his pride took control.

2

"Mom?" Jaclyn Cooper held tightly to the large ceramic mug of hot tea, her breakfast hardly touched, her appetite nonexistent. Her body on an overdose of numb with a fuel tank of empty when it came to energy. Words were few, conversations circling around safe topics like the weather. How long could this go on. . .

Lexi immediate set down the paper thin computer tablet, gave her full attention. "Yes."

Everyone was so over attentive to her every whim. Standing on the balls of their feet for an impending something. It made her feel guilty. Another problem to deal with.

"Would you mind if I redid my room. Packed up the high school stuff and cleaned up the walls a bit?"

"Redecorate the shrine to the All-American Cheerleader flying ace?" Jaxson acted astonished as he crunched on bacon.

"Not if it makes you sad, Daddy." She backpedaled immediately.

"Of course not," he assured, holding out the end of the bacon for her to finish. She did. To please him. "I love the idea." He took her hand.

"It's a wonderful idea." Lexi took her other hand. "Should we call your Aunt Cara, ask her for ideas? She'll fly up. Do what she does best—interior design a new masterpiece in fourteen by fourteen space. Bring the girls. They'll love the trip."

"Sure." She gave a nod. "I'd love to see my cousins. Maybe Samuel would come too."

They both squeezed her hands.

"How are your levels?" Her stepmother asked the all-important question about her hormones as she picked back up the tablet to read. The Eros was still sending her cycling in abnormal directions that Dr. Ida Depaul was keeping a close eye on through daily blood tests.

"Fine," she answered vaguely, rubbing her fingertip. Even the finger pricks for blood tests no longer hurt. Her levels were up a bit. She didn't want to talk about her LH. Or how she was feeling today. Or that she woke up screaming again from a nightmare she couldn't remember. She might never remember the facts. Ares, that blessed narcotic, had kept her in a dream world, detached for most of the horror Viper had put her through. She remembered the addiction, the need for the needle prick of Ares more than she remembered the details of what the Eros had driven her to do with him.

But some part of her knew. It woke up screaming. It put that look on her little brother's face as he raced into her room. Placed heartache in her father's voice as he comforted her. Created an urgency to bathe and face the fact that no matter how hot the shower was or how strong the Dial soap, she never felt clean.

She was ashamed. Was Joshua? Is that why he didn't call her? He was ashamed of what they'd had to do together to fight off the Eros. The thought made her extremely anxious. She touched the cross around her neck, Joshua's cross. He'd given it to her, refused to take it back. She'd never take it off. "I'm going for a walk."

She was home, she repeated the words with a sigh into the sunshine. Putting her hands in the pockets of jeans gone loose and wondering where to walk. She just couldn't make a decision about anything. Kept feeling stuck. On pause. Life on hold. Frozen. Numb. Please help me, Jesus.

She rehearsed her prayer of thanksgiving. She was home. Rescued from the Viper's hell. Redeemed from his venomous poison and given life. Returned to her family. Joshua Fury had found her, freed her, fought for her, then almost casually, said goodbye and released her into her father's care. She'd been given a second chance. She was overwhelmed at the grace of God. Grateful. Praise remained on her lips. A smile tight to her face. Her mind fixed on what God had done. Fixed and frozen to look no further back then the great victory. She was home. Help me, Jesus. She still felt trapped in a new type of hell.

She strolled through the sunshine. Fall was late to arrive to Texas. It was still hot here on the CX Ranch. Washington had been chilly for weeks. She watched their weather. Wondered where Joshua was. He must be fighting on another mission for Stratia. When he was back, he'd call. He would. She knew he would. He'd call her. Soon. Once he was back. He'd call her. Please keep him safe, Jesus.

"Hello, senorita." The words startled her. She looked up. In the barn. Her father's foreman held a stallion in the alley on a strong leather lead. Xtreme was standing calm in his care. The giant thoroughbred was a winning racer. A sleek dark beauty. He snorted as she gave his neck a careful stroke, ran his breath over her as he took in her scent, explored, dominated in his own horse way.

She practiced her Spanish, asked his handler, Juan, about his family. Was his mother feeling well? She asked him to thank her for the tamales she'd sent over. They were her favorite. The conversation continued as they walked down the alley.

"He'll get frisky now," Juan warned her. "He knows it's time to get to work."

She looked ahead. Saw the mare. Stopped. She'd seen the horses bred. Too many times to count. The barn housed many studs. Mares were sent every week from clients around the world to be bred by her father's stallions. It was a careful process, an exact science. An expensive business when you were dealing with animals worth more than seven figures.

The mare was slim, her muscle tone classic, her back beautiful. The bay was young and by her frantic eyes trying desperately to find a way to escape. But how could you run when you were hobbled and hedged in for your own protection and the protection of the stallion. There was a flash of memory. Handcuffs. His breath on her neck. The taste of fear overwhelming her mouth. The scream backing up in her lungs, bitten back. She'd refused to scream. Ever angry. Glaring. Biting. Hissing. Clawing. Fighting . . . like a tiger . . . until the Eros. Then she'd refused to scream. Even when the desire overwhelmed her, she'd refused to make a sound.

Anger was suddenly ripe and roaring. She was striding down the alley. She held her hand up as she passed Juan, took hold of the mare from Pete with the authority that was her right as the owner's daughter. Her voice was low, gentle. She'd been here before, helping, holding, talking to a mare, helping to guide a stallion. She'd been here before, but now she understood the animal and the biology. Understood what hormones of estrus demanded of the female. The instinct of the animal's will overruled by the biological drive to mate—to let sperm penetrate egg, create life, reclaim peace. The drug Eros had done that to her. Cycled her up to a pitch of tension. The Viper controlling even her biology in his sick possession that pushed her to the edge of sanity.

But God . . . He had freed her. Delivered.

I love you, O Lord my strength.

She was about to free the mare when the horses called to each other. The mare giving a thrilled whinny. The stud now at a prance of power, his nostrils flared and full of her scent. The mare flagged her tail, whipped it up and she backed toward the very power she was afraid of, rubbed the chest of the stud, accepting him in the courtship ritual.

Frozen she watched. Numb she stood as the instinct made the mare stand, accept, endure. As instinct made the stallion mount, drive, give all his strength, his life, making life with her.

He slipped off her back weak and vulnerable. The mare tossed her head, watched him. There was a whinny. A snort. The great animal seemed to bow to her, then stumble a step. The mare was wrenching her neck, anxious to keep the male in sight as he was aided away by Juan. He gave a snort, a toss of his head, a show of strength. The mare gave a low whinny of approval.

Jaclyn stroked her beautiful neck. The horse calmer now as life took root and her body cycled immediately into a new hormonal shift. Jaclyn's words were nonsense, the same soft babble that Joshua had whispered to her, assured her with when they'd fought Eros together. When he'd provided what she'd needed, protected her with his life, directed her faith, sung over her with his prayers and assured her God was with them.

Had God been with them … during that?

"Jaclyn."

Her father said her name. There was anger in his tone. Regret.

She turned to him with her fixed smile.

"She's beautiful." She told her father as he came close, his hand a loving touch on her back. "Gracie's Fancy is her name. Juan said she won some races."

"Yes." He gave the mare's neck a long stroke, his gaze set on his daughter.

"She was a maiden. Frightened. Xtreme was gentle. Juan's careful that he is. He teaches them to respect the mares. He's good with them, Daddy."

"Yes," he agreed softly. "You don't need to be here, Jaclyn."

"I'm okay." Her attention was on the mare. "I helped her . . . though she was ready. She backed into him, accepted him. She'll breed a beautiful—

"This isn't the place for you right now. I need to protect you. Let me." He took her arm, called to Pete.

"Thanks, Miss Cooper." Pete stepped up to take the mare. "She's good with the mares, sir."

"Yes," Jaxson agreed but he led her away, out of the barn and into the day light.

A crisp breeze blew the bounty of her hair around her face. She fisted it, long waves of burning brown. Understood her father's pain. Feeling the heavy weight of a guilt settle deeper on her shoulders. She'd prayed that God would comfort him. From the day Viper had taken her, she'd prayed for her father's faith, understanding his great love for her would be shaken in the circumstances of her abduction. Now freed, they stood together at the fence line, words that once easily flowed now frozen. In silence they looked out across the paddock where mares and foals grazed with too much to say and no way to speak it, knowing they had to start moving past this or be forever stuck by evil's violation.

"Joshua was gentle," she said what she wanted her father to know. "Careful. He always respected me. It's important to me that you know that about him. He saw me, saved me. When the Eros did its worst, tried to destroy me, Joshua helped me… it was okay with him. He made it be… a battle instead of intimacy, he made me feel in control when I could control nothing. He helped me see God in a place I thought God wouldn't come near—God was with us, Daddy. It was okay with Joshua. He made it okay. He protected me, all of me, and I accepted him."

Her father gathered her close. His emotion surprised her. The gasp of breath. The tension in his body. The power that suddenly oozed out from a pain he held hidden and private, just like the scream she tried to keep trapped inside of her so she wouldn't wake the house with her nightmares, a small sound slipped free. She clung tight as they worked through the pain of her past.

"You can talk to me," he assured her. "Tell me anything. Or if that's too hard I'll find the right person for you to speak with." He held her close. "And I'll just keep praying."

"Don't you know yet that your prayers brought me home?"

"Yes." He nodded. "God brought you home."

"I'm home."

He pressed a kiss into her hair. "You're home."

"It's all I wanted when he had me." But now she realized home wasn't enough.

"And now?" he asked her, looking into her eyes, knowing as parents do. She could only shake her head, silent to the answer. "God is going to heal you. He healed you from the poison. He's going to heal the rest of you."

She nodded. "I'm grateful. So thankful, but . . . frozen up."

"Are you afraid?"

"I don't know what I am yet. You?"

"Fear tells me to hold you tight and near. For a while I will, but faith won't let us stay afraid too long. God will show us the way. You know that now."

She nodded. "I know you're wise."

"I'm also angry," he told her the truth. "At what God allowed you to endure. I'm angry and yet I'm immensely grateful. It's a complex paradox." He brushed her hair back, kissed her as he searched her eyes. "I need to work on the anger as I continue to increase the gratitude."

"You can talk to me. Tell me anything. Or if that's too hard, I'll find the right person," she repeated his words. Smiled. "And I'll just keep praying."

He slowly smiled back at her. "I'm here for you, always, Jaclyn."

"If I know anything, I know that Daddy." She hugged him tight.

Jaxson sprang out of his bed, noting the time. Three a.m. He raced to his daughter's room, his eldest son already there. Levi helpless to wake her up. Jaclyn was plastered to the headboard of her bed, curled into a tight ball, her eyes seeing another world as she screamed in terror with overlarge unfocused eyes. "Go to your mother," he told Levi as his attention stayed on his daughter. "She needs you. This … frightens her."

"Jaclyn," he called to her with words—careful, slow and cautious with his actions like he tended a spooked horse. "Jaclyn," he said again.

"No." The word screamed into the room. "No. No. No." Now she babbled. Her body recoiling deeper into shadows.

Jaxson prayed as he spoke. "Jesus," he said out loud. "Jesus, wake her up," he said again before he called to her. "Jaclyn Marie!" His voice snapped this time with authority. "You're dreaming. You're home. Safe. It's dad. I'm here."

She made the sound of a wounded animal, her body closing impossibly smaller, her eyes black pools, colorless, haunted. Her arm oddly held up and extended against the headboard as if she were tied there.

She sobbed very quietly, "Please comfort my Daddy, God, please help my daddy." Her head bowed her words a mumbled chant that brought a bitter pain to his heart.

"Jaclyn." He touched her, fighting tears.

"No!" She jumped now, baring teeth, glaring eyes, crouched like a cat. The word repeated as she retreated. Banging her head, falling in the tangle of sheets as she tried to flee from the bed, yet one arm held up against the wall tethering her to it with strong invisible links.

He lunged for her, she fought him. He held her tight, his voice calling to her, demanding now, "Wake up. It's daddy. You're dreaming. Your home. I'm here. It's daddy."

"Daddy?" She suddenly saw him. Clung to him. The whole of her curling up into his arms as she began to tremble then weep. "I smell you," she made the strange statement. "It's you." She clung to him, repeated as he assured her. Slowly the trauma and terror of the storm dissipated. "Joshua," she called his name like a question. Her body sinking into him in exhaustion. Her mind fuddled between the surreal and real. "Jesus, keep him safe."

3

The Fury of *Stratia* saw the readout, stood in the midst of a debriefing. There was a growing group of militants in the Baltic, modern-day pirates who robbed merchant ships and killed innocent mariners. Across the globe, there were bodies floating in Russian rivers. The latest, Ivan Wilcynzski, a Russian biochemical expert had been found in the Viper's province yesterday. His time of death corresponding coincidentally with Jaclyn's poisoning—or miraculous healing from being poisoned. He was still mad at himself for impulsively removing the Viper's tattoo from her flesh without thinking it through. He knew better. You didn't make the mark of a prince without earning it and you didn't remove the mark of a prince without consequences. There had certainly been consequences. When the laser hit the green ink in that snake it had released the venom of an adder into her system. No one was sure what had kept her alive. The anti-venom had been much too late to save her from such a lethal poisoning.

But God had delivered his wife.

And he had obediently delivered her back to her father. Given her time. To heal. To choose her future. She, ignorant to the sacred covenant he held with her father. He now ignorant about much of her progress. Trusting Jaxson Cooper. And taking his phone calls when they came no matter the time or place. Fury stepped out of the room, walked the carved granite hall of *Stratia's* command center as he answered the phone, "Sir?"

"Joshua."

"Yes." He heard the concern then began to pace as Jaxson described the past few nights. "No, there were no nightmares, sir." He closed his eyes, listened, prayed. Suddenly thankful for Duchovny's overflowing fountain of information on PTSD. "She's dealing with post-traumatic stress disorder. Ida will know who to call. She can guide you, make a plan of attack for the physical systems. I'll be in prayer over the spiritual battle," he encouraged.

"She calls for you," her father told him. There was a shaky sigh. "She screams no, plastered against her headboard, her arm held up, extended in imaginary chains, fighting. When I tell her it's me, she tells me she's sorry. Prays that God will comfort me." His voice broke. "Then she calls for you. I couldn't help her. You did."

"God did. His love for her sent me. To help her escape, to bring her home. I can't help her now. Your love will, sir. Your love will help her heal. She needs her father's love not my protection."

"I don't know, Joshua. She's calling for you. When the terror settles and I'm holding her, she's asking for you."

He stopped, in the quiet dark hall he stopped, closed his eyes. For just a moment he imagined what it could have been. If he'd have taken her home as his wife. If they were together. What he could give her. All the things he could not. He opened his eyes. Trusted the Divine directions. "She needs her father to heal. I'll intercede for her, sir. You have my word on that. My prayers will cover her. Your love will keep her close until she can stand. She's strong, courageous, faithful. Remind her that God loves her, that Christ is longing… for her healing. That He is jealous over her well-being. That the Spirit is actively working to give comfort through the Word of God and work this for her good. Use the scriptures for truth and hope, sir. For the power to overcome the enemy. This is a spiritual battle."

Joshua's words came back to him at the next crisis. It came in the most unexpected place. During worship on a Sunday morning. The song was one of her favorites. The Charles Wesley hymn speaking of the love of God. He'd turned to smile at her, but her gaze was fixed, too gold in a face gone deathly pale. "How could He love me and let that happen? How can He love me after what I've done?"

He'd moved quickly, tucking her under his arm, holding her to his side, protecting instantly. He tried to keep singing. Fame had its own wages, and had taught him long ago when he played for the NFL that the world was ever watching. He knew she felt that. Even in this church, she felt the curiosity of the world watching when what she needed most was privacy instead of pity, prayers instead of gossip. He tried to sing, but her tears had bled through his shirt to touch his skin.

That's when he felt his oldest son. Levi's hand at his waist, his body shifting to shield, his arm around his sister, his hand assuring his father. His voice singing for them the words she needed to hear. A father needed to hear.

My chains fell off, my heart was free, I rose, went forth, and followed Thee. Amazing love, how can it be that Thou, my God shouldst die for me…

"God loved you so much He died for you. You are free." Her father's voice spoke the charge. "Believe."

"I believe," Jaclyn answered, curling tighter into his warmth. Hiding against her father, her hand circled her wrist, rubbed at the old imaginary raw rings that his handcuffs would leave. She could feel the abrasions. She knew nothing was there. Her wrists were healed. Whole. Yet she could feel the invisible scars of his bondage at her wrists and the angry flesh of her skin where they'd burned off his tattoo on her back. The only thing she could feel was the scars. The imaginary echo of her wounds. "I am free," she repeated the truth. She was free from the chains. Why didn't she feel free…why couldn't she feel anything.

Help me, Jesus. Please help me past this numbing insanity of doubt and confusion.

It was a photograph, an old one. A favorite one. The boy well remembered. Once deeply loved. He'd been handsome and smart with a dry wit over smooth edges. He'd played golf, not football, but her father had liked him. She had loved him. Once upon a time. She had fallen in love with him in high school. They had waited because love waits.

Evil takes.

Anger popped, blazing like a burst from a champagne bottle, foaming up, spilling over. She saw red. Blood red. It flared like a match to fuel as she hurled the photograph into the trash with a vicious shatter.

"Jaxie," Lexi's tone was confused, carefully she questioned, "We can store that, honey."

"Why?" she'd asked turning away from the old treasured picture from her senior prom like it was discarded trash. The crush on her high school sweetheart long over, but the memories revolutionized. "So I can remember what a mistake I made not sleeping with him?"

Lexi's gaze moved to her sister-in-law. Her cousin Samuel's mother was Christie Cooper-Stone's older sister and an interior decorator. Aunt Cara a master at transforming a room into spectacular comfort or chic suitability. She understood teenage girls, having two daughters after Samuel. As the victim of incest, Cara also understood evil and violation.

"Mistake?" Cara questioned, carefully slipping the photograph from the carnage of shattered glass and wood. "Let's see this boy." She tugged Jaclyn onto the bed, studied the photograph. "Well, he's certainly handsome, Jaxie. This is the one you brought down to the Chevaux on the Fourth of July before your senior year, right? I do recall a certain measure of charm in the young man. You were inseparable at the ranch."

"We thought we were in love."

"Um," Cara responded.

“I was in love with the idea of being in love. He was in love with my body.”

"Jaclyn," Lexi censored.

But Cara laughed. “Well the three of us certainly understand that misplaced love, being put together the way God saw fit to make our voluptuous bodies. I believe it makes the devil quite jealous how beautiful God made Eve. The enemy likes to turn the table on us, I’ve told my girls. He gets good and mad that we’re so beautiful and uses beauty against us anyway he can. Lust isn’t what we’re after, but because of the fall, beauty must be aware of its own reflection.”

“And its power. With beauty comes the added responsibility to maintain a certain modesty.”

”So you’ve always said, Lexi.” Jaclyn was up, pacing the room, seeing the chaos, feeling it invade as anger bubbled up. “I was always—responsible. Modest. It didn’t stop that snake from taking me. Raping me. He said he saw me at Babel. He liked the way I gave the men there nothing. He watched me… and my modesty only made him value me more.”

Her mother had gone pale. Cara wasn’t distracted, her voice steady and strong, “And you believe it was an irresponsible mistake… not sleeping with?” She held up the picture.

“Cody,” she finished. “Yes, a big mistake.” Jaclyn turned and looked at her mother. “At least I’d have lost my virginity to someone I was madly in love with.”

“At the time.” Cara shrugged when she looked at her. “Now where is… Cody?”

“MBA program at OU.” She narrowed her eyes.

“But he’s not with you anymore.” Cara dumped the photograph back into the trash.

Jaclyn looked at the trash can. “No. He’s not.”

“Just a picture. A feeling you can rehearse in a sweet memory.”

"I've got nasty memories now." Her gaze was sharp on Cara, the anger ripe, the hope great that her aunt, because of her own past, would somehow understand when many others couldn't even begin to comprehend what she could rehearse. Aunt Cara and Christie's father had been a devil. Their home growing up filled with incest. Both had escaped, survived, healed under the care of the Cooper family. "And those memories ruined what I waited for."

"If you let them." Cara stood. "Keep rehearsing them to hurt you. I don't think you will. You won't let evil have the power to shame you or make you bitter. The woman I know you to be won't let evil ruin anything else." She lifted her chin, her hand firm and loving. Her emerald eyes sharp, sparkling, wise. "You'll deal with the anger, work it free along with the bitterness, believing the truth that you are cleansed. Unashamed, you'll be better, stronger, wiser. You'll look at the picture of you and Cody and you'll be proud of that young lady who waited. Who honored herself and respected her husband. When he comes," She smiled now. "And come he will. A worthy, incredible man our God has for you." Her gaze was alive with hope, confident and sure. "Then you'll give, the gift you've kept just for him. You will give yourself. Pure. Strong. Courageous. Faithful." She carefully wiped away the tears that had fallen onto Jaclyn's face. "Nothing can take that from you, Jaclyn Marie, who you are in Christ. Nothing." She smiled, picked the picture up out of the trash and stated confidently, "We'll find this picture an extraordinary frame so that you remember who you are." Tucking it under her arm she asked, "What color did you decide for the walls?"

The three of them stood, Cara had linked her arm behind her back. Lexi wandered over to the wall, her back to them as they looked at the samples of colorful paint patches. There was a bold red, sunflower yellow, a pale aqua, a warm buckskin. She wiped her eyes, wondered what color Joshua liked as her aunt spun her ideas into each color's palette. They had never talked about colors, or furniture styles. He always wore black, ate anything, and had no time for entertainment she was sure. Her hand found his cross, the sacred gift he'd given her to keep. Held it tight, felt sad. Exhausted. Guilty from her explosion of temper. Temper?

The realization came. I felt angry.

Jesus, are you here?

She thought of all the times Joshua had helped her see God in insane places. Unholy places. Beautiful places. God was here. In her anger. Helping her feel, something, finally past the numbing scars, she could feel something. Tears came. Sweet and hot on her face. *I felt something. Thank you, God. You're here. With me. In this. Thank you.*

"Paint on the wall. Good sign of progress." Jaxson flashed dimples from the door yet studied his daughter.

"What color do you like, Daddy?" She wiped at her eyes.

"Oh, no." He came to her side, his arm slipping around her, still smiling at his sister. "Don't get me involved in something I know nothing about, daughter."

"He knows how to pay for it all well enough," Cara laughed, her hand grasping hold of his forearm, holding tight with love. "He'll do that and we'll shop for the linens. You'll find your way once you see the right thing. That's how it always starts." Cara smiled. "There's a beginning, the paint color can be the end. Let's find the beginning."

There was truth in her aunt's words. Finding the beginning began to move you toward the end. She'd felt anger. A hot striking bolt of it as the world rushed with a red heat. She decided red was a good color for the walls. The newly decorated room got her in a frame of mind for other new things. When her father suggested she speak to Ida about the nightmares she was open to the suggestion. Obedient to the course of action to adjust her sleep patterns. The paint fumes helped. Moving into another room for a few days. Setting an alarm to wake her up twice a night and switch her

REM sleep cycles. Moving back into the newly decorated suite. The transition had met success. The nightmares were learning to be controlled.

The dietician was next. Physically she was having to learn to be tuned to her body like never before. She'd always been thin, but now she watched what she ate in the degree to what effect it had on her physical well-being. Caffeine and stimulants didn't help keep her system in control. Sugar and carbs gave her a rush of energy that quickly dropped off. Protein was safe. Fiber and fruits. Eating healthy foods began to give her an added edge of physical control.

Physical fitness was her third step. An outlet for repressed emotions, Ida advised. She'd always been fit. Now she trained. With weights, running, swimming and martial arts. There was a growing need to learn to protect herself. Even though there were now men assigned to protect her on a growing security staff for her family, headed up by a man name Atlas. She was not to go anywhere alone. Ever.

It was a reason to argue. To get angry. To feel something. She couldn't believe her father thought she was going to spend her life surrounded by men in black with ear buds who watched her every move like hawks. He did. And apparently so did Joshua Fury. It was the first time she'd heard his name.

"Joshua screened the candidates."

"Cool. He'll know what to look for, sis," Levi added. He'd become her sidekick. Golden retriever friendly. Continually coming around to entice her into something fun. "The Dude is tight, Jaxie."

"The Dude?" His enthusiasm irritated her. The hero worshiping tone both pleased and annoyed. The fact that Joshua hadn't called her yet, troubling.

And now finally her father spoke his name as Levi defined, "The Fury, sis."

"Fury. Um." She lowered her brow. "So this is his idea? A personal armed guard for me twenty-four seven."

"He cares about your safety."

She was pacing her father's study. Passing the footballs, helmets, photographs of his MVP career, Super Bowl wins, the Hall of Fame induction where she stood by his side as a teenager. Now she turned on him and demanded, "You've talked to him. Fury put you up to this, Daddy?"

"I asked for his help screening the candidates. Atlas is on loan until we settle this."

She crossed her arms. Realized of course, Atlas would be *Stratia*. He wore black. Always. Was no-nonsense intense. And his body was honed to acute perfection. She felt the beautiful surge of temper, the tug at her heart, the flow of heat. "Atlas is *Stratia* and Fury screened the candidates. When were we going to talk about *this*?"

"Jaclyn, *this* isn't a negotiation. You will be protected. Anytime you leave the house."

"I'm not leaving the house."

"I didn't raise lazy laggards." It was one of her father's classic lines. "You'll either be in school or start working by January."

"What am I going to tell a boss when I show up with a sidekick?"

"Two sidekicks. Protocol demands there will always be at least two men with you."

"Two! How am I supposed to go to law school with at least two guys trailing me? Will you put the three of us through Harvard, Daddy?"

"Is that what you decided? Harvard in the fall, sis?" Draped over one of the leather arm chairs, Levi looked up with an excited smile. He palmed a football. It had been his constant companion since the age of seven.

She hissed at him, stealing the leather. "Knucklehead, like Daddy's going to let me go to Boston."

"Boston's fine. You can study anywhere with the security force we'll have in place."

"Who lives like that? With strangers walking two steps behind you. Making you and everyone around you know you're different. Making me think about *it*. *It*. All the time. I'd rather be a lazy laggard than try to explain *it*. How can I explain *it*. To a boss, a professor, a friend. No," she slammed the ball down. It flew high. Bounced off a shelf. Tackled a chess set. Slammed into a picture. There was a shatter. Glass broken over a family portrait.

"I'm sorry." Immediately she looked at him. He at her. "I didn't mean to do that, Daddy."

"You'll fix it, daughter," he told her. "Give you a chance to see you can go to the frame store with two sidekicks, ask them to replace the glass and never have to explain *it* to anyone."

She crossed her arms. Felt the heat. Narrowed her eyes. "No."

"Levi, remind your sister how we respect and obey our parents when we disagree with them."

"We, answer, 'Yes, sir'," he picked up the football then looked at him, "Sir."

"That's right. We say, 'Yes, sir'." He rose. Walked to her. His hands took her shoulders. "We say, 'Yes, sir' because we know our parents make the rules to protect us because they love us not to make our lives miserable or be a killjoy. You will have security. A personal guard. Who knows what to watch for and how to keep a young lady of worth safe and protected from the evil of this world."

"Is that what he said. It sounds like something he would say."

"He?"

"Joshua. The Dude. The Fury."

"We both agree your safety is a priority."

"You both know God can allow—

"We will keep you safe." The words had a sharp bite. A finality. His hands tight now. "This is no longer a discussion. It is a direction. If you disagree, then you should pray and ask God to move my heart, Jaclyn. You need to submit and obey."

"The Fury?"

"Your father."

"So I have no say in *this* at all? *It* is going to happen."

"You'll make the final selection from the candidates for your personal guard. In three days we're going to *Stratia*. Marc and Christie have made it a priority. You need to change your attitude. Realize you should be grateful instead of angry that God has provided what you need through provisions and family positions to keep you safe. You'll have the very best, Jaclyn. He's made sure of that. He loves you."

"He?"

"God."

4

"Wait here," her father instructed, exiting first, Levi following. In a moment he opened the door of the limo, his hand helping her mother out. Jaclyn was the final one to be gathered from the car. They were in an underground parking lot surrounded by cement and chilly air. A squadron of security men had their suited backs to them banking the short distance to the door. Her Aunt Christie was the first to greet her. A tight hug. Her Uncle Marc leaning close for a kiss before her father urged her forward through the door to safety. It was the ever present priority. Her safety. Her father obsessed with this personal guard. Plural. As in a legion of black-suited men around her whenever she so much as stuck her big toe out the door. She tried to resist. Argue. Negotiate. She glanced at her stepmother.

Lexi had been the one to tell her she was being extremely selfish. Her father was worried. She'd said the word acute. Linked it to sensitive. Then included her brothers. Levi even now a step behind her, football for the first time the furthest thing from his teenage mind. She took his hand, squeezed it. Agreed with Lexi that it helped him deal with what happened to her to have a part in protecting her.

"I'm glad you're here," she told him, trying to be obedient, sensitive.

He was tall as their father now. The serious over-achieving firstborn male. Xavier had her father's playful side. Max would be the family charmer. But Levi was already using those wide Cooper shoulders to carry a burden he shouldn't have to bear. She'd go along with this for him, she smiled as he tucked her under his arm and held her close to his side. It broke her heart when she looked at him sometimes. Saw the difference, the change in him, the worry over the awkward steadfast brotherly love. She leaned against his strength, sinking her hands into the pockets of the long wool overcoat.

She was suddenly cold. Tense. Acutely nervous as she walked the winding halls of *Stratia's* command center. She'd been here only four weeks ago. Recovered in their hospital. Said goodbye to Joshua on the curb. It had been four weeks since she'd seen him. No one had told her if he'd be here today. She hadn't asked. Couldn't. He still hadn't called her…

Her family was escorted into a conference room. They circled one side of an oblong table. She took the chair at the end. Pulled Levi down beside her. Her parents and Christie took the chairs in the center. Marc was now missing. She glanced at the dark glass on the wall. Knew there were people behind it, observing. She burrowed deeper into her coat. Colder. Brittle. Detached as the first few candidates were brought in. They were all very qualified. She'd had no questions. Just listened. Nodded. Let her stepmother do what she did best, negotiate through a discussion. Her father asking a few questions of each man. They were all middle-aged men in suits. Highly qualified to take a bullet or deliver a kill if called for in their protection of her.

"Next man is Tias Keyes," her mother read off the application. "Goes by Tiki."

"As in Barber?" Levi perked up, leaned over to look at the paperwork.

Lexi curled a smile at her. "That got his attention."

"Football always gets their attention." Christie smiled at her.

"Tiki played some ball back in the day, Jaxie," her father proclaimed. "Mr. Keyes is a retired Ranger."

"Texas or Army."

"Army," he smiled at his wife. "Fifty Two." Jaxson nodded. "Has a reconstructed bionic knee from college football. Played for the Horned Frogs of TCU. Finished his last marathon last month in under three hours. Athlete. He included his testimony and a statement of faith." He handed Jaclyn the application and she opened it, began to read. "The good Baptist was widowed two years ago. Wife died of cancer."

Christie advised, "He tested very well. He's quick with a gun and accurate with his decisions. Didn't hesitate to shield."

Jaclyn glanced over the testimony of a life lived by faith through rocky times then looked up as the man was ushered inside. An African American with an athletic build. Clean shaven. Bald. His dark suit immaculate with a simple necktie. His shoes shined. His voice had a subtle rhythm to it as he answered her father's getting to know you questions. Confident. Honest. Secure in himself but humility was clear as he answered Lexi's harder ones. Then Christie gave her pop quiz and the interview drew to a conclusion with her father's statement, "Well you are very qualified, Mr. Keyes. Jaclyn?"

She was cued. Before she'd never asked a question. But she'd forced her mind on his application and his testimony had caught her attention. A line of text on the paper she held. He'd said his wife had been a refining fire, turning a lump of coal into a diamond. He missed his life in her fire. Without looking up from the paper she asked him, "How many people do you think are watching you through that glass?"

"I'd guess four, ma'am, based on the width of the pane, but that's only a guess. The room could be deep."

"Is he right, Daddy?"

"He's close," he answered. "We all want the best for you, Jaclyn."

There was a sudden strike of anger, a resounding echo of heartache. A bittersweet acceptance that this was her life. She looked at her father. His gaze was steady, sure, certain with a love that issued a well-meaning authority.

"Yes, sir."

She looked back at the application. "Personally I think this is over the top, Mr. Keyes. I'm prickly about having a shadow twenty-four-seven. I think if evil decides to do me harm, my only true protection is God. And if He allows it," she swallowed, forced the words, "You're not going to be able to protect me even if you're the very best."

"Jaclyn—

"Daddy," she said respectfully, reopening the file. "It's okay to be honest." Repeated. Reminded the room. Herself. "It's okay. We're blessed to have the means to provide for this kind of security, Mr. Keyes. Most victims don't get this kind of peace of mind. I am grateful. Just angry that it's even necessary." She studied the paper. At that certain sentence on his testimony. Refining fire. There were five things God said that He was—life, light, love, spirit and a refining fire. "You miss your wife."

"Every second."

"Every second," she repeated. Nodded. Suddenly caught a deep breath. Emotion surfaced, like the sun striking from behind thunderclouds. She touched Joshua's cross, holding it, missing him. "I understand that."

There was a stark silence. Booming in the observation room.

Fury saw his reflection in the two-way glass. Looked through it, focusing on his wife. She was tense. Tiny, wrapped up in that dark coat. She'd yet to take it off. She was cold. Always. Beautiful. Beyond imagination. She had a way of stealing his breath, and his words. He never knew what to say around her. It had been a constant problem. He didn't know how to act around an audience with her included. And he had one now. A room full of gifted psychological observers who were ignorant to the covenant between him and her father and his sacred position as her husband.

So he stood stoically silent as a warrior who had once been her guardian. Listened. As her Uncle Marc, his commander the Bull, talked in a low voice. Asking questions of a woman who put his warrior mind on high alert and his emotional armor on maximum. The *Termite* was in the room. The expert profiling psychiatrist was a warrior-at-rest's worst nightmare. Her blond soft beauty a deceptive cover. The woman had an obsessive compulsive disorder to lift and look under every emotional rock, and telepathic tendencies to know exactly which stones needed to be turned over. She was more terrier than termite. The woman just knew stuff. Stuff no one should know. Like a dog on a scent, she had a way of sniffing things out. Her senses too keenly developed to miss as much as a breath held a second too long. Thankfully, she was focused on his wife. Since the moment Jaclyn walked in the room, Dr. Lisette had been giving Marc an oral evaluation.

"Family unit is strong. Father giving her space. That's commendable this early. Oldest brother peace making and over protective—insulating her from both the parents and the unknown public. Being part of the process helps him heal. Good idea. Mother calm. She's strong here, feels in control in this kind of environment with the interviews. Christie's a good counter. Puts the men a little on edge, they feel her authority when she asks a question. Jaclyn is withdrawn. Bit defiant. Is more concerned with who's behind the glass than who's sitting in front of her. No eye contact. Leaving the decision to her father. She's not going to have an opinion. She's against this. Not indifferent. By refusing the idea of security, she tries to convince herself life will get back to the old normal. If she accepts this, she must accept the new normal. That's why this is hard. She's not spoiled or ungrateful. She's not afraid of the world or even her enemy. She's afraid of the new world he's created. The change he's forced. That's the real enemy here. Change." She shifted her stance, angled toward him now. "She's still in her coat. Do you know why, Fury?"

"No, ma'am. I'm a warrior, not a profiler."

"Best guess," she required.

"She's cold, ma'am," he answered.

"Yes, she is cold. Fear makes us cold. Anger hot. We'll have something to work with when she starts to warm up, takes off that coat. Sometimes it's all about turning up the heat. Did you know hate and love have the same biological chemical reaction in the body? Nothing like getting hot and sweaty when you're trying to heal. How long will it take to train the Tiki guy? He's the one she'll choose."

"Yes, he's the one. Our choice too. Three months," Marc stated. "Jaxson wants him ready in January. She'll be starting law school."

"Law school. Where?"

"To be determined but he's determined she go forward with her plans. Move on and into a routine she's used to. She's a good student."

"He's determined she go?"

"You sound surprised."

"I am."

"He's a man of faith. He knows it's the right thing to do. Keeping her close will only suspend her healing." Marc had crossed his arms, resolute. "Protective measures only intensify a bomb blast. Right, Fury?"

"Yes, sir."

"Will you speak to her, Fury?" the Termite asked him.

"No." The answer was too quick. He added, "Her father can handle this."

"He doesn't think he can," she told him. "Or he wouldn't be here. At *Stratia*. Asking for help."

"He knows he can." This time he looked at her reflection. Felt the energy. Knew his eyes were a fiery blue.

"It's warm in here." She fanned herself. Looking back at him in the glass with a smile.

"You turned up the heat," Marc answered and Fury looked back at Jaclyn. She'd shifted in her seat, crossing her legs, that coat completely wrapped around her. A tiny foot showing up outside the edge of the table in some skyscraper heel with thin black straps crossing every which way turning her foot into a delicate work of art. He looked away. Focused on the conversation. It was ending. Her father was taking charge and issuing an offer for Tiki to undergo some training.

There were handshakes then everyone was moving out into the hall.

"She knows you're here." Lisette spoke as the room emptied. "Staying in here tells me something."

"And going out there?"

"Something else."

"What's the best thing for her?"

"Assurance."

"Then I'll pray for assurance, ma'am." He turned to look at her and knew it was a mistake.

Lisette searched him. Like an internal scan, bumping up against his mental fortitude. He blocked her. Blocked everything. With furious resolve. Added the smile.

Then she smiled. "Interesting." At the door she said quietly, "Not seeing you signals yet another change. The rescue is over. Real life has begun. You could say a few words. Assure her."

"As in?"

"This is a good start toward your future. She'll believe you." She closed the door.

He stared at his reflection. The room was empty. The clock on the wall ticking. His arms were crossed, locked in place, his brow brooding. His heart hammering. He could hear them in the hall. He closed his eyes and prayed. He never knew what to say to her. He didn't know how he could let her leave again. The last time had almost killed him. Opened a wound, resurrecting the grief of all his losses. He prayed, for a strength greater than his own. He'd never been a coward or selfish. Trusting God he opened the door.

Jaclyn saw him immediately. Dressed in classic *Stratia* black, he came out a door. Dwarfing most men. Large, like her father. His shoulders wide, his eyes so blue they blazed. He bowed subtly, greeted her stepmother. Then shook Levi's hand. There was the bump and grind of male conversation. He smiled at Levi, that very subtle turn at the corner of his lips. Her heart fluttered. It just rose up and budded, warm and full and beautifully at peace with the sight of him. He liked her brother. She. Missed. Him. It caught at her heart and squeezed brutally. The pounding a pain that reminded her she was alive.

"Jaclyn." Her father was looking at her. Cueing her. She felt his arm around her. His support. Saw his prompt. They'd been talking to Mr. Keyes.

"I'm sorry." She smiled at Tiki, tried to focus. "Yes. Please send me updates on your training. I'll keep you in my prayers as well, sir."

"I'd appreciate that. You'll remain in mine. I felt called to this job." He revealed the information with a smile. "Appreciate the opportunity to serve you."

She nodded. Let her father lead them on. "Here's Joshua."

"Sir." The handshake between the Fury and her father. The nod with the subtle bow to her. "Miss Cooper."

"Joshua," she said his name. Felt her smile. "How are you?"

"Blessed," he answered. "You made a decision?"

"Mr. Keyes," her father answered.

"Congratulations." Joshua extended his hand to Tiki. The men shook. Spoke. She watched Joshua. From under her father's arm, she watched him talking with Tiki, taking in every detail. The sound of his voice. Its tone and tempo. The strength of his arms, stretching fabric. The length of his lashes, dark and far too long and dense. A contrast of softness on a warrior whose bold blue eyes were the telling sign of his internal zeal.

Marc announced, "The car is ready."

The group began to walk, the men still talking. At the door was the security group, lining the way to the waiting limo. The door opened. She felt the chill. Time slipping away. Anxiety ignited. She reached out to him, terrified. Touched his arm. Found his hand. Clung.

"Has your hand healed?" She looked at his palm, saw the scar from Viper's dagger, the defensive wound he'd taken from the death blow meant for her. She ran her finger over it.

"The scar reminds me of the victory."

For a moment she saw his eyes, the color beautiful and steadfastly vibrant. Then her body was rising, her arms reaching. Here was his smell, warmth, here, close to him was everything she wanted. Too much of what was missing. Tears were sudden. Unsuppressed. Her body yearning. Clinging. His rigid, tense. He patted her back. She wept. Words unable to come. Bottled up. Frozen. Numb. Just silent tears. Like dripping ice.

"Sh," he whispered. His head bowed to her, his voice quiet and near. "You're okay. You did good today. A good first step. A great start toward your future. You chose well. Tiki will watch over you. Allow you to walk forward into your future with courage. I'm proud of you, Jaclyn. You're doing hard things with courage. In Christ you are strong, courageous, faithful. Beloved."

There was pain. A lance of it. "I can't feel. Anything. Like a block of ice. It's horrible."

"Then know." He spoke Psalm fifty-six. "Focus on what God promised. My prayers cover you." His words changed. The Hebrew a soft sacred prayer. Then his charge, "Be strong in the Lord. Trust your father." It was Joshua who placed her into the car. His gaze brutally bold. Blue. Fixed on her. Alight with a staggering energy. Faith. Hope. Gently he wiped away a tear. His resolve a single nod of assurance. "Remain in God's love. God is for you." He was gone.

In a moment her father was beside her. He tucked her into his arms and she sank down deep into her coat, holding onto Joshua's cross, her face cool from the tracks of tears, from the warmth of Joshua's hand. She closed her eyes. Turned her head. Her father gathered her close. She was exhausted.

Joshua put his hand in his pocket, her tear like a sacred jewel in his palm. She was gone. Placed into her father's care. Again. In moments his hand would be dry.

While her tear lingered in his palm he let the Word echo from Psalm 56 that he had told her. *You have seen me tossing and turning through the night. You have collected all my tears and preserved them in your bottle! You have recorded everyone in your book. The very day I call for help, the tide of battle turns. My enemies flee! This one thing I know: God is for me! I am trusting God-oh, praise his promises! I am not afraid of anything mere man can do to me! Yes, praise his promises. I will surely do what I have promised, Lord, and thank you for your help. For you have saved me from death and my feet from slipping, so that I can walk before the Lord in the land of the living.*

Those who sow in tears will reap with songs of joy. Soon, Lord, let the harvest come. May your beloved sing.

5

It would take twelve weeks until Tiki was ready and then he'd still have to pass Marc's test and approvals. In the meantime, Atlas and a team rotated on call at her disposal. Two men waiting in the wings even now as she spent time at the family's heritage known as the Chevaux Ranch. She'd come to thank her Aunt Cara and to spend time with her grandparents. Samantha Cooper was wise, her grandfather, Honey fun loving and affectionate. She spent time with Samuel, her closest friend and cousin, one of her favorite pastimes.

It was abnormally warm for October in the Texas hill country. The Chevaux Ranch was stubbornly fighting off fall with a bout of ninety-degree weather. They were pool side. Samuel in his element, surrounded by women.

Both of Samuel's sisters were tall, blond, built versions of their mother. Cassidy was the baby. At seventeen she was blooming with possibility and had the practicality and patience of her father, Beau. She liked numbers, business, order and wanted to study accounting in college.

Jenna was older, two years younger than Samuel, her eyes that startling emerald of her mother and Aunt Christie. She had Cara's eye for design but she was using the flair in a different direction. Fashion. She was a student of style and Samuel's current honey was giving her a lot to study with her

South American heritage. The Brazilian beauty was impossibly tucked into less than four inches of material.

The pool had settled into silence. Music, soft and Latin, created a mood. Maybe she would go out tonight with Samuel and Yarah. Of course her security entourage would be watching their every move. Her father was firm on that account. She couldn't leave the family property without security now. It was a new part of her life she still wasn't used to, being flanked and followed everywhere, driven in secure cars, baby sat by suited-up, armed and dangerous defenders like she was the queen of Sheba. She was no queen. She glanced at Yarah. There was a queen. The queen of Brazil. She'd come to shop for boots in Texas and met the heir to the Chevaux. Now they sunned by his pool and tangled fingers under the wrought iron lounge chairs. What a story. She snickered.

A PDA hummed on the table. Tucked in its leather tooled cover it danced like a bucking bronco. Samuel had a message. She wondered if last week's Houstonian beauty was having trouble saying farewell. Jenna said he'd had a time cutting loose from her pretty claws. Smiling, she slipped the PDA free from its holster, glanced at her cousin belly down with his fingers tangoing under the chase lounge with Yarah. Mischief began to dance out a chorus of ideas. He was totally unaware. Samuel's attention firmly on the queen of Brazil. She looked at the read out. Saw his name.

FURY

Simple. All caps. So understated.

She narrowed her eyes. Opened the message.

Back from the Baltic. Heard it's hot in Texas. S'up?

She glanced at Samuel, typed.

Nada. Pool side with a Brazilian. Yarah definitely brought the heat.

Yarah? What does Houston think of Brazil?

Houston is history.

Use my trick?

Avoidance?

Truth.

Um.

She regretted that word, quickly typed. *As the sisters say*. Added. *How was the Baltic*?

There was a pause. Then the phone vibrated again. He was calling now. She saw the read out. Sprang up, ran off a few steps, holding the PDA against her skin. Stared at Samuel. Knew she was in trouble.

Truth, huh. Okay. She took a breath, paced away to the far edge of the patio.

Answered, "How did you know?"

"Um," he answered.

"Right."

"Should I ask where Cletus is?"

"Should I ask how you know my cousin well enough to . . . correspond?"

"We became friends while you fought that . . . fever. I thought you knew that."

"No."

"Um."

"Right." *What are we?* She just said it. "What are we now? Enemies?"

He said her name.

"You're avoiding me like I had the plague and it's contagious."

"I'm not avoiding you."

"It was poison not a fever and you're not telling me the truth either. This feels like a bad break up. I thought we'd be friends."

"We are."

"Um." She felt emotion rise up, mastered it. She'd gotten really good at mastering emotion. Keeping everything in the neutral zone of numb-ville. Trapping tears gut deep and turning anger to sarcasm, fighting fear with bravado and sucking down screams from nightmares. "You talk. On the phone. To Samuel."

"No one calls him Samuel but you and his mother."

"And our grandmother. No one calls you Joshua either, Fury. You text Cletus? I must have missed your calls. Right."

"I've been gone."

"The Baltic." She let it go. Too afraid to hear the truth he was famous for. "How was that?"

"Successful."

"Who went?"

"My team."

"How's Petra?"

"She's good."

"Still fussing with Eli?"

"Always."

"And Seth?"

"He's learning his way."

"Slim and Vin?"

"In sync. And Pax is doing well. How are you?"

"Fine." She said the word quick. Too quick. "Better. Focusing on believing what I know."

"Good. You're spending time at the ranch?"

"The Chevaux. Yes."

"Give me a visual. I want to see you."

She blinked. Surprised by the request. Immediately her hand went to her hair. It was a mess. Gathered up into a clip. She didn't have makeup on. No lipstick. Her swim suit was old. She tugged on it, frowned at its ample, modest coverage. More practical than stylish. Looked at Yarah. Felt dorky. "I'm a mess," she said. "Call back tonight and I'll give you a visual."

"If we're going to talk let me see you."

"Joshua."

"No one calls me Joshua but you. I'll rat you out. Cletus will—"

"Samuel's already in big trouble with me. How long has he had your number?"

"Since the hospital. Let me see you."

"You first."

He came on screen immediately. Wearing a black T-shirt. The Potomac River behind him. His eyes so blue. Her heart went soft like warm butter.

"Where are you?"

"I don't see you."

Against her better judgment, she gave in.

"Wow."

"What?"

"How big are those—"

"Those what?"

"Sunglasses."

"They're Jenna's." She pivoted them into her hair. "She's a designer."

"Ah, there you are."

"Where are you?" she asked again.

"Hangout by the river. We've got a great day here. They call this season fall outside of Texas."

"You with friends?"

"Sure. You?"

"Family." She swept the scene with the camera eye then came back to him. "And Brazil. Catch her?"

"He said she was something. What do you think?"

"She's something. Not sure what. Samuel's fickle," she said quietly, but looked at their joined hands. Envied that it was so easy for Samuel. That his charm kept his life over full with dates. He never knew a lonely day. "You're doing okay?"

"Blessed. You?"

"Incredibly grateful." She blinked, felt emotion rise in her, studied him. "You look good."

"You look stronger."

"I miss you." There was sadness. Bittersweet and pure.

"Tell Cletus I called," he said it quickly. Flashed a smile. "You'll enjoy that."

She just nodded. Fought the tears. Pulled the sunglasses back on to veil them. "I always thought you'd call me," her voice was too soft, she cleared it, asked, "Do you have my new number?"

"No."

"You talk to my father. Samuel."

"Yes. If you needed me, I'd know. You're okay. Your father's keeping you safe. Your security is the best."

"Yes. You saw to that—"

"What's wrong?"

"You ever have security on your tail night and day. Stupid question."

"Get used to it," he said it with the same firmness as her father. Neither would be moved. "You'll be protected. Kept safe. You're safe now in your father's care."

"You can call me," she said it softly.

He spoke over her. "You're strong. Courageous. Faithful." His words reminded her of their time together, of the days when she'd felt secure. Now she felt wounded and unsure. Numb. "Beloved by God. He loves you, Jaclyn."

How could this be love? For the first time she wasn't sure she believed him. She felt weak, afraid and unbelief often dragged her into doubt that God was really for her at all. Why had He saved her to live like this? To live alone. Sleep haunted. To long for a man who didn't have her number and would never call her. To feel so ashamed and dirty even the blood of Jesus couldn't cleanse her.

Her heart lurched when her phone rang three days later. No one knew her new number. Maybe it was Joshua. Finally calling since the ice had been broken and she'd extended the invitation. She looked at the blocked number. That would be him. His way. Smiling she answered, "This is Jaclyn."

"Jac-que-line."

She stopped breathing. It's what kept her from screaming. As his voice hissed and spoke with such possessive authority. "My Tigrissa. I will have you back. Soon. Surround yourself with your father's men. They are nothing to me." He laughed. "I love your fear. How you hide. But I see you. There. In your father's house."

She hit the panic button by her bed. Thinking of her stepmother, when she needed men, their strength and protection, she thought instead of Lexi's wisdom. You didn't negotiate with evil. She said nothing. Refused his game.

"I hear you. There. Breathing. My Tiger. I remember the smell of your breath. How hot it could get. Your body. It is mine. Soon you will know. The power of your need. For me."

Atlas burst in. Armed.

Jaclyn pointed at the phone. Her temporary head of security came to her, thumbing commands into his PDA, his weapon holstered, his phone scanning, tracking the call, working. Her heart a painful panic in her chest. It broke at the sight of her father. His face was ablaze. His own gun poised then tucked into his waistband.

He took the phone as Viper told her he was coming soon.

"Come on, then," her father said. "I'm ready. We kill snakes in Texas."

The thought took root and budded with intention. Jaxson was alarmed, yet not surprised how easily his money got results. He'd had the license to conceal a handgun for years and never used it. Now he kept a new Sig holstered on his shoulder. Another small Glock on his ankle inside his boot. But it was this weapon he'd been waiting on. A black market graphite gun that could be broken apart and stored inside the secret compartments of a state-of-the-art laptop computer to be taken anywhere. The semi-automatic had enough firepower to take out a village. The gun was stealthy enough to walk through even the highest level of security and not be detected. He shot the weapon. Every morning. It was the first appointment of his day. His trainer was an expert on covert military operations. His aim was brutally accurate. He'd even worked with an eye doctor to improve his aging vision. He had a new personal trainer in combat survival who was blending the lethal trinity of Krav Maga, Jiu-Jitsu and Judo together for practical self-defense if he found his hands were ever empty of a weapon. He could kill without a gun. He found an outlet for the growing anger in preparing to protect his daughter.

Just as Jaclyn was preparing with his wife. After the phone call, she'd gone to Lexi with a certain resolve. She wanted to learn how to negotiate. How to use her words as weapons. There would be no better teacher than Lexi. No better training ground than law school for his daughter to channel her energy and find her purpose. His own mother had done that. And Christie. They'd both used justice to heal from their victimization. His father had continued to encourage him that Jaclyn would heal as well. She would. He could see the early progress. How her work, the routine of getting up and going to the office with Lexi was already helping. She had a purpose. And so did he. Sooner or later, it would come to pass. He would kill Yrasrevda the Viper for what he had done. He would avenge his daughter. "So help me God, I will avenge my daughter," the vow echoed each time he shot his illegal gun.

6

The nightmare imploded before she could surface. The memories dissipating, sucked back into that subconscious black hole with a compelling force. Her body was afire. Desire a foreign kind of insanity to her ingrained values and pure upbringing. The climax echoing through her body in a gasping release.

She panted, holding Joshua's cross, feeling the after-effects of intense pleasure, but seeing the contradicting calm seascape picture framed on the wall as the nightmare dissolved into her subconscious. She saw the soft colors of the oil painting, the ocean's waves that never stopped coming over the sunrise. Peace. God's faithfulness. She fought to relax, to understand this horrid battle between her body and spirit, her mind and emotions. Rubbed her head, there was a nagging headache behind her left eye. It was the residue from a painful week with her period but finally she was through that and the PMS that had brutalized her emotions. In a moment the dream was gone, beyond her grasp and an exciting day was ahead. She dismissed the headache and rose with purpose.

In five minutes she'd meet her father for their dawn run. Lacing her runners, she did the standard blood test. She could prick her finger and test her levels with one hand now. Her LH was a little high, she countered it with Ida's daily prescription: a melt away capsule of hormones under her tongue every morning. She washed the residue of the cherry flavor down with a mug of hot decaf tea. Smiled as her father came out in his grays with an old football T-shirt on. It's what he always wore. Her outfits changed every day. Today it was navy and lime green. Ear muffs like a headband. With a goofy grin her father slipped an ear bud into her left ear. As they ran they listened to music. Today it was his choice. Sports rock she called it. The music you heard during the down times of sporting events. She'd grown up on the pump it up tunes. They were familiar as old friends. So was the wireless ear bud system where she could talk and listen, hear and be heard. And the security force. Two men, running with them.

With a lively conversation about the cold snap in the air, they fell into step for the three-mile jog. Fall had slipped into winter without a fight. The chill slipped off her high tech fabric. Her father was still in fantastic shape. His body lean, sculpted with muscle. His shoulders wide, his waist narrow, his belly flat. Under the ball cap his hair curled a bit. She touched it, smiled. Thought of Joshua with his overlong hair, dark as midnight, just as thick.

"Need a haircut," he told her.

"You're cute," she answered.

"Little old for cute."

"You're not old." She bumped him. "You're prime, Daddy."

"Prime," he mimicked. "Tell that to my knees."

They talked about her brothers. Levi's junior varsity team had a game tonight against the school's rival. Her father was proud of his high school start as quarterback. Enthusiastically coaching Max in his last year of Pop Warner. Watching from the sidelines as Xavier played his first year of middle school ball. She was looking forward to Levi's game tonight, too.

Back in the kitchen he said, "Good run."

She wrapped her arm around her father. Love suddenly deep and vibrant. The moment reminding her she was free, with her father, when just weeks ago she had been imprisoned and losing hope of ever seeing him. She just wanted to be near him. Love on him.

"I love you, Daddy."

He held her tight, stroked her hair. "Love you too." Gave her a kiss. "Better get going," he looked over her shoulder at his wife. "Heard your boss is hard to please."

"Um," Lexi replied. "I heard your daddy is a softie."

"Cutie," she corrected with a wink. "He's totally prime, Momma."

"Um." But Lexi smiled. The love real and sweet and a bit sexy as she slipped her hand around his waist.

"Um-hm," she sassed, bobbing eyebrows at them. "Might want to take ten and check him out. I'll feed the knuckleheads." She sashayed past her, called out, "Who wants pancakes?" She repeated one of his favorite lines, "Life is too short to procrastinate," as she gave her daddy a look.

She chuckled as her father took the bait and tugged Lexi behind closed doors.

"Oh, yeah." Jaclyn danced as she made the batter, poured it, flipped the pancakes, ate a stack as she waited and cooked, and wondered how marvelous it would be to have a man like her father for a husband, a marriage like her parents, still vibrant and sexy. She thought of Joshua, of his smile right before he laughed, of his tenderness when she cried, of his strength and the unforgettable moment when he'd sang over her, the sacred words as he'd draped his cross over her head. She touched the necklace, treasured the gift. Wondered yet again over the Hebrew words, what they were he always prayed over her.

"Sis," Levi greeted her.

"Levi, looking good," she praised him as he slipped onto a bar stool dressed up for game day in shirt, tie and trousers. "I like the shirt. Shows off your shoulders. You have dad's shoulders. Great shoulders. Quarterback shoulders," she said like an announcer serving him up pancakes. "Carry the world on those shoulders. I'm so proud of you."

He blushed and shrugged and started eating with a soft, "Thanks."

Max was next. He came in like a burst of energy. She loved him best because he was still shorter than her. She grabbed him up, squeezed him tight. "I made you pancakes."

"No way!" His eyes sparkled the brightest with his childlike excitement.

"Tell me you love me." She held up the plate.

He frowned then smiled. "You know I do."

"Say it. Mean it."

"I love you already," he gasped as she squeezed him.

She smacked him with a kiss and he moaned, struggled, wiped it off as she laughed.

"Don't you dare wipe off my kisses!" she threatened, but handed him a plate, called out her middle brother's name. "Xavier."

"Yeah. What?" He slumped into a barstool, his head on the bar.

She draped an arm over him. "Wake up, sleepy head."

"Where's mom? You're too happy in the morning," he growled it even as his arm slipped around her waist. "And you're getting shorter."

"You're just getting taller." She argued. "And I'm in runners not heels, boy."

His blue eyes locked with hers, his smile coming slow, building until his father's dimples winked at her. "You look good in heels. You made pancakes for Max?" There was charm. He'd been born knowing how to use it.

"No, just for you." She countered with her own, whispered, "Max got the leftovers."

"Darling shoes," he whispered their mother's saying, hugging her tight. "Like the outfit."

She set the plate down, watched them with wonder. They were so handsome. Levi with his shoulders. Max with his bright blue eyes under that fall of their mother's thick dark hair. Xavier with his charm and that overly handsome face. She had some kind of brothers.

Her mom came back, greeting, touching, cleaning. “How’s the pancakes?”

“Great. Good. More,” her brothers answered.

“Please,” Lexi prompted, meeting Jaxie by the stove.

“How’s Daddy?” Jaxie grinned.

“Um.”

”Um-hm. He’s totally hot, mom. You should see him run.”

“I think we’re partial,” she smiled.

“And look at his boys. Are they growing handsome or what?”

“Totally handsome,” she agreed. “Love the way they shovel in the pancakes and chug that milk then wipe it on their sleeve.” She checked her watch, called out the warning to depart for school. “Five minutes. Get those plates in the dishwasher. Grab your back packs. To the car.” She turned to her. “Better get in the shower. We’ve got a jet to catch in an hour.”

“Yes, boss.” She saluted her, kissed her brothers as they protested. On the move she chugged a glass of orange juice and ate a dry pancake wrapped up like a tortilla as she headed to the shower. The orange juice was unsettling. Eventually her system refused the acid. An after effect from the serum sickness was how easy her stomach could decide to get nauseated and vomit. She threw up. Felt better. Took some meds for the headache and kept going. She was tired of her body being in control of her life. She had things to do today and a new outfit from Jenna she was determined to wear. Aunt Cara had helped with the design, encouraged her to deny evil the power to fear her beauty and embrace who God had created. She was strong, courageous, faithful, beloved and beautiful. She fixed her hair and wished Joshua could see her in this, see her living out her faith with courage. Viper wasn’t ever going to stop her. Scare her. The Name of the Lord was a strong tower.

An hour later she emerged in new boots. They were definitely not made for walking far. The four-inch heels were pencil thin, the black suede butter soft leather rising up to her knees beneath a tone on tone, black on black, houndstooth skirt that was split over the center of her left knee and then fell tight and straight bursting out at the bottom back to almost sweep the floor mermaid style. The blouse was a soft black suede vest that was form fitting and zipped like a jacket. Incorporated into the vest were sleeves of fine gauge cashmere. The houndstooth collar stiff enough to stand up open at her neck like the petals of a flower, the sleeves belling softly at her wrists to mirror the hem of her skirt. The vest's zipper pull was a tassel of strands of tiny strung rubies that were also found on the boots. The outfit was a statement. There were moments when she loved being a girl, and this was one of them.

"Wow," her father said as she walked into the kitchen. He was dressed in business casual and preparing for his own meeting. His new laptop slipped into its case.

She bowed. "Presenting Jenna Cooper's latest. She threw this together for me while I was at the ranch. *Mae New West*, she called it. What do you think?"

Her father studied every detail as his brow lowered in degrees. "I think we need to add another man on the security team when you power up."

"Daddy."

He tugged on the tassel to zip the vest up higher.

"That's as high as it goes."

"She forgets you're short."

"Short?" There was a snort. "She knows my proportions. Jenna said this was perfect. Aunt Cara said it was modest. Nothing is showing." She glanced down. "I'm totally covered. Head to toe, Daddy."

"You're covered, but somehow," he shook his head, "You're not."

"You're beautiful." Lexi came to the defense. "Let me see those boots."

"Oh, man, here we go," Jaxson teased.

"Hush," Lexi warned. "They're darling shoes."

"Darling shoes," he mocked as his wife purred over the boots.

"What's this?" he lifted the suede strand around her neck.

"Joshua's tags and cross. Jenna gave me some new ways to wear them." She held up the black shot beads wrapped around her wrist. "I heard he's back from the Baltic," she said it casually, checking her handbag. Wishing suddenly she had taken her father's PDA while he was behind closed doors, checked it for messages from Joshua. She could have sent Fury one asking him to call his daughter. "Have you talked to him?"

"Um."

"Is that a Um- yes?"

"Yes."

"And how is the Fury?"

"He was glad to hear you're working with your stepmother. Thinks you'll be a fine lawyer."

"She'll be successful at whatever she decides she wants to pursue."

"He could pursue me instead of Daddy." She looked at her father. "Tell the Fury that next time he calls you to check on me. That he's got the green light along with my phone number."

"Does he?" Jaxson cocked his head.

"Dad." Jaclyn lowered her lashes a degree. "Are you making it hard on him?"

"I'm your father, of course I am." He laughed.

"You'll scare him off."

"I doubt even your father could scare off Joshua," Lexi told her.

"Tell him to meet us for lunch. We're in his neck of the woods." She looked at him. "I'd like to see him."

"I thought you were in New York today. Is it Washington?" he asked Lexi.

"New York," Lexi clarified.

"A stone's throw from Washington, Daddy, even on the train. I miss him," she said softly. "Please call him, he'd come if you invited him. He can check out the security force. See how well I'm doing."

"I can't do lunch today, sweetheart." He drew her close, kissed her. "I have a meeting but I'll miss you today."

"Ready, Jaclyn?" Lexi asked.

"Um," she answered but wrapped her arms around her father's neck. Her eyes linked with his. Her mind wondering how she could get his PDA and send Joshua a message. Deceitfully tell him to see her today for lunch. Where was his PDA… she frowned as his smile grew and flashed dimples, his words unheard until, "I love you." He kissed her.

"Don't stop talking to Joshua," she kissed him back. "I want you to get to know him. You'll like each other."

"I already like him."

She smiled now, clung close to him and held on for a long moment. She pressed into his neck, whispered, "I love the way you smell." There were several breaths, then softer still she told him, "I remember how Joshua smells. Isn't that strange. That you can remember a smell, find comfort in the way a man smells."

He held her closer, nodded.

She finally pulled back, told him, "I love you, daddy."

He kissed the tip of her nose. "I love you." She held on, the room waiting in silence. "You can stay with me today, be my assistant. I'll take you to lunch."

"No, I'm okay. It's not my first rodeo with Atlas and the A team on high alert."

"They've got you covered. You know that."

She nodded. "I'm not afraid. And I want to go with Lexi, meet Mr. Webb. I've enjoyed talking to him about today." She gave a nod, a smile, but still held on, still trying to think of a way to get to Joshua.

"Ready, Jaxie?" Her stepmother cued her again.

"You'll do great." He gave her a squeeze then Lexi a look as he commanded, "Stay safe."

Jaxson walked them out to the car. They both kissed her father. Lexi lingering a moment, talking privately to him as she waited now, then her mother told him, "We'll be back before game time."

7

They commuted to New York City on the supersonic jet in under an hour. It was an important meeting. A delicate deal as her mom put it. The Washington Nationals wanted a pitcher from Chicago but were going to have to deal with the Yankees to get him. She'd been working with her mom's team all week to get the deal done before the trade deadline at midnight. Jaclyn was assisting. Observing, would be the better word. Her mother needed no assistance. She was the country's best contract arbitrator in the sports world. Jaclyn was soaking up everything she could as she watched Lexi work the complex contracts.

During the past four negotiations she'd watched her deal with the NFL, NBA, a soccer team from Spain and a major athletic gear company. Taking notes and studying her body language, the responses, the innuendos, the contract wording. The language of the law fascinated her, the art of the negotiation an endless study of psychology and posturing, timing and tactics.

Her mind was following her mother's opening words, the value of the player clicked off in stats for the room then summed up by three points. Brett Webb had excellent strikeout numbers, didn't allow many walks and keep the hits on the ground creating more easy outs.

One of the men stated, “We’re not here to debate the ground ball impact.”

After working on this case, Jaclyn knew what that meant now. That ground balls could be the new strikeout in baseball.

“There’s no debate Mr. Webb also knows how to win the Series, gentlemen.”

And gentleman ... let's not overlook the fact that he fills out an Armani suit and knows how to pick out a tie.

The thought just popped into her head out of nowhere. She wondered if he had a stylist, if he bought off the rack or had a tailor. Maybe he had a male version of Jenna in his life. Someone with an eye for the right tie, shirt and suit combination. Jaclyn bounced the pencil that had been poised for any notation on her mom’s process, her ears tracking with every word, but with the summation finished, her gaze had shifted to Mr. Webb with her thoughts on fashion.

Brett Webb was looking back at her. Smiled. The subtle pattern in his tie picked up the green in his hazel eyes.

She smiled back. They’d talked on the phone several times this week. In the middle of his career-changing situation, she found him to handle the pressure with grace and respect. He was charming and their last few conversations had progressed past business issues to personal questions. He was twenty-eight, single, a Christian, from Maryland originally, the oldest of four boys who loved baseball and also gave a lot of his time to the Boys Club of America and the FCA. She’d looked forward to meeting him today. She’d been surprised and suddenly very charmed when he’d taken her hand in a gentle handshake, smiled and told Lexi it was good to have them both in his corner.

She’d appreciated his confidence. Refused to dwell on the obvious chemistry since she wasn’t interested. She was interested in learning how to negotiate. Watching Lexi who sat between them. Deciding Brett’s hair was red enough to be called chestnut. His eyes a smoky hazel. His shoulders wide. She realized she had a sudden fascination with shoulders. That's why his suit had caught her attention, it fit his shoulders really well, slimmed down his athletic body in that inverted V. The man had really great shoulders. Strong, like her father's and Levi's and Joshua's. . .

There was a flash of Joshua, the width of his shoulders, the strength of his arms. She shifted her thoughts before they had her imagination sinning, shifted in her chair, away from Brett Webb as she re-crossed her legs in the other direction. She began to jiggle her foot, wondered why Joshua wouldn't call her, angry suddenly that Joshua was avoiding her that he couldn't have lunch with her today. She fed the heat, loving the warmth of feeling and emotion that melted away at the numbness. She should have stolen her father's PDA, sent Joshua a message, "Call Jaxie. She misses you."

She shifted in her seat. Re-crossed her legs. Jiggled her foot. Bounced her pencil. Pouted her lips as her boot kept time, rowing the air. Energy restless to move. She'd lost track of the conversation. Felt like she suddenly had ADD. Worried about it for a moment, her inability to concentrate as troubling as her frozen emotions. But she was angry. Now. Maintaining the frustration, feeding the pout, really stewing. Getting hot. She wanted to see Joshua.

She felt Brett Webb's attention. Looking at her. Her gaze connected again with him. His eyes weren't that intense unreadable blue; they were hazel, a nice clear calm hazel. She smiled and those hazel eyes turned like a kaleidoscope, darker, delighted, so easy to read. Unlike Joshua, he was attracted to her. "Great boots," he mouthed silently.

"Thanks," she could only answer back silently and then force her attention back on her stepmother. She took notes. To concentrate. By the rebuttal he'd caught her attention again. His hand on his empty glass had a large signet ring from a World Series. Viper had a ring. A heavy gold ring with a large green jewel. She turned her thoughts away at once.

Her father had a ring. A Super Bowl ring. Brett had a ring, a World Series ring. She studied his hands. Brett had strong hands, capable of striking out over thirty percent of the batters who came up to the plate, his fingers long, almost elegant. Strong hands—strong man. She liked the correlation. Wondered if it was true. Brett was not Viper. He was like her father. A successful athlete. She wondered if he was a strong man. Strong enough to steal her heart from the Fury…

She glanced at the crystal pitcher but her mother had already moved to lift it, fill Brett's glass, right in step with the conversation about the three players who were being offered to New York from Washington and the four from New York that would go to Chicago for the single pitcher.

"Thirsty, Webb?" A man across the table from them asked.

"Something has his mouth watering," A man from Chicago threw in, glancing at her. He was young, rich entitled as the owner's son to talk like an idiot. *Knuckleheaded fool.*

"Actually," he countered, "I have a headache, Ned."

Instantly people responded. A bottle of Tylenol presented on a plate with a fresh water.

She felt the beat in her own head, behind her left eye. She felt the heat in her face, shame. Felt the tiny ripple of anger that came off Lexi. It was subtle but she knew her well enough to know Lexi's claws were coming out in quick defense along with a red pen that she used to alter the contract. This could get brutally ugly for Chicago if her stepmother went grizzly bear. It did.

Ned from Chicago paid big. Brett seemed to like that. When the papers were signed, he tossed him the bottle of Tylenol. "Think you might need that, Ned." He stood, made his rounds around the table shaking hands. He stopped at her side, smiled at Lexi. "Ladies, can I buy you lunch? I've got reservations upstairs. I knew you'd have this done by noon, Lexi."

"Give me a minute to snip a few loose threads." Lexi fingered her fat pen. "I'll meet you at the restaurant." Lexi quickly turned back and told him, "I've got security at the door. Take them with you."

Brett laughed then said, "You're serious."

"Very." Lexi's gaze was direct, her voice flat. "In about ten minutes the media is going to be on top of us."

"Where to?" Jaclyn asked and Brett walked with her into the hall. Paced her toward the elevator. The lunch hour rush had a group waiting. Her personal guard stepped in behind them as the elevator door's opened. They all did a dance to find their places in the crowd. Brett ended up behind her. Atlas beside her.

Jaclyn thought of the International Inner Port City, of the elevator ride with Joshua. The way he'd growled at the audacity of a man who dared to look at her when she was tucked under his arm. Joshua had incredible arms. Power. She looked at Atlas. Shoulders wide. Muscles breaking the clean lines of the dark black suit. Did Atlas know the Fury? Surely, he did. Coming from *Stratia*. He'd know Joshua.

"Hungry?" Brett's voice was low, interrupting her thoughts. Rich and warm. Private.

"Yes." She turned her attention to him. Could feel her stomach rise and fall quickly as the elevator surged up a floor and halted with a deflating surge that had the crowd groping for balance.

She squeaked. Immediately men moved. She had everyone's attention. Brett's hand on her back. She smiled at him. Told the crowd, "Some elevator."

The doors opened and they were pressed closer as more people joined them. The elevator took off with a lurch and she swayed, out in the middle, nothing to grab hold of but air. She caught her breath over another extremely female sound, looking up into those hazel eyes.

"Okay?" Brett asked softly, a gentle touch again for balance at her back.

"Miss Cooper?" Atlas was talking to her, looking at Brett and waiting for her signal.

"I'm okay," she assured Atlas. Told Brett, "Thanks."

"Sure." She felt the brush of his jacket, the loss of his touch as the ride smoothed out. She remembered his wide shoulders, his elegant hands. The lift stopped again. Fast. She swayed and Brett's hand was at her elbow. A few more crowded into the elevator. She stepped back. Looked up at him. Smiled as the whole group adjusted within the tighter space. As they took off his hand held her against him for support.

"You smell good." His voice whispered through her hair. "Really good. Like a flower. That pretty red one."

"A rose?" She'd looked up to smile, tease, then eased against him as she felt the coming stop. Heard the bing. Felt his hand find her elbow, secure her to him for balance.

"No." His gaze held her. The hazel green and focused. "Not a rose. Something else." He'd leaned closer. Inhaled. "Something, tropical. Really red. Cinnamon."

"Um. That's a spice, not a flower."

"You're right. And the scent is more brilliant. Like a diamond." He swept her outfit. Saw the details, smiled. "No, a ruby."

"Does a ruby smell?"

"Yes." He smiled. "It has an incredible, beautiful, red, spicy, tropical, cinnamony smell."

"Cinnamony? Is that a word?"

"Yes. Absolutely. Triple point scrabble word."

"You do smell really good," a stranger told her. He stood beside them. Smiled at Brett, looked her over. "What perfume are you wearing?"

She named the brand. Squeaked as the lift launched them at rocket speed again and her eyes went wide, her focus on Brett, her body turning toward him, away from the stranger. "Sorry, Brett. It's impossible to find any grace at the moment. This is like an unpredictable ride."

He'd moved closer if that was possible. Drew her nearer. He gave the stranger a look. The universal look that said, 'Back off, Dude. Mine.'

"Okay?" Brett asked her, his gaze a sharper green. His hand at her elbow had moved to her waist, tucked her closer.

"Perfect. Now." She smiled at him. "My boots are—

"Great." His attention was spectacular. Their discussion soft. Private. His gaze locked on her eyes.

"But they're a little high. I'm off balance when the lift starts. Sorry."

"I have you now."

Yes. He. Did. Mr. Brett Webb who wore Armani like he was their cover guy, with his wide shoulders, strong hands and hazel eyes did indeed have her. Now. She could feel the strength of his chest, her body cupped against him. Close enough to smell his cologne—expensive, innovative, American at its brightest potential—kind of scent. To feel his body heat. Sense his protective nature. To know that this was how it could have been. Months ago. Before. Now.

"Okay?"

"Um," she considered, looking up at him and finding a gentleman asking for permission. His face close, his pretty eyes changing color like hazel eyes could do. He was a Christian. An athlete. A man of integrity, from a strong family. He wanted to make something of his life past just being a famous pitcher for the Washington Nationals. Give back. Give. He was a giver. He would call her on the phone. See her. Tangle fingers under the lawn chair. Give what she needed. He was what she would have been looking for. Before. Now. "Yes. I think. You have me. Now."

She took the tiny step that was there to be made, came fully into his arms, accepting. Their fingers linked. She felt his ring. The wreath of laurel to the victorious athlete. Like her father's Super Bowl ring. Not like Viper's ring. Brett was like her father. A Christian. A man of worth. A good man. His hand tangled with hers. A playful caress, like fingers tangoing under the chaise lounge chair… she smiled. Not alone anymore. She had his attention. Undivided. Consuming. Possessive. Very male attention. Something bloomed in her. Power. Pleasure. Singing through her blood. Wanting. More. Yes, give me more…

She was irritated when the door opened, when the crowd gave them room, when she had to step away, separate, stand at a proper distance. She gave a frown and a huff and a sweep of lashes at the security team as they held the door and bid her off the elevator. Then she smiled. Brett claimed her again, stepped right up, his hand at the small of her back after he'd been so gracious to let others go first.

He was greeted by name at the restaurant. She liked the way he handled people. With humility but authority. He asked for a certain table, they were shown there. It was draped in white linen, in the center of the wall of windows that overlooked New York City. "We're honored to have you today, Mr. Webb," the waiter announced as he seated them. Brett held her chair out, tucked his own close to her. Dropping his napkin in his lap he asked her, "You follow baseball?"

"The Rangers," she answered. "My Uncle Layne's team."

"Layne?"

"Lexington," she answered. "My stepmother's big brother."

"Layne Lexington," he said with awe. "Right." He cleared his throat.

"Do you know him?"

"Just a hero of mine. He's a hall of famer, Golden Glove, one of the best shortstops to play the game. Now a U.S. Senator."

"I can get you an autograph." She teased.

"Really." Now he grinned. Then he stared at her mouth, lowered his voice to a whisper as he picked up his water, "My mouth *was* watering. You're . . . really beautiful, Jaclyn." He took a long drink. "I'm not sure what to do about that."

"What do you usually do? Beside stand up for a girl in the middle of a bunch of male chauvinists and protect her by claiming a headache. I thought that was very honorable." She leaned toward him, the desire to be close to him driving her there. The thought that Joshua had never told her she was really beautiful suddenly troubling and tempting her to anger, revenge. She took Brett's hand, tangled their fingers. Needy. She had to feed it. More. She clung tight. "Thank you, Brett."

His gaze swept her face, traced her lips. The internal motor in her body jump started with a rush as she interpreted the male body language. There was a driving urge, the energy manifested in a need to move. Her foot began to tap a ceaseless pumping rhythm of restlessness.

"What do I usually do?" There was a smile then he leaned closer to her, shared a secret. His mouth a whisper away from her ear. "Usually, I'm not falling for the daughter of my agent. You tell me?"

"Um." She leaned her face into his mouth. There was a kiss. The wetness on her skin magic. The place by her ear a tingle with sensation. Joshua had never kissed her. The anger flamed. Her body set fire to her feelings.

"Do I need to talk to Lexi?"

She lowered lashes, brought his hand up to inspect. He had very nice hands. Strong hands—strong man. "I stopped asking my parents' permission to date a few years ago."

"Maybe I need to. We do business together."

"This doesn't seem like business."

"You work for her."

Now she looked into his hazel eyes. "I'm observing her, trying to decide if I'm going to law school."

"Law school?"

"I'm smart," she confessed with an unapologetic, confident smile. "I've been accepted to a few schools. Georgetown. Harvard. Stanford."

"I believe it. You'd make a good negotiator."

"My mom said I could create a subtle distraction today. We agreed the boots would do it," she shrugged. "She's apparently not too fond of Ned."

"The boots are subtle, your beauty," he smiled. "Well …" He shook the ice in his glass and her gaze darted to it. Memories surged. Another man, holding a glass of ice, with a heavy gold ring. She was suddenly tense, troubled. Terrified.

"Jaclyn, did I offend you? Are you okay?"

She blinked, his hand had found hers. She clung to it as she saw Brett. Brett not Viper. With soft hazel eyes, adoring her. "Sorry, your ring—

"Ah." He frowned. Blushed. "It's too big. Too much—

"It's nice." She forced a smile now. "An accomplishment."

"I don't wear it very often. Today, Lexi said I should." He played with her fingers, picked up on the conversation, "Ned stung us two years ago."

"Yes, Lexi told me the story. She takes that personally." She tried to relax, stay focused.

"She's good."

"She cares."

"Which is why I do. I want to make sure she's okay with this."

"This?" She lifted a brow, held his gaze, pumped her foot. Thought about the elevator ride. His shoulders and his hands and the way his body fit to hers. The shape of his mouth. The way it had pressed to her face. Joshua had never kissed her. Never called her. She wanted him here. With her, for lunch today. She wanted his attention. There was temper that wanted to have a sudden tantrum. Now. Brett was here. Adoring her with a single-minded affection. Where was Joshua Fury?

"This," he said and he pressed that mouth to her hand, holding her gaze through the kiss. She was like a sponge for his attention. "I want to take you out. Tonight. Stay in New York."

"Um." For a moment she considered it, strongly, staying with him… then she said, "Tonight, my brother Levi has a football game. He's a freshman. Quarterbacking the JV team against their rival. It's a big game. I don't miss them. Come home with me." She smiled. "If you want permission from anyone, that would be my father. He's protective but you've got character to stand up against the inspection. He'll like you because Lexi respects you. Plus, my Uncle Layne will be there. We can get that autograph. I know it sounds strange, a high school football game, JV at that."

He chuckled. "High school football. It's been awhile."

"Did you play?"

"Sure. I have an arm. They used it."

"Quarterback."

He nodded.

"Levi and my Uncle Jude will like that."

"Jude?"

"Jude Dake, my dad's best friend. His dad will be there too. Uncle John doesn't miss a game."

"John Dake? As in, the John Dake."

"My family likes to play football." She wrinkled her nose and whispered, "We can get his autograph too. What do you say? Up for it?"

"I'm up for it, honey."

"Ah," she shook her head. "You can't call me honey. That's my grandfather's name. Honey Cooper. He was a bull rider."

"Right. Is there anyone not famous in your family?"

"I'm not famous." She lifted a coy shoulder, shrugged it slowly as he watched. "But I understand what it's like to live with a famous father. Why the entire room is fascinated with you."

"Us," he corrected. "And I'm certain it has nothing to do with me. Your boots are distracting, remember?"

She laughed now. "It has everything to do with you. These boots are certainly a distraction but they're under the table right now. You," she smiled, "Have that distracting smile out for everyone to see."

"For you, Jaclyn." He adored. "Most of them don't know who I am, just that I'm famous."

"Famous," she said with understanding, "It can be exhausting. Dad calls the recognition—ministering opportunities to share Christ. He sprinkles in a little Jesus whenever he can, gives some character talks, helps out, of course. And we were instructed to follow suit. Rudeness wasn't tolerated. Ever. My dad said it was being ungrateful for what God had given us."

"I'd like to meet your dad."

She smiled. "Here's Lexi."

Jaxie held on tight to his hand but then released him as he rose with respect. Lexi took her seat beside her.

"Brett's coming back to Texas with us. Going to Levi's game," she stated right away with a big smile. "He wanted to talk to you first, but I assured him I don't need permission anymore to invite a boy home. He's worried about your work relationship."

"Um."

"I told him I don't work for you. Just interning a bit before law school. Brett thinks I should go. That I'd make a good negotiator." She looked at him, smiled.

"You will," he agreed, then looked at Lexi. "I also want to make sure Lexi is okay with me seeing her daughter."

She looked at her daughter. "We'd love to have you in Texas. So you've decided on law school, Jaxie?"

"After today. How can I say no. I love how you work a deal. It's so . . ." she took a deep breath, smiled. "Stimulating."

Lexi smiled, lifted her menu. "What are you having?"

"Oh, we haven't even looked. Brett?" She leaned against him. Under the table she tangled their fingers, led them to her leg. "I'm sure you're having steak." She pointed. "Am I right?"

"Absolutely, big steak guy. What would you like, babe?"

"Babe," she purred softly behind the menu, "Love that. The Ahi tuna looks good. I like it rare."

"Lexi?"

"Caesar salad." She rose. Her hand on Jaxie's shoulder. "Why don't we freshen up, let Brett order for us?"

"Yes, ma'am." She rose, marched obediently beside her stepmother to the bathroom as one of the security guards followed. Because the laws were so strict on privacy, she'd been told the bathroom was an incredibly dangerous place and she was to wait to go in and not come out unless the man was still at the door. If he wasn't there, there was trouble and she should immediately call for help. At the door, Lexi told him to make sure they had privacy.

8

"What are your levels?" Lexi asked the minute they were alone.

"They're good," she answered slipping into a stall immediately and pricking her finger because she had no idea.

"When did you check them last?"

Jaxie inserted the cube of blood into her PDA and stalled with a sigh, "Lexi, a minute here. I really had to go and its totally complicated holding up five yards of this *Mae New West* skirt."

She was guessing she'd be at a level eleven, maybe as high as twelve. Ida liked her in the single digits, a nice simple seven was acceptable. But she'd had a soda, the caffeine would kick it up. And then there was Brett. She smiled. He was kicking her up. She felt great. She blinked when the read out came. Impossible! She couldn't be a nineteen. There was no way. She'd eat and check it again.

She faked the flush. Came out smoothing and tucking. Her stepmother was waiting.

"What's your level?"

"A little high. Why?"

"What is it?" She pressed on lipstick.

"Nine," she left off a digit, felt the guilt of the lie immediately.

"High," Lexi stated. "How are you feeling?"

"Fine." She lifted a brow, knowing she asked, "Why?"

"Honestly?"

"Yes."

"I'm worried. You're not yourself."

"Who am I?"

"You're charming him, Jaxie."

"It's in the blood."

"Not yours." She frowned. "You're—

"He's attracted to me, Lexi. He's gorgeous and smart. You know him. You rep him. I've gotten to know him the past week. I think he's great. A solid upright born again Christian." She pulled out her own lipstick and applied the dark red color. Lexi was watching her. "What? There's more, I see it in your eyes. So, what? You don't want me mixing business and pleasure? You want me to stay away from clients? Is he off limits? The first man that's been attracted to me since…" she trailed off, looked at her as a sudden emotion filled her eyes. "Is Brett off limits?"

"I just—

"You're worried. I know you." She turned and requested. "What is it?"

"I thought you were interested in Joshua. Where does he fit into this? We know there's a connection."

"A connection? He connects with Daddy. He connects with Samuel. He's never called me. I thought he would." She looked away now.

"Maybe he's just giving you time."

"Time?" She paced, needing to move, not wanting to think about this.

"He knows you need time. He cares about you."

"Of course."

"Maybe you need to give yourself some time."

Time. She was so sick of time. How slow it went, how fast it moved her away from Joshua toward a certain loneliness. She didn't want to be lonely. The ache was excruciating. Anger came like a hot flash. A lightning bolt at Joshua Fury. She wanted him, now. And he'd rejected her with that quiet, solid, certitude. Her father had told her no. They wanted her alone. She couldn't do it.

"Maybe I need to feel normal. I was raped by the Viper." She saw the flinch, was strangely glad her words had affected Lexi. "Repeatedly. Then thank God, rescued by Fury. I did things with both of them I never thought I'd do outside of marriage." She gathered a breath, emotion rising with facts she didn't want to disclose, didn't know how to say. "You're right, I'm not myself. I'm never going to be myself—the self I wanted to be. That's the truth and I'm dealing with all it means, but is it so wrong to tangle my fingers with a man I'm attracted to? Samuel tangles fingers with different girls every other day." She sighed. "Is it so wrong to have someone kiss me? Joshua never even kissed me, Lexi," there was a little gasp of pain then anger as she pressed on with the truth. "He did his duty, helped me through the insanity of Eros, he protected me, he cares about me. But he's not attracted to me and he's not interested in me or he'd call me. Brett is." She smiled now. "And frankly, it feels pretty good today. Can you let me have that for a little while? A good feeling? Some regaining of my confidence? Some attention from a handsome man? I need that. I need some attention right now." Her breath caught with a stab of pain and a thought she didn't want to face. She forced it back, took control, demanded, "I need to know someone is going to want me after all this—

"Jaclyn." Her name was to stop her line of thinking.

"It's a rational fear, don't you think?"

When her eyes went from anger to hurt Lexi stepped to her with great concern. "Of course, but it's unsubstantiated." Her stepmother took her hand. "Joshua—

"Don't," she whispered. "I wanted to see him today. I asked Daddy. He said no, in his own way, Daddy said no to me seeing Joshua."

There was a troubled look on her mother's face, a regrouping as she told her, "Your father is not going to be happy about you seeing Brett. He's very protective of you right now, Jaclyn."

"Maybe next time he'll understand." She looked away. "When I hint . . . maybe next time he'll realize that I'm not a little girl, that I know what I need. Who I want . . ." she just shook her head, exhaled, restless suddenly, urgently. "Before. Now. I was okay. I need to be okay again."

"You're not a little girl nor are you a woman to charm a man and play games. Brett is a fine man."

"Yes, he is. A very fine man and he thinks I'm beautiful. Very beautiful, he said." She brushed away a tear. "I'm not playing any game that he doesn't clearly understand or want to participate in. We're attracted to each other."

"Physically."

"Okay, sure." Jaclyn shrugged. "It happens to Samuel every other day."

"You're not Samuel."

"Of course." There was impatience. "I'm a woman and in this family we have our designated roles." Now there was a bite of indignation. "It's a double standard if you ask me." She crossed her arms. "So what do you want me to do, Lexi? Backpedal. Step aside."

Lexi's voice held the emotion she was doing her best to disguise. "I just want you to be careful."

"I'm not staying with him in New York, I'm taking him to Texas. We won't be alone, we'll be with family. I'm not going to do something impulsive and stupid that I'll regret. I won't get myself in any trouble. Trust me."

Lexi had closed her eyes, she knew she prayed. There was a soft and long exhale then a nod. "I want a code word," her stepmother said as she looked at her. "Something unique that lets me know if you need me. If you're in trouble and I need to negotiate you clear of a situation with Brett, or anyone else, a doctor, friend, family, security, a stranger, anyone. Give me a word so that I know you need my help."

"Softball contract," she answered spontaneously.

"Softball contract?" her mother repeated. "Okay, that will work. It's unique and something we wouldn't normally handle but no one would know that. Softball contract." She smiled now. "Promise me you'll use it when you need me. Anytime, anywhere, with anyone."

"Even dad?" she grinned.

Lexi frowned. Deeply. "You're on your own when you introduce Brett to your father. That's hardly a softball contract moment."

Jaclyn laughed, hugged her. "I love you, Lexi. Thanks for understanding."

Lexi nodded as Jaclyn made up her face, coiffed her hair then they returned to the table with a smile and a light and lively conversation. Her stepmother asked Brett questions, centered the conversation on him, and showed Jaclyn that she was supportive. It turned into a wonderful lunch. The three of them sharing a slice of cheesecake towered with juicy strawberries, she fed her mother, she fed Brett. She licked her lips after his fork forced upon her the last bite.

Under the table she held Brett's hand. His fingers tangling with hers. They had a chemistry, a rhythm, an energy that was thrilling. He made her smile. He made her feel incredible. She was disappointed when lunch ended. When Brett stood and his hand no longer played within her fingers under the table, she felt a flash of resentment, an obsessive need.

"Babe," he held his hand out, smiled and he was redeemed. His arm went around her waist, his hand a light guide for her mother. The three of them stepping out in front of the security team. She smiled when she saw the crowd for the elevator. Lexi sighed, commented on how crowded, fast and furious the elevators were in the building.

They made Lexi a little sick.

She could hardly wait for the ride. She backed into Brett, butting up tight against him. She felt the ring on his finger tap her hip bone and she wasn't afraid, she was thrilled. He was strong, the heat of his body braced tight to her, the strength in his hands holding her close, steady. Those hazel eyes adoring her. She smiled, delighted as he whispered, "I have you, now."

She didn't need Joshua Fury. Now.

Determined not to break contact, she clung to his side as they walked into the lobby. The midday light was bright. Brett slipped on shades, so did her mother, glancing at the security team, waiting for the cue that their car was ready.

"Let's wait in the sunshine. It's a gorgeous fall day," she persuaded them. There was a spring in her step, an energy coursing through her body that urged her to move. She was taking three steps to his every one, snuggled to his side. She had an urge to dance, she had an urge to shout to the sky she was happy. Joy was bubbling over into laughter now. They all were laughing about the crowded elevator and the way it dropped and brought the cheesecake rising to the top of their stomachs.

"Actually I believe the strawberries were on top," she told them. "I love that elevator," she purred into his ear privately, "Love the way you hold me."

His hand slipped back to her hip, strong and possessive. He was smiling, that darling, daring, smile of his, she bowing up high against him, returning her own. Up on a toe, the other foot kicked back, the slit showing booted leg. The lighting perfect. The picture couldn't have been better if they'd poised. And the photographer was happy to snap up as many as he could get of them.

The machine gun sound of the shutter at warp speed had her detail reacting before Jaclyn even realized what was happening. They blocked with the wide-built bodies they'd been hired to use. Atlas at once a shield of defense.

But the paparazzi had their shot of the new Washington National pitcher who had secured the Yankees four players from the capital city. He had Brett Webb and he wanted her name.

"Brett," he called out with a huge smile, "Chuck from the New York Globe. Who's the hot girl with the great boobs . . . I mean boots? Let's call it a rack."

Brett stepped forward, pointed. "You. Watch your mouth."

Atlas moved as well. Cutting off. Pushing back.

"Get in the car," Lexi insisted but Jaclyn only clung closer to Brett, watched him defend her with a certain giddy pleasure.

"How many millions did you get from Washington?" Chuck followed up skirting to the side, still shooting pictures. Jaclyn poised. Her attention on Brett. Her body locked to his side.

"Will you win the series? Earn your keep? Lot of pressure Mr. Webb. Is your arm up for it?"

"I'm up for it." Was the only comment he gave before he followed the girls into the car. "Sorry, Babe."

"Publicity. You deserve a little. Lexi's the first to tell you not to pass on advertising. You're a product, right?"

"Um."

"You're not," Brett said frowning and protective. He linked their fingers. "I know better. They got us, Lexi."

"Oh, yeah," Lexi agreed. "They got you. Good." She shook her head as she took a deep breath.

"Really?" Jaclyn smiled.

"They'll want her name." Lexi was looking at Brett. "Your publicist will call within the hour asking about her."

"He'll be demanding an apology from Chuck from the New York Globe for his disrespect to her. No one is talking to her like that. I'm furious."

"Um." A thought suddenly crept past. Jaclyn asked him, "Is anyone back in Chicago going to be furious about this?"

Brett laughed. "Oh, yeah."

"She means a woman," Lexi translated.

"No." He sobered. "No," he repeated, looking at her. "No," he assured. "There's no woman in Chicago."

She smiled. "Well then, feel free to give them my name."

"Jaclyn," Lexi interjected, "Let's talk to Marc."

"Marc? Is he going to be furious?" Brett teased.

"Marc handles my security," she answered, looking out the window, resentful that her life was guarded, that the Viper was still a threat. Joshua could handle the Viper, that's what he cared about. He didn't care about her, just her security. "Then talk to him, Lexi. Whatever you think is best." She cuddled into Brett's side. "Are you up for it?" she mocked the photographer, became his cheerleader. "You are so up for it. You'll clean up in the playoffs. Has he ever seen you play ball? Please."

"Have you?"

"Not in person."

"Then maybe you'll come."

"Maybe you should invite me."

"Invited," he answered.

"I'll be there." There was staring, silent and penetrating.

"One block to Mr. Webb's hotel," the announcement came from the driver.

She glanced at her stepmother as Lexi worked buttons on her PDA. "I'll go up with Brett while you reconnect with the world, Lexi."

"I'm trying to connect with your father." She looked up, the words processing, a warning look in her eye. "Oh, no. I might need you."

"Please, if you can handle the Yankees," she waved off her warning. "You'll be okay for a few minutes," she spoke in code. "We'll be right back." And they slipped out together as Lexi warned to watch for more photographers.

Security followed at a jog. They were moving fast. They were bombarded at the door. The click and flash of cameras like rice after a wedding. Three bellmen and security stepped in instantly cutting off the questions, the camera angles.

"This place got an elevator?" She refused to let the media affect what they were feeling.

"Glass. It's slow. But the view is showy."

It was. She stood against the glass looking out as Manhattan sunk below them and Brett braced tightly behind her. "What a gorgeous day. The view is beautiful."

"You should see it from my room."

Security checked it first, then waited in the hall. His suite was large, the view on such a clear day went on forever. She went to the window as he changed out of his suit. Found landmarks, and followed streets and the Hudson. Thought about what it would be like to be here with him, in this room. Saw her reflection, a cunning smile. Suddenly remembered…

The wall of glass. The tower of Babel. Up so high. Only clouds. Sometimes the horizon. Alone. Naked. Always. He'd be coming. Back. Soon. She needed the Ares. Where was Borg? She glanced around. Saw the door. Opened it.

Reality. It came back in a blink. "Miss Cooper?" Atlas stepped up. Brows drawn. Eyes looking past her into the room.

She was here. Now. In New York. Not Babel. Viper was gone. These weren't Russians. They were her men. Her security detail. She was safe. With Brett. Where was the Fury?

"We might be a minute." She smiled.

Atlas frowned. But he wasn't Borg. To give her orders. He was under her orders. Now.

"You're *Stratia*." She poised, against the door, lowering lashes, looking at him through their wealth. "Do you know the Fury?" At his nod she asked, "Did he send you to watch me?

He gave a single nod.

"Do you talk to him . . . about me?"

"He talks to your father."

"Tell him..." She gave a cunning smile. "He should have called. Been here. With me. Now..." Anger was hot enough to boil water. She closed the door. Searched. Now. "Babe?" The bedroom door was open. She pushed her own boundary, her boots striding slowly into a new territory she'd never pursued before. She saw him shirtless. Her gaze a study of him as she shifted her hip and poised with a certain posture. "Now. That's a gorgeous view."

He smiled back. "How cold is it in Texas?" He showed her the choices.

She didn't look. She didn't know she had such power. When her hand reached out and touched him and she watched under lowered lashes his body respond. "You've had surgery?"

"Yeah. In college."

Her fingers traced the scar. "Tommy John surgery?"

He nodded. "My parents thought lengthening the muscle would help lengthen my pitching career, better my chances. It did."

Their eyes met. His hand brought her unhurriedly close. "Shirt? Sweater? I'll wear what you like, Babe." She took the hangers and dropped them both on the bed.

"This is nice." Her hands measured his naked shoulders. "You have great shoulders. I've been . . . truthfully . . . a little mesmerized by them."

"I've been mesmerized myself." His hand was on the tassel to her vest, he studied the rubies. "These look real."

"Um," There was a smile. Her lashes low, her eyes hot. "They're real."

There was a sound. Male. Hunger. "I meant the jewels."

"I know what you meant." She closed her eyes, sank into the kiss. Deep, deeper, sliding. She melted, burned. Gasp, erupted.

There was a growl as she was gathered up into his arms. She could barely breathe, her eyes slow to focus, then finding him. There was heat in her face, a blush of innocence that made him confused.

"I," she tried to speak, tried to think. Shook her head.

He took back her mouth. The kiss was deep, drugging, discovering as his arms held her body against his own. "We need to stop. Go. Now. Your mom," he caught his breath, laughed. "We need to go." He pulled back. "Thank God for your stepmother." He shook his head. "I… we… you," there was a groan of frustration. "You are," he glanced down her body, his hand moving back up, "Incredible."

Immediately she bowed into his hand as a moan escaped.

"Babe, we've got to go. I want things," he shook his head. "You."

"I wanted…" *Joshua.* "A kiss," she corrected. Just to be kissed. But too late, she'd gotten more. Now she stood with her breast in his hand and her body craving so much more. "Just a minute with you. A private minute." There was a little frustrated gasp. "Brett." A pout.

"What Babe?" He was so attentive to her. His eyes a smoldering green, looking into hers, waiting.

She shook her head. He nodded, kissed her.

"I know. We need to do the right thing. Go."

"Stay close to me," she requested softly. Fear and frustration producing an unclear chaos. "Discreetly," she demanded, handing him the hangers. "I like you close," she zipped up her top, straightened her clothing, smiled at him. "You have great shoulders." She decided on the sweater. Watched him shift his shoulders into it, spread the thin black cashmere across his chest and let it mold over his muscles. "Um." It was a helpless little cry of wanting. "You'll drive me to distraction." She turned on a heel, sashayed to the door as he chuckled she deserved it. She held the knob, waited for him. "Coming," she tossed over her shoulder with her wealth of fire brown hair, watched him put on the leather jacket as he walked to her with heavy eyes. At the door, he pressed up against her and she purred.

"Close you said?"

"Yes. Like this." She gathered him to her.

"Like this?"

"Just like this." She took his hand, rested his ring on her hipbone. "With your hand here."

"Right here." He nuzzled her ear with kisses as he promised, "I'll be discreet. Respectful. Lexi will keep us honest. We don't need to be alone, Babe." His gaze was direct, holding her own and she understood what he was saying. "But if you like me close, I'll stay right here."

9

The guy was close to insanity. The combination of his cousin's beauty and sensuality delivered at him with such adoring attention, a man would be helpless to be unaffected. And Jaclyn's charm was on full throttle. The couple locked in a crowd, of family nonetheless, when it was so obvious they needed to be alone.

They'd be anything but alone, Samuel decided, sidling up close to the famous pitcher. He didn't like the man. He didn't know him, but he was certain he didn't like him despite what everyone was passing around. Great guy. He scoffed. He was a guy, a rich and famous guy, and he was bewitched by a pair of high heel boots and a sparkling tassel of red rubies predominately placed where they shouldn't have been. The fit of that black suede jacket and slim skirt giving curving guidelines to be filled in with living color. And his cousin had a whole lot to fill in, including that edge of hip bone Webb was so determined to rest that World Series ring on.

He was going to have a talk with his sister, Jenna, about this sexpot skirt design—how she could interpret something modest into that kind of trouble. He was not going to let Jaxie out of his sight. He'd never seen her like this. Maybe it was good. Her not being afraid. Stepping out. Dating. That's what his mother was saying. This was good. He thought about Fury. Frowned.

"Donde esta Yarah Silva?" she asked him with a glance, her attention on her brother, Levi, as he warmed up before the game. One hand was on the fence, the other tangling loosely with Webb's hand at her hip. Their positions like her outfit, modest, but somehow the chemistry around them was totally immodest.

"She's back in Brazil."

"So soon. I liked her."

"You did not," he scoffed.

"Brazilian beauty." Jaclyn described her to Brett. "I'm glad she didn't come or I might have a hard time keeping your attention."

"Babe," he denied, whispered something in her ear that had his cousin's dark red lips smiling with satisfaction.

"Levi's tossing the ball well. Got anybody that can catch it on the team?" Samuel turned their attention to the field.

"He's got three good receivers."

"Looking forward to the year when he can throw to Xavier. Your brother's got hands like your dad."

"Um. That will be a great year."

"They wanted to move Levi up to varsity, I heard?"

"Dad said no," she stated. "It was right. Don't you think, Brett? Holding him back. He's only a freshman. Lot of difference between fourteen and eighteen. He could get hurt."

"Your dad would know. Did you play ball?" Brett asked him.

"Do they have a choice in this family," Jaclyn chuckled, nudging back with a shoulder and a cock of hip.

"We all have a choice," Samuel defended, taking notice of the way the man caressed that hip and locked her to him.

"But he played. Brett was a quarterback," she told him proudly.

"I liked defense best. Free safety." Cletus locked gazes with the man, swept Jaxie then came back to his gaze with an open challenge. "I liked intercepting the pass. You'd understand the play."

She understood the man code too and openly challenged him, "Samuel, don't make me kick you with these boots, they'd hurt." She leaned back against Brett and covered his hand with her own. They talked football, baseball, Texas, and the weather. They moved to the stands, took a seat with Jaxie between them and their family around them. He watched him as he met the infamous among them and he watched him when he met the common. He studied him as he met their women, the young, the married and the beautiful. He was constant, confident, polite. And protective, he kept Jaxie tucked tightly to his side.

At halftime they rose. "We're going to the concession stand," Jaxie announced. "Want anything?"

"Don't eat too much, I've got ribs waiting with the brisket," her father reminded her.

"You don't have chocolate," she smiled at her stepmother. "I'll bring you M&Ms."

Samuel stood and her stare was enough to sit him back down next to her father with a, "How's it going Uncle Jax?"

He watched them walk away. Brett's hand tangled loosely with hers, attentive to her careful steps in those hideous boots down to the even surface when he tucked her to his side. Samuel crossed his arms and muttered quietly to his uncle, "He's on her like sticky on tape. What's up with her?"

"I've been told to let it go." Jaxson said quietly but took his arm and pulled him up. "I'm suddenly thirsty. You Cletus?"

"Parched." Their boots strode in a quick step down to the concession stand. He was surprised to find air between them along with a 10-year-old boy. Brett was signing his ball cap, carrying on a conversation.

"I'm surprised you recognized me. I don't get to Texas very often."

"Sure. You're the best. Your sinker, rocks, Mr. Webb. How do you throw that?"

Brett explained it in simple terms then shook his hand. "Good luck, Colin."

Immediately three more kids were on him and Jax chuckled as they approached her.

"Price of fame," Cletus said.

"He's great with them." Jaxie actually cooed with pride. "Don't you love it, Daddy?"

"How long have you known him?" Cletus took her arm and tugged her toward the concession stand.

"Um."

"Um-hm. That's what I thought," he looked at her dad.

"Don't you even start, James Samuel." She stomped a boot and backed up with narrowed eyes. "I guess Brazil was your high school sweetheart?"

He tugged her forward, got nose to nose. "Oh, I'll start alright. With Jenna when I get home. I'll bust that sewing machine apart." His gaze swept her from roots to boots. "This—

"This what?" she growled, bumping back suddenly. "And don't you dare touch Jenna's machines—

"Hey," Jaxson stepped in. "Manners." He walked them forward, smiled at the concession mom. "Hey, Janice, we need some chocolate." He ordered the M&Ms and sodas. "Water?" he asked her.

She nodded, looking over her shoulder.

"He'll find you," Samuel grumbled.

She lifted a brow and took the candy, leaving the water. "Brett."

"Ah, here's my girl, now."

"My girl," Samuel mocked.

"Just an exit line, Cletus."

They watched them come together. "He's smooth," Cletus stated, "So subtle with the hands. You can find her waist easier than you can that hip bone," he frowned. "That has to get a daddy's temper up a bit."

"Nothing inappropriate." But Jaxson was tense.

"Lexi's holding you back. I can tell. Jaxie never flirts and she hardly knows this guy."

"Lexi knows him." He put a hand on his back and led him on. "Game's on."

"Game's on," he repeated to her as they passed. That would get her moving.

Instead she said, "We'll be up." They watched the second half from the fence. The pitcher snug to her back, whispering in her ear. Her parents keeping track of her as they tracked the game almost as closely as he did. Everyone was tense. Jaxie was all smiles.

"Find out her levels?" he heard Jax tell Lexi as they were loading up the cars and suddenly Cletus realized this went beyond a defense of her honor.

"Have you checked your levels?" Lexi discreetly asked her at the sink. She was expected to sound them off. She was expected to help serve the meal. She wondered sometimes why they didn't have help to do this. They were rich after all and there were always friends scattered in with the family, time for socializing not getting stuck in the kitchen with all the women in the family tradition of hospitality. Stuck in the kitchen while the men sat on the patio. Stuck in the kitchen away from Brett. There was an obsessed irritation she couldn't rationalize that had a bit of a bite to it and a wild sense of impatience.

"I'm fine. I need to get back to Brett. He doesn't know anyone."

"He's fine. He's in the club." Lexi assured. "He knows their language."

"Football," her Aunt Tori added, "Just baseball with a southern dialect. Right Ellen?"

"Absolutely. Layne loved him by the way."

Jaclyn smiled. "Uncle Layne is one of his heroes. Don't tell him, he'll be totally embarrassed, but he was freaking out that he got to meet him. I'm getting him an autograph." She laughed. "Think you can help me out?"

“Anything you need.” Ellen conspired quietly. “Does he have a younger brother,” she whispered, “Julia thought he was adorable and she never notices anyone.”

“Really? He’s the oldest of four. What will the Senator think about a baseball boyfriend for his medical school daughter?”

“What does your dad think?”

“Well, Lexi kinda works interference.”

Ellen laughed. ”That’s always been how we do things in the family.”

”Yes, and with that said, I’ll leave you ladies to what you do best and join my very handsome Washington Nationals pitcher.”

“You need to eat,” her stepmother called her back. “Really,” was said with a serious note. “You’ve had not a thing since lunch and you picked over your fish.”

“I had chocolate and soda.”

“Exactly.” Lexi gave her the look. “Stimulants.”

It’s what had her blood racing, her hormones spiking and her mood edgy. She didn’t want to worry about her levels. They were high, she knew that without painfully pricking a finger. She looked at Brett, smiled as he held out his hand. He was eating on the patio, a fire dancing in the outdoor fireplace to reflect the one dancing with her anticipation to be back to him. The area was crowded with family and friends who had come to celebrate her brother’s win. Brett sat on the padded nook, she took his hand, snuggled down beside him. His body warm. His sweater soft. He smelled clean and rich. Classic American success story.

Levi sat down beside her, forced her closer to Brett. She loved her brother. Told him so. How proud she was of him. He smiled. She introduced him to Brett.

Levi shook his hand, said very matter-of-factly, “If you hurt my sister, I’ll kill you.”

In the awkward silence she laughed.

Levi stared only at Brett. “I’m serious, sir.”

"I believe you." Brett nodded.

Levi released his hand, rose with a single nod.

"Kid's got a handshake." Brett told her with a smile. "And a future. He's a great player."

"Yes," she agreed, watching him walk back to his table of friends. Troubled. Embarrassed.

But Brett smiled, squeezed her hand, praised her father's cooking. She shared a rib from his plate. They had a conversation about smoking beef. She just enjoyed listening. Her daddy was serious about his grilling. The topic and the function a constant competition among the men in her family. They guarded their "secret" recipes. Her father still not ready to pass his along to anyone yet. The fact that Brett had an opinion interested the men. They debated the country's steakhouses next. She snuggled in, her foot tapping out a beat of energy. She needed to move. She whispered about the horses that he wanted to see, reminded him. He nodded. They rose, began to move into the night.

"Get enough to eat?" Samuel stepped up. There was another conversation about the great meal. He held out a cigar, nodded to the edge of the patio where several of her uncles were lighting up. "Smoke?"

"No," Brett shook his head. "Thanks though."

"Enjoy it," she said and turned. If he followed her a step she was going to kill him. He did. She turned. "Daddy could use a cigar. Since you have a spare," she glared at him, "And he's out." She mouthed, "I'll kill you if you follow us." Then she told him, "You do owe him. Big, for all the times he's had a spare for you over the years."

It did the trick. He stopped. Knowing it was true. She'd covered for him with his mother more times than either of them could remember.

"Dad has three barns," she began the tour. "Mares. Studs and then his personal horses." She leaned on him, her feet were starting to feel the day. She cuddled tight to his body.

"Cold?"

"You're warm." She led him to the first barn. The stalls were big, the stallions poking their heads out to investigate. "The stallions. Strong, temperamental, unpredictable. They're bred every week but the young ones can be feisty. Like you, RexRacer," she laughed as the stallion tossed his head, called out loudly, then pawed the earth. He paced in front of the door. "Beside him is Xtreme then thexFactor. You can tell my dad has a thing for the letter X." She smiled, introduced a few more as they passed but they both knew why they were here. At the end of the barn he turned her into his arms and they kissed.

She sighed as he moaned over the first taste. He was tedious, slow, attentive. He spoke against her lips. "You're so beautiful." He looked into her eyes. "I've never been with anyone that makes me feel what you make me feel, Jaclyn." He kissed her. His words coming between their kisses. "The way you . . . do what you do. Need me, want me." He shook his head. "It's incredible, the chemistry. You're an incredible woman. I want to see you again. Build something with you. Soon. Tomorrow." He laughed. "Tell me you'll see me tomorrow."

"Tomorrow," she repeated the word, her mind thinking about what she wanted now. She couldn't speak. What she felt, if said, would sound crude and wicked, but it smoldered in her body, hot and bothered and needy and was communicated through her kiss. She could have wept when he filled his hands with her breasts. He pleasured her until the sweet eruption came that had her surging higher into his arms and finding that brutal moment of peace.

She was breathless and weak as she sank back down and uncurled her toes. Opening her eyes she found him smiling.

"You smell so good." He murmured her name. "I want you. I can't believe I'm talking like this, telling you this, doing this. But the chemistry . . . this connection. I want you. Jaclyn. . ."

She was breathless, they both were, standing there, staring into each other's eyes. And the moment spoke, in the silence, lust whispered the great looming potential of utter pleasure. There were decisions that could be made, here . . . right now in this instance. Here in the dark shadows of night they could hide, find that moment of fleeting pleasure. He said her name in a way that warned her how weak he was, how dangerous it would be if she didn't decide. Now. If she wasn't strong. Now. "Show me . . . the mares," he requested.

"I . . .I'll show you the mares." She took a step back. Led him by the hand then drew close to him immediately. They walked again, into the night, down the road a ways to the bigger barn. Here the stalls were smaller, with charts and temporary name cards for the visiting mares to be bred. She passed Gracie's Fancy. Read the card. The two live covers last month by Xtreme. The vet checks. She was pregnant. She smiled, gave her nose a pat, told Brett, "She won some races. Her owner had her bred to Xtreme. They'll foal a winner for sure."

They walked down the barn she explained the breeding process. "An owner sends their mare to be bred by one of the studs. They determine when she'll be in heat."

"How do they do that?"

"They can do a clinical test, but she'll give off signs. Restlessness. She'll flag her tail. Winking occurs that has nothing to do with eyelashes. They bring her and the stud together for several days. They walk him around her. They both show off their stuff and act up appropriately. They'll call out to each other from the barns. Irritated to be apart."

Brett chuckled as one of the mares made a loud long call.

She grinned. "It's funny, really. The way God designed the process, even in animals. But it's appropriate. Either one can refuse to cooperate if they decide they don't have a thing for the other. The teasing period is important. It assures that they'll mate and when the mare moves into standing heat ... that she'll accept the stallion."

"Teasing?" He read off a mare's card. "So this one's been teased by RexRacer but not bred yet. No wonder they're both restless and pacing their stalls."

She looked, Brett tucking her in front of him like she liked, his hand on her hip bone, his body close behind her. "The chart shows she'll come into heat tomorrow."

His mouth was on her ear, sliding to her neck, his body tightly fit to hers. He chuckled now then sighed. "Babe, we're like these horses. Restless and wound up from a day full of teasing. I swear, the way my body is misbehaving, my flesh demanding you. We're in heat."

The blind could see. The day replayed like a slide show. She watched the mare, pace, flag her tail, call out with irritation to RexRacer and heard the stallion's reply. Felt Brett. His strength covering her. His mouth pressed to her. His foreign scent surrounding her. And her body fit to his, wanting...

A greater strength. The first kiss. A familiar scent. Instantly she understood.

Eros.

Her hand swept under her hair, below her neck, where the tattoo had been. The Eros had been removed with the tattoo, but somehow it was back. The truth a terrible revelation.

Her soul cried out for Joshua.

She felt Brett and revolted. There was nausea. It swelled. Swift. She swallowed. Her hand went to her throat, closed around Joshua's cross as the mare let out a shrill high demand. She remembered Viper's threat, that she would never be free.

She said His name, the only name that could help her with a silent screaming plead.

Lord Jesus, help me, it's back.

10

"Babe?" Brett was still. "What's wrong?"

"I… I, don't feel good." There was a rush of reality, with it overwhelming regret and shame. She was mortified. So mortified, she was paralyzed. Frozen with fear. Sick. She was going to be sick. She lunged away from him. Vomited on a bale of hay. Emptied herself, over and over again until the dry heaves doubled her over.

Finally it stopped. He was there, helping her to stand.

She couldn't look at him. "I'm sorry." She began to weep.

"Shh." He brought her close. "I'll get you to the house."

She stumbled. He scooped her up into his arms. "Jaclyn," there was deep concern.

"I'm sorry." She clung to him, needing him, hating it. "Forgive me. You're a good man."

He took her to the house. She pointed to a side door away from the party on the patio, there was a pool bath. Once inside she asked him softly, "Will you find Lexi?"

"Sure."

"Just tell her . . . I need to talk to her about the softball contract."

"What happened?" Lexi asked as she slipped into the bathroom.

She couldn't answer, just lunged into her arms and cried. "Did he do something? Tell me?"

She shook her head. "No. It's me. You were right. I'm off. My levels." She showed her the read out.

Lexi gasp. Grabbed the PDA, studied the high number. "There's a mistake."

"I did it twice." She shook her head, began to cry. "I'm cycling. I don't know how but I am. It's bad."

"Okay." Lexi paced. "Okay. We'll call Ida. She'll know what to do."

"I did . She wants me to come right now to Virginia."

"I'll go with you."

"I need you to handle Brett." She took her hand. "I want you to tell him. Everything. I want you to explain what I've been through and do it so he doesn't feel any guilt or responsibility for today. Will you do that for me? Take him to the jet and tell him I'll call him when I get through this. Thank him for today. For respecting me. Tell him I understand that this is just too much for him to deal with. He can walk away without any hard feelings. You know what to say. How I feel. You know."

"Yes. Okay. I'll talk to him, use discretion. Are you sure you want me to tell him?"

"Yes. The truth. He'll have to deal with it."

"I'll explain it in a way he can understand. Okay?"

"Thanks." She squeezed her hand. "Go take care of Brett. He's worried. I got sick. He had to carry me back from the barn."

"Did he do anything to you? I need to know."

"No." She shook her head. "Please. It's me on Eros. I did everything to him. You can't understand." She walked away, pacing the small bathroom, reminded of the train and its narrow pathway in their compartment. "Trust me. Do what I asked. I've been through this. Believe me, I've been through this before."

"Okay."

"Go. Please. He's worried." She turned back to her. "And I need him to leave." Looked into her eyes. "He has to leave or I'll be all over him because I don't have Joshua."

Lexi blinked, then took a deep breath and left. Jaclyn paced the small bathroom, waiting until she knew enough time had passed and they were gone. She raked her hands through her hair, avoiding the mirror, ashamed to see the face of the girl who lusted. She felt the urgency in her body, the restless demanding need. She could hear the mare calling out with her shrill high demand. She could hear Viper's taunts.

Only I can keep you from roaming the earth and becoming its whore. Do you want to be the whore of the earth? I have put lust into your body and it cannot be silenced even by your God. You are mine forever.

She heard his voice. Felt the hiss of Viper's breath against her skin. Rubbed the back of her neck where he'd marked her with his tattoo. Saw the woman he'd turned her into. She fled the room.

"Hey." It was Samuel who cut off her flight to her bedroom. "Where did Spiderman go?"

"Who?"

"The pitcher, Webb—Spiderman."

"New York." She detoured to the kitchen, glad it was empty, searched the refrigerator for water. When she closed the door Samuel was waiting, caging her in the corner.

"Back to New York? I thought you were joined at the hip."

"Don't." She lifted her chin, lowered her lashes. His eyes were dark blue, focused on her own, intent. "Please," she said it softly, "Don't." She tried to slip by, he stepped up, looked down at her. "I have a headache, Samuel."

"What were you doing today?"

She ducked under his arm and put her hand up. Marched away. He followed her into her bedroom.

"We're going to talk about this."

"We're not." She drank the water, rubbed her head then the spot on her neck. It was burning. How long had it been burning?

He'd been talking. Talking and walking behind her as she paced. His words just babble. Babble until he said, "Joshua."

"What does he have to do with this?"

"He's going to have a come apart when he hears about Spiderman."

She growled, lunged, ripped at his shirt as she tugged him up against her with a power she didn't possess. There was a voice that came out of her, a voice of an animal. In Spanish she cursed him violently. Said all the things she'd been holding inside against him for becoming Joshua's friend, for being the one he called, for betraying her somehow. She'd kill him if he ever talked to Joshua about today. He wasn't her cousin if he did that. He wasn't. She was sobbing when she finished. Shaky. Ashamed. She let go of him, backed away, stumbled as she turned her back.

He caught her with care, tender now, seeing something as she tried to turn away. "I got most of that. You were talking faster than I could translate, Jaxie, but I got it. Sit down," he said it softly. "Your feet have to be killing you in these ridiculous things." He pulled the tassel on her boot, unzipped it and tugged it free. He massaged the arch of her foot. "Have you taken any meds for your headache?"

"No."

"I'll get you some in a minute." His hand was magic, she closed her eyes, felt the muscles quiver in her arch. "I'm going to talk to Jenna about these boots. She's got no idea what it's like to walk around on five inches. Squeeze her toes into a fifteen degree corner." He kissed her foot. "You've got pretty feet, Jaxie. Give me the other one."

His hands were strong and sensual. His lips full and sexy, the kiss hot and wet on her arch. She needed that mouth, so many places on her body . . . She blinked, seeing him. Her cousin, Samuel. Terrified. She pulled back, stood up, paced, limping from foot to boot. "You need to go."

"What did I say?" He stood. "Come on. I let it go. Jaxie. I love you. Want to protect you."

"I don't need protection," she tossed over a shoulder. "I've got a personal guard for that."

"Sometimes you girls just don't understand. Your beauty. What you do. Your power."

"I understand. It's a double standard. You get Houston. Brazil. Anybody you want to tango your fingers with under the lounge chair and I'm supposed to stay home and be safe, alone!"

"That's right. You're to be protected from guys like me."

"You're a great guy."

"That's not what Houston would tell you. I'm fickle. Fast to move on. I hurt people because I can be carelessly selfish. Is that what you want to do? Be? Selfish. Careless."

"Just leave!" She turned into the corner, there was nowhere else to go. She was trapped, by angry red walls, her own choices, her body on Eros. She couldn't look at him.

"Jaxie." He was behind her. A hand that turned her.

His hand was on her shoulder. He had strong hands—strong man. Wide shoulders. His eyes, no one's eyes were that fine a blue. True blue. His lips full. His face so pretty. She'd ripped the buttons off his shirt. It hung open, his chest sculpted, dusted with dark hair. The trail centered into his six pack strong abs, falling into his jeans. She closed her eyes, a tear fell immediately, the shame caused more and more as the lust ran overwhelmingly hot.

He said her name, pulling her into his arms. "I'm sorry. Whatever I did, said, I'm sorry. Forgive me."

She could smell him, feel him. She trusted him. He would help her.

She jerked, gasp. "Please, Samuel. Please. You have to leave." She skirted him, fled from him, unbalanced, tripping.

"Jaxie." He had her, helped her. "Sit." He cursed her. Jerked the zipper down, tugged the second boot off. His hands, the feel of them on her legs made her want to fall into his arms. She sprang up. He grabbed her close. "Tell me what's wrong. Now."

She just looked at him and moaned.

"What did I do?"

"You're a man." She pulled away. Her gaze ran over his chest again.

"Yeah. We're jerks. I was a jerk."

He was gripping her shoulder. There was a fire. "You're . . . hurting me."

"Sorry." He let go. Pocketed his hands. "Please, tell me how to make this right."

"Spit." She held up her palm. "Give me some spit. Just do it."

He spit on her palm.

"More." She demanded, "Give me more spit."

He did. She immediately put it on her neck. On the place that burned like a fire and she moaned. He was staring at her. She didn't care. She was beyond it in this moment as she rubbed his saliva into her shoulder and felt the fire ebb back from his male hormones.

"What can I do?"

"I need you to leave." She opened her eyes and looked at him as tears clouded her vision. "If you don't, I'll regret it for the rest of my life. Please, Samuel." She begged even as her body quickened and yearned. "You don't want to see me like this. You don't."

"Did Webb do something to you?" He cursed.

"It's me," she hissed. "It's my body, my hormones. My levels are high, escalating. I don't know how but I'm not in control, Eros is," she finally admitted it.

"What?" He stepped back, raked a hand through his hair. Paced a minute. "I'm calling Fury. He'd want to help."

She attacked him and they went to the ground, rolling and wrestling as she screamed at him.

"Jaclyn!" Her father rushed in. "Jaclyn," he tugged her off. She was hysterical then in a blink she was crushing her father into her arms, clinging for dear life as she sobbed.

"Samuel?" Jaxson asked.

"She's upset." He rolled up onto his feet. "She doesn't want me talking to Fury. She ah . . . she's off."

"Off?" He took her face, his gaze examining her and becoming troubled. "When's the last time you checked your levels?"

She told him the number.

He shook his head. "Eight you mean?"

"Fifty Eight." There was silence. "Is Brett gone?" The need for him to both be here and be gone a terrible tension.

"Yes." Her father's hand stroked back her hair, holding her close, his eyes searching her. She felt his strength. Could smell the familiar comfort of him, her daddy. She clung closer as she pleaded now in a soft whisper, "Please don't tell Joshua." There was a sob. "Please daddy, don't tell him. Don't let Samuel tell him."

Emotions surged up, over and her body escalated with the next heartbeat. She was suddenly on fire and the man that held her was all she'd ever known of love. There was a thought. Repulsive and so wicked it jolted her. Immediately she pushed her father away, told them both, "Get out! Get out of my room. Oh God." She ran away from them, turned her back on them. Her shoulder was tingling. Her hand going there, rubbing there.

"Jaclyn," her father called her.

"Now. Please. I'm begging you." She sobbed now, broken and desperate, unable to look at them. "Please, Daddy." She held out a hand for him to stop, sensing he was coming to her. "No. Sammy, help me. Please get my daddy out of here," she cried out the words, sank into a tight ball, began to pray, her hand clutching Joshua's cross. The Psalm Joshua had her memorize coming suddenly to her lips. *I love you, O LORD, my strength . . .*

It was her stepmother's voice. She started to cry from the relief then demanded as the conversation started again between the three of them, "Lexi! Get them out of here." She looked at her father, Samuel, saw their shock, their sudden understanding and felt overwhelmed with shame.

"It's okay," her father said with assurance. But she wasn't sure if it would ever be okay again.

11

Jaxson watched his daughter until she was escorted onto the jet, watched his wife give a wave and then duck inside. He was powerless to help, grasping to understand, shaking with the revelation that his daughter's body was out of control. He'd seen her eyes. He'd thought the night terrors would be the worst of her healing. He'd been wrong when he'd seen the Eros. This was worse, to see her fight the evil that oppressed her from within. An echo, his wife had told him the doctors were already calling it. Eros.

Samuel was shaken but steadying. He'd known something was off and now confessed instead of watching Webb he should have been watching Jaclyn. He wanted to help. Staying with his sons as Jaxson followed Lexi and Jaclyn to the airport. His family was already at his house. His parents. His best friend, Jude and Tori. Samuel. They would be there for his sons. But his daughter…

Her eyes had been overwhelmed with shame. Her hand clutching Joshua's cross.

Jaxson prayed. Closed his eyes. Shook his head. Remembered this morning. She'd asked for Joshua. Just a lunch date. He'd not listened. Not realized. Even as his daughter had clung to him, holding tighter than normal, needy. He'd misread her. Thought it was nerves about stepping out with Lexi, going to a negotiation, representing a client . . . She'd wanted Joshua, he'd sent her to Brett.

He opened his eyes. Grabbed his PDA. Made a call.

He just caught him. Running to the private jet they'd chartered to send him back to New York, ducking inside. Brett was staring out the window. Troubled. Then startled as he saw Jaxson. He tried to rise but the seat belt held him down. He yanked it open, stood. A handsome man, with hazel eyes and an athletic build. A man who had proclaimed Christ in his profession and honored God through his livelihood. A few months ago he would have been exactly the kind of man Jaxson would have esteemed for his daughter. Now ...

"Mr. Cooper."

Jaxson raked an unsteady hand through his hair, nodded. "Mind if I share the ride with you?"

"Sure."

Jaxson took a seat, motioned for him to do the same. "I just caught you." He buckled up in the seat across from him as the leer jet began to move. "Had to run. Glad I've still got some speed left." He tried for a smile, knew it was forced.

"How's Jaclyn?" Brett asked him.

"Lexi's taking her to Virginia. Her doctor is there."

He nodded.

"I know she spoke to you but I wanted to have a conversation. It's not an easy one to have, but we've got some time on the flight to New York." There was a pause. "I don't know what Lexi told you, so why don't we start there."

"I'm not sure what she told me." Brett shook his head. "It was fast." He looked confused. "I know Jaclyn got sick. She said something about a drug ... a drug that elevated her hormones to a dangerous level and she was having a relapse. Lexi said that Jaclyn wanted me to know she ... thought I was a, ah, wonderful man. That she respected me." Now he looked troubled. "But that today, she wasn't herself. The drug relapse was causing her to experience an elevated sense of … desire." He quickly said, "Lexi said Jaclyn knew this was a lot to deal with and since we just met, I could walk away. She'd understand." He took a breath. "Lexi told me she was sorry. I could tell she felt responsible. She was upset. And concerned. I'm concerned. Is Jaclyn alright?"

"She will be."

"She got sick. We were standing in the barn … talking about the horses and she just went stiff. Then she got sick. Really sick. I had to carry her back to the house."

"I appreciate that," Jaxson told him.

"Then she asked me to get Lexi. I did. I didn't do anything to cause this, did I?"

"No," Jaxson answered. He'd prayed. He'd listened. He trusted his wife's wisdom. They'd discussed the situation on and off all day since lunch. What was right. What they should do. How they should help direct Jaclyn, if they should at all. Joshua wanted her to have choices. Once she healed. She was far from healed. Jaclyn had told Lexi she wanted an opportunity with Brett. He had thought perhaps she was stepping forward, but her first choice had been Joshua. Brett had been an alternative. It was time for truth.

"My daughter was abducted this summer," the statement was flat, the story short. He gave the facts. About the Viper, Eros and Ares. Some still hard to say. He kept to the facts and left out the details of her rescue and of Joshua. He finished with, "Lexi told me you're a man of faith."

"Yes, I believe in Jesus, was raised to do my best to follow Him …" he looked past him. "I tried, Mr. Cooper to respect your daughter. The ah, chemistry between us was like nothing I've ever experienced."

"That was Eros," he corrected. "The Eros was driving my daughter. On a normal day you'd find her charm much more subtle."

"We'd talked on the phone, before today. We had several conversations. I felt the chemistry then, when I saw her there was attraction. Once we acknowledged it, she didn't want me a step away."

"That was the drug, it demands."

"She wasn't demanding." Now he argued, defended. "She was incredible," he began to smile then suddenly realized. "You daughter is beautiful. She has a way about her."

Jaxson realized the man had fallen hard. He tensed. "Were you intimate?"

"No." His posture had straightened, he sat back, shook his head. Jaxson wished for his wife, for her ability to read people, for her intuition. "No," he repeated. But the word only made Jaxson more tense.

"Was there foreplay?" he asked flatly then with emotion, "Did you touch her?"

"Sir, I," he took a breath. Jaxson watched him think then watched him find the courage to speak the truth. "Yes. With respect to Jaclyn, I think you should speak to her if you want the details."

"No." He exhaled. "I don't want the details. I need to protect her not shame her. The drug turns her into something that she is not, something that she hates. She'll be burdened with a great deal of shame from today. She'll have to work through that. As a man of faith I hope you can forgive her for deceiving you."

"Deceiving me?" He shook his head.

"The drug deceived you," Jaxson stated. "That was not my daughter. Jaclyn is self-controlled not sensual. Jaclyn," suddenly his voice broke, emotion taking his words.

He shook his head, looked out the window. Memories flooding every sense—of his baby girl, his little girl, his teenage girl, his beautiful daughter. The days he'd spent raising her, the dreams for her future. The girl she'd been and the look in the eyes of the woman Eros turned her into.

He suddenly thought of Rachel Cruz, her birth mother. Rachel with a body passed on to his little girl. Rachel who used that centerfold body to both lure and seduce. Rachel who once caused in him an obsessive sexual craving, who had commandeered his lust when his spirit had been weak and immature and exploited its desires. Rachel, the great sin in his life. Jaclyn the great blessing. Through Rachel God had finally taught him the truth of physical passion. It fades away. Three days of sexual gluttony finally finds its empty end. Lusts disappears like the morning mist in the strong light of mid-day. But love He spoke the words of first Corinthians thirteen out loud, for both of them to hear. "*Love never fails. Prophecies, they will cease; tongues, they will be stilled; knowledge, it will pass away…but when perfection comes, the imperfect disappears.*" Now he looked at Brett and said, "*When I was a child, I talked like a child, I thought like a child, I reasoned like a child. When I became a man, I put childish ways behind me. Today . . .we see but a poor reflection as in a mirror; then we shall see face to face. Today . . .I only know in part; then I shall know fully, even as I am fully known. And now these three remain: faith, hope and love.*

"*But the greatest of these is love,*" they finished together. Jaxson nodded. "Love never fails." He testified of God, telling his story of Rachel Cruz, of Jaclyn and of his wife Lexi.

He looked at Brett, realized it was imperative he understand, "You haven't met my daughter, you've met Eros. The drug is a powerful personification of lust and she fights to take you from God's will. My daughter Jaclyn fights to remain in God's will."

"Then I'd like an introduction to your daughter Jaclyn," Brett stated.

"It might be awhile," Jaxson made no promises. "She's been through hell and now she'll have to take another trip through this echo."

It had been a hellish ride to Virginia. Her emotions raging higher than even her hormones, her tears causing her body to escalate and accelerate further on a course out of control. Her stepmother tried to comfort her, but in the end it was firmness that caused her to find control. They needed to focus, not fall apart. There would be time to fall apart later, not now, Lexi had demanded she stand up and stand firm. She'd paced. Paced as Lexi spoke through an ear bud with Ida, taking orders and making plans with Christie. Jaclyn paced, as fear rose up over shame, and insanity scratched at her door. She was losing it. Losing herself in this raging rush of hormones that was belligerently demanding. She felt possessed as her mind urged her imagination toward sordid thoughts and memories of Joshua, even the Viper. Her body was overcome with the lust, tossing her from brokenness to belligerence.

She clutched the cross and tags at her neck and just said her Savior's name. Psalm Eighteen came back to her lips, *I love you O Lord my strength...*

There'd been a race from jet to car in the dead of night. Her Aunt Christie had said very little, only steadying her into the back seat of a small sleek sedan as she drove like an Indy driver into the night. There was no hospital, just a building tucked back among trees next to a park in a quiet suburb. Ida was there to meet them when they first walked into the place called, Heatherwood. Calm and ready, the woman from India took her hand and said only, "It has been a day for you, child. Come."

They walked down a gently lit hallway, there were doors, solid wood and closed tightly. There was no nurse's station. No windows. No waiting area. No noise. No security. At the end of a hall a door was open, a bedroom waiting.

"This will be your sanctuary. It is secure and completely private." She'd explained. There was a bed, a vid screen, a console for music. There were built-in drawers and above them shelves of books. Two chairs were in a small alcove.

"Let us talk," was the way Ida had started the discussion. "This is a very private fight and we respect what it must be for each person here in Heatherwood who battles with Eros."

She'd held on to Lexi, fear gripping her as she scanned the room. She'd expected the normal hospital. IV's and nurses poking and prodding as Ida gave the orders for medication. "I just need medication. Hormones to counter this."

"We are past that. It would cause you mental and physical distress… It is this way, Jaclyn. It is as if a car had driven down a narrow road carved away from the rock with twists and turns. It is very close to impossible to back that car back down the road but we can more successfully continue forward and find the end of the cycle."

"No," she shook her head. "Back me up. I don't want to cycle."

"To back up the car we will tax the transmission, the brakes, the steering and leave scrapes and dents on the surface not to mention put a crick in your neck. We will go forward to the end and you will see that it will be okay."

"I have been on this road before, I never want to drive it again."

"The road is different this time. You are a woman driving a car. The road will not be rocky with dips and pot holes, it will be smooth. You can drive alone, I will give you everything you need and teach you how to use it."

"No."

"You fear what you yet understand."

"I understand perfectly." She rubbed her shoulder. "I'm possessed with a demon and you're going to let it have its fun."

"You are not possessed," Christie broke in with passion. "This is a drug and we'll fight it."

"How can it be back?" Lexi questioned.

"It is what we call an echo. It can occur for several reasons. Eros overstimulates hormones. I am analyzing her levels, tracking the progress but it seems she is ovulating and there was a spike yesterday that overrode her medication."

"I threw up," she suddenly realized. "Yesterday morning. After I took my medication. So this is all over orange juice?"

"If there was a failure," Ida bowed, "It is mine, Jaclyn. Forgive me for not monitoring you, preparing you for this."

"How can it be beat?" Christie asked with determination.

"With medication to help stabilize her and sperm."

There was silence then she asked, "I have to cycle. All the way," she glanced at Lexi, moved away, paced, her shoulder burning, screaming. Her mood turning edgy, angry. "So what, you'll send in, who?" She turned, glanced at Christie, then Ida as some kind of sick anticipation rushed. "The Fury?"

"Here," Ida opened a drawer and unsealed a pot of ointment. "Rub this on your neck, where it is burning."

She touched the ointment, it felt like a buttery moisturizer. She collected some and applied it. Instantly there was a cooling sensation. "It has the testosterone and the enzymes your body is seeking. It can be put anywhere." She put the pot into her hand.

"If you have synthetic male spit you must have sperm?"

"We've not been able to reproduce that." Ida smiled. "But I do have sperm."

Jaclyn stepped back, fisting the pot of ointment.

Ida took her arm, led her away to another drawer. She opened it. It was cool, the vapor rising up. Inside was a medical tray with a label that had a number on it. "This is your number. Your privacy is always secure. And this is the sperm stored for you. It is the Fury's," she said softly. "He is your donor."

Her breathing quickened. Her gaze on the six capsules. Ida closed the freezer drawer. She placed a hand on her back and slowly opened another drawer, explained the process of the application. Then she turned to a communication center. "You initiate any correspondence with us. If we need to reach you, the light will come on and all messages come via text never voice. You can use your personal PDA but I would advise caution and discretion with very little video. Text works best at this time, not voices and pictures. Food and drink can be ordered through this touch screen."

She turned to the wall, pushed a button and a door slowly opened. It was a dumb waiter. "Blankets, pillows, deliveries, they can all be sent to you through this dumb waiter system." She took her hands and told her, "Above all, we rigorously protect and respect your privacy. And I am here for you as well. Do you have any questions?"

She could only shake her head.

"I will ask for your levels as needed and send any medication through this drawer." She showed her. "Unless you ask for me, I too will respect your privacy. Together we can decide when you are ready to go home."

"Would you talk to my stepmother and explain this?"

"Certainly."

"When will I reach the worst of it?"

"Soon. When you need to be alone, ask for your solitude."

She nodded. Accepted. Surrendered.

[illegible]

[illegible] Do you have any questions?"

[illegible]

[illegible]

"When will I [illegible]?"

[illegible]

12

The simulated battle had been unforgiving. The gunfire coming from three sides, his team split. Two wounded. An army of masked militia had cornered the Fury, riddled him with fire, the hits stinging like a blast of volcanic rocks, tearing into his flesh. Wounds left him immobile and out of the game, dependent on others. Eli had to take control, it had been planned that way. In the end he did the job, in his way, but he did the job and got them out, blowing up half the town and exposing something meant to be covert, but the mission was accomplished and everyone had survived.

The debrief was always brutal. Always. First from command, then from each other. Mistakes were exposed, tactics criticized, weaknesses revealed, strengths stated as they re-watched the battle on the vid screen. It was always about getting better, doing it better, faster, more efficiently. Criticism was just part of the sharpening, and it came bluntly, often with laughter, always with truth. He rubbed his chest, the sim suit doing its job enough to leave bruises and a lingering sting from his virtual hits.

"Heart hurt a little, Fury?" Joel, a lead chair in Command, asked with a grin. He was used to hearing his authoritative voice and it was always a little weird to match his jolly face to it. The man smiled a lot and liked jokes and pranks.

Joshua leaned back in the conference chair. "The tech guys need to stop working so hard. Those bullets feel real enough already without the bruises."

"Thought it might be the cover of the Globe that gave you the sucker punch." He hit a few buttons and the cover of the famous New York Paper popped up on the big screen. "Never seen a Hummingbird dressed in boots before, have you?"

There was a response, immediate and electric from the team. Where was she? Who was he? In the end they were all looking at him. Him with his hand frozen over his chest. His heart lurched painfully from its momentary pause, then his fingers tugged the shirt, rubbed once and moved away to rest on the arm of the chair.

"Has Marc seen this?" he said without emotion.

"Not sure," Joel answered, "He's not in yet."

"Neither is Christie," someone added.

"Who is he?" the Kid asked with a protective edge to his voice.

"Brett Webb," was the answer. "Cy Young-winning pitcher, just got himself traded to the Nationals from Chicago."

"Eight digits," was the ridiculous salary someone called out as members of the team debated the new last ditch deadline for MLB trades prior to the playoffs.

"Just got himself the hottest little Hummingbird to ever fly—" There was an ugh, and a mutter, and a request for respect. Then someone stated, "The reason we do what we do is to put smiles back on pretty girl's faces, boss. She looks happy."

It was Petra who stood. Her accented words told them things weren't always what they seemed. "She is his friend. Nothing more."

Another page flashed on screen. "You think?" Joel questioned. The three snapshots showed the couple at the hotel. Webb and her in silhouette as they entered. Her tucked in Webb's arms in shadow as they rode the glass elevator of the famous hotel. Webb pitching in the fifth game that won Chicago their series two years ago.

She waved him off. "They can make those pictures tell any story. You know that Joel." She looked at Joshua. "Are we dismissed?"

He nodded. Stood. Someone had left a copy of the paper on his desk. A sticky note asked, "Who's the soon-to-be-dead dude?" Dr. Duchovny had left his scrolling signature.

He looked at the man in the photograph. Not his smile, not his cloaked eyes behind expensive shades, not his Italian suit, or the way his body would size up against another. Joshua looked at his hand. On her hip. That tiny angle you could find if you knew where to hunt. It held there, possessively, fingers spreading out to cover a space too intimate for the hold of a friend. Petra was wrong. This man was not a mere friend. He was an intimate and he was very happy about it and the fact that he'd just increased his net worth and been traded to a team that was in line to sweep the playoffs and fight for the series.

He fought the jealousy. It was a new feeling but he pushed it back by confessing it. Spoke the truth that God's will would be done in their lives. Decided if he loved, there wasn't room for envy. But God was jealous ... the Spirit very jealous ... love could have a righteous jealousy.

He finally looked at her. The boots. The poise. The shot made it look as if she'd just soared into his arms, up on tip toe, her other leg bent, the slit showing off the long line of her leg, the slender length of her body, the fullness of her breasts as she leaned against him for support. Their gazes were synced. And her smile...

He lifted the paper, studied it. Turned the page to 6A, looked at the other two shoots. It was the same. This smile was not about being happy, it was about hunting.

He said, "Delilah," and tossed down the paper, still staring at the shot.

"You okay?" Eli leaned against the door.

He nodded, already pulling his PDA out.

“You’re calling Marc?” He stepped into the office now. It was small, he was hardly here. “That Russian will see this.” Eli nodded to the paper. “With a little luck, he’ll get possessive and come here to take her back and we’ll catch the arrogant snake.”

Joshua looked at the paper, realizing he had only been thinking of himself. Where was Jaclyn? “I need to talk to Marc.”

Now Eli smiled but Joshua closed his eyes and prayed.

”What can I add to your prayers to increase their power?” Eli asked.

Joshua shook his head.

“Look, Fury. I was there, remember. There when we first saw her, chained to him, enslaved, drugged, disrespected. I’d have killed him in another step. Killed him just for the arrogance of his entitlement to oppress her with such evil. But you stopped my arrogance and reminded me God worked in other ways. Now what can I add so God can work this another way?”

“I need to know what to do. If anything.” He opened his eyes, opened himself for just a minute. “Maybe our job is done. Maybe this is her father’s concern . . . not my business. I need to know.”

Eli’s words were simple. He asked for wisdom and he covered the spokes of the wheel that came from it and surrounded her in God’s mercy and asked for God’s will.

“Let me know the answer,” he lifted his hand from his shoulder and with a nod was on his way. At the door he turned and said, “Sometimes this job lingers after it’s done. You know that.”

He was still watching him, looking out the glass wall and into the hall when the PDA vibrated in his hand. The message from Marc was direct.

Come to my office.

He took the newspaper with him. The walk was short. Marc’s office large and accommodating for the business he did. The Bull stood at his desk, a data screen in his hands.

"Have you seen this?" Joshua's focus was single-minded as he held up the Globe and walked to the desk.

"Lexi warned me yesterday. Let me see." Marc took the paper.

"This is going to get Viper's attention. We need to track that snake and keep a sharp eye out on who he's working with. He'll have a plot together in a day. Could send men or even come himself. He's not going to like this." He felt his emotions narrow into a hot anger. "His Russian pride will be ignited. And the way she's cuddled up to this peacock," Joshua thumped the paper, where the pitcher's hand was attached to his wife's hip. "That Russian possession is going to demand that he get her back. I don't like it!" he growled.

"I'm sure you don't," Christie came from behind him and took the paper.

"Ma'am." Joshua's posture popped.

"I'm sure he doesn't like this one bit, brother." Christie's green eyes stayed on Joshua for a beat then looked over to the window where her brother stood. "Have you seen this, Jaxson?" She held the paper up for Jaxson.

"Sir," Joshua acknowledged, further startled.

"Your instincts are off, Fury," Christie criticized as Jaxson joined them.

"His focus is right where it should be and you were out of his peripheral. Don't mess with my men, Doc," Marc defended with a rare narrowing of his eyes to his wife. "I've already calculated the risk when they took the pictures. Already moved men on the alert. Yrasrevda's being tracked."

Joshua nodded. "Her security?"

"She's untouchable," Christie answered.

"She's at Heatherwood," Jaxson finally spoke and Christie made a hiss. He touched his sister, his gaze firmly connected to Joshua's. "She's had an echo."

"Yes, sir. I could see that from the pictures."

Christie immediately lifted the newspaper. "How? Show me."

"Attitude, Doc. She's acting Delilah."

"Delilah," Christie took a step to him. "I don't like that assumption, Fury."

"It's the truth. It's not Jaclyn, it's the drug. She's not brazen. She's not provocative. And she was taught not to pout."

"That's true," Marc nodded.

"Delilah pouts and pushes. She has an edge, a tone and an approach. She wants his hand here," Joshua pointed at the newspaper, to the cover shot. "Here on her hip. Not her waist, or her back. Here, where her ovaries are heating up." He flipped the paper open to the shot in the elevator. "She wants him here, behind her, close. Which I don't need to explain. Was her neck bothering her? Here." He showed him where Jaclyn's hand rested on her own shoulder in one of the shots.

"Yes, after she sent Brett away. She made Cletus give her some spit, put it on her shoulder there. She was . . ." Jaxson paced now, his hand racking through his hair, the man obviously upset. "I've never seen her like that. It was horrible." He stood with his back to them. "I need a minute with Joshua." He turned to them now. "Do you mind?"

"No." Marc and Christie walked out together, closing the door.

Jaxson stood for a while with his back to him. The room quaking with silence. When he turned, his eyes glistened with emotion. "She asked for you. Yesterday morning. She asked me to call you. She wanted to see you." He shook his head, closed his eyes, fought for a moment. "I didn't realize. I failed you both."

"No, sir."

"I didn't protect her again. I should have been with her. In New York."

"No one knew she'd have an echo."

"I didn't know the signs. Neither did she. Subconsciously maybe. She asked for you, I sent her to Brett Webb."

"She has a right to choose. It's what I wanted for her."

"She chose." Jaxson looked at him, standing stiffly at attention. "She wanted you. She substituted. When she realized what was happening, she sent him away. Samuel sensed she was off, tried to defend her. She was screaming at him when I found her. She sent us both away. Her eyes . . . she wasn't herself then when she was . . . she's consumed with shame." There was grief. "I wanted to comfort her but she sent me away." He wiped his eyes. "That wasn't my daughter." For a moment he broke, gasped in the silence. "Who beside my Lord can I tell this to?"

"You can tell me, sir," he answered.

"Please, call me Jaxson," he insisted on a weary sigh.

"She's at Heatherwood?"

"Yes, Lexi is with her."

"She's safe there."

Jaxson looked at him, glanced back to the desk and went and picked up the newspaper. "I've been more worried about her health than her safety. You think he'll see this? In Russia?"

"Yes. I think he's obsessed with her because she beat him. I can only hope that Russian arrogance will be what God uses to humble him. That he'll come and try to grab her and we'll ..." Joshua reached for Jaxson, a hand on his shoulder. "Sir, she's safe." He'd gone pale, his eyes unfocused. "I assure you, she's safe."

"She's right. Only God can keep her safe. She needs you," he told him. "I don't know what you know about Eros. How to read her. How to help her. How to defeat her enemy." He looked up at him with great emotion. "She needs you."

"No, sir," his words were soft assurance now. "She needs her father. You know her best. You'll direct her best and help her to heal and be whole. If she had me, she would be dependent on me and not God, she would never conquer her fear or completely heal. She needs you—your wisdom and love—if she is to ever have me."

For a long moment the truth resonated in the room. Jaxson just looked into his eyes. Processed. Prayed. Then he blinked, spoke. "I was worried about her health, grieving her emotions. Now I'm overwhelmed with her safety."

"Pray for her safety and trust your God. Then do the practical things Marc tells you to do. Leave the rest of the worry to *Stratia*. I'll watch over her, do everything in my power to keep her safe. Trust me," Joshua told him. "I'm trusting you with her health and her emotions. Guidance and direction. Be her father, you know how to be that, you're a very good father, Jaxson."

There was a smile, slow and sure. His eyes filling with life and an odd joy. "'Bout time you called me Jaxson."

"Sir?"

Jaxson chuckled as he slapped his back. "I thank God for you, Joshua. I felt helpless again, unable to do anything but pray and wait."

"Sometimes that is the hardest thing God asks us to do."

"And the easiest is to worry and regret, doubt that God is still in control of even this. You've strengthened my faith to remember we each have our parts to play and God oversees it all."

Joshua gave a nod.

"I am sorry about this." He held up the paper, folding it closed. "I know that's not a position a man wants to see his wife in."

"She is to have a choice."

"You're my choice. God's choice." He paced. "Her choice. She just needs time. And I sense this echo could do some damage, put us back at square one." There was an exhale, then faith. "At least two steps back with her health, but maybe a step forward with her safety if he responds and you capture him. You're right, I'll let you and *Stratia* worry over her safety. As her father, I have an idea for some damage control for her emotions. Care to take a walk with me?"

Jaxson guided him into a never-never land of extraordinary curiosities most would consider over common. "Pick one and I'll be back," Jaxson encouraged as he walked away. Joshua swept the aisle full of stuffed animals more crowded then Noah's ark. He touched the paw of a yellow giraffe that reached out to him. Soft as down. He was amazed. Put his hands in his pockets. Walked the aisle. There were the classic teddy bears, their modern versions, then the vast spin offs of dogs, kittens, rabbits, and the rest of the zoo. Fury couldn't remember ever being in a toy store. A missionary's son. A third culture kid. A global nomad who didn't fit in here or there. His toys had been found in nature, the playground more often imagination. Mass materialism was still mind boggling to him. He was overwhelmed by the selection. Prayed. He saw what was chosen. The large lion, its coloring classic, its paws like a rag doll that made his form soft not stiff. He'd never had a stuffed animal. Just his brother. Now no one …

Jaxson was back. A hand on his shoulder. A confident smile. A father who loved his family. His father-in-law. With a hand on his shoulder. "Find something?"

He nodded. Swallowed as he reached out. Chose. Realizing he was never alone. He had Christ and His family, the church. *Stratia* and now Jaxson Cooper.

"A lion. Alright." Jaxson held up a greeting card. "I found what I needed." Now he flashed dimples as he showed him the card. As they walked to the checkout he told him the story. "Jaclyn was always very smart."

"Yes, sir."

"But because of an ear problem she was slow to talk."

Now he smiled. "She's good at talking now."

"Well, she couldn't say oink." He chuckled. "She had all the other animal sounds down, but not the oink. It came out oh-in-ee. Been our little joke ever sense." He showed him the pig card.

They paid the necessary credits and took the box back to Command. On the elevator Jaxson told him, "When she was little I'd have to go away to training camp for weeks playing football. As a single parent, I hated leaving her. Talked to a specialist about how to handle it best. She told me to take the stuffed animal she slept with—Whiskers the bunny—and rub my scent on it. That she would identify my smell and be comforted. Yesterday when she left she said something about loving the way I smelled," he looked at him. "Then she said she could remember what you smelled like and it brought her comfort. Put your scent on that lion," he directed.

If someone saw him they'd think he was a pervert as he rubbed the stuffed animal over his body. The enemy told him he should be embarrassed, which is why he decided not to be. He covered the lion in his scent, finally taking its face and rubbing every part of it against the related parts of his. Holding its thick mane, he looked in its jeweled eyes and prayed for God to comfort her. He packed the lion in a white box and carefully scripted the card, then awkwardly tied the pink satin bow. With a final prayer he handed it to Christie as Jaxson gave his sister a pink envelope that held his card.

"Call me with an update," Jaxson told her. "We'll be here waiting."

Her stepmother's voice was even and constant as it read the classic words of "Hinds Feet on High Places." Occasionally she would glance over her reading glasses and they would catch gazes then she would read on. Jaclyn was relaxed, the drugs effective to take the horrible edge off, yet she prowled the room listening to the allegory of Much-Afraid and her journey from her family of Fearlings. It was a story she liked and related to growing up with her large family with its many characters. But her focus kept wandering from the peaceful words, coming to the physical irritations. Her loose lounge wear suddenly tight, seams brushing against over-sensitive skin. She glanced at the door, she felt imprisoned. She was safe, she told herself. Safe from everyone but herself. She tugged on the top, the fabric brutal. She looked at Lexi. It was almost time to be alone.

The message light went on. A soft dull light that blinked. Her mother stopped reading, checked her watch. "It must be Christie."

It was almost lunchtime. Just yesterday they had been circling the clouds, eating with Brett. The thought of him shifted her body into another realm, her mind understanding the process, her emotions preparing.

"Go eat with Christie," she told her. "I know you're hungry." They looked at each other, her stepmother rising and setting the book aside, understanding what she said.

She nodded, took her face and pressed a kiss onto her forehead. "Can I get you something? A salad? Pasta?"

"They have a good selection. I'll be fine now."

"Okay." She held her gaze. "I'm praying."

"I know you are." She nodded. Watched as she moved to the door. There was a panel there where she had to type in information. There was a click as the door unlocked, a final look.

"Lexi!" She felt the terror, of being alone then saw it reflected on Lexi's face and instantly found her courage. "I love you."

"I love you," she said it with a fierce conviction.

Jaclyn nodded. Her stepmother slipped out. The door closed tightly shut and the locks engaged. She prowled again, her hands working the fabric with worry, finally shedding it to grab up a light blanket and wrap her shoulders. She rubbed the ointment on her shoulder. She took her levels, the medication had slowed the ascent but they were still climbing, nearing the limit. She sent them off to Ida through the PDA then took the designated medication that was sent through the drawer. Ordered soup and salad. Had two spoonfuls of soup and a bite of a cracker. Paced. She found music, filled the room with praise choruses, did her best to sing along but her mind wouldn't focus. She was restless, she was strangely sleepy, but understanding it was the medication. She laid down and closed her eyes.

She thought of Brett. She wondered if there was anything real between them at all or if it had all been some hideous trick of the Eros. Smoke and mirrors.

She wanted him, his hands on her flesh, his kiss on her mouth. His body against her back. His hand on her hip, possessive and stretching across her womb. He knew how to fit her against him. He would kiss her and come into her arms and love her as a man loves a woman.

He would love her . . . would he? Or would he take from her. Take the only thing she had left to give. Open arms, the sacred place. The place Joshua forbid himself to go. The place he'd told her belonged to her husband. Did she want to marry Brett?

The thought was overwhelming. Then it was simple. No, Eros wanted to have sex with Brett. The drug wanted those wide shoulders and strong hands and sexy mouth. Wanted his hazel eyes shifting colors with desire and the sound of pleasure he made when he kissed her. Lust. It had been round after round of teasing. She was in heat…

I have put lust into your body and it cannot be silenced even by God.

She heard the hiss of the snake, knew how true his words could become. She could easily become the whore of the world without Ida's help to silence the chemical lust in the safety of this place. She loved Joshua but love had not mattered yesterday. Eros wanted only pleasure and its available preference whether Viper, Joshua or Brett. She cried now, with the shame of yesterday and the growing demands of today. She felt the oppression. The darkness of loneliness. The pit of despair. The evil of Eros. The deceptive power of lust. The filth of shame. She was back in Yrasrevda's house, locked in a room. Utterly alone and terrified, drugged and desperate. Powerless to change anything, even her intense desire for the Viper when he'd held her captive and made her wait until she was mad for him. He was here. So close. In memories. In this wicked desire. She opened her eyes so she wouldn't dream of him.

The light was on, signaling a message. She lifted the PDA.

You have a delivery.

She was expecting lunch. Pasta or a salad with smoked chicken. Something from her stepmother, not the white box with the pretty pink bow that filled the little elevator.

She took it out, pulled the card free from the satin ribbon. There was a pig on the front. Pink and cute that asked her, "Do you know what a pig says?" When she opened it there was a loud and startling oink. She laughed, at once. He'd signed the card, "There's a k on the end my one and only. You're going to be okay. I'm praying for you. I love you forever, Daddy."

She cried, fighting it, knowing her emotions only fueled the Eros like a stimulant. She opened the card again, let it make the long oink. Then again. Until she smiled then she lifted the lid off the box. She was startled at the discovery. She expected a pig not a lion. His mane dark, his head large, the eyes like jewels. She pulled him free, his legs like a rag doll that could be flopped on a bed or over a chair. His fur soft as down. She clung to him, smelled Joshua's power, his presence somehow in the fur of the pretend. She tore open the card.

You're strong. Courageous. Faithful. Beloved.
Make present Christ as you believe and trust.
You're never alone. God is with you.

He'd signed it Joshua. The penmanship clean, dark, engraved letters. He'd written it with a fierce stroke of a pen. She could feel the indention of each letter. She turned the card over and found his business card. He'd underlined his number.

She wiped her tears away as she smiled.

"I'm strong, courageous, faithful, beloved," she told herself and the room. "I believe I'm never alone."

With courage she finally followed Ida's instructions and found relief.

Holding tight to the lion she closed her eyes and drifted off into peaceful exhaustion. She could smell Joshua. She buried her face in the soft full mane of the lion. She could smell him . . . she remembered him, how he'd hold her, how he fought to help her, how he prayed over her, sang her to sleep, pointed her to God as he repeated the Word.

The lion, no one dares to rouse him … She slept in peace.

Thank you.

The two words sat on his screen, staring at him to respond. It was nine o'clock. He was stretched face down on the floor of the Ancient Place of *Stratia* yet his hand held onto the PDA and he could only thank his God for an answer.

Slowly he rolled to his back after hours of prayer. The white marble cool and unyielding, a constant reflection of light in the empty room. The PDA resting against his heart. He asked that she be finished. Forever. That God's will would be done in their lives. Then he asked for the Spirit's perfect guidance for his words. He never knew what to say to her, in the end Joshua typed simply,

How are you?

Better.

Levels?

Lowering.

Lion?

Smells like you.

He smiled now, typed. **Sorry.**

Like it. Comforting.

That was my prayer.

You're my donor. Again.

Yes. The neck?

There's an ointment that kills the burn.

Emotions?

Not good. Shame.

Forgiven. Never your fault.

Regret. Feel possessed.

Can't be. You're sealed by the Spirit.

Oppressed then.

Battle with prayer. Use the Word.

It's been a battle, worse alone.

I've been praying.

I can tell.

I know it's hard.

Hard to face my family. You. Anyone. After today.

Lift up your face.

There was a pause. He prayed. Wanting to be with her, to physically lift her face and pray over her. His spirit struggled to surrender to his place in this battle. He was a man of action but at times the battle was spiritual alone. He steadily typed the words of truth.

You are His beloved.

Give me a visual. I need to tell you.

Her words sat waiting on the screen for his answer. She should only have text, he should respect what medically he knew was best for her. She didn't need to see a man. He leaned against a wall. Prayed. God said yes. He said, "Visual."

She came on screen. Her face fragile in its natural beauty, her eyes weary, slowly filling. She just looked at him, for the longest time, she searched his face and then said, "I'm sorry, Joshua."

"No apologies," he reminded her instantly of their mutual rule. Understood her need to see. Be seen.

"I was worse than Delilah—

"I know the woman you are, Jaclyn. I know what you fight. You're surrendered to Heatherwood, allowed God victory for you." She looked at him, tears swelling, slowly blinked back as he said her name. "Don't cry."

"I know . . . it freaks you out."

"It's harder for your body to relax," he defended.

"Um." She wiped her eyes, tried for a smile. "Right. Thank you, Joshua. For everything."

"I understand."

"I know." There was a nod, an inhale, a show of confidence. "You're the only one who really can."

"God understands. Everything. You need to rest. Eat. I'm here for you."

"You're not," she countered, cuddled the lion close, "Just the lion."

"Hold on to him."

"I am."

"Lift up your face. You are not to live in shame as Christ bore it for you to be free," he commanded. "Walk in victory. You have it in Christ. You're more than a conqueror."

She nodded, asked softly, "Can I text you again?

"Anytime." Then he reminded her, "God keeps you."

She laid her head down, cuddled the lion. Her fingers typed out,

His love for me sent you.

True. I still fight for you. In prayer. Be at peace.

Fury rose, bowed, backed away with respect and exited the holy room of the Ancient Place.

Below the stairs at the incense bowl another waited. He was robed, his head bowed. Century-old eyes looked up, the violent violet color catching hold of him. Energy connecting. Unmistakable.

"Wisdom." Fury bowed with respect to the leader of *Stratia.*

"The Lord has bestowed strength on the warrior. Shouts of joy and victory resound in the tents of the righteous: The LORD's right hand has done mighty things!"

"In God we make our boast all day long, and praise His name forever," Fury answered.

"The LORD is gracious and righteous; our God is full of compassion. The LORD protects the simple hearted; when in great need, he saves. Be at rest once more, O my soul, for the LORD has been good to you."

Fury repeated the praise, with a deep exhale, "The Lord has been good to me."

"The Fury of *Stratia's* wife has found victory."

He bowed his head. Nodded.

The old hand touched the pendant he wore. It was Wisdom's wedding ring, cut open, stretched flat, a cross bisected the thin strip of platinum that hung with the tiny ID tags on the black shot beads. A month ago he'd placed it as a ring on his palm, knowing the warrior had obeyed without exception. Taken the woman as his wife. He'd given him a ring, but Fury refused to claim his wife publically. Now the ring laid flat against his chest, open and broken, smoothed into a shape it had not been destined to be.

"Pain is part of the cost of a sacrifice." Wisdom's hand laid upon his back while the silence was filled with their separate thoughts. Prayers. Then he spoke again, "Switchbacks are bitter, but still sovereign. God will use this echo in her healing, for His glory."

"He works all things for good."

"We can use this to His glory."

Fury lifted his gaze. Wisdom's ancient eyes were ablaze.

"Let us walk together." Wisdom set the course. He spoke of the plan. Then he laid his old hands upon the Fury's head and blessed him.

13

Brett Webb had agreed to meet with them. Jaxson had established the meeting. Marc had made the arrangements. Fury had spent several hours in prayer to prepare himself. He wasn't sure he should be present. Jaxson had requested it. Marc had ordered it, told him Wisdom had tested the man. Fury didn't know how. Wisdom knew. And those chosen to be involved in the delicate and detailed process.

Brett Webb had passed their tests. Now he was here. In a room of *Stratia's* selected best. Including the Termite. For once he was glad Lisette was on his side of the battle. The Eagle was present, Curtis Lexington often behind the glass now sat at the table with his men from Intel and IT. They were all the spokes of the wheel. Behind the two-way glass was Wisdom. The driver.

Joshua entered the typical rectangle conference style room. The three walls housing the vast vid screens that could flash up information and the other with the two-way mirror where others would sit and decide. In the far corner, he greeted Ida DePaul, Jaclyn's specialist dealing with the Eros. The medical talk comforting as he waited impatiently for the man to show up.

The black *Stratia* sweater itched his neck. This whole situation made him uncomfortable. He hated diplomacy and politics. The game of it slow like… baseball. The world's slowest sport… except golf. Maybe golf was slower. But baseball was like theater, each player spotlighted in the pitch and catch of the game. The drama playing out in the count of the umpire, to the swing of the bat and the catch of the fly ball. The double play and the catcalls of fans. It was nothing like hockey or football or combat. He prayed, running his hand over the back of his neck, feeling the wool of the *Stratia* sweater he was forced to wear, the length of his over long hair he was forbidden to cut. He did not want to be here. Duty made him stand. Firm in the faith that God's will would be done in their lives and that he would be enabled through this difficult meeting.

Jaxson escorted Brett Webb into the room. He looked like a man who would attract Jaclyn Cooper. He wore a suit well. His handshake was firm. His eyes hazel. He was courteous to Ida, taking her hand gently and giving her a beautiful smile.

"This is Jaclyn's doctor," Jaxson told Brett and Ida gently bowed her head.

"We're thankful that you came," she told him sincerely.

"I'm glad to be here." He looked at Jaxson. "To help. In any way." As she guided him in conversation Jaxson took Joshua aside.

"Full house." Jaxson scanned the room. "I wasn't expecting it. Who are these people?"

He clicked off the short list.

"Termite," Jaxson repeated, looking at Lisette.

"Profiler and psyche evaluator. Short answers work best to her questions. Yes. No."

Now he smiled then he said discreetly, "You've got the final word with me, regardless of their evaluation. Just give me a yes or a no and we'll move forward."

"God will show us."

"Why don't we sit." It was Curtis who took the lead. "Brett did you meet everyone?" he asked, still standing while everyone sat.

He held a remote in his hand, used it to make his presentation. There was a quick but thorough vid show on Yrasrevda and his history on a wall-size vid screen. Then a recap on the Globe article with their photograph. The news had spread and they were shown where. "Apparently Miss Cooper's outfit has sparked interests with the fashion world. The shot is now going viral through social media." Several more slides were viewed of just Jaclyn. "There is no doubt it's reached Russian readership. There is a sixty-three percent probability that the Viper will have a response. That jumps to eighty with increased media exposure."

"Does he have a new girl?" Christie voiced the question.

"He has a stable of girls."

"Then why is he still interested in her?"

"Because she escaped. Twice. Once from Babel. Then from his poison." It was Lisette that gave the profile. Educating everyone on the Russian princes, their illegal businesses and practices, their personal preferences. Then she focused on the Viper's prolific history of indiscretions and his deviant behaviors. They were told the psychopath was a narcissistic egomaniac. A game player. "He hates to lose. Will seek a rematch. Revenge. He must show his power and prove himself."

"And we've invited baseball's finest during his busy season to play what part for us? A bull's eye?" A man from IT asked the Bull with a subtle grin.

"Brett needs to be forewarned," Marc stated. "He's touched what the Viper claims to be his. Strolled in front of the earth's window with his escaped tiger. He'll need protection until we eliminate the potential threat."

"Agreed," Intel stated.

"I can get my own protection," Brett told the room.

"We appreciate the offer," Marc nodded. "But you'll need more than a body guard. We've got people who are trained to watch and they know how to respond."

"And if I see Miss Cooper again?"

There was a static pause then Marc answered, "Are you planning to do that?"

"That would raise the Russian's response to eighty-two percent likely probability," one of the analyzers ticked off the new statistic.

"They get media exposure again," another analyzer was punching buttons with a sudden greedy anticipation.

"We can keep that from happening," Christie answered.

"Not always," Marc countered.

"Eighty-six percent probability." The analyzer looked up from his PDA. "You antagonize with more of the same sexpot shots and we're edging toward ninety. He'll come to take back what he feels is his."

"Come to the states?" Jaxson questioned.

"Yes."

"He's too powerful to come himself. He has hundreds to do his bidding," Joel debated.

"And he could have moved on. Without Intel to counter that he hasn't, how can we assume he'll come hunting her?"

"Because he's arrogant," Lisette answered. "Possessive. And believes his power usurps the law. He paraded an abducted American woman of high birth back into the spotlight of the world in Babel. Wearing the Czar's Serpent that was stolen from the Louvre." The necklace of diamonds was flashed on screen. "This was beyond bold. And a claim. He is above the law. Wearing the diamonds, she was shown to be above all his women. She was his choice. She also escaped in the presence of his enemies, which he soon killed off. Czenky the Bear of Moscow was dead the next day. No doubt Viper has claimed he allowed the Tiger to escape so that he could hunt her."

"He's convinced himself now it is a game," Christie agreed.

"Yes. A game his father played, and now he's addicted to. The Swan," Marc punched a button on his PDA and caused a file to flash on screen. A platinum blond was captured beside the Russian. "Viper's name for this woman. The Swan was the last woman he kept for any length of time. We don't know her origin but we've followed their history. It was similar to the last few weeks he held Miss Cooper. The Swan was pregnant the last time she was seen." A grainy photograph showed the image. "If Jaclyn shows up in the media, the lure will be too great for him. He'll come to claim his rights," he told the room. "And we'll be waiting."

There was a discussion, in the middle of it the door opened and Pearce Harrison walked in.

"Sir!" It was Joel Bondi who popped up first at attention. The ex-military in the room on their feet at once. Even Lisette was caught off guard, mouth open then quickly closing as she also stood in respect. Pearce Harrison had watched six presidents come and go during his tenure in the CIA. Most thought he was retired. Some knew he was not. Everyone understood he wielded great power. Respected his wisdom. And those who had served with him admired his strategy in tight situations and his chess moves on the world's game board. He was a liaison to *Stratia*, working with the Eagle.

"Please. Sit," he gave the order in his usual style, circling the table to Brett. He shook the man's hand. "Harrison," he introduced himself. "Glad to see you in Washington. About time those Nationals did something right. I'm expecting a sweep."

"Yes, sir."

"Fury." He nodded at Joshua. "Still got you in those itchy sweaters." He groaned. "Surely someone can do something about that over in supply, Marc. We know how the boys hate those sweaters." He stood beside the Eagle. "I've looked over the information and the current Intel you sent me. The Viper hasn't moved. I agree, he will or he'll send eager men in search of glory and you'll be ready. Guard the pitcher, I've waited too long to lose a world series. Jaxson, how's the daughter?"

"Improving."

He shook his head. “I’d bomb that snake pit if I still had the authority, but we’d take out a lot of civilians. More likely a lot of innocent women. Instead, we should all sit down and play a game of chess or perhaps we should call it baseball."

"Mr. Webb are you interested in sacrificing your own desires to help out Miss Cooper and pitch a few balls for us?” Curtis, the Eagle, asked him.

“Yes, of course.”

“That’s what the data tells me, too, that you’re a man we can trust with the task.” He nodded. “I won’t lie. We checked you out. Tested you. Do you agree, Lisette?”

She cocked her head, looked at Brett. “I have just one question, sir.”

“Ask it.” Curtis looked down at his report.

“Did you bring Miss Cooper to climax during your day together?”

The room full of saints imploded in silence, gazes dropping to the nearest report. Brett glanced at Jaxson. Fury began to pray. He fixed his mind on Lamentations as he looked at a spot on the wall. His heart crying out with the prophet as words he didn’t want to hear were spoken out loud.

“We weren’t intimate. I’ve discussed this with her father and her doctor.” He looked at Ida.

“That’s not what I asked you.”

“What you ask is very private. Why should I answer you?”

“Because the answer matters.”

“She was on Eros—

“Yes,” Lisette sighed now. “We know the facts and most of us here understand what they mean. Just answer the question please.”

“Yes,” he answered.

“How?” She kept her gaze locked with his.

“You said one question.” Christie reminded the room. Her gaze had remained locked with the Termite. Joshua knew her loathing for the woman was never concealed. The three looked at Curtis Lexington. He gave a nod and Christie narrowed her heated eyes.

"How?" Lisette asked again.

Brett narrowed his gaze and leaned forward. "I won't answer that and I wonder—

"I wonder if it has haunted you? Ignited fantasies?" She folded her hands and asked him, "I wonder if it made you proud? Surprised you?"

"What surprises me is that you would disrespect a woman that the rest of us would defend with our lives. She was a victim. Of that snake. And his drug. It was Eros. And I won't be fooled again or discuss that evil, let alone rehearse it with such a disrespectful conversation."

Lisette studied him. A long, sweeping scan. Then a smile. "He passed."

Several shook their heads and Christie snarled but Lisette cut her off. "You're a man of integrity but I'll warn you, Mr. Webb, not to think of the memories of that night. Lust will tempt you, fortify yourself by renewing your mind to the present task of respecting her. Obey our instructions and I believe, if Mr. Cooper does the interfacing, and Mr. Webb meets with the Fury on regular appointments, then I can concur." She sat back.

Christie said very clearly, "Lisette, you are a nasty little Termite."

"I do my job and I believe you might be too close to this particular case, Peregrine. Perhaps you should nest." There was a lift of her brow that lit a fire in Christie's green eyes.

Jaxson must have known the look for he stepped in. "Look, I know I'm too close to this case," Jaxson spoke. "She's my daughter and I never dreamed she'd be in the center of anything like this. I can only trust those that do this for a living—that every part of the work is vital for the mission even the extremely personal questions."

Jaxson looked at Fury. It was the moment of truth. Yes. Or. No.

In a single sweep Fury looked at Jaxson, Christie, Ida. His gaze moved over Lisette and the Eagle, then to the Bull who with a shift of his chin told him his take on the plan. He looked at his reflection in the two-way glass, knew Wisdom watched. Had orchestrated the plan for the good of his wife. Knew God was over all of it. *May His will be accomplished...*

He looked at his father-in-law and nodded then Jaxson signaled to Curtis agreement. "This is hardball. There's a risk, Mr. Webb, I won't lie to you. This isn't a vid game, it's real and it's dangerous. If you step into this game, date Miss Cooper, allow the paparazzi to shoot your picture. You need to know what you're up against. The Russian can hit home runs off your best curve ball. So you'll throw what we call. You wait for the signal. And you keep the action to first base. You try to steal second with Miss Cooper and I'm gonna know about it. This isn't about dating a beautiful woman or falling in love. This is about luring out an evil enemy and protecting a very fine young lady. Understood?" Curtis asked.

Brett nodded.

"I need more than a nod. I need a yes or a no. If you need time to decide—

"Yes."

Curtis turned to the table. "Appreciate all the work on this and the inter-department cooperation. You'll be linked in as necessary as we move forward and duty calls for your expertise. Mr. Webb and Mr. Cooper, would you join me for lunch?" The Eagle leaned down and spoke confidentially with the Bull.

"Fury," Marc spoke his name and Joshua understood the order. He was to wait.

"Is she always like that?" Brett asked softly, his gaze focused on Fury.

"She?"

"Lisette."

"Ah, she is a Termite." He sighed. "And they do have their purposes."

"I don't understand her purpose, or the question."

"She's trained to evaluate."

"What, my prowess?" Webb stood and buttoned his jacket, glanced at Jaxson. There was anger. "Or a father's grief? Perhaps the concentric effects of Eros? She has no idea what that drug does. No one would believe it unless they saw it."

Fury could only nod as Jaxson moved Brett forward and the room emptied. As they walked to the private room where lunch was served, Marc told him discreetly, "You're to befriend the Spider. Develop a relationship. Keep watch. He'll check in once a week with you."

Fury stalled, his flesh in immediate rebellion. His spirit whispered the familiar announcement, "This is a test" and he was given the right of man's free will to obey or resist. Marc's hand went to his back, his words soft. "It's for her best."

"Spider? Is that the best you could do?"

Marc grinned. "I suggested Peacock since we could use his feathers to catch a snake's attention. I was told were weaving a spider web."

"Spider," he repeated now with a sigh.

"What is a Spider to a lion but an irritating sting?"

"Spiders bite."

"Do they? I thought it was more of a sting." They debated the fact. Marc said he'd have to ask his wife. By the end of lunch the friendship had begun.

14

The flowers were waiting in her room when she came home to Texas. A huge vase of vivid red roses. The buds opened and fragrant but four days old. They'd been sent from Brett. She opened the card pinned to the ribbon.

> Please call me when you can.
> I'm not walking away.
> I don't have any expectations.
> It's important you know how much I care.
> I've been praying for you.
> Brett

She sighed, her hand shaky, her emotions not ready to think about Brett Webb. She longed for the lion, to bury her face in the lingering scent of Joshua and hold on to him. But she'd left that at Heatherwood. Left the lion in the sanctity of that place. Left the lion, knowing now the high possibility that she would return there in the future to battle again and she needed its strength on that day, not every day as a crutch.

She was left alone, not trusting herself, or her feelings. Tomorrow she would be stronger, sure, more courageous. Courage came in small steps. It was odd that the first involved her father. Seeing him again after that horrid night. But she lifted her face and she trusted his love. He opened his arms to her, reached for her, then held her gently.

"I'm so glad you're home."

She squeezed him tighter.

"You're my heart," he reminded her. "I was crazy here, waiting."

"I know. I'm sorry. Forgive me."

He lifted her chin, looked into her eyes. "No, not for something that was outside your control. You're not responsible."

"I had a part. I drank orange juice, threw up my medication and then didn't take my levels seriously. They were rising and I didn't call Ida. I let Eros deceive me. I won't do that again. In fact now my PDA sends each reading to Ida automatically. She'll help me to adjust if I need to and she changed my hormones. I'm taking injections for a while until I get more regulated."

"That sounds like a good plan," he said and smiled.

"Mom's been through the wringer," she told him. "She could probably use some attention. If you held her for a minute she might let it loose and cry."

He kissed her, assured as he drew her closer still, "Might need to just hold on to you for a minute."

"You can cry," she told him, holding him tight.

"Done that, now I want to rejoice. You're home again, better." He kissed her. "We're going to learn how to fight this fight better. I have some ideas of my own. A game plan." He brushed her hair back, looked into her eyes.

"A game plan?" She lifted brows. "Diet, exercise, hormone injections, counseling sessions, personal guard and a dad with a game plan." There was an exhale of honesty. "Great."

"Hey. You haven't heard the game plan yet." He flashed dimples. "Your birthday cometh."

"Yes?"

"We're going to celebrate this one. Big. All of us. Together. Gifts."

"Shoe party. Tight." She kissed him as she chuckled.

"Anything," he whispered it now holding her face, the sincerity bringing a sudden silence.

She looked into her father's eyes, whispered from her heart, "I want to honor Joshua . . . his team. I want to . . . share a meal with him, meet his family. Could you do that? Honor me that way by honoring God?"

He gave a nod, she watched him think. "I think I might be able to do that. I know some people, who know some people, who can probably make that happen in a very honorable way."

"Thank you," she could only whisper it. "I miss him," was said even softer. Her father drew her into his arms again, held her.

"You needed him that day," he told her softly. "You were trying to tell me. I didn't understand. I will, in the future, I will," he promised her.

She held tight to her father, nodded silently. There was emotion, hidden and sacred that welled up and came forth then there were words that she needed him to understand, "I don't understand myself yet. Who I am now. Where I went when the Eros took over. What I wanted or did. I'm sorry, Daddy. I didn't want you to see me like that. Or Samuel."

"We love you, Jaclyn. We want to help you. I won't let you hide." He'd taken her face, forced her to look at him. "Feel ashamed at what you're not responsible for."

"I do," she confessed, "I was all over Brett."

"We talked. I rode with him to New York and explained things. He's a good man, Jaxie."

She could only nod. "I put you and Lexi through the ringer and I was mean to Samuel."

"He loves you dearly. He'll come the minute you call."

"I want to see him."

Samuel came with Jenna to Austin. They met her and Lexi for lunch by the office. It was still the headquarters for the Lexington Agency. The staff now numerous, their clients select. Samuel didn't wait around for their reconciliation. He jogged to her, taking her up into his arms and holding her tight and silent. She cried, and in the end so did he, with soft words of apology and love. "Forgive me," he'd asked her.

"Only if you'll forgive me," she'd countered.

"You weren't yourself."

"There were parts of me that misbehaved. I'll take account for them."

"Feeling better now?"

"You've no idea." She smiled. "I feel so much better."

"You look good." He nodded. "I brought Jenna." He buried his face back into her hair, held her tight again. "I was nervous." He laughed. "Now I'm not." Then he moaned. "And I promised her a trip to the fabric store if she'd come with me."

"Well then you'll take her." She grinned up at him, stroked his handsome face. "Hungry?"

"Oh, yeah." He released her and Jenna stepped up, hugged her tight.

"She has a few things to apologize for." Samuel nodded. "Don't you Jenna Ann?"

"You wouldn't mean this!" Jaclyn flashed the cover of a pop culture magazine and squealed. "Unnamed designer causes an October East Coast trend." The picture of her with Brett Webb was compared against several knock-off versions of her skirt, vest and boots on pop culture's brightest stars. "Unnamed designer," she scoffed. "We have to do something about that. They're all over you with this outfit. They love it. We have to launch you."

"No," Jenna immediately argued, glancing at Samuel. "I'm not having that night . . . launch my career."

Jaclyn snorted. "Please. The outfit was a total hit. The boots darling."

"That outfit was part of the problem. You were a booted bombshell."

"I was totally covered up, James Samuel. From head to toe."

"You were covered, but the outlines were—

"What?"

“Do I have to explain this? Just trust me. The get up was bombshell.”

“Lexi,” she punted to her stepmom. “The boots were not bombshell, they were darling, tell him.”

“Absolutely, darling. I must have a pair, two inches shorter. I can’t do five inches anymore for more than an hour. I had no idea you were making shoes.”

“I just started.” Jenna smiled. “And you know I don’t do knock offs, only one of a kinds. I’ll come up with something else darling.”

“I know you will.”

”In fact I heard we have an occasion.” Her smile was electric.

“Award ceremony at the White House. Little formal dinner. Can I do your dress?”

“Yes! I was thinking suit.”

“Ohhh.” They were arm in arm. “Cletus is taking me to the fabric store.” There was a moan. “Come with us. We’ll find the material. I have an idea.” Jenna drew the jacket on a napkin as they ordered. Samuel made a few alterations. “Absolutely no cleavage,” he told his sister. “None of the Cooper women get cleavage. Give that to the Dake girls—Shannon and Laurel. They can show all the cleavage they want.” He grinned and Lexi tossed a napkin at him.

“Pig,” Jenna wasn’t so kind. “You are such a pig. You’d have us Cooper women in sack cloth with are heads in burkas while the Dake girls are on parade.”

“Way it should be. No one should see your hair either.”

“He needs a wife,” she told her aunt. “So he can bother his daughter.”

“Not having daughters.”

“Are too,” she waved him off. “You are such a girl’s guy.”

“I am not a girl’s guy.”

“Tell him, Jaxie,” Jenna insisted as she drew another sketch.

“You are,” she said it flatly. “Another reason you need to hang with the Fury more. He’s a guy’s guy. Seen him lately?”

"He got called out."

"Where?" She felt the dread. Like a brick in her belly.

He took her hand. Squeezed. "He couldn't say. I just got a message, gone to work."

She nodded, looked at the napkin, holding tight to him. "You can talk to him. It's okay. I won't be mad that you're friends. He's a great guy. Jenna, that's pretty. Look Lexi."

Lexi agreed.

"What do you think, Cletus?"

"Where's the burka?"

This time ice flew as they all said, "Pig."

The invitation came on expensive paper, tucked inside two envelopes. It had a seal you took notice of—gold leaf on blue. The eagle brilliant and powerful. The words summoning him to a formal reception that would honor *Stratia.* His PDA was bulleted with messages. The team was looking for direction. Why did the president want to honor them? Did they have to wear formals? Was this a must attend? And just who invited their parents?

"My parents can't come," Vin told him in his office. He'd come from special forces, with a turbulent upbringing and a strength of character that had made him rise up above it. "They would embarrass me and you," he scowled. "They don't understand protocol and chain of command. My mom might steal the silverware or something. She's not a believer, sir. Far from it in fact, but you don't want those details."

"They've been invited," he told him what he'd been told. "The invitations mailed out without our editing of the list. Apparently the country feels like your parents have a right to see you honored as their son." He command, "Be there and trust God to deal with the details."

"Sir," he popped to but slouched as he went out.

"So it's really a go?" Eli asked him.

"Afraid so. I've been told it's a mission, *Trust God to deal with it.*"

"Trust God to deal with it," Eli repeated. "I better pull out the uniform."

"It's in your locker. Supply saw to it all. Along with the travel itineraries for everyone's folks and the local accommodations."

"Great. Out of luck then."

"Totally out of luck."

"And this is supposed to be an honor? Yanking our pants down? I'm not sure there's anything that makes a person more vulnerable than having them bring their family around and get an inside look into their past. Is this political propaganda?" He paced. "I know it's not from *Stratia*. We don't serve just the country. And we only honor God, never ourselves. Who did this?"

"Don't know."

"Find out." Eli's gaze was narrowed. His mouth a grim line around a toothpick. "Because I'm going to kill them, sir. Very slowly. And you'll understand my motive when you meet the folks." He groaned, "This is no honor."

"You'll *deal with it*. And trust God with the rest."

Eli forced out a sigh of irritation. "Deal with it, huh? Well they can deal with it later. I'm going to find a way to get us 'beeped' out of there if all hell has to come loose to do it."

"We won't be 'beeped' out of there and hell will be contained for the evening."

He grinned, slowly. "Tried that route already?"

"I did." He frowned. "I was appropriately put in my place. So I'll pass that on if necessary since I've now been held accountable to the whereabouts of every chest getting pinned by the president. We are to be honored and grateful for the opportunity to salute the Commander in Chief of this great nation under God. You can pass that down as executive officer, Eli."

"But I'm not an American."

Now he growled. The warning he was getting impatient.

"Yes, sir," he sighed. "My neck's already itching." Eli cursed as he exited.

Joshua felt like a fish out of water. His shoes pinched, his neck itched and he was suddenly cold. For the first time in five years, he was out of gear and cold. SEALs didn't know cold, but he felt the chill of winter through the fancy getup they were forcing him to wear as he slipped out of the car and prepared to meet his family at their hotel. It had been several months since he'd seen them but they had never seen him like this. Nervous. He didn't like praise. He hated being recognized. Standing out. And his men were right, this whole arrangement made him incredibly vulnerable. Pants on the floor. Meet the parents …

Denise and Nathan Oliver weren't his biological parents. They were his family. His only family. He'd been eleven. Caleb nine, when providence had placed them. The couple understood grief—how painful their loss had been even if they never knew the details of his parents' death. They'd lost an only son, two years before to leukemia. The complexity of relationships had been the easy part. Being a family. Doing life. Healing. The simple had been tricky. Titles. Mom. Dad. Son. They were sacred. Denise. Nate. They were dishonoring. Ma'am. Sir. Worked most of the time yet often fell too short. And the pattern of not knowing what to say just went on, didn't it … Wife… Jaclyn … Miss Cooper… Baby Girl…

"You're handsome," Denise told him with a tight hug that just made his neck itch more. She was a pretty woman, letting the gray slowly invade into her golden hair in soft highlights. Keeping her body healthy with her swimming and biking. Her mind was sharpened with the medical students she taught in her chemistry classes. Her leadership skills put to good use in a local Bible study and then there was their prayer group. Since Caleb had joined the Navy there had been the SEAL team lapel pin and the prayer group. They were what strengthened her to stand after losing another son. "You hate this."

"I do." He nodded at her, kissed her. "This collar has my neck itching like crazy. Sir." He shook Nate's hand. "How was the trip?"

"Good," Nathan Oliver answered with a smile. He'd always worn a suit well. After thirty years of consulting and teaching at Georgia Tech, he was comfortable in a suit. Comfortable in a crowd with his quiet confidence. He'd become more silent over the years since Caleb was gone. He'd aged as well. The grief was an unspoken part of them all. They kept topics between the lines, discussing the things that made them fuss and kept their attention off the things that made them hurt. It was the way things had become. The way they survived.

"Sorry I couldn't get you at the airport."

"The car service was nice." Denise slipped into the sedan at the curb.

"How do we look?" Nathan wanted to know, riding shotgun. "Presentable?"

"Sure."

"Well it is the president."

"Not every day you get a medal and a dinner at the White House."

"Right."

"We're proud," Denise said seriously. "Are we picking up your date?"

"No date," he answered.

"Are you seeing anyone?"

"Haven't had a lot of time to . . . socialize."

"You have to make time." There was a quiet sigh.

"Joshua's always been focused," Nathan defended. "Medicine, the SEALs, now this special military assignment. He doesn't need a wife right now."

"Well, I'd like some grandbabies." Her gaze was direct in the rearview mirror.

"Denise," Nathan chuckled. "Can we find the wife first?" He said it like they spoke of this topic often. "She's got the prayer group praying for grandbabies. I always follow the request up for the wife. I'd personally like to have the wife before the grandbabies, myself. Call me old fashioned."

"Nate, the wife is assumed. The good Lord knows the way of things. Give Him credit. Besides, I'm weary praying for his wife."

Looking at those blue eyes he wondered what she'd think of the grandbabies she already had frozen on ice, tucked in a secure vault at Heatherwood. He wondered what Nathan's conservative values would think of the ethics of the whole situation with Jaclyn.

"Are there any interesting ladies at work?"

"That's never a good idea," Nathan argued.

"Church then? Or your neighborhood? Give me some hope or I'm going to start saying yes to all my friends who want to set you up."

He was gentle. "Can we let God handle the wife and kids?"

"Yes," Nathan agreed. "Denise, look there's the Capitol."

"I love Washington. It's always beautiful in its patriotism."

Joshua tugged at his collar, sighed. He longed for an ear bud for the voice of direction to help navigate him through the next few hours with his family and mission, *Trust God to deal with it*. His mouth tightened, he'd personally strangle the one behind this whole thing if he could find them.

There was a receiving line, an official photographer. The president wore a dark suit with a red tie, the first lady a red suit. After them were a few senators and statesmen, then the line of military muscle. He saw *Stratia's* leaders—the Bear, the Eagle, the Bull—wearing suits and mixing in with generals, admirals and intelligence. He presented Denise and Nathan, let them talk and shake hands. They were better at it than he ever wanted to be. Slowly they made their way down the line. Before the president an elderly man stretched forth his hand and introduced himself, "I'm Brad Bennett," he told him.

He had eyes of distinct violet, hair of white, a face that was still handsome though he knew him to be in his nineties. There was a quiet power in his handshake, a sincerity as he closed a second hand over the joining and quietly told him, 'Blessed be the man."

"Sir." He nodded, received the blessing of the first Psalm then introduced Denise.

"There is always a great mother behind strong sons," he took her hand.

"A praying mother," she told him humbly.

There was a discussion about her prayer group.

"May I introduce you to the president." Mr. Bennett did the honors, Joshua stepping back as his family was introduced. The president took his hand, the group posing for a photograph. The first lady detaining them for a little longer, talking to the Olivers about the prayer support they were involved in for the military.

Next came the policy makers. Senators and congressmen who supported and scrutinized *Stratia*. Denise had taken over the spearheading of their progress; he was happy to acquiesce and follow.

"Joshua," Denise caught his attention as he ran a quick finger around the tight collar of the torturous wool jacket. He came to attention and smiled. "This is Senator Lexington, from Texas. His wife is an orthopedic."

He shook his hand, nodded to his wife. "Doctor Lexington."

"Joshua is also a doctor."

"Where were you trained?"

"The Navy."

"Wonderful," she answered. "My father-in-law was a Navy pilot."

"The senator played baseball. Remember? For Texas. We're Braves fans, but we always did enjoy when you came to town."

"I'm the beginning of the end," he told Joshua with a smile. "Just the family left. They tend to keep us at the back of the line because our protocol can start to break down." He held him up a minute. His eyes suddenly intense. "You'll hear it a lot tonight, but I personally wanted to thank you." He leaned closer, and a card was slipped into his hand. "Keep that for the future. If you ever have a need I can assist you with. I'm here for you."

"Thank you, sir."

"My father said that black coat itched like a heat rash. He was a Navy pilot." Layne smiled. "I'm still not used to the coat and tie myself. Rather be in a baseball jersey."

"Yes, sir."

"Wife nags me all the time about squirming in my suits. Just can't quite get comfortable with silk tied in a tight knot around my neck."

"No, sir."

"Joshua," Denise called again. They both smiled.

"Proud mamas. Mine's down the line somewhere. She'll be calling my name in a minute too."

"Layne," his wife censored, but smiled. Doctor Ellen Lexington was a beautiful brunette, her eyes a crisp emerald, humored and intelligent. She took his hand and softly said, "We're very thankful for what you've done for the country and our family."

The two words echoed as she let him go. He suddenly realized exactly who her family was. Beside Ellen was Bennett Lexington and his wife, Cheyenne then her brother, Jaxson Cooper. He began a long line of family that all had their eyes on him.

Innocently, Denise led the introductions, "Jaxson and Lexi Cooper. Their three sons, Levi, Xavier and Max. And their daughter, Jaclyn."

She stepped forward. What she wore was simple but that made her only more stunning. Fitted jacket, a little flirty sleeve that fell over her hands, a length of silk legs from a pencil skirt just at her knees. The shoes a takeoff on men's patent dress shoes stacked up four inches high. The suit buttons were some red jewel. And in the open lapel was his cross and tags on a cord of red suede.

She looked at him. Their eyes connecting. Something in him relaxing and yet tense with anticipation as he realized why they were all here. Who was here. What the honor was for. How far her family reached. And who was behind this.

Too bad he couldn't strangle his wife …

"Miss Cooper," he gave a nod. Couldn't help the little grin that surfaced.

Her smile widened, she held out her hand, "Joshua."

He accepted it, his other hand going to Denise's back as he held Jaclyn's hand. Her attention had immediately turned to Jaclyn the moment she had spoken his given name. And suddenly this moment became intensely important. "Jaclyn Cooper, this is—

"Denise." She stepped in immediately.

"Mrs. Fury," Jaclyn immediately responded.

"It's Oliver," she corrected with a beautiful smile. "Everyone makes the mistake."

There was only a blink. "Mrs. Oliver," she repeated. Her smile was soft, her eyes connecting with Denise's as her hand moved from Fury's to hers. He remembered her words on the train. When they'd role played a story, learned about each other. He remembered when Jackie asked Josh if his mother liked her. "I'm honored to meet you. I have the greatest respect for Joshua."

Denise looked at him, scoped to his heart as only a mother can do then she turned back to Jaclyn. "I'm honored to meet you, too," she told her. "This is my husband, Nathan."

"Why don't you stand with us, Joshua," Jaxson requested. "Introduce your team again."

Lexi asked, "Denise, have you been introduced to many of the people Joshua works with?"

Lexi drew Denise aside as Jaxson talked with Nate. Fury stood in line with her, silent, searching for something to say, between handshakes. There was small talk, her soft casual conversation that held his interest. A side bar, she whispered privately that made him smile. She always found a way to make him smile, laugh, to draw him closer. There were stories shared with his men as they passed by. There were questions from her brothers as they crept closer to hear the stories from soldiers, their attention pushed them another step closer. There was a great awareness of her, everything about her.

Her hand was on his cross when she asked about Caleb. "Did your brother make it?"

There was that moment of excruciating acceptance as he vocalized what was still so hard to accept. He looked into her eyes, the soft gold of them and said the words he hated, "Caleb was killed three years ago in Damascus."

She blinked, shaking her head, denying his words, then reaching past them, to him. Her troubled eyes holding his gaze, her touch connecting as her hand covered his, held firm. She said nothing. There were no words. Just held his hand, his gaze and then was forced to move on, to reach out again to another team member as they came down the line.

His grief was soft, more a deep regret. That she would never meet Caleb, that he would never get to tease and interfere about Jaclyn. Caleb would have prodded, he would have seen, known, understood.

Because he wasn't here—and because Caleb was why he was the Fury—there was honor above all the other emotions as the president presented him, then his team and gave them a simple civil medal for a job they could discuss in front of family and friends. They had found a missing American, brought her home. There was applause then another line, a smaller line that started again with Brad Bennett and ended with Jaclyn Cooper. She handed him a box as her father said, "Just a token of something that can't be expressed in truth. I'm very grateful for what you did."

15

Denise Oliver watched the young woman embrace the son she had been given. Jaclyn Cooper had hugged all the men and the one woman, Petra. There had been affection and smiles and real gratitude. They had freed her from an oppressive evil. The president telling a simple version of what she could only imagine was a very complicated story. Her family was politically connected. Famous in many of its members. Blessed, extremely blessed by anyone's standards and obviously gave all of the glory of what they had achieved to their Lord. Now they were giving thanks for answered prayer and the team who had delivered a daughter home.

Her heart noticed the way her boy kept his hand to her back, bent his head, saw him whisper something and the girl nodded, holding his gaze. In her eyes there was emotion. The kind that comes from the soul and between them was a connection that came from the heart.

The moment she sensed it the elderly Brad Bennett asked them all to stand. He lifted his hand and gave a prayer. His words blessed God then the ones who served Him. He asked that their arms be strengthened for the fight and reliant on the true source of victory. He asked for wisdom for the administrators and protection for the fighters. He asked for comfort for the families who sacrifice and wait, that their faith would be sustained through the battles. He asked that all might have courage as they waited for the glorious hope of Christ's appearance.

"Amen," Denise agreed and looked at her son, watched as he slowly released the hand of Jaclyn Cooper and the two stepped away from each other in slow degrees of separation. The young woman fingered her necklace, watching him go as another family member stepped up to her side.

Back at their table Joshua said immediately, "Ready?"

Nathan stood at once. "I know you can't wait to get out of that monkey suit."

They made their way from the White House, she was quiet as they drove back toward the hotel. Nathan talked him into coming up to the room. The dog a good lure.

Harley D met them at the door. It always amazed her how his stocky little serious self could suddenly turn excited at the sight of Joshua. She still had no idea how such short muscled legs could run so fast, but run the English bulldog did. He raced off to find that gopher and brought him back to Joshua. The two kept busy playing tug of war and fetch. Nathan finding drinks. Joshua losing the jacket and getting on the floor in his undershirt and trousers. In moments like this she kept expecting Caleb to come into the room at any minute. Her heart ached as she watched his dog play with his big brother.

The television went on, Nathan catching up on the sports recap. They talked football. They talked about Jaxson Cooper and his Super Bowl wins.

"He didn't wear any of the rings. Did you see that?" He asked their boy. "Humble man."

Joshua nodded, his attention on the dog.

"Tell us the story," she said, turning down the volume on the TV.

"Story?"

"Of how you met Jaclyn Cooper."

"You heard it."

"I heard the abbreviated presidential version."

He went back over it. Man style. Brief bites of information, places, dates, events. He moved them from point A to point B leaving out the details. "Mission accomplished."

When he finally looked at her, she saw that he saw. "She's wearing your brother's cross."

"Yes." He stilled, his arm around the bulldog. "I gave it to her."

There was emotion, she didn't fight it. "She must mean something to you to give her something that important."

He looked at the dog, gave it attention. Denise felt her husband's gaze yet she couldn't let this go. She couldn't and kept at him. "Why would you give that away?"

"I'm not sure you can understand."

"Does she mean something to you, Joshua?"

"Yes." His answer was honest, yet closed. His attention on the dog. Her husband silently urging her to stop pushing as she met his gaze.

Looking at Nathan she asked, "What?"

Joshua looked back up at her. "I was chosen . . . to protect her. The man that took her isn't happy that I took her back."

"You're in danger?"

"Denise, we're all in danger. We could die tomorrow in a car accident."

"I'm talking about danger, Nathan, not accidents. Who is this man?"

"If I told you it wouldn't mean anything."

"What is his name?"

"Yrasrevda. He calls himself the Viper. He's a Russian prince and very evil."

She nodded. Sighed, clasping her hands together so she wouldn't wring them.

"Please don't worry."

"I do," she answered. "But I pray. You're still protecting her?"

"God protects her. The cross reminds her of that."

"And your tags. What do they do?"

"They were with the cross when I had her put it on. Now she tells me they remind her to pray for me."

"A person shouldn't have to be reminded to pray."

His face tightened and he stated, "You gave me the cross."

"Yes. Caleb would have wanted you to have it."

"Now you're angry that I gave it away."

"Maybe," she agreed, explained, "I get possessive about the things that were Caleb's. I don't want them to be lost."

"She would never," he stopped. She leaned closer, waited but his attention fell back to the dog. "I think he'd be glad that she wears it."

"Did she know your brother?" his father asked.

"No, sir."

"He'd have liked her." Nathan smiled then he gave a nod. "Caleb would have liked to see his cross on such a beautiful girl, Denise."

"Tucked in such a beautiful bosom you mean?"

"That's not what I meant at all." But he smiled at Joshua all the same.

"You think I don't know my boys," she stood, tossed the gopher with a burst of anger and Harley D pursued it like a linebacker after a quarterback. "Caleb liked a beautiful girl, and I haven't heard Joshua complain. Though a girl built like that makes a mother of sons a bit anxious."

"Who could complain?" Nathan asked her. "We'd think you'd be happy. Earlier you were drilling him about finding a wife. He gave his tags to the girl. Trusted her with Caleb's cross."

"Are you in love with her?" Denise frankly asked the question as she took a seat.

"I, ah—

"I, ah," she repeated as the stagger became silence. Waited, watched as he guarded and finally leaned forward and lifted a brow. "You don't know yet."

"Maybe he's not ready to tell us yet."

"No," she studied him. "He's not ready to tell himself. Overanalyzing the whole affair. Probably made a flow chart of all the reasons why this shouldn't work—" Her nostrils flared. "You have!" She stood. With hands on hips. "Being a warrior does not disqualify you from having a life, Joshua. Look at David. He was a mighty man with a house full of wives."

"He was a king." His head was bowed, his arm around the dog.

"Is that what it's about then? Tell me you're not believing the lie."

"Denise," Nate tried to break in.

"No," she stopped him. "I did not raise stupid boys, Nate. Joshua," she demanded he stand. He did. A grown man in a warrior's body but she still saw the wounded 10-year-old boy in his over serious eyes as she took his face into her hands. "I don't care what this world is doing. Separating people into classes. The haves and the have nots. The served and the servants. Don't you believe it for a moment that your worth is in what can be seen—power, beauty, position." She took his hand. "Gold watches and rings. You are invaluable in Christ. Worthy. And no matter where He's placed us, we all are servants of the Lord Jesus."

"I know that."

"Do you believe it?" Her gaze penetrated his. Ignited that fire. She squeezed his hands. "David was the youngest son. A shepherd. An uncommon warrior. A friend to a prince, a court musician. A leader of mighty misfit men. A husband. A father. And a king. Don't pigeonhole yourself into a single role. God is constantly growing us in new directions. With us in every stage of the process." She squeezed his hands. "And don't apply love to pencil and paper. It can never be figured out with reason. Look at me and Nate, only God could have placed us together."

"Only God, darling." Nathan spoke over her shoulder.

She kissed him and signaled the moment of truce. "I liked her, her family, not that it matters what I think."

"It matters. More than you know." Joshua brought her close.

She held him tight. Charged him, “Don’t be afraid to love, Joshua Fury. If we’ve taught you anything, surely I’ve taught you this.”

He confided softly, “Keep praying for my wife.”

“I sure will.” She rubbed his back, agreed as she pulled away. “And this business with the Russian will need to be resolved.” She sighed, problem solving. “She’s young. How young?”

“Twenty three.”

“Young. I heard something about law school.” She pulled back and looked at him. “Is she going to be a lawyer?”

“Yes, ma’am.”

”A smart girl then.”

“Very smart.”

“We like smart.” She nodded to her husband.

“We like beautiful, too.” Nate took his son close. “You could do worse than a beautiful girl with a bosom that makes your mother worry.”

”Nathan Oliver!”

“That’s what Caleb would say.” He smiled at her.

“Caleb would have already stepped in and stolen her heart.” Joshua grinned.

“Joshua Daniel,” Denise gave a laugh. “He’d have given you a push, that’s the only reason he’d ever be your rival. Surely you know that now.” There was a tender smile then the haunting silence.

His dad patted his back. “We’re proud of you. It was nice to see you rewarded.”

“Will you wear the watch?”

“Where? I don’t dress up.”

“It was a very nice gesture from her father to your team.”

“It’s worth more than my salary.”

“It will be an heirloom.”

He nodded.

"Make sure she knows what that cross means to you. Your family. It's not worth much but it's your heirloom." She was firm. "I'd rather it not end up in someone's jewelry box forgotten in a few years."

When he got home he took the elegant gold watch out of its famous box and ran his finger over the engraved back.

To Joshua Fury
With Gratitude and Respect.
Jx. C.

He put it on, let the synchronized perfection tick silently from its oyster face. The engraved message tight against his skin. He looked at the presentation. Gold winking from the edge of his cuff. Is this what it feels like to be a rich man? To feel the dramatic weight of gold heavy on your wrist … to feel important. Noticed. Envied. Judged well to do. A man above others.

He didn't have the eye to discern such things on others. But he knew he was uncommonly detached from materialism. A Third Culture kid. Not fitting into Africa, not fitting into America. A global nomad misfit. He knew that's why he found belonging in the team structure of *Stratia.* Home more about people than places. Comfortable in rough surroundings. Uncomfortable in society. Guilty in plenty. Angry with greed. Merciful to the poor.

He'd dreaded this night. He'd been surprised. Blessed in many ways. He took out his journal, drew a picture of her as he would remember her tonight. Caleb's cross delicate on her skin, her beauty vibrant. She'd been strong and steady tonight. Like the night when they'd all had dinner on the aircraft carrier. He turned back to that page, past the sketch of her face pillowed on the lion. He liked her in the dark cable sweater, her hair full and loose around her face. He turned to the page with her draped in the blanket on the train—she'd been vulnerable. Then to the first image. Just her eyes, haunted behind heavy kohl lashes, when they'd first connected and she saw hope. Feelings rose up in him intense and possessive. He was no closer now than then in understanding them. He glanced at the page. At his flow chart of reasoning. Words jumping out at him.

Rich. Poor. Warrior. Lady. She deserves someone better. Let her choose.

Denise was right. He took his pencil. Added to the page.

Invaluable in Christ. Worthy. Servant. She was chosen for me.

He closed the book. Glanced at the watch winking from his cuff. Rose and went to the Ancient Place. Went through the cleansing ritual then mounted the steps into the large white empty room of brilliant marble. He laid prostrate. Prayers lifting high. Communion a warm wonderful joy in worship. Then he opened the stiff new clasp of the beautiful watch and slid the heavy gold links from his wrist. Gave the reward to his Lord. For it was His glory. A great victory won for his wife.

"Soli Deo Gloria," he said aloud. Placed the watch on the floor. Beside three others. Pax. Petra. Eli. Had already come. Presented. Before dawn there would be more. Not all. But more. The Lord teaching hearts at different levels. Fury rose and made his way.

Invaluable in Christ. Worthy. Servant.

They were all still learning, weren't they…

"Hey." It was Jenna who found her in the lonely quiet spot on the patio of her Aunt Christie's house. There was a fountain flowing with its peaceful endless tune in the center of a fall garden. Above a canopy of stars were bright in a clear sky. The men had gone to Curtis' house, the women of her family staying here. She was longing for her father, unsteady, too full of emotion and things to process. She felt the edge of desperation. Could this be the last time she saw Joshua? He'd said nothing about a future. No, see you soon. I've missed you. Let's get together. She held his cross. Her gaze unfocused, her body tense, her heart a lonely ache. "Aren't you cold?" Her cousin Jenna wrapped an arm around her. A pretty hand-knit scarf was shared.

"Um." She blinked, smiled at her. "The suit was a hit. The first lady asked me about it."

"Wow, okay." Jenna looked up at the stars.

"It's going to happen, you know. You'll be designing for real people soon."

"Um," she echoed.

She was looking out at the garden, the mums glazed with frost, the bright-faced pansies a surprise of color as her cousin stated, "He's tall, dark and handsome. Brooding. The mystery in the room kind of guy. You could feel the energy change when he walked in. The Fury . . . I don't think the name comes from an anger problem, he's powerful. Did he like your suit?"

"He never comments on my looks."

"His mother was pretty."

"Yes. She talked with Lexi. I listened in. Nervous. All night I was nervous."

"Jaxie, why?"

"It's his parents. And him. Then I thought he would be disappointed in me. What I'd done with Brett."

"No. He wasn't mad." Jenna hugged her closer. "He was compassionate, tender even. I saw that, wondered over how a man like him can be who he has to be and still look at you with a tenderness in his eyes. His eyes are very blue."

"Yes, they're very blue." Jaclyn studied Jenna now. "He looked at me with tenderness? You saw that?"

"We all saw that. It's a contrast, like a waft in a weave. He's serious, stern even and then he leans down to listen to you and there's this sweet tenderness on his face. When I saw that, I couldn't help but like him. Samuel already raves. He thinks the guy's the brother he never had."

Her hand went to his cross. "He told me his brother was killed."

"Killed?"

"Three years ago, he said, but on the train he talked as if he lived. He was part of our stories." She confided in Jenna. "We were told to tell a story of how we could have met. You know, I told a part and then he told a part and it became a story. It was supposed to help us get to know each other and build trust, I guess. Anyway, I put his brother in the story. I said he was there when we met, playing softball."

"Softball?"

"Yes, isn't that strange. The way I told it, Caleb was pitching. Joshua catching. I was up to bat."

"Home run?"

"Yes." She looked at Jenna.

She smiled. "I'm no shrink but it is a metaphor for ..."

"Oh," she laughed totally embarrassed. "Do you think he thought of that?"

"Um. Isn't that what men are always thinking about?" There was an edge in her voice.

"Jenna, how stupid am I?"

"You're never stupid." She squeezed her tight. "So his brother's name was Caleb?"

"He died three years ago, he said. It made me sad."

"Of course." They held each other. In the silence she thought of words he'd said. Of being young with blond hair. Of brothers named Joshua and Caleb. He mentioned a dog. She'd mentioned a girlfriend for Caleb named Emily, he'd simply nodded and agreed. "He misses him. They were close when they were young." She fingered the cross. "I miss him," she said it. Softly.

"You found her." Three aunts stood at the door. It was Aunt Cara who said, "It's cold out here. Come inside girls."

"We've got music on," Aunt Tori told her.

"With the boys at our house, Sophia insisted it was a night to dance," Aunt Heather informed them and Jenna's hips immediately started swaying as classic Motown drifted out.

Her ears perked up. "A little R-E-S-P-E-C-T," Cara sang out.

"Find out what it means to me," Jenna answered. "R-E-S-P-E-C-T. Take care, TCB."

Arm and arm they went inside. Jenna at once kicked off her heels onto the pile of expensive stilettos and raised her hands above her head, clapping. Holding a bottle of sparkling water as a microphone, it was her cousin, Sophia who took her hand and sang her into a circle of family, of aunts, grandmothers, cousins—all singing backup and dancing.

16

Ida greeted her with a hug, then took her face in her small, tender hands. Her eyes were dark, like onyx. Her hair a fat, single braid down her back. "I so enjoyed our night at the White House. My husband can't stop talking about it."

"He's a wonderful man. I liked meeting him."

Ida laughed. "He loved you and all the young ones on the team. It was a special night for us both. Thank your father again."

"I will."

"How are you today?" was asked in her soft soothing voice, drawing her into the office.

"Fine. Good."

There were twin chairs. Comfortable and large that sat back in a small alcove. They'd begun to sit and talk after her counseling appointments, sometimes before. Today, they ended here, talking, sharing hot tea.

"You seem a bit . . . weary," Ida told her.

Jaclyn gave only one nod, slouching with a sigh into the chair. "More edgy," she confessed, "I talked too much today. First with the post traumatic expert then *Stratia's* evaluator, Dr. Lisette Frances. She asks a lot of question about Joshua."

"Oh?"

"Personal questions." She took her first sip of tea. "I told her I wouldn't talk about Joshua. I'd tell her anything she wanted to know about the Viper or my nightmares, but if she wanted to know about Joshua's prowess, she should have a consultation with him. I'm no shrink but some of her questions made me wonder what she was after."

Ida only nodded.

"I was rude."

She sipped her tea.

"I'm not giving anyone at *Stratia* information on the Fury, Ida. Even you."

"I respect that."

"He protected me. I will protect him. I'd prefer to just speak with you."

"I'm a gynecologist, not a psychiatrist."

"You understand me, Eros and I trust you," she told her. "If I don't trust who I'm talking to, how can they help me?"

"They want to help you, Jaclyn."

"They're *Stratia* people."

"Yes, chosen to serve God," she reminded her. "How are the nightmares?"

"I've stopped screaming. Waking up the house." She looked away. "My dad still asks me every day if I slept okay, if I dreamed. He worries. And my oldest brother, Levi . . . he's become very protective. They all worry."

"Of course."

"I hate that. I've used the practical tools. Adjusted my sleep cycle. Learned to handle the nightmares with God's word. I have three people who I know pray for me every night. I feel stronger with the tools."

"You seem stronger." She smiled now.

"I think I'm doing better, what do you think?"

"Yes. Physically, I think you are doing better. The injections are maintaining your levels. Are you comfortable with them?"

"Point and shot." She smiled. "Prick my finger then pop the blood sample in the PDA. It's becoming systematic."

"Are you feeling more like yourself?"

"I'm not sure who 'myself' is anymore. So much has changed."

"This stage of your life is about finding one's self. You're thinking about law school?"

"I've enjoyed working for mom."

"Do you like the work?"

"I like the routine of it. I guess I like the idea of the routine of school. I'm comfortable with school. I don't mind studying."

"You excel at it, so it is a good place to be while you heal physically and emotionally."

"I think it's a better plan than just sitting at home." She rose, walked to the table poured more tea. "I want things to get back to normal."

"What is normal?"

"It's not living with my parents. That's not normal. I'm twenty-three. I should be on my own. My parents should be concentrating on my younger brothers not me right now. It makes me feel guilty." She looked at Ida. "And I'm self-conscious. Of the nightmares, my emotions. Especially knowing my hormones could get out of control again."

"You know the signs."

"I ignored them, Ida. I know that now. I could ignore them again."

"I'm here to help now. You're trusting me and I won't ignore them. If I see something is off, I will alert you and your father. It's what we agreed to."

"Yes, it's what I want. I don't trust myself yet."

"It will get better with time and experience. I promise Jaclyn."

She nodded, watched the steam rise from her cup with its light smell of spice and just said it. "I'm thinking of coming here to school. I've been accepted at Georgetown." She took a drink and watched Ida, looking for a reaction, a warning or disapproval, excitement or encouragement. "What do you think?"

She smiled. "Tell me instead what you're thinking about?"

"I'd be close to you and Heatherwood. I'd be on my own but still close to—" she drank, knowing her real motive. After seeing Joshua, she couldn't stand the thought of not seeing him again. "People I care about—Christie and Marc. My stepmother says school has a rhythm I'm used to and she thinks the routine will be helpful. My dad thinks law is a good fit for me. He's brave enough to let me go with the personal guard in place. I'm not sure what they'll think of me going this far. To Georgetown."

"It seems you have given this some thought." She smiled. "Thinking through an important step toward what's around the next corner. What has God said about this?"

"I thought I was going to Austin or Southern Methodist in Dallas. But suddenly it's . . . Georgetown. He laid it on my heart, keeps the thought on my mind, and the doors just keep opening. I can start in the spring, mid-year and catch up at summer school. They don't offer that to many people."

"Ah, that is His way when we seek Him. Circumstances and open doors. A peace, not of simply calmness but of knowing it is right. Divine direction comes from divine favor."

"Should I wait to start? It's too soon, surely."

"When the peace of knowing comes and the doors open we should have the courage to trust God and walk with Him in the direction He is showing us. You are courageous. A strong woman, cooperating with God to heal. You are doing what many wise people are asking of you. And as I watch this process unfold, I see that your father is maintaining a good balance. He is a man of faith, trusting God and not himself for your protection and purpose. Most would try to hedge you in or hold you too tightly, but because of his great love for you he is trusting God. Your father has learned many things through this, too. Received a greater faith and thus a deeper love of God and an understanding of Him. There is blessing even in the most difficult circumstances, yes?"

She nodded.

"Something I've learned of you Jaclyn is that once you hear the order, you are not one to procrastinate obedience. You are a woman of intention and purpose. I think this also comes from the teaching of your father and shows your trust in God and your individual courage." She smiled proudly at her.

"Speaking of courage," she said quietly. "I'm going to see the man that was with me the day of the echo. I'm dreading it, truthfully."

"It is necessary though, you understand it is better to resolve a difficult situation than to avoid it. And you are not a procrastinator."

"We're having lunch tomorrow. I'm anxious."

"Of course." Now she smiled. "In some ways you wish it were today. You don't like to dally, being intentional you can be impatient. You like things to move along, to find their purposes and be resolved. It is hard to learn patience, to exercise tolerance and perseverance as we wait for God's timing."

"And you said you weren't a counselor." Jaclyn shook her head. "This is the most help I've received all day."

Ida blushed softly then laughed. "It is the Lord. I ask for His words and wisdom. I, too, was a bit anxious today. The physical is my field of expertise, not the emotional. I am trusting God as you do." She stood and promised, "If you'd open your heart to the others they would help you as well."

"I'll try harder. Thank you, Ida."

"It is my honor to stand with you." She smiled.

"I appreciate your wisdom."

"When you see Brett, allow God to give you wisdom and strength, to allow forgiveness and second chances, to open and close the doors here too."

She was nervous. Incredibly nervous. This was something she really wanted to avoid. But she was courageous after her talk with Ida and trusting God to help guide her. She'd brought him a gift, thanks to Aunt Ellen, it was wrapped in simple brown paper. She'd dressed in neutered layers. Slate gray sweater under a black jacket. Slacks with a simple boot. They were meeting for lunch. Her security detail at the next table, Lexi and Christie shopping a block over. They'd be close by if she needed them.

She was waiting for him in the booth. He'd still come early. She stood as he approached. Smiled as he smiled. They sat across from each other.

She began. Her opening line well-rehearsed. "I'm sorry about what happened and I wanted to thank you—

"Please," he stopped her. "Don't say you're sorry."

She was immediately off balance.

"Your parents told me what you've been through. And I did some research of my own on Eros and its effects. I talked with a doctor about it." He shook his head. "It wasn't you, Jaclyn. It was the drug, and I'm surprised it wasn't worse."

"It was bad enough." She felt the shame. Remembered in detail what she'd put him through. Her eyes lowered, her chin following, her attention on her napkin and its stitched edges.

"Babe?"

She looked up. He smiled. "I know this must be hard for you. If someone failed, it was me. I say I'm a Christian. I didn't stand in Christ that day but followed my flesh."

"Please don't—

"I will." He stopped her. "I'll tell you what I learned. I could have been stronger. A better leader. Prayed more. Fled when I got in over my head. Kept you in the car with Lexi instead of taking you up to my hotel room. Not walked out to the barn alone. Kept my hands and my curiosity to myself. I made a lot of mistakes and take full responsibility. You need to know that I recognize them now. I want to earn your trust and I need your forgiveness."

She could only nod.

"We don't know each other well and this is really personal. It would be easy to just walk. It would have been easy for you to forget me." He held onto her gaze. "I told you, on the card with the roses, I don't want to walk." He smiled. "Don't like walks anyway, I'm a pitcher. We throw strikes."

She smiled now.

"Could we start over? Wipe the memory, clean slate? First date. No expectations." His hand went over his heart. "My word, Jaclyn, I have no expectations."

"I could be a bore."

"You have a great personality. Before the meeting that week, remember? You'd call me about some detail and then we'd get to talking. We connected on the phone, I remember those conversations. We talked about God and family and brothers and trials."

She nodded, remembered.

"Just be yourself."

"Truthfully, I don't know how to act. I'm not sure I can get past it. Be myself."

"Truthfully, the only way to get past it is to be honest and build some trust. We could talk. Phone calls and this," he pointed back and forth between them. "Friendship. If you want to take the next step, tell me. Friends, want to try that?"

"Yes."

Suddenly his security guard was up, intercepting a fan as he came to the table. "I'm sorry but Mr. Webb wants to have a private lunch. If you give me your name I'll get you an autograph."

"I've got security right now," he explained. His voice was firm, his gaze watching the scene play out then it came back to her. "I'm still trying to find my way around the city. Find some safe places to call my own where they respect my space and treat me, you know, normal."

"Normal," she thought of Ida's question, then asked him. "How's that going? Lexi said you found a place."

"Yeah, apartment. High up, view of the river. I like it and the neighbors."

"How's the new team?"

"I know a few guys, meeting more."

"Warm welcome?"

"It helps when you win right away. It's time to be serious, with the series on the line."

"You sailed through the playoffs," she smiled, praised, "They've got to like that as they start the series tonight. You had a good game Saturday."

"Want to come tonight?"

"Um, I don't want to make you nervous," she told him.

"I won't be pitching." He smiled. "And you'd never make me nervous, just a show off. I can get a row up from the bullpen, they're not the best seats but—

"You could show off."

His smile grew, his hazel eyes an easy gray. "I've missed you." He just looked at her for a long moment. "You look pretty."

"I brought you something." She pulled the package wrapped in brown paper out and laid it on the table.

"You didn't."

He knew. She nodded for him to open it. Layne Lexington's autograph was framed in a nice showcase.

"Wow," there was real excitement. "Babe, this is nice. Thanks. I've got a place for it."

She said her line now, all of it. "I'm sorry about what happened. I wanted to thank you." He looked up, his eyes finding hers. "For your respect. A lesser man would have taken advantage of the situation. I was horribly demanding, very disrespectful of you. Aggressive. Please forgive me, Brett, I wasn't in control of myself, Eros was."

He nodded. Said simply, "Forgiven."

She took the brown paper and folded it carefully around the picture, tied the string back to secure it.

"Jaclyn," he told her, "I love this. Thank you."

She nodded.

"What are you hungry for?"

"I was so nervous," she looked away. "I wasn't sure I could eat."

"Two friends having lunch. Don't be nervous."

"It's not every day a girl sits with Brett Webb and has lunch." She smiled.

He waved her off and lifted the menu. "They've got great pizza here. Should we split one?"

"Order for us."

"Sure. I know what you like. Let's see anchovies, pineapple, and goat cheese sounds good."

"Great," she gave a little moan. "I can pick off what I don't like."

He looked at her grinned. "I really like you."

The camera caught her between innings, one of the huge vid screens had a caption that said, "fans of number four." There she was, larger than life, chatting with their new ace over the railing, her and Marc's son, Cutter Stone wearing Webb's number sharing a red snow cone.

"Look, boss, the Hummingbird's here."

Seth pointed at the screen, Eli frowning. Both of them looking at Fury. "Did you know she was coming?"

"Where is she sitting?" The Kid was searching with the glasses.

Eli directed the binoculars with a push in the right direction. "There, Kid."

"Where?"

"She's by the bullpen." Eli watched the big vid screen.

"Those are Marc and Christie's boys," Joshua told them.

"Cute kids."

"She likes kids," Seth chuckled. "The little one on her lap has his sticky hands all in her pretty hair. Ah, he just spilled his snow cone on her jersey. She's laughing. She's got Webb's jersey on."

Eli elbowed him. "We saw it, dude. Give me the glasses."

He took a look. "She's got security on the aisle and up. They've got ears. Eyes alert. I'd have sent more than two in a crowd this big."

"Her father is here. Marc and Christie are with her." Joshua took a bite of his hot dog, watching the game.

"And we got their seats." Eli leaned back. "The job does have its occasional perks."

"She's dating the pitcher then?"

"Dude," Eli looked at the Kid. "Who invited you?"

"Fury did. Did you ever play baseball, Fury?"

"The game was too slow for me," Joshua said. "I liked contact sports."

"Are you actually wearing your watch?" Eli shifted the conversation.

"Yeah," Seth answered. "It's the nicest thing I'll ever owned. I'm wearing it when I'm not working. What are you supposed to do with it, keep it in the box?"

Eli crossed his arms, his black military timepiece ticking off silently just like Fury's. "Lay it down, Kid," was said with a quiet reverence.

"When I look at it I think of all the things God did. How he helped her and us. He's a redeemer of sinners. Look at her." Seth pointed to the screen, where Jaclyn sat with Cutter Stone sharing snow cones. "And look at me. With you. Serving in *Stratia*." He shook his head. "I still can't believe sometimes what He's done with me." The Kid gulped suddenly, emotion caught up in his words. "So er, ah, Fury… think the Nationals can pull off the series?"

"With the best pitcher in the league and all the fan support, absolutely."

It was late when they got home. The Stone boys fast asleep, Christie too. Marc winked as he carried his wife in, told them he'd be back for the boys. Her and Lexi grinned at each other, her mother tucking her under an arm. "Christie will never live that down."

She could see the sparkle in her father's eye as Christie came into the kitchen the next morning.

"Sleep good, sis?" Jaxson asked her.

"Um." Christie looked at the coffee pot and frowned.

Jaxie tried to hide her smile but in truth this really was going to be good. Her dad and Aunt Christie could get a real tit for tat going.

"Too bad Tori missed it, huh Lexi?" Jaxson looked at her stepmother.

Christie's lifted a brow at his tone.

"Oh I called her and filled her in." Lexi's smile widened.

Christie studied it then asked the two. "Okay, what's up?"

Marc chose that minute to walk in. He poured himself a cup of coffee and was just about to drink it when he stopped. Christie was close to a glare. He set it down then reached out and curled a hand around his wife's neck, his body moving close, his mouth giving her a kiss then whispered a secret.

"Morning, girls. Jaxson how'd you sleep?" He set the coffee untouched in the sink.

"How's your back?" Jaxson asked him.

"Fine." He was perplexed.

"Do you carry Aunt Christie upstairs every night?" Jaclyn jumped in with the question, knowing where this was headed.

Now he smiled.

Christie's brow furrowed, the word low, "What?"

"You fell asleep on the way home," Jaclyn stated.

"Marc carried you to bed." Jaxson shrugged.

"He did not," she looked at her husband.

"How do you think you got to bed, Christina."

"I certainly would never let you carry me and you'd never dare to do it."

He shrugged. Lexi sighed. "It was so romantic. I called Tori."

"Showed her the vid clip." Jaxson held up his PDA.

"Gone with the wind, we named it. Marc sweeping up those stairs and your hair flowing. I was humming in the background." She hummed the soundtrack from the famous old movie.

"I was asleep." Her gaze moved to Jaxson. "And you did not vid that."

"Um."

She snorted. "What is on your face, Jaxie? I swear, girl, if you think this is something to smile about." She was on the move, bumped her husband and jerked up the coffee cup from the sink. She was about to take a drink when Marc claimed the cup and gave her a look. Now Christie stated, "There is nothing funny about a man's slow and torturous death."

"You fell asleep." He shrugged. "You were tired, baby."

There was a growl. "Why didn't you just wake me up?"

"He tried," Jaxson cut in. "We all did. I even roused you a bit. It was either leave you in the car or carry you to bed."

"It really was romantic, Aunt Chrissy. He just plucked you up and carried you off to bed."

"There is nothing romantic about being plucked up and carried." She pointed. "And don't you ever forget that. We raised you to be strong and level headed. No man is sweeping you off your feet."

"Always make sure you get your eight hours so you don't fall asleep during a World Series game too, Jaxie," Jaxson added. "You were cuddled up on his shoulder at the fourth inning. That's when I shot the first picture. News flash, Dr. Christina Cooper Stone cuddles in public."

She growled.

"Dad sent the first message back." Jaxson checked his PDA. "What's gotten into Chrissy girl? Then Cara followed it with, 'Isn't she sweet. Asleep.' Tori told me to wipe off the drool."

"Are you done?" she crossed her arms.

"Well there's more. Don't you want to hear what Jude said?"

"What I want is a cup of coffee."

"Here." Jaxie was up. "I'll make a fresh pot."

"Don't you dare." She pointed at Marc. "You are in so much trouble."

"I didn't touch the coffee."

"For that too." She narrowed her eyes and blistered him with a glare. "You are loving this, Marcus and I swear you are going to pay. Big!"

The threat only had him drawing her closer. She struggled, they wrestled a minute then amazingly she gave in, her neck bending to accept his kiss.

"Call the doctor!" Lexi was on her feet with mocked concern. "She's sick, Jaxie."

"I am pregnant!"

"What?" There was shock. Jaxson on his feet with concern and joy.

Christie smiled now. "I've been off caffeine for a week. Is there any wonder I can't stay awake, brother?"

"Pregnant!" Lexi smiled. "Christie, that's wonderful. That's—

"He thinks it's fabulous." Suddenly there was an elbow, a tuff, a readjusting that had Marc's arms firmly around her waist. "He loves me pregnant. A year stuck in the office."

"Two years," he corrected. "Remember, you like to breast feed the offspring."

"I remember how much you like the side benefits."

Marc shrugged. "A few things get . . ." There was a very male grin. "Bigger."

"Marcus." She glanced at Jaxie. "I was talking about me staying home and out of your way as you run the world."

"Ah!" He kissed her softly. "I hardly run the world and I could never do it without you. She wanted this baby. I gave in."

Christie shook her head, looked at Lexi. "He so wanted this baby and I gave in."

Jaxson reached out to Marc and they shook hands, smiled.

Now she smiled. "He told me it would be a good reason to move to the country. We've outgrown the brownstone. We're moving to the farm." Their farm was nearby in Virginia, set back on a quiet country estate where Christie's horses grazed the rolling hills of the pastures under the canopy of ancient trees. "I want the boys to grow up there. Slater starts school next year. We're going to become commuters."

Marc groaned.

"What was that?"

"Yippee."

"That's what I thought the father of my baby said." She looked at her brother. "Now what were you saying about me last night, Jaxson?"

"Okay, you got me."

"I did." Christie beamed.

Suddenly Lexi squealed. "A baby." There were hugs as they rejoiced. "Surely she's a girl."

"I've got my girl right here." Christie hugged Jaclyn tight. "In fact, goddaughter," she looked at Lexi. "Marc and I want you to consider taking the brownstone if you come to Georgetown."

"What?" she blinked, astounded. "This place is huge!"

"It has everything you need," Marc told her. "It's close to school and most importantly, it's secure."

"It's huge."

"Apparently not big enough," Marc looked at his wife.

“It’s perfect for single people,” Christie said. “There’s a place for Tiki and the cook’s quarters. The master suite is like a small apartment and there’s three bedrooms for family visits.”

“Um.”

“No pressure,” she told her and looked at Jaxson. “But we’d love you to have it.”

“Daddy?” She’d taken his hand. He drew her close, his arm wrapped around her shoulders, tucking her in tight. There was joy in the dazzle of his blue eyes, they held her own as he smiled.

“It’s up to you, Jaxie. I think it’s a great idea. You. Here. Georgetown. It’s only an hour away on the jet for me and your mother. You’ve worked hard these past few months. You’re ready.” He hugged her tight. “You’re ready,” he assured her quietly as she rested in his arms. “Fly, baby.”

He’d said that before, the first time she left him for college. Now again, he was letting go and she was launching off from his nest of security. There was peace. In the decision. She was going to law school at Georgetown. She was moving into the brownstone on Sullivan Street. She was taking another step forward through the doors God was opening in her life. And a peace ascended of knowing… knowing it was God's will for her life.

17

"Sir?" Joshua's knuckles rapped the door as he proceeded into Marc's office. The chair was turned, its large leather back to him. He waited just inside the door.

The chair turned to face him. It was Christina Cooper-Stone's dark emerald eyes that connected with his as she held up a finger. "The Fury's here." She smiled as she stared at him. "Oh, I can assure you he has a few questions about it. I love you, darling. Take care that I don't have to come and retrieve you from the nether parts of New Zealand with this baby in my belly. Yes, I'll kiss the boys goodnight. Bye." She set the PDA on the desk. "Fury. Happy New Year. Enjoy the holidays?"

"Yes, Ma'am. Feeling okay?"

"Pregnant." She smiled. "But we've been here before."

"Yes, ma'am." He vaguely remembered her with a tiny belly and a huge appetite when she was pregnant with Cutter. "I thought there'd been a mistake but I'm sure now this assignment comes from you."

"Oh?"

He held up his PDA. "Ballet. Tonight. The Queen of Norway's niece or something like that. I'm to baby sit. Is the Secret Service over extended?"

"Um," she replied. "The Queen's granddaughter needed an escort and *Stratia* was called. She's a high priority as far as our country is concerned.

Her parents will be at the White House for a state dinner and she would like to attend the ballet. The president was impressed with you and he asked for a favor tonight."

"And you chose me?"

"He chose you. It's a duty you should be honored to obey. She's beautiful."

He watched her eyes, kept his neutrally disinterested as she studied him.

"You'll need dress blues."

"Blacks," he corrected. "I'm on loan from the Navy, ma'am."

"Of course. Black. Blue. I was never military and Marc still hasn't revealed exactly what branch he got his training under in Scotland." She rocked in the chair. "Rank, medals." She waved. "All the bells and whistles will be loaded on your *Blacks*. Supply has seen to it. Should be in your locker by now. You'll pick up the princess at the Ritz-Carlton. She doesn't want a limo, so take your pick from the garage."

"I got all the information when I downloaded the assignment."

"Good."

"One question?"

She lifted a brow.

"Why me?"

"Why not you." She tilted her head. "The president called *Stratia* for the best. I'm sending our best to keep the hopes of Norway protected."

"I know how to protect but I'm horrible with politics. You know that. I don't small talk very well and I tend to scare people."

She only lifted a brow. "Exactly why you need opportunities to strengthen those weaknesses."

There was silence. Then she lifted a brow.

"Yes, Ma'am."

"Send me the report." He could feel her smile as he turned his back. "And Fury."

"Ma'am?" he held his breath, turned back to give her his respect.

"Nights like this keep us humble."

"Yes, ma'am." He nodded then left to meditate on the strength of his pride.

Jaclyn smiled at the woman as she held the door open to her brownstone on Sullivan Street. Dena had coffee brown eyes, ancient as time itself. Of Cajun French heritage, she had a dialect that was like a changeling depending on what she was cooking. Christie had hired her and Jaclyn was smart enough to understand Dena was skilled in greater things than running a household and cooking. "Senorita Cooper," she greeted with a very authentic Spanish accent. The spice of jalapeño peppers in the air. "How was your afternoon?"

"Fine."

"It's a cold one." She muttered Cajun French words, taking hold of a few of the many shopping bags Tiki was carrying, trying to get them in the house and not let too much of the heat escape as she closed the over-tall door.

"Yes." Her voice echoed up the high cathedral entry of the brownstone. The address was on a famous street. More mansion than house, the space old money intimidating to her Texas ranch upbringing. It was too large, too empty and now too filled with strangers who all wanted to serve, assist, or protect her at a moment's notice. She'd been here two weeks. Four days now without her parents. She was lonely and alone and not handling it very well.

They'd known. Lexi leaving a list. Jaclyn too practical to be pampered but her stepmother had given her strict steps to follow. The spa, shopping, and statistically relevant navigating. She was to take care of herself, furnish her house, and learn her new city. She'd shrunk and needed new clothes. It would be colder here, Lexi had warned her, and she wasn't used to the winter or the walks in its blistering icy wind.

Time seemed to crawl and there was another week before school started. She'd prayed today would be better, but today as she meandered the high end shopping along the streets of Georgetown, she felt incredibly empty, achingly lonely, and absolutely certain she'd made a mistake. She should have stayed in Texas. She should have never agreed to the security detail her father was navigating around her. She was not to go anywhere without full protection. Her father had told her the next two weeks it was important to go and do and let everyone practice out their roles on the job before she started classes. Her father had left another list of places to go to and things to do every day. She was to cooperate with the training Marc had outlined for her security.

Any spontaneity was out for a while. People had to be put on notice. Tiki was required to have her schedule and daily agenda. How did someone plan ahead a whole day? It had been difficult. They promised that she'd soon forget they were even there, but now she was mindfully aware of them. Especially in this getting to know you stage that had her awkwardly trying to communicate with people she was supposed to ignore. How could you ignore a tall, bald, athletic African American man suited up in an elegant trench coat, who kept three steps behind her as she shopped for new underwear and winter hats. He took her bags. He opened her doors. He stood guard at the restroom door and even threw away her paper cup after she had her favorite decaf latte. What would Tiki do when she sat in law classes all day? Or spent late nights at the law library? Would he turn the pages of her books? Her recently massaged shoulders began to tighten up with the unsettling anxiety of it all.

"The ballet is tonight." Dena broke into her thoughts. She gave her a smile. "Sleeping Beauty. You'll leave at seven?"

"Yes."

"The dress arrived. Jenna said it's dreadfully ugly."

She laughed. "Can hardly wait to see dreadfully ugly."

"I put the garment bag upstairs." She pointed.

"Thank you."

"Call me if you need any help."

Jaclyn jogged up the stairs. Curious and excited. On her bed was the garment bag. The Chevaux's brand embroidered across it. She unzipped the protective fabric bag revealing copper silk, translucent yet heavy. As she pulled it free she realized the variation of the fabric, the undertone of gold, the rich texture that gave it movement. She called her cousin. "Jenna?"

"Did you get it?"

"Yes. It's dreadfully ugly."

"Isn't it."

"I love it. The color."

"Did you see the bra yet?"

"No." She looked around, saw the silk bag. She drew open the drawstring, pressed the phone between cheek and shoulder, peeked inside. The lingerie was the same color as the dress. A bold copper with gold embroidered bejeweled fairies.

"Do you see the fairies? You know there are fairies in the ballet tonight?"

"Yes. Of course." There on the lingerie were the gold, silver, sapphire, diamond, and lilac fairies.

"I hand-stitched those little sprites."

"Jenna, this is so beautiful. I can't believe you did this just for me."

"You're my number one client, cuz. I think I'm getting into lingerie next. Anyway, the shoes are ridiculous. I'm loaning them to you. They're a prototype."

"Um," she grinned, balancing the stiletto on her palm. "My foot's two sizes smaller than yours."

"Um," was echoed back. "There's directions for your hair. Mom insists you wear it messy and falling loose from that clip I sent. You know the style? It will show off the dress. Take a picture for me."

"I will."

"And have a spectacular time."

"Why don't you come? There's time. And Uncle Marc can't make it. He's still out of town."

Jenna laughed. "I have nothing to wear!"

"Come on."

"I wish I could, cuz. Go. Enjoy. Call me later."

She bathed, took her time applying makeup and curling her hair. She gathered it up, let it spill from the jeweled clip. The dress floated down from the careful tucks that moved around the narrow empire bodice. There was no show of cleavage, only a vast length of leg. She took out a necklace from her father. Seven strands of gold, layered and falling with forty-nine beaded diamonds scattering the strands. On an exaggerated long gold chain she attached Joshua's cross and tags.

On the way to the ballet she got the message from her Aunt.

I have to cancel. Forgive me. Something is critical at work. But I don't want you to miss Prima ballerina Nadia Katrinivik dancing as Princess Aurora. This was my first date with Marc so many years ago… I want you to enjoy it since duty calls me elsewhere. It's why we fight so hard. Call me tonight. I can't wait to hear what you thought. Aunt Christie.

Something critical…Fury. She closed her eyes. Prayed. Afraid. For him. Knowing first-hand the evil of their world and his zeal to fight it.

"Miss Cooper?" Tiki was waiting. The door open. His hand ready to assist her from the car.

Clutching a beaded bag only large enough to hold her phone and a tube of lipstick, she let Tiki escort her inside the Kennedy Center ten minutes to show time. She released his arm as she entered, knowing he'd stay close, and let her eyes take in the abundance of the scene. It was hard to find places where people still dressed up for an occasion. She enjoyed the parade of the beautiful crowd. Noticed as attention came and went her way as she people-watched in return, and slowly proceeded down the Hall of Nations to the Grand Foyer. The carpet was a regal red, the bronze bust of the famous president welcoming the dignitaries to view the Potomac as the sun set on the lush lawn. She casually strolled to the door, took her seat up in the Box Tier. The orchestra was warming up. She reviewed the names of St. Petersburg's magnificent company of Kirov dancers. Noticed the many men in black at attention along the back wall. Earpieces in place, eyes on the crowd. Servants of security, watching over the royal and the rich and the politically placed . . . and young women who had escaped evil Russian princes.

She sat on the aisle. The seat beside her vacant. For a moment she was lonely. Felt oddly isolated in a room filled with people. For a moment she thought to text Tiki, to tell him to come and sit with her, but that request would be denied. She'd learned already he was uncompromising in his duty to her father. She refused to complain so she used the wait to text Christie and tell her what she thought so far.

"I wonder where she is?" The woman beside her scanned the crowd with pearl handled opera glasses. "You know the eleven crystal chandeliers? The famous Hadelands in the concert hall. They were a gift from Norway. Her parents are at the White House tonight. State dinner. She wanted to come to the ballet. Smart girl, don't you think, Bill?"

"Yes," answered the man beside her wearing military blues and a patient boredom in equal good measure. Giving her a nod he said, "Good evening, dear."

"Good evening," she answered. "Thank you for serving our country, Sir. We're here tonight because of men like you."

The woman smiled. The man nodded.

Tchaikovsky's music began and she fell into step with the magic of the ballet. She was clapping when intermission turned the house lights up.

"Bill's favorite part of the ballet," the woman said as she rose. "A good stiff scotch to get him to the curtain call."

She grinned at the four star general when he winked at her. "Please join us."

She walked with the couple, declined a drink. Mary Margaret and Bill Thatchery introducing her to the many high-ranking Washington officials as they waited by the bar for their drinks. "Oh, look," the older woman touched her arm. "There she is." She nodded to the left. "There with the Navy captain. Isn't she lovely?"

Jaclyn began to walk, later she would question her sanity, dissect every second of the next five minutes, but the instant she saw him relief had her almost running.

"Joshua." She was about to reach up and hug him when she realized there was a woman attached to his side and protocol to follow when they were dressed like this. She clutched her handbag. Her gaze brushing over the young luminous woman, then back to his eyes too greedy for the sight of him. Here. Safe. Home. Here, not out fighting something critical at work.

"Jaclyn Cooper," he seemed to announce.

The girl at his side gave a single nod, a simple courteous smile, then leaned close to him. She was tall. Blond, classically beautiful, statuesque. She could easily reach his ear. She whispered something. He nodded, looked past her.

The woman's eyes scanned her dress. Her proper English asked quietly, "Your dress is very lovely."

"The designer is Jenna Cooper, from Texas. She does one of a kind work. She'd be pleased with your interest."

There was a glimpse of a nod as Mary Margaret pressed nearer.

Jaclyn introduced them. "Bill and Mary Margaret Thatchery, my," she stumbled there.

Joshua stepped forward took Bill's hand. "Sir."

"Captain," Bill answered.

"May I present Her Royal Grace." The woman gave a small smile, a regal nod.

"Would you like a drink, your Grace?" Bill asked immediately.

"I would, yes. A dry Champagne please." Mary Margaret stepped up with her protocol. She was obviously a master with all the years climbing the military hierarchy toward the top, and there was an honored crowd quickly stepping forward to meet the princess from Norway. It left them alone outside the circle.

"Happy New Year," she finally found her voice, her manners, his eyes again. "Did you have a nice holiday?"

He gave a nod.

"How are you?" She gave him no time to answer. She knew, already she knew. "You're at the ballet." She laughed, her smile widening at his distinct displeasure. "I can't believe it."

"She . . . loves the ballet so . . . here I find myself." The princess walked a few more steps away. His eyes followed her. She was statuesque in a mist blue dress that seemed to flow around her perfectly proportioned body like moving water. His body language totally attuned to her every step. She watched him, watching her, intently.

At once the thought struck her heart. "You're in love with her." She couldn't breathe, she couldn't think. Her heart was rising into her throat.

His gaze connected with hers, narrowed at once as if insulted. "I'm on duty." His brow was heavy, the blue of his eyes intense, his words flatter than his frowning mouth.

There was great relief as her heart fell back into its place then her mind clicked the information into position. "Duty?" she repeated the word, the tone at the same time strange and fierce. "You're working?"

"Yes." His gaze went back to the woman. "I seem to be drawing the tougher assignments. I've no idea how to handle the more . . . delicate duties. As you would know."

"Being a more delicate duty." Something began to burn in her chest. Torch her frozen center with alarming quickness and fierce heat.

"Exactly." He watched the princess. His attention fixed. "I'd rather be sweating it out in a fox hole or freezing in icy waters, but tonight I'm at the ballet, unarmed and totally out of my element thanks to the . . . privilege," the word had a sarcastic tone, "of meeting the president and him requesting me for this ridiculous assignment." He moved his neck in the confines of the tight neckline. "After that night at the White House, they had to tie me down to get me back in this get up so soon."

"You look very nice," she said softly, the hurt deeper. Emotion was rising. She fisted it tightly as he looked at her, heard or saw what was unspoken. "Incredibly handsome in your uniform. Did you get your picture, with the president?"

Another nod.

She glanced at his wrist. "Do you like the watch—

"Who are you with?" He looked around, irritated. "Webb here?"

"I'm alone." She stepped away as he struck at another raw and tender nerve.

"Alone?" His voice went harder. Then he found Tiki, gave a nod. "You shouldn't be—

"I'll let you get back to your . . . duty. It was good to see you, Joshua. Always." She lifted a hand. "May God bless you and keep you," she whispered.

She walked. She didn't know how. She trembled everywhere. Acutely aware. Like a heart attack victim after a shock from a defibrillator. Feeling was back. Her heart was wailing with the pain. Hurt too deep to understand yet but she could feel it. Heart ache. Screaming. Like a vacuum dragging everything up she'd suppressed to the surface. Her mind struggling, rewinding, analyzing every word. It was his duty. She had been his duty. Nothing more. And he was mad about meeting the president. Not wearing the watch. Not glad to see her. Tonight just another ridiculous duty...

The Fury pressed a hand to his earpiece as a catcall split his eardrum. Joshua's voice had been muted, now, with a word, Command could hear him as he gave a warning growl, clamping his teeth.

"Was that the Hummingbird?" Joe's voice held the m's and rolled the r's. "Is she beyond beautiful or what?" he growled. "Who wears dresses like that? Was it gold or copper, Fury?"

"Like he'd know. The fool's color blind," Zhara's voice chimed in next. "I caught the bling though. Gorgeous rocks. That necklace was fab."

He turned aside, coughed, spoke quickly, "Eyes on the iceberg."

"You're watching her, the rest of the building is watching the Hummingbird fly," Joe corrected. "Geez, that tiny thing can walk in those stilettos fast. You'd think you made her mad or something. She's soaring across the carpet."

Joshua glanced over his shoulder but she was off his radar now.

"She's heading toward camera four. Give us a look at those golden eyes. She's got spectacular eyebrows— What the heck?" There was silence. A ripe pause of it.

Zhara's followed with a volume of rage. "What did you say to her, Fury?" She called him an idiot. "You've got her in tears, you pig."

He coughed again. Walked away a step and growled, "Eyes on the iceberg, Joe. Zhara follow the Hummingbird. Don't leave command until I get there. And not another word unless it's business about Norway."

There was a click of static from the Command center as he turned back to the group. He watched the princess drain her goblet, nodded at the general's comment about the weather while duty alone held him in place. He did his job, suffering through the backstage bravos and meet and greets of the dancers and the privileged who were invited to meet Her Grace. It was after midnight when he stepped into Command. Zhara's gaze swept him with disdain from shiny shoes to the eagles on his epaulets as Joe gave out a whistle and hollered, "Look what the cat drug in."

"I need you to file my report on the iceberg." He plugged in his PDA and let it download into one of Joe's many computers. In a very soft voice he told him, "You disrespect Miss Cooper again and you'll have a hard time talking. We clear, Joe?"

"Clear, sir." He swallowed and gave a stiff nod.

He turned back to Zhara. Her arms were crossed, below her afro her dark brown eyes were stewing and she was glad for him to see the attitude behind the voice.

"Get the iceberg to bed?" She lifted a brow. "She was priming you all night. Anyone with eyes could see the progress."

"I slipped free of the trap. I'm not sure it was done very well. I said no and left." He unbuttoned his jacket. "You know I'm not one for decorum and it's not something I care to learn. I hate politics and escorting princesses is now on that short list."

"Did you leave Her Grace in tears too?"

"I have no idea what I said to Jaclyn but I'll figure it out and make it right. Show me the vid."

She typed in some commands and films began to run. A dark luxury sedan pulled up to the curb and a man was helping her out. "She came in at ten minutes to show time." She'd isolated her entrance and highlighted her face. "Alone, after her security man opened the door for her, escorted her into the Kennedy Center." Adjusting the speed up by four times, they watched Jaclyn quickly make her way into the opera house. "She sat in the first row left of center, box three on the aisle. The seats belong to Marc and Christie. She came alone," she repeated. "Had a short conversation with General Thatchery and his wife. Obvious by her body language she enjoyed the ballet." She warped the speed. "Progressed to the bar at intermission with the General and wife. There the Hummingbird spots Fury."

"I don't need your report. I was there."

He watched his wife spot him. The smile, the joy. She was going to hug him. He saw the moment she pulled back, stood back, clutched her handbag. "Pause tape," he ordered, studying for just a moment her dress, her beauty, remembering the effect it had on him. "Proceed." He crossed his arms. He couldn't remember what he'd said. She'd surprised him. He'd been embarrassed. He liked to be in control. He was anything but that dressed up like a peacock and strutting awkwardly beside a princess at the ballet.

She'd thought he was in love with the girl. He didn't understand that. They were from different worlds. A servant and a princess. Besides, the princess was too young. Totally not his type. Jaclyn's assumption made no sense. He'd clarified it by telling her it was work.

"She told me I looked nice then she got upset," he reasoned aloud. "I saw it happen and didn't understand. I asked who she was with."

"She came alone," Zhara said again.

"She told me."

She was shaking her head.

"What did I do?" He met her glower with one of his own.

"Don't ask me." She pressed her lips together and jagged her shoulders. "But you said something." She typed in another command, used her finger on a wheel to advance the tape. "She walks away. Clearly shaken. Holding it in. The girl's fighting hard here. She's walking faster, looking for a safe place. See her look right? Camera four picks her up."

It was like a knife. Brutal and violent as the camera grabbed her face. Her eyes full of liquid. Her face pinched with the effort. Her feet quickly taking her into the ladies room.

"We really need to get that privacy law reversed. You can never get a warrant in time to be effective. The whole world knows you're off camera in a bathroom. The most dangerous place in the world if you ask me." She typed out more commands. "Fifteen minutes later, everyone is back in their seats enjoying the second act and this guy steps from the wall, knocks on the door. He's security. Hers."

"Yeah, he's hers."

"He waits outside the restroom. Picks her up without a word as she comes out. Together they walk outside. She's got classy wheels waiting again. Her man helps her in the car, rides shotgun and away she goes."

Her chair spun his direction. "Now what did you say, Fury?"

"I swear. I said nothing."

"Go through it again. I can promise you, you said something."

"Fine, okay, sure. She says, hey."

"Hey? No. She doesn't say hey. She says?"

"Joshua," he answered.

"She calls you Joshua not Fury?"

"Yeah."

"Brave girl. What next?"

"You're at the ballet. She's surprised. Amused. The General steps in. Shake hands, introduce Her Grace. The crowd is transfixed." He sighs, shakes his head. "I watch the curious move in closer, keep my eyes on the iceberg. Jaclyn asks me if I'm in love with her." He tilts his head. "Okay, that was totally out of place and weird. I tell her I'm on duty, that it's work. Then something about the assignment and that I'd rather be sweating in a foxhole than shouldered with the more delicate duties. That I wasn't very good at it and she'd know." He waved his hand in front of his suit. "Getting all dressed up like the night at the White House again. I said you had to tie me down to get me in this. I was trying to downplay it. She said I looked nice in uniform. That's when I caught the emotion. Then she steps back and says her, good seeing you. Always. God bless and bye."

He looked at her shrugged. "See. Nothing." He paced. "I tried to tell her I was on duty. I couldn't give her my full attention. She's not used to that. It upset her."

"Did you tell her she looked nice?"

"No."

"That you were glad to see her?"

"No."

"Did you ask how she was?"

"No."

"God bless? Take care? See you soon?"

He shook his head.

"Eyes on the job. Doing your duty." She nodded. "Great job, Fury. Anything else you need to see?"

He leaned against the desk and looked at her. "I have a job to do."

"You did it."

"I took care of her. When it counted most. I was there for her. And anytime now. She knows that."

"She's in love with you."

There was silence.

Zhara shrugged. "She'll get over it, with the rest of what happened. Eventually, once the shrinks do their work. She's strong."

"She's steel."

"Then don't worry." She touched screens, buttons, dimmed and redisplayed terminals. "If she was crying then it's a start. She saw the truth or heard it and she's dealing with it. That's what girls do. We cry when we get our heart broken. Like you said, she's steel." She put her headset back on. "You're not a pig. That was out of line." Zhara gave a nod. Her official apology.

18

Jaclyn lied. Said she was sick. She wasn't a very good liar. She couldn't look at Tiki. Didn't look at anyone as she went upstairs and retreated behind a closed door. She curled up in the window seat and looked out the window at nothing but her empty reflection. She felt comfort at the window. Trapped, yet somehow secure. Looking in more than out. Feeling too much. Holding tight to herself as inside the few pieces that she'd put back together seemed to fall apart.

There was no reason to be in Georgetown. She'd go home, back to Texas, to her father's house and protection. She'd been Fury's duty. Nothing more. He'd taken care of her. Now he'd moved on to take care of someone else. She'd embarrassed him tonight. He'd not known what to say. How to handle the past coming into the present. She was his duty.

She was in love with him.

She felt the rip of that. The brutal horrid cleave as part of her was torn and left with Joshua Fury. It's what her parents had warned her about. What intimacy did outside of marriage. How emotionally damaging it was to the woman. How she was to protect herself from something God never intended to happen. Two made one then separated. She felt it. The wound of it spirit, soul, mind, heart. She wept, the pain greater than anything she'd ever imagined.

If she'd been wiser, it would have happened sooner. But she'd lived in a fantasy world where any day now he was going to figure out he missed her and he loved her and they should be together. He'd start calling her. She moved here to Georgetown, hoping for it. They'd run into each other. Well they did and it wasn't what she expected. She was so naïve. They were never going to be together. She was his duty.

She was up pacing, as her tears fell again and her hands ripped into her hair and pulled the clip out to free her hair. She was so ignorant to the ways of love. How did a woman pursue a man like Joshua? If she wanted to fight for him, how would she do it? She wasn't one to be coy or manipulative. She knew how to be honest and she didn't think that got you very far in love. She knew how to pray, to ask . . . she'd asked God to help her, to cause Joshua to call her, to help them start a normal relationship.

He was a good man, a man of God. Pure of heart. Committed.

She was a delicate duty. Delilah . . . a whore. Ruined now. A man of God like Joshua doesn't want to remember, but forget what he'd had to do…

The shame was fierce, the flash of memories like a slide show. She tried to turn her thoughts away. She walked the room, saw the walls and felt suddenly caged in again. It was disturbing now, not safe. This was her home, hers. She commanded the whole of it. No one told her what to do or would question her if she decided to go home early from the ballet or wear a formal dress as a nightgown just because it was so pretty.

She yanked opened the door, found her way to the kitchen. The house was too big for a single woman. The many rooms empty and dark that she passed on her way down the smaller back stairs. She went into the wine vault, found a bottle of red. It took her a few minutes of searching to find the bottle opener. She knew any minute Dena would emerge from the dark to help her out. That in itself was disturbing, that she wanted to be alone but wasn't. That she needed to be safe but felt imprisoned. She poured the glass of wine, took it outside to the patio. She needed the air. Needed to know she could stand outside alone.

She liked the patio. There was a fountain here. Running water in a garden covered in winter's sleep. Time passing. Soon there would be spring. The awakening of renewed life. It had been weeks now since she saw him last at the White House. Weeks turning to months as Christmas passed into a New Year and her old life drifted so far away. The pain made her afraid.

She looked at her phone, wanted to call her father. She needed to hear his voice, to process her heart, to cry long distance on his strong shoulder. She stopped herself. She just couldn't put him through it. He'd been gone four days. Four days… and she was falling apart.

She could deal with this heartache. It was common to all and one thing she wouldn't burden him with tonight. She sat in a chair, watched the water work its way through the levels of the flowing fountain. Wondered why God had brought her here. If she'd been wrong, misread the open doors, the signs, the feeling of peace.

She wished for a girlfriend, someone to talk to about everything. But who could understand this? Abduction, rape, Eros, Fury. That was too much for Jenna. Too personal and sinful for anyone unmarried. To late a call for Ida. To short a time away for her parents. She thought of Samuel. Her thumb worried over the phone, finally typed in a simple message to her cousin.

She drank. Watched the water, brushed another tear away as she realized how far she'd fallen in love with Joshua. How this would be another thing to work through in the tangled complexity of everything else that had happened to her.

The beep alerted her of the incoming message. Samuel must be available. She looked at the message.

I didn't get the chance to ask- how are you?

She stared at the words, at his name. Started typing before she could stop herself.

I'm drinking wine, why?

Where?

Home. Back patio.

Let me in the front door.

She just stared at the words, then realized he would know where she lived now. He would have been told. He was here and he was serious. She rushed to the restroom. The mirror reflected the tear-stained mess of makeup on her face. She could only clean off the smudges before the phone was telling her.

I'm at the door.

She opened it. Still in her dress. He now in jeans. Tiki had joined them.

"Good evening, sir."

"Tiki," Joshua answered. Tiki nodded, disappeared.

"I'm not used to all this." She waved toward the door where Tiki had faded back through. "I'm sure there are rules. And I'm probably breaking them. I should have told him I was opening the door."

"Just live your life. They know what to do. They won't take chances either. You're safe."

"How did you know I was here?"

"Marc told me."

"Um."

"Great place."

"It's big."

"It's safe." He looked past her. "Drinking on the back patio, you said."

For a moment she was confused then it clicked and they went outside.

He refused a drink, walked the large covered patio, around the strategically placed seating areas of thickly padded wicker furniture. His booted feet silent on the fieldstones, his gaze scanning over the perimeter, passing over the garden to study the thick stone walls at her border, noting the cameras and their angles, looking for any weaknesses.

She watched him as the winter wind flirted with his long hair and the sound of water filled the silence. She took a sip of wine, waiting for his attention, longing suddenly for his love.

When his gaze came to her she smiled and said, “Are we going to talk?”

“Depends on what I did tonight to make you cry.”

“Who said I was crying?” She took another drink.

“There were tears in your eyes when you said I looked nice.”

"You did look nice.”

"I hate that get up.” He stretched his neck, looking off, away. “It makes my neck itch. You know how those uniforms feel, BioWatch is too tight, the sweater too hot and every jacket they button me into itches my neck.”

“Um.”

His gaze snapped to her now, impatient, edgy. He had an edge tonight she’d not seen before.

“Is it so hard to be handsome, Joshua?” She met his gaze, held onto it with a challenge now. “Accept it. God gave you a handsome face and a strong body.” Turning a smile, feeling that energy of connection, that sudden charge of female power she told him with an unsubtle glance, “You fill out a uniform, Fury.”

He frowned. His lashes—too thick for such a man, such a contradiction unless you knew the center to his heart that was soft and sensitive—lowered, shielded, deferred the compliment. He countered her comment. “You looked…” he nodded at her dress but didn’t look at her. “Look…” he finally chose a word, “Nice.” She’d forced him into it, he’d never commented on her appearance before in a compliment. “I should have told you. I didn’t have time to small talk. It upset you. I saw that. I wanted to explain. Want you to know I’d never intentionally hurt you. I need you to know that . . . I care about that.”

“How so?” She held tight to the wine glass. Her hand suddenly slippery, her body shaky. She took another sip, watched him watching her.

“You drink.”

“Sometimes I drink wine.”

“When?”

“When I want to.” She shrugged. “Do you have a problem with wine?”

"You're upset."

"I'm not drinking to get drunk. That would be sin."

"Why are you drinking?"

"Why are you here?"

He walked over to her, picked up the bottle, read the label. "I'm not good at this, Jaclyn."

"Neither am I." She added softly, "I don't hide my feelings very well, obviously. I don't know how to be what I'm not. I'm honest." She was only brave enough to say a half truth. "I care about you."

"We knew that would happen. What we went through together. I'm sure it was hard for you to see me with someone else, protecting them, my attention on them."

"I misread your . . . attention. It's intense." She drank again, realizing suddenly, with more clarity and a much deeper heartache. "I thought . . . you were in love with. . . her. The princess," she clarified.

"No."

"Just a job. Duty. A delicate duty, you called it. Like me?"

"You were very different. A divine assignment. You know that."

Something in his tone gave her the courage now to say the full truth. "What I know is that I'm in love with you."

His voice was soft as he said her name, his gaze holding hers. "After what happened, your feelings are confused. Once you work through this, heal, you'll stabilize back into your right realm of influence and be able to make clear choices."

"What did you just say?" The wine glass clicked against the table as she set it down. "Was that medical mumbo-jumbo? Or General Fury's commando talk for I'm crazy and out of my mind right now? I tell you I love you and you think I'm crazy?"

"Confused."

"Confused? Oh. That must be the politically correct way of telling someone they're un-stable and crazy."

"You're not crazy."

"Unstable, you said."

"I said stabilize," he defended now flatly. "You've been through a lot. You're still dealing with the fallout of the drugs, the memories of what he did and what I had to do. I want you to forget those things."

"You're telling me to forget you?"

"Because I knew this would happen. It's called Nightingale syndrome—because I helped you—you attach to me, bond with me, need me and not God. He needs to heal you, Jaclyn, I can't. I can't," he told her firmly.

"I'd never put that kind of responsibility on anyone. Not my father and certainly not you. I'm not asking you to heal me. God is doing that, through counselors and doctors and my time with Him. My feelings for you aren't related to what happened."

"They are. Most definitely they are and you'll come to see that in the future and be able to make clearer choices."

"I connected with you and it has nothing to do with the past, everything to do with what I want in the future. I want a relationship with you."

"I want you to be free . . . of the drugs, the fear, the evil. I want you safe to heal, to find your way clear of this, to be able to make your own choices and see God's will for you. I don't believe a relationship with me right now is going to give you that freedom."

"And that freedom is in a right realm of influence? What in the world does that mean?"

"God's will is always the right realm of influence. I'm a warrior who lives in dangerous circles. You're a woman who needs to be protected from evil. I'm poor, I'll die young by the sword. You're wealthy, full of promise, with a long life to glorify God."

"Opposites attract." She waved off his excuses. "And none of that matters."

"It will. In the future, it could really matter. Make a difference in your choices." He looked past her, said with firm authority. "I don't want you hurt."

"You're hurting me."

"I'm a warrior, Jaclyn."

"And I'm a woman who might never be able to have children, Joshua."

He looked at her, with intensity and tenderness. "You don't know that."

"You don't know your destiny either," she advised him. "But you trust God."

He nodded. "God will determined His will—"

"You're not a prophet, you're a warrior. Don't tell me what God's will is unless He's revealed it to you. Has God told you no? Have you talked to Him about me?"

He was silent.

She looked away. "You don't have the right to tell me how I feel or determine God's will for me."

"It's my opinion that you need time to heal, so what do you want me to say?"

"I want you to say," she whispered softly as a tear appeared, fell slowly down her face, "I love you. I want to see you tomorrow. I've missed you. Every day we're apart, I miss you."

He said her name, with that male sound of frustration, closed his eyes. She looked down. The hurt powerful enough to take her breath away and flood her eyes now.

He slowly pulled her into his arms. He held her there, in silence, his head bowed, his prayers his own. Her tears harmonizing with the fountain's flow.

Softly he whispered, "I don't want to hurt you, disappoint you, but in time you'll understand." He pulled away, held her face up to look into her eyes. "For now rely on your father, study law, work hard, stay close to God. He'll heal and protect you completely. Learn your passion and purpose.

Know that you're strong, courageous, faithful, beloved by Christ. Accept there's so much more ahead for you than what you see today. Date the pitcher," he commanded.

She pulled back as if he slapped her. "What? No." Now she pleaded, "I never wanted him," she quickly explained. "It was the drug, Joshua."

"You've seen him since."

She shook her head.

He lifted a brow. "Lunch."

"I had to make amends."

"The Series, game three and five."

"How do you know—" She narrowed her brow, something sensed something else. "You're jealous."

"No."

She moved a step. "Angry with me."

"No."

"You think I betrayed you."

"It was an Eros echo. You'd never had one before. It was the drug."

"Um?" She countered, lowered her brow to study him. "And I betrayed you with Brett."

"No," he repeated and she saw the truth, was confused again.

"No," she agreed now. Stared at him, searched him. Hurt and confused. "I don't know how to do this with you," she argued now. "I'm adrift in what feels like a turbulent ocean and you stand there so steady. Knowing everything yet not hearing me. You're the Lion and I'm," she frowned, "The Hummingbird. Twittering around. Confused and unstable."

"Jaclyn."

"We're friends," she snapped at him. "Brett is my friend, Joshua. That's the truth. I'm in love with you."

"Did you tell him that?" He sighed, looked past her then his gaze came back steady when she was trembling and unsure. "Don't. He's proven himself worthy. Pursue what it could become."

"Don't say that."

He pulled away now. Stepped away. "You should date him."

"You can't mean that." She shook her head.

"I do."

"You want me to date Brett Webb? To build some relationship with a man you think is worthy of me because he bounced back well after a horrifically embarrassing brush up with me on an Eros echo?" She marched toward him. "You want that? Me to 'pursue what it could become' marry some guy like Brett Webb? Let him father the sons of Joshua Fury?"

"You have eggs."

"They'll have to get in line behind the sons of Joshua Fury because those children are my first priority."

"No."

"Don't you dare stand there rock steady and tell me no! I'm healthy now. I was healthy on the aircraft carrier. I should have let God make the decisions. Not man and medicine. I shouldn't have frozen those babies." Her voice broke, pain and fear battling at once. "I want children. In a few years that could be impossible. Now it's not. I could have the first next year if I wanted to."

In a very firm voice he told her, "That would not be God's will, Jaclyn." He stepped to her and lifted her face to him. He slowly lifted a brow. In the silence she glared at him, her chest heaving, her heart breaking. "His will is for your healing. Your progress forward, not back. You're not a child you're a woman. You're not childish, you're growing wise. Wisdom yields to God through your trust in Him. Trust Him now, cooperate with him fully. Do what's right. Walk ahead. Don't look behind you."

"You're not behind me. You're always," her voice caught, her gaze clinging to him, her hand over his cross now. "Always here."

"I pray for you, always. For your healing, your future," he told her. "God has a great plan for you and I trust Him to carry it out, but it's not with me right now."

The realization that he was rejecting her was suddenly too evidently powerful.

"I can pray too," she finally said pulling away. "I can ask that you're totally miserable without me, Joshua Fury. You want me to date Brett Webb? Okay, I'll oblige you and pursue what it could become. I hope you don't miss a date when we're together." She stacked her arms.

"The way the press catches the two of you," his blue eyes were a sudden fire, his energy fierce and hot. "I'm sure it will be easy to keep watch. And I will keep watch over you," he vowed with a nod and she answered it with a hiss of irritation.

"Then keep watch if that's all I am to you. Watch us on the trash tabloids and any big screen they want to throw our vid up on when we're at some sporting event. Watch me kiss his handsome face because you refuse to kiss me. Watch him tell me I look beautiful. Because you refuse to look. Watch him text me and call me and do everything friends do because you won't even be my friend." She pointed at him now. "You're right. I am beautiful and I am very smart. I'm strong, courageous and faithful too. You're not the only one who's faithful, Joshua Fury. God listens to me too. I am his beloved!" She wiped at her tears with a fist. "So you keep calling my daddy and Samuel and Tiki—anybody but me—to check up on my security. If your delicate duty and divine appointment was only about keeping me safe, then keep watch. Keep your hot blue gaze right on me." Her voice challenged him, her emotions raging. "Believe me, I can give you something to watch."

"If you're going to be childish," there was a patient sigh, "Then obey your father." He gave her a nod, calm, cool and collected. The lion. She the hummingbird.

It infuriated her into a hiss of rage as she told him, "That won't be hard since my father doesn't issue orders like the Fury!" She mocked his growl.

He smiled suddenly and she felt her own fury rise as he laughed. "Your father loves you, perfectly, Baby Girl. And I trust that love." Suddenly he stepped close, his gaze on the cross as his fingers gently lifted it from her skin. There were words in a language she didn't understand. His eyes were closed, slowly opened, he gently let it go, stepped away. "I will keep watch. You will be safe, Jaclyn. Always."

Then she watched as he vaulted up the giant wall, walked upon its ramparts a few steps then disappeared on the other side into the night.

19

In the morning Christie found her wrapped in a blanket on the window seat in her room. "Well, how was it?"

"Aunt Christie?" She rose, startled.

"Tiki let me in." She looked over the room. Jaclyn had made it her own, eventually the rest of the brownstone would follow in the same way. "How was the ballet?"

"Wonderful." She gave a nod then told her. "I left early. I wasn't feeling well."

"Oh?" She came closer, began to see. Took a seat. "What's wrong?"

Jaxie sat back down, looked out the window. "I saw Joshua."

"Ah, with the Norwegian princess." There was a grin. "He wasn't too happy about mission, 'Iceberg.'"

"Yes, he told me he'd rather be freezing in a foxhole or sweating on some desert."

"Did he?" she gave a challenging look. "What else did Fury say?"

"Not much, he was on *duty*." She rose with the word. "Delicate duty, he called me."

"You or the princess?"

"Both of us. Apparently he's had enough babysitting."

"Did he tell you that?"

She turned and looked at her. "He told me I was crazy and unstable."

The emerald in her eyes instantly jolted up in intensity. "He told you what?"

"Don't," she put her hand up. "I can't talk to you about this. He works with you, it isn't fair."

"You explain what he said or he will."

"He thinks I'm confused."

"About?"

There was a pause. Christie waved her on. "Come on. You can trust me. More than anyone, even your father right now. I'm a step away and impartial."

"You're not." She smiled softly. "Impartial, but I know I can trust you. It's just that," another pause. "You're not going to like it?"

Christie was suddenly impatient. "What?"

"I'm in love with him," was whispered.

"Fury?" Christie let it sink in. She'd known, subconsciously she knew the moment she'd seen them together. She understood. She also understood Joshua. "You told him."

"What an idiot." There was heartache. "I told him and he said I was confused." She laughed. The sound of the mocked and jeered. "He said once I work through this I'd stabilize into some right realm of influence or something ridiculously Joshua-ie sounding, doctor military talk. Then I could make clearer choices." There was a sigh, then her eyes filled. "He said I was his duty. I thought there was more, Aunt Christie. I really did. He's so intense about his work. I thought he was intense about me. I thought he was in love with me." She paced, her hands raking through her hair. "He also told me to date the pitcher. That Brett had proven himself. Whatever that means. Like Fury is going to get final approval on the men I date." She blew out an exhale. "This really hurts." She held the blanket tight, her lip beginning to quiver. "Getting your h-heart b-broken."

Christie rose, held her close, remembered the feeling of being heartbroken. The devastation, the paralyzed despair as her niece emptied her tears on her shoulder. When it was done she opened the blanket and said, “Is this the dress?” She looked at her eyes. “Jenna did a good job. You look beautiful. And the man is a fool.”

“They’re all knuckleheads.”

“Every last one.”

“I’m angry. He won’t be moved. I know him. He’s going to let me go to law school, heal, stabilize, find my realm. He’ll sit back and watch while I date the pitcher and anyone else who comes into my life. He’d even smile at my wedding and tell me, told you so. But he doesn’t realize I have a stubborn streak too.”

“Um.” Christie nodded. Sat. Rubbed her belly, the baby her own Waterloo of sorts in a clash between her own stubborn streak and Marc’s incredibly irritating patience.

“Of course he’ll be there in a second if trouble comes. Protect and defend,” she stated. “And when the Eros gives me another echo. He’ll be there. His frozen sperm donated just for me. His lion tucked in my arms.” She raged for a minute. “I’m furious. This could be so easy and he’s going to make it difficult. And when I’ve stabilized and healed and found my realm, there will be another excuse. The job. My money. Can you believe he brought up my money last night? Like that matters.”

“It matters,” she told her. “Don’t think it doesn’t. He could never earn what you already have, Jaclyn. His pride will have to deal with that, just as Marc’s did.”

“Okay, so let him deal with that, the rest is ridiculous really.”

“Um.”

She turned on her. “Um? No, um. I’m right, Christie.”

"Time will tell. Date the pitcher.”

“Please.” She held up her hand. “Don’t make me think about that.”

"Maybe you need to. Maybe you need to see that you can live a normal life with anyone of your choice despite the Eros. Maybe Joshua needs to know you're not settling into what's easy or safe. That you love him despite his role in your recovery. Only time will show him that."

"Time." She huffed and stomped. "I don't want to waste time. I love him. I miss him, every day. It's horrible how much. He won't even talk to me. He won't be my friend."

"He can't. He knows you're beyond being friends, you'd become intimately more very quickly."

"Well that just stinks," she raged, her anger a sudden burst of words and tension. Her mind realizing the intensity of her feelings were both emotional and physical for Joshua. "I'm furious." She seethed. "So mad I can't find a way to handle it. Everything just comes out mad right now."

Christie stood, told her, "Change out of that dress and put on your workout clothes. Go on," Christie insisted. "I know the best way to handle anger and frustration. How to purge out a heartache and the heat of your anger."

She led the way to an elevator hidden behind a wall in her closet. She smiled at Jaclyn's wonder. "I wanted to show you this and where it could take you."

"Bat cave?"

"Something like that." She nodded. Together they rode down. Beneath the house was another world. A gym, a lap pool, an open area with a padded floor. "When I first moved into the brownstone, your Uncle Curtis lived here. He was recovering from an injury and I was recovering from my break up with your dad—which is another story we'll talk about another day. Anyway," she reached into a cabinet and brought out Virtual Reality headgear. "I was angry. It was the only thing I could feel at the time. Curtis turned me on to a way to work it out. Want to try?"

"Sure," she nodded.

"It's like live martial arts."

"I have my black belt."

"That will come in handy." Christie smiled. "Just beat up the bad guys. Ready?"

Together they donned the masks, zipped on sensor suits. Christie warned her that the VR was as close to reality as technology could take them and she'd feel the hits. Jaclyn nodded then her aunt spoke a few commands.

The room altered, they were in a designer shoe store. Jazzy music, pretty ladies browsing, shop keepers eager to help you find your size. Glass shelves lined the wall showcasing shoes of every style. Glass round top tables highlighted more.

They were dressed up. Even Christie had on stilettos. She held up a shoe. A strappy black number. "Darling shoe," Jaclyn said.

"It could come in handy in a minute." Christie smiled.

It happened fast. Three men came in the store. The first one pulled a knife.

"I don't like knives." Jaclyn backed up.

"Pause," Christie called out the order. She looked at her niece, dressed up in some designer digs she'd never wear outside the VR world and crossed her arms. Around them the virtual world was frozen, people like still life. It was freaky. "Jaxie," she gained her attention. "Forget the knives, we have shoes, girl. We'll be fine."

And they were. Christie took the knife right out of the big guy's hand with a single toss of a shoe. She used the long straps of a sandal to choke another one. The little guy was left to come at her.

"Use what you know. Attack him."

She did. With a round of kicks and several good hits. Then he pulled his switch blade. He started swinging at her. She screamed and squealed but she kept fighting. Brett would have been impressed with her arm as she threw shoes like fast balls, then she used the glass from a small round table to shield herself and finish him off.

Exhilarated she looked for Christie. She found her aunt sitting on the counter by the cash register with her long legs crossed. She smiled.

"How was that?"

"You fight like a girl." She hopped down. "But we can change that."

She pulled the VR mask off and they were back in the basement. "I fight like a girl? I hurled those shoes at him, beat him with the glass top table. That thing was heavy."

"You squealed like a piglet. High female little shrieks. No man does that, but we've time to fix the dramatics and the audio." Christie tucked her under an arm. "Most importantly, how did it feel?"

"Awesome." She let out a breath. "Really awesome. This is tight, Aunt Christie."

"And it's yours. Just yours." Christie looked at her. "And it's our secret. You and me only. You can't tell anyone. Anyone. Do you understand or I'll have to lock you out?"

"I understand. It's our secret." She nodded.

"This is linked in with *Stratia*'s training programs. They think we secured it when we left. I programmed in a loop hole. Originally for myself. I like to train in private when I'm working through a problem. I prayed and felt called to include you. I think it might be beneficial to your . . . healing." She put up the VR gear. "There's a man who can teach you a few things. Liu Xuing. I'll give you his address if you're interested."

"I'm interested."

Christie smiled. "Lexi won't like what I'm doing. She fights with words and wisdom. She wants you to be safe in the courtroom. Strong and independent, a lawyer."

"I'm going to law school."

"I went to vet school. Nothing wrong with educating your mind and expanding your intelligence. God likes wisdom. He trains us through education as well as experience. Being smart and disciplined always helps you out of a jam."

"What are you saying?"

"I'm giving you an opportunity to see if there's more than law to negotiate."

"Like what? *Stratia*," she gasped, came up on her toes, suddenly excited. "Like Petra. I could be a Petra?"

"There's only one Petra." Christie smiled.

"How do you get into *Stratia*?"

"You're called," she told her. "Recruited. There are tests that determine qualifications. Time will tell—if you're interested, in the meantime, train. Hard," she told her. "It will build your confidence. It will help you work through the anger and process decisions. It will teach you about the Fury and more about yourself. Train."

"Train?" She paced. "Will you help me?"

"What do you want?"

"I want what you have. I want to be strong not just with words and wisdom. I want to be more than safe. I want to fight back. I want . . ."

She waited, watched her, finally asked her, "What do you want, Jaclyn? Just say it."

"I don't know." She shook her head. "I thought I did. " She closed her eyes. "I think I do." She looked at her aunt, shook her head as she fought tears. "I don't know."

"Indifference."

"Indifference?" Jaclyn shook her head.

"To everything but God's will. That's a good prayer to begin with. Asking for indifference when we don't know the way yet." Christie came close, her hands framing her face, wiping tears. "You couldn't bear it yet if God revealed His will to you, so for a while it's okay not to know yet. God knows." She kissed her and said, "We're deceived if we ever think we know what's good for us. Sometimes what we want isn't what is best. Sometimes, in fact, it's the very opposite of what's good, it's bad, it's worse than bad. And we're outside of God's will, headed the wrong way. Good is the enemy of the best. But God knows exactly what He has planned for you." She smiled. "And it's the very best. Trust Him, not yourself now. Him. He'll show you. Moment by moment. Day by day. You're right where you're supposed to be. Abide in Him. His love for you. It's what He longs for from us. To abide in His love. To obey today and trust Him for tomorrow. Ask to be indifferent to everything outside His will."

"Okay. Will you help train me?"

"If you'll listen, I'll train you."

"Of course I'll listen."

"Date the pitcher."

"What? Brett? What does he have to do with training?"

She lifted a brow.

"I'm listening, I just want to see the correlation."

"Part of this kind of training is obeying, even if you don't see the correlation. Trust my wisdom. Go to law school. Work out with Lui Xuing. Date the pitcher. Come here in the morning. I'll leave you instructions. We're on a three-year plan. A very covert three-year plan. This whole thing is between you and me. No Marc, no Dad, No Lexi, or Samuel. Definitely, no Fury."

She paced, thinking, processing. "Okay," she turned to her aunt, gave a nod of decision. "How do I start?"

"We just did."

Christie watched Marc tuck their sons beneath his arms, read from their favorite story. The burr of his homeland thickening his voice, shortening the words. Skipping over vowels, rolling the r's. She smiled, the sight of them the most beautiful thing in the world to her. Slater studied the pictures. Cutter watched his da. When the story ended they begged for another, but Marc was good on his word. He hoisted them into his arms and off to bed they went. Soon he was back, slipping an arm around her waist. His hand palmed the globe of her belly, held there as he pressed a kiss to her neck.

"I missed you."

She turned her face to the kiss, met his lips, held there. Anticipation building. He'd barely been gone three days and it was too long now. The pattern of their lives, its harmony and rhythm, skipped beats when he was away now.

"I missed you," she answered. Turned into his arms. Her hands cupping his face. The question on her lips. "I want to ask you something."

He murmured his approval.

"Fury." She looked into his eyes.

Silver separated from blue. Marc's eyes so often shifting like two edges of a sword.

"Is there something you're not telling me, Marc?"

His body shifted, closer, fitting her to him. "A'bot?"

He was the Scottish Bull now. She fully aware of his stubborn standards. "My niece."

"Which niece." There should have been a smile. There was not.

"You know what I'm talking about, Marcus. Do you know something about them?"

"A'bot?" Now his lips curled, as her eyes flared. He was bold enough to smile. "Aye dinna 'ave any idea what your askin' me."

"Is he in love with her?"

"He'd tell me that?"

"You know something. Fine. So do I." She smiled now. "More than before."

Marc shook his head. "I said no'thin."

"You said plenty in all that no'thin."

20

Enough of the love story... He looked away from the sensual spectacle. He wanted action. War. An angel of light, he lusted for the power to rule—not the beautiful woman that was led away from the room.

He watched the Pendragon follow her naked back. Her long dark hair like the silky tail of a horse that switched proactively over the ripe slender curves of her bottom. Her beauty, until now only legend, had been revealed in full to their prince in a scandalous unveiling by his half-brother.

Standing against the wall, in a room where a dozen dark men did the bidding of their prince, courting his favor with their devilry and deeds, only the foolish dared to look at her as she walked past. The rest kept their gaze on his father. They'd proven themselves loyal, gained positions and titles of distinction branded in colorful symbols on their flesh. Tattoos of roses and stars, skulls and spider webs, mixed with crosses, portraits, and cathedrals of the holy and somewhere on each of them—the vivid green of the Viper, stamped with Russian words. Vor V Zakone, the old ways of *thief in law*, when men's crimes had been told in black and white stories, written from prison cells. Now the old tradition was painted in new color with high-tech lasers by artists' hands. But there was still nothing new under the sun. The tattoos were histories, holding grave meaning and conviction on the flesh of a man's loyalty and a ruler's favor.

At thirteen, his Russian bloodline had been carved into his fair skin in distinct scrolls of black, expectantly waiting to see what he could color between the lines and make of himself. He glanced down at the intricate lines that curled out from just under the French cuffs of his fine tailored shirt. The beginning and the end of his markings traveled from wrist to wrist, up both arms and across chest and shoulders. Barren ink only black, they marked him a boy in a man's world. His father's world, where he was admitted but not yet included much less respected.

Within him, his motives were as dark as the ink, boiling with heat but his handsome face was emotionless, his eyes fixed on his father with the flattery of adoration. He showed his world nothing, but inside he frowned fiercely, jealous of this room's tapestry of colored ink, the images of their rankings, the deeds earned, the names given. Inside he narrowed the unique blue eyes of his mother, glaring at the man who held his future in the snap of his fingers. Inside he growled, coveting the power of the heavy gold ring with its green stone and the hand that beckoned action with a mere wave. Inside he bowed up his chest, lifted his chin, defied his father, too ready to make his mark, take his place, to usurp, rule.

At that moment his father looked at him, into him. His discernment terrifying. For a moment he feared. The feeling came to the surface, was enough to cover his intentions and make the Viper smile arrogantly.

The hand lifted, the heavy ring flashing as he bid him over. Obediently he came.

"How is school?"

"It is fine. Thank you, Sir."

"Your English is good." There was a nod. "Your grades surprising, considering your French mother possessed only beauty."

He held his gaze, stayed silent. Unless there was something to say, you stayed silent.

“Did you think the Arabian filly pretty?" Viper asked without a smile but the words were merry, just merry enough to make him think long and hard of his answer.

"Her beauty was legend."

"We shall see if she lives up to the hype. How are the girls in England? They are known for their bounty of breast.” There was a smile. It was reflected around the room. When the prince smiled, so did his lieutenants. There was an inside joke with his English half-brother, their laughter made jealousy flare hot as Viper suggested an Arabian filly be added to his brother's tattoo.

His brother had earned his colors this summer while he’d been stuck in his books at Oxford. Earned his colors and his name. He was Pendragon now—the standing serpent-tailed beast with a forked tongue and the canny ability to lure out a legend and gift his father with what most would consider an untouchable woman in the Arabian princess.

His brother liked the idea of the new tattoo but in the middle of the conversation Viper tired of it and turned back to him. “You ask to go to America? What interests you there?”

He played his smile, knew its power came from his father. “The girls, of course.”

“This is not a holiday.” He held up the piece of paper. “It is a bill of sale for an apartment in America and warehouse space.”

“You’ve said it is the land of much opportunity, father.”

“Opportunity?” The Viper steepled his hands, looked over them with lifted brows.

“If America holds your interests, we should hunt for . . . opportunities.” He used the smile again as those dark eyes intensified their study of him.

“What has caught your interest in America?”

“Baseball,” he answered and suddenly his father’s interest sharpened over the surprise. He explained, “The Nationals won the series last year.

They have an amazing pitcher in Washington D.C. Their ace has been on the tabloids."

"Has he?" He frowned. "I detest cricket. It is slow enough to kill a man of action." His fingers rested on his lips, his eyes steady and dark. "You have no experience." He slowly pointed toward his brother. Waved him over, moving his attention. "Pendragon. Perhaps a holiday in America would be opportunistic for you."

"No!" He stopped the words, then his movement forward. Holding fast to his emotions as his father slowly moved his gaze back. This time the smile was telling.

"Yes, perhaps America is a good idea for your brother. They don't like the French in America."

"I am Russian."

"Are you?" His father tilted his head.

"I am Russian," he told the room with passion. He stepped forward with boldness, lowered his voice to a soft confident level. "I have secured an apartment across the hall from a famous pitcher, already made initial contacts with him."

"Why should this . . . pitcher interest me?"

"Are you gay, brother?" Pendragon had stepped up to challenge.

"I am loyal to my father." He glared at his brother now and spoke bluntly. "The dead were careless and allowed a certain tiger to escape. Give me six months and I will return her to you."

There was silence now. A deathly silence. The room holding its breath as it collectively took a step back from a subject no one was daring enough to speak about. The Viper wore the smile that caused a man's stomach to boil with trepidation. He lowered his lashes a telling degree as his eyes darkened intensely. Then he laughed. "If I wanted a tiger caught, I would have a tiger *here*!" The last word echoed across the room. "Or dead," he added with indifference.

Viper picked up his glass of vodka and drank until the ice was drained and left to clink against itself with alarm. Fear rippled through the room as men tried to anticipate the Viper like a farmer fleeing from a tornado. It was the Pendragon who boldly spoke first. "It was I that gave Father his rival's beautiful filly, the races have been jolly good sport." The Pendragon smiled, his Queen's English irritating. "The Sheikh's legendary beauty fast and hot blooded." His brother casually leaned a hip onto their father's desk, facing off against him. "She is dark and lean, long in leg and back, bountiful in breast. Beyond description. Father enjoys the sport of kings. She gives him a fine race."

He ignored his brother. Kept his gaze on his father. He'd studied him for too many years. He knew his love of games, of competitions, of controlling his chess board, toying with and destroying his enemies. He knew also his vanity, his greed, his curious patience and ruthless pride. And of course his lust. He made his move. "You no longer favor hunting, Father?"

"I love to hunt."

"Fast horses are common," he made the statement. "The exotic," now he smiled. "You told me once, hunting what is rare would teach me patience and the successful hunt has great rewards."

Again there was silence, like the hollow haunting of catacombs.

"My patience has limits." There was impatience. Then a shrug. A glance—hope. "But I will reward success for what is rare."

"Did I not secure that Sheikh's filly? I could hunt down a tiger in three days." The Pendragon stood up boldly now as he sensed opportunity.

"That is ignorance, Pendragon," Viper answered with a hiss. His gaze on his younger son. "I reward initiative and like this strategy. Your younger brother will have a head start." He handed the real estate deeds to his captain with a nod of approval. "And his apartment and warehouse." Viper laid out stipulations and restrictions. "International laws are slippery. The United States justice system restrictive to my way of business. You can catch a tiger by the tail with any trap . . . but it takes creativity to avoid the game wardens of her world. Do not bring trouble into my Russian house nor shall your name be linked with mine if you are caught breaking laws."

He nodded at his father, accepting the terms.

The dark eyes penetrated him and he feared even as he lifted his chin ever so subtly and accepted his father's handshake. It was a vise grip of brutal strength and power, he released him with these words, "I would not mock the dead with your boldness when you have yet to find loyalty, boy. Your mark is blank." In a violent move the Viper ripped his sleeve, showed his heritage and immaturity. "Loyalty is earned." The Viper's fist punched out exposing his forearm of color that he held next to his black and white flesh. "Your name yet to be made, nor mine given." He waved his hand at his marked flesh. "That pattern means nothing more than that you are one of many sons of the Viper, a Russian bastard born from French beauty." Then he waved him off, dismissing him.

In a single move, his brother picked up the gold cuff link that had fallen to their feet. He looked at the design, at the same light green stone that was held in the Viper's ring, then his eyes rose up to confront him with a grin.

"Adieu, LaRue." His brother gave a mocking bow, pocketing the cuff link with a vicious smile. "Good hunting, little brother."

21

Jaclyn began law school with courses in Contracts, Constitutional Law, Criminal Procedure, Legal Writing and the Evolution of Ethics. The intellectual challenge was stimulating and familiar compared to the physical disciplines Christie introduced her to that were foreign.

She was expected to sign in at five every morning on the basement computer system. Sometimes there was a simple regimen, sometimes there was a long detailed list to complete throughout the day. She was to be prepared to upload her personal schedule, including tests and school assignments. There were never conflicts but there were days when every minute was filled to capacity. Time management was crucial. Free time was minimal. Her training multifaceted and taking her places she couldn't have imagined.

Her aunt would call and command, "I have tickets to, or I have an invitation for, or let's go to, or meet me at," and there she would be at an event or a political affair or a restaurant or a cultural engagement and the next day there would be an exam on her observations. Everything was an opportunity to train, to learn surveillance skills, develop instinct, discernment, situational awareness, self-defense and the confidence to attack. All the while monitoring her hormone levels and insisting her body cooperate at crucial times while completing the most difficult year of law school. In between it all she was expected to study, socialize, and to slowly develop a relationship with Brett.

It had begun with coffee. Progressed to lunch. In their third week she'd accepted a dinner invitation. Cameras had caught them together at the posh new restaurant's opening night. Washington's infamous World Series ace pitcher and the unknown darling dressed down to her boots. The shot would make the headlines again. Jenna's plum coat and short swing dress a backdrop for the patterned boots studded with amethysts and jet crystals that covered her to her thighs.

"Sorry, Babe," Brett apologized, slipping into the car beside her. He seldom drove, the parking in the city hard to come by, his notoriety at a level that demanded security now. He had a team. She had Tiki and her personal guard. They followed Brett's driver in another car. She'd agreed to see his place tonight. She'd been putting it off but knew it was time. Brett had invited Tiki to take a look at his building, to come up and see his place as well. He wanted her safe. She saw that it was a priority. She wondered if her father had insisted on it privately or if this was simply Brett's initiative.

She asked the question. "Did my father ask you to keep Tiki with us?"

"We talked about your security, how you were never to be without Tiki. I understand the reason, Jaclyn. I respect the wisdom behind it. I'd never want to put you in danger or make you feel uneasy. I'd like to think I could protect you, but Tiki knows how to keep you safe. He's trained."

"It's a lot to deal with, me and all my baggage."

"I'm a lot to deal with too. I can't hit the street now without a camera clicking off rounds. When we're in public it won't be simple. Price of fame, you understand that, me and my baggage?"

She nodded, assured. "I do. Sometimes it's easier not to go out."

"Exactly. That's why I wanted you to stop by my place. Let Tiki check it out, give you a chance to trust me. If we need chaperones to make you feel comfortable, that's okay."

"I'm used to dating in groups."

"Then we'll find some friends." He smiled at her.

"I'm not used to being at a guy's place alone."

"That's why Tiki is here." He took her hand now. "If you want to call this off tonight, it's okay."

"No, I want to see your place."

They talked about the weather as they entered the lobby of his building. Brett shielding her beneath his arm through a brutal wind. Men were at once there to open the doors. "Good evening, Mr. Webb."

There was security in force, three men standing and greeting him from behind a counter deck. He introduced her and Tiki, his own man standing behind them and to the side.

"Jaclyn should be cleared to enter any time," Brett told them.

"But I'll always be with Brett," she assured the men.

"She'll always be with Tiki," he corrected as his hand touched her back, his gaze waiting for hers, his voice soft. "You might not always be with me. You might come over for dinner . . . or maybe want to surprise me." Now he smiled. "You're free to do that, Babe, and they'll have your name on file. And your thumb print."

A man at the counter showed her where to place her thumb, let the system scan it. There was a brief conversation about building schematics and procedures for guests entering and leaving. Brett ended the instructions with a charge, "Jaclyn is to be protected. If anything looks suspicious you're to call it in. She's incredibly important to me… and others."

"Yes, sir," they assured him.

A man was at the elevator, he held the door as they entered, told her, "It's an express, it moves rather abruptly, Miss Cooper."

"There's a rail," Brett said, looking up at the numbers, standing opposite her and far away. As the doors closed she felt the sudden uneasiness, it amplified to stand like an elephant in the space with them.

She took hold of the rail, was glad when Brett asked Tiki his opinion on the NFL playoffs and the elevator blasted off. Like Brett she looked up, held on, spoke her own opinion of Dallas' chances, of Washington's hot streak, of the ever-threatening underdogs and the overrated favorites, tried not to think about the elevator or her and Brett's pastimes in them.

The doors opened as they came to a gentle stop. Before them was a square lobby with five doors. Two on either side of the elevator, one on each of the other three walls.

"I'm C," he told them as door number B opened. A man was backing out, a huge barrel-chested rottweiler on a thick choke chain between his legs. He was cursing the dog, trying to hold a cellphone between shoulder and cheek amidst the tug of war.

"Sweetheart, Brutus has me in another tangle." There was a carefree laugh, a subtle but elegant accent to his words. "Let me phone you in a few or come now. Swiftly, surprise me with something fabulous. I'm insane for you." The phone fell free into his hands, blue eyes looking up to find them from an over handsome face even as he scolded the dog in a heated curse. He blushed, raked a hand through a fall of platinum blond hair to push it from his eyes and gave the leash a firm yank as he commanded, "Sit!"

The dog did immediately, tilting its large block head to the side to study them with his tongue hanging out in a heavy pant of excitement.

"Sorry." He smiled at them. "Didn't know we were on parade or, ah… intercom."

"LaRue," Brett greeted his neighbor.

"Ignore him," LaRue urged immediately in confidence. "I'm not sure I have the strength left to hold him off. How have you been, friend?"

"Excellent," Brett answered. "Meet Jaclyn Cooper. Our friend Tiki."

LaRue nodded with a wink. "Please take the wink as a handshake. How's the weather below?"

"Windy," Brett advised.

“Ah, the majordomo has the night off. I’m to myself with yours truly. Pray I’m not half way to Philly once the door opens.”

Jaclyn smiled at the dog.

Immediately the rottweiler surged. Tiki stepped into the gap. LaRue giving a command that had the dog at an immediate halt.

“Ah, she smiled.” He commanded, “Sit, Brutus. He’s harmless. Affectionate. Has no idea he’s supposed to be mean.” He tried to hold him back. “He loves a pretty girl. Likes to put his nose in all the wrong places.” The dog was reaching desperately toward her, tongue hanging out, eyes excited, his stub tail wagging his entire back side. “Get the lift for me, Webb, before the beast drools on the beautiful Jaclyn or worse.”

They were laughing together, the men trying to herd the dog into the elevator. LaRue waved at her with a charming grin as the doors finally shut.

“Wow.”

“LaRue is great,” Brett told her. “He’ll stop by later. You’ll love him. He’s French. An importer. Travels all the time.”

She nodded, following Brett into apartment C. “This is home,” he told them. There was a brief tour. The apartment was large with its three bedrooms and study. The open living room combined into a dining area and kitchen and a separate media room had theater seats and a wall vid screen. The colors bold but classic, the style masculine but warm and inviting.

“It’s great.”

“I still need a few things,” he told her. “Some artwork, a rug, some knick-knacks here and there. Maybe you can help me shop.”

“Sure.” She nodded. “I like the view.” There were lights spreading out to the horizon.

“If you have to live in the city, live up high, I guess. I’ve got the lights, the spread of the city. Tiki what do you think?”

“It’s secure, sir,” he agreed. “If you don’t mind, Miss Cooper, I was going to ask a few more questions downstairs.”

She nodded, knowing if she needed him, she only had to call. If she really needed him a single button on her phone would alert him at once. As Tiki left, his neighbor entered, "Brett." LaRue smiled. "Come over for a minute, I want to show you what I found."

They entered apartment B, it had very little walls, more like a warehouse. Back in a corner was a huge bed, so immense it looked medieval. Fit for an ancient king with drapes hanging high from the canopy and heavy masculine pieces of furniture walling off the area. The bath was likewise left in the open, a shower of glass, a marble tub like a bathing pool, mirrors suspended in air over vanity tops, the toilet and bidet in full view as well, with a feminine table between them that housed a frilly lamp.

In contrast to the antiques was a vid screen of theater proportions. It played an international channel across the entry wall, a British voice reported news of London, while stocks ticked off below from the Japanese market. Before the huge screen, luxurious couches in black leather were positioned around the area. Puddled on one was a lacy negligee, on another was a blanket with a hunting plaid pattern and Brutus. He only lifted his gaze as his teeth gnawed along a bone that looked like a plump turkey leg.

"Ignore him," LaRue whispered, shielding her immediately. His eyes both exasperated and humored as he told her, "He'll be on that bone for an hour. Come." He led them into the kitchen. It alone had structure in the space, stainless and high tech. A large island stood secure in the center with a cooktop and a mobile of stainless pots with brass bottoms. There were bar stools along a counter and again an immense and masculine dining table looking every bit stolen from King Henry VIII with obese candles melted down on gaudy sticks. Above a chandelier glistening with crystals hung low before the windows competing with the city lights.

She loved the place. A masterpiece of color and art and clashing centuries, she told him.

"Ah," he waved. "It is a mess of mismatched pieces but home, for now. Look what I found—the Sizzle." He held up a bottle. Presented it to Brett then stepped back and said, "A magnificent Cabernet Sauvignon." He set out three glasses.

"This is the wine you told me about."

"It has been waiting for you." LaRue seemed to stroke the uncorked bottle as he received it back from Brett, telling its story, "The summer of 2003 was very hot in Tuscany and early ripened the Merlot, so the owner after consulting with an oenologist omitted the blend and chose the best Cabernet Sauvignon and Sangiovese from the estate—some included the cherished 70-year-old Sangiovese vines." He poured the wine into their glasses. "This *Oreno* was aged in new oak barrels for eighteen months, and then rested a year before release. It was a once in a lifetime blend. I came upon a few bottles this week. What do you think?"

The three of them each took a taste.

"Jaclyn?" he watched her, waiting for an opinion.

"I'm afraid I don't know much about wine."

"Ah," and he nodded respectfully, "Everyone must be taught. The taste buds educated." He smiled at her, took another drink, moaned softly with pleasure. "This fabulous red is called the Sizzle."

"It does," Brett agreed.

"And I know the most decadent accompaniment." He grabbed hold of a skillet handle above him and with a flourish brought it down. "Sit. Where did you take the most beautiful, Jaclyn tonight?"

Brett smiled at her, pulled out a barstool as they both took a seat and LaRue seemed to perform before them. They discussed the new restaurant they'd dined at, LaRue wanting every detail as he whisked milk and flour.

"The Globe got us on the exit," Brett took a drink of the wine, watching her. "Jaclyn has a fashion following."

"You have a fan following," she countered Brett.

"Lovely frock. Who's the designer?"

"My cousin." She talked about Jenna then told him, "You'd like her and she'd love your place."

"Then we must meet." He was melting something sweet in a small pan, flipping something thin in the skillet, stirring something else in another small pan as if he conducted a symphony. The crepes were stuffed, then drizzled with chocolate before presented to her with a garnish of raspberries.

"Take a bite then try the wine. Beef would be better, the taste of rare rich meat." He shrugged, "But chocolate works as well."

The crepes melted in her mouth, a taste of cheese and chocolate, then she took a sip of wine. There was a bit of a sizzle across her taste buds now. She moaned softly, applauding the cook. She forked up another bite, fed Brett. "These are wonderful."

LaRue gave a regal bow. "Merci, Mademoiselle." He toasted Brett. "I will teach him this." He winked. "Women love a man who knows how to work the kitchen. Does your father cook, Jaclyn?"

"He grills." She smiled, sipped more wine, shared the dessert. Enjoying the company and conversation. Intrigued with the way hazel eyes could change colors so quickly. Brett's were now green in the stainless kitchen, his hand warm in hers, his attention sincere and sweet, leaving her to wonder why in the middle of this night she could think of Joshua—stubborn and serious with blazing blue eyes too often narrowed on her with a look caught between exasperation and displeasure.

"LaRue!" His name was suddenly called out from the door.

"Sweetheart, we're all in the kitchen," he answered.

"I love a man that cooks." A tall blond struck a poise in a full-length mink. Her lips were full, her eyes half mast, heavy lashed and strained on the man with the skillet. High stiletto heels clicked off the floor as she did a little jog dance to get to him.

"Jenny Brooks," LaRue made the introductions only a moment before she locked her lips over his. There was a very long and hot kiss.

"Ou, crepes. And red wine." Her hand was waving at his wine glass, beckoning he share. She took a bite, a drink then kissed him again, whispering across his lips as long red fingernails scratched down the placket of his shirt. Then there was a shriek.

"Brutus!"

A dance. Cursing and female outrage with LaRue's unmet commands. There was a bobble of the rottweiler's square huge head rearing up. The jingle of the chain collar. The flash of flesh, breasts and belly, naked beneath mink. Red nails clutching at fur. LaRue tugging on Brutus' collar, swearing.

"Oh, the rogue." She pressed high against LaRue.

"Forgive his nose."

"It is his tongue!"

Now LaRue laughed, stepping in front of her, shielding more as he tried to control the dog. "The dandy. He is sorry, sweetheart."

"He is most definitely not."

"I gave him a bone."

"He needs a girlfriend."

"Find him one." He laughed, petting the dog with strong strokes.

"I'll find him a vet with a strong emasculating knife."

"No." The word was firm now, his affection genuine to the dog. "He just smells you, your scent, is jealous of your adoration for me." His mouth closed over hers with whispered promises that floated erotically across the room.

"LaRue." Jenny nudged him.

He looked at Jaclyn and Brett, blushed, swore in French. "Mon Dieu." He told Brett, "It has been a long week, man. Forgive us."

Brett stood.

"No, no. Finish your wine. Please." He took hold of Brutus' collar, told them all, "I'll put him in my majordomo's room." It took quite a bit of strength to take the dog off. Jenny's hand held a firm grip on her mink, the other draining the wine in the silence as she watched him struggle with the dog.

"He is a sweetheart."

"Me or the dog?" LaRue asked as he came back into the room.

"You," she cuddled close.

"Ah." His arm went around her, his gaze on Brett as he filled their glasses. "To the Sizzle." He held up the glass and they toasted.

They left the impatient lovers quickly after their glasses were drained. Brett gave the classic excuse, "It's getting late."

In truth it was. There was a warmth wrapped around her, an easiness when before she had been both stiff and uncertain. She felt a bit of guilt, of confusion as she cuddled close to Brett now, but pushed it aside. She was free to drink in Christ. Each man's conscious their determining factor of freedoms in disputable matters, Paul had taught. Hers was clear, the wine had been savored as a delicacy not downed like shots of bourbon bingeing to get drunk. And she had every right to this man's affection, to have his arm around her and his attention centered on her. To feel adored and beautiful. To forget about Eros and Joshua Fury.

"I like your neighbor," she told Brett as they strolled into his apartment to get her coat. They talked about the night. Laughed about the dog. Agreed they were both full from the rich pasta and the late night snack of crepes. Sleepy now too, she told him, leaning into his arms.

"It's late," he told her, helping her slip into the plum coat, watching as she lifted her hair clear. It was late, she'd stayed much later than she expected to, but they hadn't been alone, and perhaps LaRue had also helped ease them both past the initial phase of the rebuilding process of what this could become. Now she felt the nerves assault her again, the uncertainty.

"I had a good time," she admitted to them both, smiled up at him.

"Did you?"

She nodded.

"I want you to." He was holding her gaze but his words began to stumble. "Want you to feel okay ... comfortable . . . relaxed." He took a breath. "I, ah . . . I'm waiting on you, letting you lead, make the first move . . . if you want this to move."

"I know as much about first moves as I do about wine, Brett." She was looking at him, into those hazel eyes, told him honestly, "I'm not sure . . .

He kissed her then. Softly, with no demands.

It was a sweet kiss.

"I like you, spending time with you, Jaclyn. The past few weeks have been great." He drew her closer, hugged her gently, whispered now, "I hate leaving you. Two months in Florida. Spring training already." He sighed. "I'll miss you, Babe."

"I've got my first round of tests, a lot to do."

He broke the contact. "You'll do great. You're smart and disciplined. I really admire that. I'm going to keep in touch." He grazed her cheek. "Bug you every day. Okay?"

She nodded. Smiled.

"When I get back, we'll celebrate those tests. Opening day. You'll be there?"

"I'll be there."

Brett led them out into the hall, pushed the elevator button. Jaclyn felt the sense of dread as the elevator rose up to the command with a humming surge of energy and a flashback to their past.

"You don't have to go down," she told him, pressing into his arms, holding him for a moment.

"You don't have to be embarrassed about what happened in the elevator," he whispered.

"I am. It's hard still."

He nodded with understanding.

"Tiki's coming for me." She pulled back from him. "I had a wonderful time."

"Will you call when you get home?"

"I'll send you a text."

"See you soon," Brett told her.

The doors closed slowly, Brett standing with his hands in his pockets, smiling at her. Seeing everything he wanted, remembering how it had been, how it could be again. He glanced at her thigh-high boots, the long tassels to the zippers that teased just beneath the length of the subtle swing of her dress. He remembered the ruby tassel, the weight of her breasts, the sound she made when she'd surge against him, how she could demand from him, burn against him with that fire.

He shouldn't think about that. Lisette, that Termite, had warned him. He shouldn't compare either, but he did. Now she was cool. Slick and cool as the stainless finish of the elevator. He saw only his reflection in the doors—a man with hands in his pockets, wanting more than she was ready for, more than this assignment allowed—as the lift hummed and his memories surged and his body burned. He shouldn't think about that day, but he remembered…

He heard a scream. Jenny Brooks in obvious delight. He turned to the door with the large cursive B. Thought of her mink coat, of the flash of her naked body, of the pleasure behind the closed door, of what the world considered casual and the believer sacred.

He let his imagination wander as he prepared for bed and laid his hot body down in his cool sheets. He began his prayer. But in the quiet darkness, voices traveled through the thin apartment walls. The sound of pleasure, hers, his. It was like a movement of music, cascading high, running hard and strong then softer to silence.

In his dreams it gently built again, a tangle of Jaclyn and Jenny Brooks. Wine was flowing and chocolate was dripping off the chin of pretty Jenny. His tongue enjoyed the flavors, his hands finding the jeweled tassels of thigh-high boots and glorious cleavage. But each time flesh was exposed it was Jenny, not Jaclyn. And the frustrating maze of trying to find her left him exhausted.

"I hate to bother you," LaRue was at his door early the next morning. "I thought I heard you up."

"No worries, I've been up a while. I'm off to Florida today. Spring training."

"Ah. The life of an athlete. I was hoping you had two eggs. I used my last few last night—"

"Oh, sure." He waved him in. "I always have eggs. Part of the daily diet to get in the protein I need." They walked into the kitchen.

"Part of being neighbors, I guess, popping in and out at all hours."

"We enjoyed last night. Thank you again."

"My pleasure."

Brett handed him a carton. "Take these."

"You have serious intentions toward her," he stated, smiled. "I can tell when a man has decided on marriage, he is above reproach."

"Oh." Brett was startled and a bit embarrassed but LaRue quickly went on.

"She is exquisite, Brett. A rare beauty indeed. I would understand your careful respect. She is young?"

"Twenty-three."

"Young." LaRue shrugged. "Cultured, educated, wonderful style. She understands beauty, highlights it without the fuss or flair. That is exceptional these days, to see a woman with such a body unrevealed and modest. Most do not understand men like to solve the mystery not have it revealed like the last page of a whodunit page turner in the opening paragraph. Who wants to read the book when you've solved the crime?" He sighed and suddenly sat as if exhausted in a stool at the counter facing him. "Nor do they understand that the conquest leads too soon to the rebuttal. My fair Jenny will soon be cursing me, I fear. She's given all and wants more than I can offer her. Mind if I smoke?" He pulled out a package of

French cigarettes, lit the tobacco quickly and took a long draw. "Jaclyn liked the wine?"

"Yes. She doesn't drink much."

"It relaxed her a bit." He took a long draw, blew the smoke away. "She'd warmed to you, by the time you left she was happy in your arms. Wine is one way to help a respectful woman relax. Are you intimate yet?"

The words were there. His faith easy to explain, defend, stand up for. He just had to open his mouth, say the words, tell his neighbor they were Christians and would wait for intimacy, share his faith and his Savior. Instead he said, "She was raped last year, before we met."

"Ah, no," LaRue shook his head, "I am sorry, Brett, truly that is horrible." His hand reached out and covered. "You are just what she needs. You will help her to heal with your strength and compassion." He smoked, his blue eyes thinking in the silence. "She is fond of you. I saw that right away. You've the patience to tend to her. She'll be tense at first, always. Try a little wine, it warms the heart, my father said and I agree."

"When we're alone she's, well, she does better in groups."

"Let me join you whenever you need some help. I think she liked me well enough."

"She did." Brett smiled.

"Good. Then will forge a friendship. Meet often. Dinner. Dates."

"I could use . . . the help."

"Of course, she is important to you. Woo her, use romance, build trust. Soon she will be helpless in your arms and you'll love her gently. Once you get past that first encounter, she will be who she was."

He took another long pull from the cigarette then waved the air clear of the smoke. "Nasty habit." He sighed, then smiled. "I do discern she has a passionate soul. I sense these things, being French. You just need the right keys to unlock her."

"Keys?"

"Love is a locksmith." It sounded like a song. With the words a sly smile, a promise in his blue eyes. "Alcohol always releases the first tumbler of a lock. I will bring you a few bottles of wine that she will appreciate. I have a few other suggestions, if necessary." He stood with a nod. They made their way to the door. Before LaRue left he thanked him again for the eggs then turned and said, "Respectfully, with a tender woman such as this, take care of your own needs before you see her. It is not well done to burn all evening when she is . . . " he lifted eyes of blue in an angel's face. "Anxious." There was a blush. A smile.

"Right."

"With all my travels, I've met a few women that can help you, discreetly. Fame has a price, no? Just ask me for . . . an introduction, we'll say. Where are you going in Florida?"

"Viera."

"Ah, lovely place. I have a friend there, Suzanna Santiago. I'll have her call. Enjoy the," He smiled, a twinkle in his eyes, "Sunshine."

22

It was a drill. Just a thirty-minute drill he was commanded to accomplish as Fury signed in for work. It was your standard daily training done through Virtual Reality. Decision making, navigation, leadership, control, stamina, perseverance, courage—a spectrum of elements could be evaluated and he'd be debriefed by the computer when it was over. He donned the headgear, took a stand in the center of the high-tech simulator. It began with a single word, "Engage."

He smiled. Zodiac drill. One of his favorites, being a man of the sea with SEAL in his blood there was no better way to start the day. He dropped down the zip line into a turbulent sea with a giddy kind of anticipation. He was the second to land, secure his spot at the aft and wait for the rest of the boat. They came falling from the pitch dark sky, the boat alive with restless energy. You'd need sea legs to survive this kind of boiling ocean and strong arms to row in the next few minutes. The last man was small and a bit out of control falling more than securing his spot. He'd keep his eye on the man.

In a moment the small man had been knocked to the center of the boat. There was a call from the helm to get back to his spot. That wouldn't happen while the man was throwing up nor would it be accomplished as he slid his way through the mess and bounced off half the men spreading it around within the small hull of the zodiac. He was reaching for him when suddenly, as all things seem to happen, the boat lurched and the newbie was up and out with a splash.

"Man overboard," was the call, the command was to retrieve him.

Joshua was in the water. It felt like a hurricane. The pitch and roll severe. He needed night vision to find the body heat, to aid in the rescue. The man was struggling, in a panic, they could both drown if he wasn't very careful. He grabbed him firmly from behind, tightly to his body in a rescue swimmer hold and there was a scream. A woman. Small, weak, panicking.

"Fight me . . . and I'll let go, leave you to drown."

"No."

"Work with me."

She calmed, clung, asked what to do. He swam, instructed, together they moved. It was a fight, the boat seeming to be farther than he expected. With one arm he powered his way up and over waves through an angry brutal sea, holding her with the other. Telling her to kick, teaching her to use the waves, understanding any moment the sea could turn on them, take them under or she could panic and drown them both.

"Kick," he demanded as he saw the ocean boil with trouble. "More," he insisted and the small woman did what he instructed. They reached the boat and she was too weak to use her upper body strength to pull herself up. In a surge he launched them both into the boat. She fell in his arms, bounced on the rubber surface tight to his chest. His hand held her close, grateful, exhausted. Greedy for air, for a moment, just another moment with her as he praised God for his strength.

Moonlight illuminated and he saw what he'd known. For just a moment her gaze linked with his, recognized him, spoke his name then there was a blink. Sizzle. Hiss. Surge.

She was off screen as if she'd been a mistake.

He refused to respond. To reveal. He only recovered. Finding his position at the helm, watching the sea as the end of the evaluation concluded.

He debriefed with the computer, heard nothing. Typed in the required information. There was a bewildered anger. A moment when he wanted to hunt. Find out who'd put her into a sim with him, who was taking liberty to make something personal. Who was playing games with his head and emotions. Lisette the Termite? Marc the Bull? Christie the Peregrine. Harrison the Eagle. Or maybe Wisdom…

His vitals were escalating, his heart pounding. His mind telling him perhaps this moment was the drill, how would he react when he found the Hummingbird was the anvil his skill was struck against? Who would Fury hunt down and what would he demand? He stored the equipment and said nothing but to his God. He'd always been his advocate. He could be trusted with this too. He would remain silent. God was his defender.

He was learning to be silent. To listen to words he didn't want to hear from Brett Webb about his growing relationship with Jaclyn. To hear over coffee this morning—in the meeting he was assigned to attend with the Spider weekly—that the famous pitcher had not only secured another photo op from the Globe but had earned her trust as well.

"We kissed last night," Brett Webb had confided in him. His head had been bowed, his gaze on his coffee. His famous hands cupped around the mug. "Just a kiss. I thought I should tell you." He'd looked up. "I'm supposed to, right?"

Joshua had only given a nod. Kept silent. Very still.

"I'm leaving for two months and she's just starting to . . . warm to me, think past the first encounter, wonder if we could be something more than friends." There was a sigh, a shake of his head, a hand shifted the mug. "You've no idea how delicate this has been, how great she is, how much I care about her. I want her." He'd looked up with a smile then his words accelerated. "Want her to heal, to trust me, to be free of that monster."

"We want that too." Joshua checked his watch, instructed, "If this is moving past friendship, talk to her father." Then he stood and told the man they'd have a team in Florida to watch over him.

"Just keep her safe."

"That's what we do," he assured them both. He wrapped the Oakleys around his eyes. They were blazing. The energy raging inside of him. He was jealous. Very jealous.

Just a kiss. The man had no idea how sacred that was.

Fury had never let himself kiss her. He'd protected her. Sanctified her rights to choose from her free will, not be forced to give by Eros. Sacrificed his legal rights to his wife. Given her away. To her father to heal. Now to Brett Webb to lure the Viper into a trap.

Wisdom said he'd covet her. That his sacrifice had been sin, unbelief. That she was chosen for him and he should accept God's choice and in his weakness become strong. He hadn't listened to the wise man. He thought he listened to God. He thought . . .

Suddenly he saw them. His team. Staring at him. He'd lost track of time and space. He'd lost control. And wasn't that what love could do . . . wasn't that what the wisest had warned. Love could rage.

"Boss?" It was Pax. His name a snarl. "You cool?"

He nodded. Let himself snarl. "Anyone up for a fight?"

"Me!" came from five voices.

"That was dirty," Jaclyn told her aunt that afternoon.

"Um?"

"Putting Fury in the sim today."

"Ah," she gave a nod. "I put you in a boat. He just happened to be commandeering it."

"I made a fool out of myself. Did you see it?"

"You survived, that's what I saw. I was proud of that. I drowned the first time Curtis tossed me into the sea." Christie told her, "I fought Marc.

Was too proud to let go of the panic and let him help me, lead me. We both went under. I was furious that he'd die because of my pride instead of just let go and let me drown."

"He drowned with you?"

"He drowned trying to save me. Big difference." She narrowed her eyes. "There was nothing romantic about the way I fought him."

"He said he'd leave me. Let go if I didn't stop fighting him." She looked away.

"He is SEAL trained and a leader of men, understands what motivates them. You trusted him. You survived. Both of you."

"Was he real?"

"It was a sim."

"Was he a part of it?"

"Um."

"You know what I'm asking."

"He'll show up in your training occasionally. Count it a reward whenever you see him. You've been working hard, gaining fast."

"You didn't answer me."

"They're training just like you're training. Obeying orders even when you don't understand their purposes. Trust me, Jaxie, like I trust you to keep this covert."

With a sigh, she gave an accepting nod.

Christie read from the Globe's gossip page. "*Pitcher and his plum eat pasta*—where do they get these headlines?"

"Plum?" Jaclyn frowned as Christie pushed the newspaper toward her. "I do look rather—plummy."

"Darling shoes."

"Yes, thigh high darling shoes." She described the boots, smiled now. "I love being a girl sometimes. Jenna makes me feel beautiful. Occasionally I like to let that loose, you know. I keep it covered up most of the time." She presented herself today, no makeup, hair up, and workout clothes on. "But if the paparazzi is going to follow us around and snap pictures, the least I can do is wear darling shoes and show off for Jenna. She's gaining momentum."

"Um." Christie was looking at her now, seeing, maybe knowing that showing off Jenna was an excuse for rubbing a certain nose in Brett.

Christie handed her an envelope. "How was your test this morning?"

"It was challenging." She accepted it. "I did fine."

"Fine," Christie repeated. "That means what?"

"We'll see."

"I want excellence."

"I'm not perfect."

"I didn't say perfection. I said excellence. You get that with integrity and consistency in your daily habits." She nodded for her to open it.

"Tickets?" She read them. "Hockey?"

"Take the pitcher."

"Brett?" she made her say it.

"Brett," Christie acquiesced.

"Are you coming too?"

She yawned. "This baby is making me turn in early."

"How are you feeling?"

"Good." She rose, stretched. Her body lean and tall, carrying the weight of the child like a small tiny globe of belly. Yawned. "Keep swimming in the morning until the weather turns. Security can't keep up with you on the run."

She nodded.

"Xuing treating you right?"

She only looked at her, lifting brows then cutting her gaze. Christie laughed.

"Good thing it's winter. I'm covered in bruises."

"Your body will get used to it, toughen up. How's your dad?"

"He misses me."

"Your levels were high this morning. How are they now?"

"Fine."

"What number?"

"Still a nine."

"Ida okay with that?"

"Prick and poke. I do what she says, when she says. I'm obeying people left and right."

"How does that feel?"

"I was a kid a few years ago. I'm pretty used to living under orders."

"Want some freedom? Define the word for me."

"Legal definition?"

"Your definition."

"To live without undue restraint, restriction, interference or fear. I'm not free of the Eros. I'm not free of fear, or free to love. I'm still a slave to a few unwanted masters."

"Is freedom the absence of something or the presence of someone?" Christie gave her time to think before she added, "*The Lord is Spirit, and where the Spirit of the Lord is, there is freedom.*"

"I had a bad definition."

"It was incomplete."

"*You shall know the truth and the truth shall set you free.*"

"And *He who is restricted is free if his master is righteousness.* Abide in Christ and He'll handle your emancipation through the truth of His word." She rocked in her office chair studying her. "There's a lot to be defined in the word *undue.* You know the difference between an order and a suggestion, what is justified and permittable. Is it a good time to see . . . Brett?"

"He's in Florida, spring training."

"Already?" She thumbed her PDA.

"It's February."

"It is," Christie acknowledged with a sigh.

"I have my ethics test tomorrow."

"That doesn't factor in. You've managed your time, studied. I'm more concerned about your levels."

"I'd tell you if I was struggling with Eros in a way that would be destructive."

Christie rose, gave her a kiss, her hand falling down the length of her hair. "Then ask a friend and enjoy the game."

Jaclyn left Christie's office. She already coveted a place in the building. Had a growing desire to be a part of the *Stratia* system. Many here greeted her, knowing her association and her history. They viewed her as Marc and Christie's niece, as Fury's rescue, as a grateful and generous benefactor of the program. One day she'd show them she could be among them, God willing.

Digging into a messenger bag filled to capacity, she tugged out her phone. She read a few text messages as she walked down the hall. Her dad checking on her test. Another from her stepmom. Jenna had sent her a few new designs to look at. She was typing an answer when he said her name.

She looked up, into his blue eyes. Startled to see him, unsure how to act, remembering this morning's drill—drowning in the sea then saved, remembering the night he'd rejected her love. The hurt was strong, real, alive between them and her mood was intensified because he'd caught her off guard. "Hi," she said coolly. "I was seeing Christie," she explained her presence in the office. "I thought you were off … out, somewhere."

"We're back. Yesterday. How are you?" He nodded at Tiki a few steps behind her.

"Good. Busy. You?" Her heart was fluttering. Her gaze taking him in. He wore fatigues, camouflaged for the desert. His name stitched in black. An eagle on his shoulders. She wore her own camouflage. The tight workout pants from her session with Xuing. Her dad's NFL football hoodie sweatshirt huge and vintage hung down to her thighs. Her hair in a ponytail coming out the back of a ball cap. Wearing runners, she was a good foot shorter than him. Anger sizzled up for some reason as she squared her shoulders and felt small and inadequate. Childish…

"Law school going well?"

"Um. First round of tests. I have my last tomorrow. How's work?"

"Always training. Spending time in the gym and conditioning. You still running?"

Her PDA beeped and she answered automatically, "Swimming." She glanced down, refused the incoming call. When she looked up his gaze had strengthened, was searching.

"Swimming?"

She gave a nod, thought fast and used her aunt's reasoning. "I'm not used to the winter air and it's hard for the security detail to be on the run. We . . . I thought it was better to stay inside. My place has a lap pool. How about you? Running through the snow and sleet?"

"I've been swimming." His gaze had a grip and she was locked in it.

She smiled, batted her lashes and knew it was dirty but she had to protect Christie and he could just wonder. "I'm sure you're an awesome swimmer with your SEAL background. I'm not too good yet. Weak arms and bad kick. The short legs and small feet. Your feet have a lot to do with your power, I'm learning." She shrugged. "But I'm finding it . . . challenging." She took a chance, another risk, dared him as she stood up a little straighter and stared him straight in the eyes. "I've got tickets to the hockey game tonight. Want to go with me?"

He blinked.

She'd shocked him. A part of her gloried in that sucker punch. Her heartbeat accelerated with the growing tension that he might say yes, give in, try.

"I'm, ah." His gaze held her eyes, she watched him think, then she watched him carefully evade. "I already have plans . . . with Eli."

"Um."

"Really," he assured then smiled. It was too close to patronizing. "But, you've got a hundred friends—

"Not really." She was backing away, the hurt coming too fast to hide. Anger expanding like a rushing wind, twisting into something hard to control. "Who could understand me? You know how confused I am. How foolish and childish."

"Take Brett," he suggested.

"He's in Florida."

"Ah," he said with clearer understanding.

She smiled now, as a staggering temper sparked, flamed, burned that he would even suggest it. "Good seeing you. God bless." The anger pumped with her pulse, a need to strike, hurt, draw blood and avenge herself was demanding she say more. She glanced at her PDA as it beeped then looked back up and something made her just say it. "Oh, and good save." She looked him in the eye. "Again."

"Hey, Brett." She turned and without another look back, she walked away from him. Squaring her shoulders, lifting her posture as she put her hands into the pouch and pulled the sweatshirt up so that the swing of her hips was revealed inside those skin-tight pants she knew showed off her rear end to her advantage.

He was the kind of man who would never look at her rear end. Resentment beat through her brain with a building vocabulary over that truth. It made her follow through with an impulsive plan. She ended her conversation with Brett quickly. Found his office and called his name with a seductively sweet purpose, "Eli."

"Ma'am." He was up, standing at attention, startled, scared.

They're overwhelmed with your beauty.

You have the Cruz blood, beauty, body. Learn to use that power for your advantage.

She heard the voices of others, responded with what they'd told her she possessed. Posturing her body, tossing her hair, lowering her lashes. "Hi. How have you been, Eli?"

"Fine, Miss Cooper."

"Jaclyn," she corrected him with a smile. She used her pocketed hands in the pouch to tug up the jacket and take a slow stroll around his office. She gave him her back, a twitch of hip as she looked at a framed picture of George Washington in prayer on his wall.

"Jaclyn." He repeated cautiously, looking at the door. "Ma'am. How are you?"

"In law school over at Georgetown." She meandered closer to him.

"Great."

"First round of tests." She smiled up at him.

He gave a sympathetic groan.

"Yeah. Tough." She sighed, her body brushing against his arm. Her lashes on dramatic, her mouth a pout that slowly smiled with adoration. "I've got tickets to the hockey game tonight. Thought of you." *Thought of getting back at Joshua...*

"Me?" He frowned a minute, looking at the envelop that was already in his hands. "Maybe you should ask—

"Brett?" She lifted her brows, tilted her chin.

"I've seen you in the papers together."

"The Fury told me to date him. I'll keep it up until he cries 'uncle.'" She laughed, female and cunning. "It might be at the wedding but I trust God to put an end to the game in His time. Joshua's stubbornness is eclipsing his integrity. He thinks it's right for me, he should know it's wrong. I'll hurt Brett eventually." She waved it off as emotion began to rise over the vengeance.

"I can't go with you." Eli held out the envelop. "Fury and I—

"I can't go either," she interrupted, began to back out of his office and retreat now that her purpose was accomplished. "Big test tomorrow on the

Evolution of Ethics. You'll enjoy the game. They're great seats. Good seeing you. Tell Petra and the team hello for me. Hello, Pax."

"Miss Cooper. Good to see you. Doing well?"

"Blessed, Pax."

"True." He nodded. "True."

She turned and let the blood beat through her system with its growing heat. She was mad. Suddenly a slave to her anger. She wasn't free. Free to live without undue restraint, restriction, interference or fear. She was a slave, believing lies and bad definitions of the truth, independent of her Savior's sovereign will, rebellious suddenly and jerking on her chains. It was the first time she disobeyed an order from her aunt. It was the first time she'd struck out with intention and manipulation to get Joshua's attention. She was foolish and childish … Delilah. True?

Fury's hands were back in his hair, raking into his scalp. Dazed and frustrated. She'd come in like a hurricane. Dressed like a welterweight boxer. How could a woman look so beautiful in a ball cap and oversized fleece? Then she'd knocked him out.

A pop to the chin. "Go out with me."

A left to the eye. "Good save." Then the right hook to finish it. "Again."

The one two punch had left him flustered and confused. *Good save … again.*

"Fury?"

"Yeah." He saw Eli at the door of his office. Tried to focus and force the funny look off his face. He was seeing stars. Like a cartoon character, totally confused. He sat down. Hard. In a seat behind a desk he never used. She'd asked him out. What had he said. Something lame. That sounded like a lie. Was that the good save … again?

"Hummingbird came by." Eli tapped an envelope on his door jamb.

He nodded. "Yeah. She saw the Peregrine."

"Gave me this."

"You." He stood. His gaze went to the envelop. "This. What?"

"Tickets. To the hockey game."

He swore. The foul word blowing like a gust from a blow hole.

His brow lifted as the toothpick in Eli's mouth shifted sides. "And I always thought you liked hockey."

Their gazes locked. "What did she say?"

"Something about Brett Webb. And you crying uncle." He peeked in the envelope. "Pretty good seats here, boss. Capitals game a bit more exciting than an hour at the firing range. Really good seats." The smile grew. His blue eyes sparkling.

"What else did she say?"

"Really? You want to go there?"

Fury stacked his arms.

"She thinks you're playing a game with her. Something about stubbornness eclipsing integrity. Did you tell her to date Brett Webb?"

"He's a great guy." He turned his back.

"We going to let these go?"

He heard the envelope. Paper tapping on metal. He grabbed his jacket. "Yeah, we're going." He looked in the envelope. "Good seats you said."

"She's always going to have the best. Petra says that's the way the high born do things." His gaze was direct. A bit humored. A bit serious. "You really going to let this get to the wedding before you cry uncle. Cause she's a little worked up. Had that attitude on. The one the Kid says prowls. Feels a bit Spanish to me. Furista-ish as Pax says. And I think Slim's right, she smells a bit like spearmint. Moves like a cat. Vin hit that right."

"Why would my team be talking about Jaclyn Cooper?"

The toothpick shifted, the smile went firm. Fury's look pressed him to the wall. His brow a heavy frown over loud blistering eyes.

"You really want to know?"

"No." He immediate pushed his arms into the leather jacket. "Forget it."

"Furious," Eli said.

"No." He held up the envelope. "Who can be mad when we've got these kind of seats."

"She's Furious." He smiled boldly around the toothpick. "That's why we talk."

23

Jaclyn stayed home and programmed herself against a gang of computer-selected bad guys, downloading her ethics definitions into the system in a program that Christie had sent over called "Ethics on Steroids" to drill her on the schools of thought governing the appropriate conduct of human beings.

An ancient Greek was the first character to emerge. Plato, perhaps, with a vast knowledge of the self-defense skills of Vee Arnis Jitsu. He asked her as he circled, "What is Applied Ethics?"

"Philosophical methods to identify the morally correct course of action in various fields of life. Ethics involves the rightness and wrongness of certain actions and governs the goodness and badness of the motives and ends of such actions," she told him as she countered his strike with a kick and a thrust then a left hook had him dissolving in midair.

A gang banger rushed her. He wore leather and used a chain. She charged before he could use the weapon on her, taking him quickly to the floor and smiled in his angry face. "What is prudence?" he snarled.

"Something you should develop." Her hold was cutting off his air supply. "Prudence is the exercise of sound judgment in practical affairs. You lack the motivation to live in conformity to the moral conduct of our society, thus law and order will judge you." He went limp beneath her, evaporating into thin air and she was up to meet her next opponent.

She was a woman. Dressed to kill. She cracked a whip and Jaclyn called her a Hedonist. "You believe pleasure is the only thing that is good for a person; indeed: the only good. You justify your motivation, striving to maximize net pleasure by reducing your amount of pain. Will you decide to choose enduring pleasure or the most intense pleasure currently at hand. Should this present instantaneous pleasure be denied for overall comfort? Oh, decisions, decisions, Hedonist—there are a million angles and layers to your motivations." She let her make the first move. With the crack of the whip, she used a candlestick to tangle her up, jerk her weapon free. "Mental pleasures can be preferable to the physical ones, you know Hedonist?" And with the whip wrapped around her throat, Jaclyn strangled her of air.

Suddenly she was in fencing gear. This was new, the sword light in her hand, her opponent at once coming at her. "Another Hedonist? You think the highest attainment is power. You like competition, because victory raises the level of competition and allows you a taste of absolute power over a component. You are like the Viper." She struck harder, faster. "You seek to persuade through deceptive means. Drugs, Eros, violence. You pull us into your game, unwillingly, and make us play by your rules." She was struck across the arm, then the leg. "Pause," she commanded. "I don't know how to sword fight." She walked around her simulated frozen opponent a full circle. "Engage," she commanded. Smiled. "But I do know how to take you off your well-balanced feet." In a move the masked man was down and another simulation began.

She was one hundred stories up, balancing on a beam of metal on the skeleton of an unfinished building. "Ah, a stoic," she greeted the Asian man with a bow. "In harmony with nature yet your life is influenced by material circumstances so you practice wisdom, courage, discretion and justice. This enables you to achieve your motto, 'Endure and renounce.' You value fortitude in the face of hardship, do you?" She attacked, her feet gripping the iron, her balance perfected through years of dance and gymnastics. The man was quickly counterbalanced and falling away from her.

"Where is the Epicurean?" she asked out loud as her surroundings changed. "His good is regulated by self-discipline and he believes my religious practices are harmful and preoccupied with death." From the shadows a tall man advanced. He was handsome, dressed well, from the newspaper tucked under his arm he pulled a shiny knife. "I hate knives. And I hate the Epicurean beliefs. All men will die. Death runs in the family. You best think of that end."

"What is good?" the character suddenly said, examining his sharp weapon. "Plato believed evil did not exist, but was an imperfect reflection of the real, which is good."

"Evil exists. It bears a name. The father of lies. Deception. Satan. The Devil."

"Impossible to prove in academia." The woman was back, cracked her whip. The Hedonist said, "Does not human virtue lie in the fitness of a person to perform their function in the world?" Her whip seemed to split her hairs. "Live up to your potential and you are therefore, good."

The man looked at her, smiled. "You are beyond lovely."

"Of course. She is lust." Jaclyn moved away from the snap of the whip.

"She will lead you into trouble." The Asian was beside the Epicurean. He smiled at the Hedonist. "You are lovely though. We know that the human soul has three elements—intellect, will and emotion—each possess a specific virtue and perform a specific role."

"Intellect is wisdom," the Epicurean stated. "Knowledge of the ways of life."

"That of the will is courage," the Hedonist stated, "The capacity to act."

"The virtue of the emotions," Stoic bowed, "is temperance or self-control."

"Yes," Jaclyn frowned. "I've studied Plato's ideas. That the ultimate virtue is justice—a harmonious relationship of each part of the soul doing its appropriate task and keeping its appropriate place."

"The intellect should be sovereign," Epicurean said. "The will second, the emotions subject to them both."

"Your emotions ruled you today," the woman smiled, caressing her whip. "You tried to manipulate Fury."

"You were not just," the Stoic told her. "The just person's life is ordered and is therefore good."

"You were not good," the Epicurean decided, his hand running over the blade of his knife.

"You are right. *I know that nothing good lives in me, that is, in my sinful nature. For I have the desire to do what is good, but I cannot carry it out. For what I do is not the good I want to do; no, the evil I do not want to do — this I keep on doing. Now if I do what I do not want to do, it is no longer I who do it, but it is sin living in me that does it. So I find this law at work: When I want to do good, evil is right there with me. For in my inner being I delight in God's law; but I see another law at work in the members of my body, waging war against the law of my mind and making me a prisoner of the law of sin at work within my members.*

"*What a wretched man I am! Who will rescue me from this body of death? Thanks be to God — through Jesus Christ our Lord*!" she announced. "This is the Christian view. That a person is totally dependent upon God and cannot achieve goodness by means of will or intelligence or temperance, but only with the help of God's empowering Holy Spirit."

"The Great Commandment and the Golden Rule," the Hedonist sighed. "Love thy God and do unto others," he tsked.

"It is balance," the Stoic thought.

"It does not work universally," the Epicurean debated. "As each man is ultimately motivated by his own pleasure not the pleasure of others."

"I like the German Kant," the Stoic defended, "Act as if the principle on which your action is based were to become by your will a universal law of nature."

"Categorical imperative," Jaclyn defined. "To treat others as 'in every case an end, never as a means only.'"

"You treated Eli as a means only." Stoic frowned.

"Again." The Hedonist cracked her whip. "You were not good."

"Perhaps as Bentham explained," the Epicurean defended, "The highest good is the greatest happiness of the greatest number of people. She made Eli happy."

"Well, she is not happy. Fury is not happy. Brett is not happy." The hedonist struck the air with a violent crack of the whip. "No one is finding pleasure in her actions. She is not good!"

"Didn't Moore's *Principia Ethica* define that 'good' is indefinable?" Stoic mentioned now.

"Jesus said, 'There is only One who is good, God.'"

"How can that be proven?" Stoic asked her with lowered brow and crossed arms.

Jaclyn sighed. "Are we going to fight or debate Ethics?"

"Ah-ha!" The Epicurean announced. "She is a naturalist. Good can be defined."

"I am an intuitionist," the Hedonist defined. "Good is un-analyzable. Each man decides what is true and false of good. Pleasure is good. Comfort is good. Power is good. Blood is very good." She cracked her whip. "Boys, shall we fight the sinful Christian?"

24

In the morning she woke up on the floor of the VR room with the mask askew over puffy eyes, the dream lingering then fading like mist as she tried to remember. She was foolish and childish… she was not good.

She moaned at the time, it was seven o'clock. She didn't sign into the computer. Her levels were up again, a headache like a hangover, was nagging her and she had an irritating crick in the back of her neck. She took an injection and then took a two-hour law exam on ethics that only intensified her bad mood. She saw herself in every philosophy. She was a Hedonist.

She'd realized Joshua had his own code of conduct and he was most certainly obliging her to follow it. The thought made her mad that he'd give her orders to follow. That she'd be obedient to him, prudent. That made her good and mad. She'd become competitive for the power to decide their future. She was a definite Hedonist, no better than the Viper, wanting to manipulate.

As she left the building she didn't want to be driven home. She wanted the cold air catching her breath, clearing her head. She wanted to stroll the sidewalks, with her hands in her pockets and her thoughts given room to brood. She wanted to be alone. She wanted freedom…

For a fleeting instant she thought about rushing into the noon crowd of pedestrians, losing her bodyguard, being free. Her heart ticked with the adrenaline rush of that, pounded with the lust of excitement. She glanced over her shoulder. Tiki was a few steps behind her, giving her room, a long shadow today. A gentle nod. She turned back, rejected the idea with a single rational thought. This wasn't Tiki's fault. She wouldn't disrespect Tiki or her father that way. That would not be good…

She would do unto others as she wanted done to her. Respect him.

She redirected her rebellion. She wanted a soda, sweet and bubbly. Chocolate. Maybe ice cream or a real latte with caffeine. She was tired of doing without stimulants. She was tired of all the rules in her life. She was angry that Joshua continued to reject her. It was Joshua's fault. All this bad temper went back to him. He was so very stubborn.

Her neck pain was intensifying her mood with its screaming nerves and stiff catching ache. She moved her head from side to side, rubbed at the back of it, at the tense muscles where the crick was tight. Maybe she should schedule a massage, some time to herself without demands, try to relax instead of rev herself up with food stimulants…

No! She was tired of all the don'ts, all the no-no's, checking levels and staying in the lines because of Eros. It was Eros' fault. All of it went back to the drug. She was so sick and tired of Eros. She wanted her old life back.

She turned into a corner deli and walked the coolers. She picked a bottle of her favorite soda. It was cold, icy cold. She used to drink as many of them as she wanted a day without a second thought. Now it would be an indulgence, a huge treat. She broke open the bottle, took the first exhilarating sip. Was stunned by the sweetness. Wow. Now that was sugar at its finest. She took another long drink, strolled down the candy aisle unsure if candy was what she really wanted to splurge on with the soda.

She felt his gaze, looked up and caught his eyes strolling her body beneath a loud ball cap cocked sideways as she drank. She knew she was wearing an attitude. So was he, bold with it as he swaggered toward her, two friends behind him. All in wife beater tank tops beneath gang leather. Pride. Possession. She'd seen it before but the men had been Russian instead of American urban gang members. She had been drugged, helpless. Last night she'd taken that gang banger down in the training vid. She was no longer a victim. She lifted a brow and stood her ground.

His gaze gave her a bolder sweep. Then he spoke, rude and disrespectful words.

Tiki moved in instantly and she raised her hand.

"Excuse me, sir?" she asked for clarification with a deceptively sweet and naïve voice and a bold offensive step toward him. "Were you talking to me? You have no idea what prudence is, do you?"

There was laughter. "Zee, are you prude, man?" The three danced like bobble heads. Zee gave her a very rude suggestion as his eyes sculpted her body and his friends laughed at her expense.

She hated men. It was all their fault. They lusted, abused their power, were obsessed with sex. And Zee proved it with his next disrespectful chorus of creative language as he tried to grope her.

In a move she took him down a notch. With the first strike his nose bled, knees buckled, his hands jerking to his crotch as he sank like a puddle of pain with an intense groan.

Pleasure soared.

Eye to eye now, she asked him, "Prudence is living in conformity to the moral conduct of society. You play by the conventional rules. You respect others. You stop lusting after women, abusing your strength, obsessing over sex. Get a wife. Be a real man."

There was a swift blow to his face. *Yes.*

Her knee drew blood from his mouth. *Yes.*

Another hit took him to the ground like a tree falling over. *Yes.*

His head thudding off the hard tile floor was a beautiful sound. *Yes.*

"You better realize you aren't at the center of the universe or even the king of this corner. God is, you punk, and He makes the rules. He commands you to love Him and others." She looked at his friends, lifted a brow then waved them on. "Come on, then. He only touched the edge of my temper."

One of them flipped open a knife and God revealed her own pride. She didn't like knives but her temper said let him try. "If you can't fight a woman fair, then use your knife, you disrespectful punk."

Tiki stepped forward, he'd been calling her name, tugging her back. Her feet stepped on broken glass. There was a crunch. A memory flashed. She forced it back with rage. There was a groan below from Zee. She kicked him thinking of the Viper now, glass crunching beneath her feet. Tiki hissed her name, used greater force but she got in another kick.

With his eyes on the other boys, he demanded, "Jaclyn that's enough."

But it wasn't. She'd shut him up, humbled his attitude and his entitlement to lust after her but she hadn't stopped her screaming soul. She was hot with anger, screaming at everyone in the store. It was all their fault. The world had allowed it to happen, stood by and watched as she was abused.

She cried out, "You think you can disrespect me? Look at me like that and I'm just going to let you. Lust after me because of how I look and I'm supposed to let you. Talk to me like that and I'm supposed to take it. I'm done taking it. I am done!"

"She's done," Tiki told the store, tossing money for her soda to the clerk behind the counter already on his cellphone. Tiki didn't wait around to talk. He demanded, "Be quiet." Quickly escorted her out and around the corner off the block. Holding her arm he crossed the street, got lost in the pedestrian flow.

"You going to talk to my dad about this?" she said as he finally slowed their pace, his hand clamped firmly on her upper arm.

"No, but we're going to talk about this." He stopped at a deli cart on the corner ordered her a water. "Drink."

"I wanted a soda." She realized she'd lost the bottle somewhere in the battle.

"You don't need a stimulant." They were walking again. "Or me to tell you how dangerous that was. My job is to protect you. You could have made that hard back there if those two boys would have jumped in to help their friend instead of laughed at him."

"It would have been a fight." She nodded.

"Why are you looking for one?"

"He made me mad. His attitude." She drank. "He felt entitled to degrade me because of how I look. I don't dress to attract that kind of attention."

"No," Tiki agreed. "But you will attract attention, nevertheless." He sighed. "With beauty comes modesty and modesty is more than just dressing appropriately, it is also moderating one's behavior. With strength comes responsibility. A husband to his wife. A mother to her child. A wise man with a fool. You abused your strength. That's not like you. Want to tell me what's going on?"

"Um."

"Ethics test?"

"No."

"Brett?"

"Definitely not. He adores me." Then she looked at him. "I know he calls you. Fury."

Tiki blinked then he nodded. "He checks in. Your father cleared that."

"Of course he did. I'm sure Marc was involved somewhere to."

"Actually your Aunt, she made the call, informed me he was cleared on all systems."

"Um." She glanced in a shop window, saw her reflection, steam rising from her heat in the cold morning air. Eyes narrowed and angry. She felt huge and strong. She looked short and silly.

"Would you like me to redirect Fury to your father?"

She looked at his reflection, shook her head then said the truth. "We disagree about our relationship. I love him. He believes I'm confused. Wants me to date Brett. And I'm doing it!" There was a sudden punch of anger and self-disgust. "I. Am. Doing. It."

There was silence, then Tiki stated, "Most women I've known know their minds about their hearts."

"I'm mad about it." She took a long drink. "I'm mad about a lot of things, Tiki."

He gave a nod, stated the verse, "*In your anger don't sin.* The boy was out of line, Miss Cooper. People have died for less but you don't want to live with that on your conscience, believe me. Murder isn't a cure for anger, it's a lust for blood and the power to rule over others."

She accepted the rebuke. "I wanted to hurt him, not kill him."

"You have a responsibility to control your lethal abilities. Xuing would tell you you're stronger than violence. Silence is the high road when faced with a fool."

"Yes, sir." She rubbed her hand.

"Sore?"

"Will be."

"The first move and it was over. I knew he was done then I knew you needed to be. It was hard to get you to stop. We were on the edge of having a serious incident with that outburst. In fact I think we might need something to help you cool off. A healthy indulgence." He nudged her forward, held a door open. At the counter he ordered them both frozen yogurt.

"Thanks, Tiki."

"Discipline deserves a reward now and then."

"I'm not sure I deserve a treat after that." She sighed now. "I'm sorry. Please forgive me."

"Forgiven."

"I lied to you that night at the ballet," she confessed. "I wasn't sick. I just needed to leave." She looked into his eyes, watched him eat the frozen yogurt, holding hers untouched. "It's been on my conscience. I don't like to lie."

"Forgiven."

She nodded, took her first bite. The treat was sweet and creamy, vanilla swirled with caramel and chocolate, dotted with almonds.

"You don't owe me explanations, Jaclyn," he told her. "If you want to leave the ballet or stay at the library another hour, or cancel plans or adjust your schedule—it's your schedule, your life. I don't need the reason or rationalization. I'm not your keeper or conscience, just your protector. And don't feel like you're putting me out. This is my job. Serving you gives me purpose, Jaclyn. It might seem small to you—

"No. I know this can't be small. I mean look at me. I'm a mess. My life . . . well, being with me must be challenging."

"I'm learning a lot. Your father is an expert consultant on my client and Marc's an expert on my assignment. I couldn't ask for better training." He smiled at her.

She smiled back. They walked to the park, strolled along the river, talked about anger and evil. Tiki shared about frustration and disappointment. He'd wanted to play football, the dream was ended early when he blew out his knee. He'd gone into the military then became a detective. He told her that in God's sovereignty he protects us from the good when He wants to give us better. Often during that protection period we experience disappointment. "It's crucial to trust and be patient in the meantime of waiting."

She agreed with him but part of her wondered if God wasn't ultimately to blame for everything. Immediately she stopped the thought, thanked Him for His deliverance. She knew only God had saved her, working through men to free her. She believed that, but a part of her wondered why He'd ever let it happen . . .

Why? She whispered it, circled around and around it until she was only frustrated again. Within an hour she was watching a group of teenage boys bullying another kid.

Why did the world constantly seek the weak? They surrounded him, nudging with shoulders and words. Why did evil get to be so strong? They took his PDA away. Why was man so mean? They knocked him down. She was up wanting to fight, strike, kill. They ran from her like roaches when the kitchen light is struck. She chased, hunted the leader, took him down to the earth with her questions. He had no answers. Nor did he have the PDA. When she insisted he call back his friends, none came. They left him alone. To fend for himself against justice.

She gave him words. Crisp warnings bouncing off his shut ears. She let him go. Turned to give the bullied young man her attention but he was also gone. Tiki had taken her arm, turned her away. Asked the all-important question—what were her levels?

Ida called after she entered the cube of blood. Her PDA showed a number past twenty now. She'd had a soda, yogurt, a fist fight then a verbal encounter as she bullied back those teenage boys. Now an injection to counter the hormonal increase. Her neck was stiff, the tension growing tighter on the right side. Her headache a pounding force behind her right eye as she agreed to come into *Stratia* and see Ida.

She was restless on the drive through the Friday traffic, there had been a chain reaction pileup, five cars rear ending each other. No doubt the victim at the front of the line, none too innocent of the whole action had been distracted, texting on his phone. He was to blame. The driver in the silver coupe. She scowled at the car, the driver standing with the police on the curb as hundreds affected by his negligence crawled by in bumper-to-bumper traffic.

There was glass on the street, her car crunched through it as they crept past the destruction. The sound triggered the memory again, it shifted subtly in her mind, glass breaking, crunching under foot. The unique sound, a horrid memory. Instead of deflecting it away this time, she let it echo, listened. Graphic horror came suddenly like a raging river. His fancy bathroom. The triple floor-length mirrors. Her reflection cast everywhere. Her hair was in a complicated up-do, women working on her. Then a robe was swept aside and it was revealed for the first time. Her naked back a canvas for Viper's artwork. The tattoo embedded with the drug of manipulation, Eros. The artwork—a tiger mated by a snake—reflected in all its grotesque vileness in a baroque mirror. The symbol, his symbol, cast into her flesh forever, reflected infinitely everywhere she could see in his room of mirrors.

Fear had made her strike the reflection, desperation making her destroy everything in the Viper's bathroom that reflected the image. There'd been shock and sickness, pity in a housekeeper's eyes that had sparked an explosive rage that made the women leave like scattering mice. She'd thrown a tantrum, it was all a red blur. Glass broken beneath her feet, the sound of it like a bold alarm ringing through the house. A door left open on the patio. A flight through the garden, into his forest. Running, fighting drugs and disorientation, dizziness and despair. Terrified and tragically thinking she had a chance for escape she had run without looking back from the shadow of his grand country estate into a forest of darkness. There had never been a chance, it had been a game. He'd let her go into the dark woods only to hunt her down. And when he had found her, those dark eyes so arrogant and excited now, pleasured by her defiance, her challenge, the game . . . she had raged against him then ravaged. No longer victim, finally broken to his will and ways. Beneath him, she ravaged as he ravaged her. She could still smell the forest, feel its darkness, remember the animal rising over the dullness of the drugs, an excruciating passion and erupting pleasure. The Viper's victorious smile.

There was hate. At herself. At Yrasrevda. At her rebellious body. Hands that had been rubbing her neck now clawed into her flesh, released an instant burn of pain where the tattoo had been. There was a hate so strong it produced a taste in her mouth and brought a red tinge to everything. Her blood was a bass drum beating aloud now. Her hands clenched, every muscle straining. Shame and self-loathing pushed aside with a terrible rage. It was his fault. All the Viper's fault. And he would pay. She would kill him. She! Not anyone else. Not Fury or her father. Not Christie or Marc. Not a team sent from *Stratia* or Tiki defending her. She would kill that snake. It was what he deserved and she deserved to do it.

She was going to kill him. It was all *his* fault. God had spared him so she could do it! Let her go so she could hunt him. Justify herself. Take revenge. Quench this consuming hate.

The truth needed to be told. And it would be obeyed.

Christie would understand. Only Aunt Christie.

"Wait here," she commanded Tiki calmly, too calmly. She walked in the door without looking back. Flashed ID and was admitted into a doorway, then took an elevator. She didn't go to the med center to see Ida but down to the operations area. Coming off the lift, she only nodded at security as they greeted her and she spoke her aunt's name. She marched onto the working hall of *Stratia* toward the corner office of the Peregrine.

"Miss Cooper." Her name was announced.

She saw Eli first, his surprised smile, his quick glance to Joshua standing beside him. Petra had put a hand on his arm. Eyes alarmed. Knowing. She saw understanding in Petra's silver eyes, the woman warrior knew. Then Fury stepped forward. Those hot blue eyes of his connecting with hers, holding. At the sight of him something surged in her, dark and dangerous. He wanted to kill Viper. He wanted to do it. No! He had protected her. He had rejected her love. No!

There was desire—to grab Joshua's hair, bite at his mouth, claw his flesh, growl out her demands, make him obey her. She tossed her hair, twitched her hip into a seductive gait and passed with a silent dare. He would follow. She could smell the forest, feel its darkness, remember the animal rising up from her to ravage. Tigrissa.

There was hate. At herself. At Yrasrevda. Now at Joshua. A twisted kind of hate. Growing. Her blood beating stronger. Inside she was running. Every muscle straining. Her hands fists. The taste of blood. The image of her tattoo. The sound of broken glass. Viper's eyes, that look of competition and arrogance. The defeating laughter. The name. Tigrissa… whispered like victory, impressed into her flesh, forced upon her body, her soul. Viper was to blame. He'd given her the Eros. He'd taken away all she had wanted to be. Made her a tiger.

She was a tiger. And she would make him pay. Vengeance the only cure for this madness she felt. She would be free then. She had to tell Aunt Christie. Find her. Make them understand before they took away her rights. She heard the Fury coming, sensed it, knew it, wanted it, him, but strode on. Into the corner office, dark, vacant. She whimpered suddenly.

"She's not here," he informed.

"I don't need you." Jaclyn turned, now cornered, the whimper now a growl. Her gaze narrowing, her senses hyper, her surroundings blending, blurring on the edges to a pinprick focal point in a tunnel of red. His eyes too blue. Seeing. Protecting. "Christie will understand. Not you. Leave. Me. Alone."

The door closed. Locked.

She growled. Attacked. Something crashed. There was a slap. Her nails finding blood. Her teeth tasting it. Motions fast, furious, reckless energy.

He grunted, defended. There was the slap of skin to skin, counter attacks, left, right, right. Pain, pleasing pain. A chair skidded out of the way, rolling against another, bumping into the desk. Papers flew, something heavy hit the floor, something else fell against the wall. Another growl high and frustrated. His grunt, plead. Her name.

He pinned her arms behind her, gave curt instructions to stop. Pressed her flat into a wall with his body. Heat and strength and energy invading at once. Male. Mate. His scent like a brutal lance to her heart. Their memories flashed, fighting Eros on the train. The images set her body to fire, broke her heart.

"Don't. Please." Someone cried from a faraway place in a pitiful voice. "Please. No. No. No."

Immediately she was let loose.

He was tricked. Good. At once she turned on him, rage twice as strong, dulling everything to be released. It attacked with kicks and swings, swift and now lethal as she voiced her frustration, "I will kill him. Me, not you. I'll kill him for what he did to me, to us. I will kill him for that tattoo, for the drugs, for making me doubt God!" She was suddenly swifter, taller, faster, tangled with him, holding him, face to her face as she growled it. Golden eyes ablaze with fury as she stared into him.

"He let this happen to me!" erupted from her soul. "God allowed this to happen to me," cried from her heart. "He is sovereign. He is to blame," she declared the truth with a guttural growl of fury. "I. Hate. Him. Me. For this." There was a burst of blinding vengeance with supernatural strength.

Energy lit his eyes as foreign words spoke a litany. In a move he finally engaged his strength, countered, attacked, twisted, pinned, held her immobile, off the ground as she kicked her feet viciously into him. There was swift pressure. On just the right point. Someone was shrieking. Her vision faded to black.

She went limp in his arms and Fury took them both carefully to the ground. The air seemed thin, his lungs heaving with an unfamiliar fear. His heart aching, his arms held his wife with utter tenderness. There wasn't much time. Single-handedly he dialed his PDA, called Ida. He told her what to bring, where they were. "Get Christie," he instructed before he hung up the phone.

He prayed now, his hand a heavy exacting pressure on her artery. The other stroking her hair, taking her hand. She had little hands, long elegant fingers, pretty shell colored nails. Her knuckles were swollen, the center one cut open, her forearms bleeding, scored by her own ruthless carving scratch. He pressed trembling lips to it, prayed the strong plead of the helpless who cry out for their deliverer.

"I'll kill him." There was the softest whimper, an odd saying, "His fault. Not God, right? Not God," she gasped. "I'm not good. Wretched man I am."

"I've got you, Baby Girl. You're safe here." The intense heat began to seep from her damp body, her hand clung to his. A thumb stroke over the scar in his palm.

"Tigrissa." Her eyes opened, looked at him but not yet seeing. "Hunting me. Playing his games. Letting me go to hunt me. Catch me. R-rape me. I'll kill him." There was a sound, a battle cry from her soul. "Wretched man I am. Who can rescue me..." She panted in his arms. A tear traced her cheek. "He branded me."

"The tattoo is gone."

"I'm not good. He broke me. Made me lust."

"No." He gathered her up closer. "He drugged you," he told her softly with confidence, "You're strong, courageous, faithful, beloved by God."

She whined, shivering. "My neck hurts." She whimpered. "It's too much." She began to shake, become more aware, agitated. "Tigrissa. Hunting me. Playing his games. I'll kill him. Wretched man I am. It's too much. I have to kill him. After what he did. Me not you."

Agitation was blooming, her skin flooding with color. His hold tightened, prepared.

Then a keycard was clicking, locks sliding, the door opened.

Her gaze went wide, wild, vivid gold. She went rigid, jolting up as she demanded, "I'll kill him." He applied pressure instantly and she was again a rag doll in his arms.

Christie Cooper-Stone's emerald eyes grasp hold of his at once, he gave her only a glance, taking in both her shock and fear as Ida moved quickly. She gave Jaclyn an injection from a pressure syringe. Helped Joshua reposition her body carefully to lie flat on the floor. She had her pulse, Joshua punching a finger for blood.

"She was at thirty-two ninety minutes ago," Ida clicked off the data as he punched the cube into his PDA.

"She's close to sixty now."

"They were stuck in traffic. Tiki said it's been an eventful afternoon. She took out a ganger in a convenience store, then took on a group of bullies at the park. Anger to rage, reacting in a moment. He didn't realize it was an echo."

"An echo?" Christie was beside them now. "This looks more like . . . a, ah," she was looking around her office, then at him. "A temper tantrum on steroids."

"Ever seen a hummingbird angry? They're furious little birds."

"Interesting adjective." Christie had taken Jaclyn's hand, ran her thumb over the swollen cut knuckles. "Furious."

"Sixty-seven." Fury told Ida the readout, ignoring Christie.

"I need to get her to Heatherwood. Can you get me an airlift?"

"Absolutely." Christie was on her feet, calling out orders on her PDA.

Ida was also on her PDA, calling the Termite. "We're in the Peregrine's office."

"No one's coming in here," Joshua made the statement flatly.

"I respect your need to protect her," Ida bowed her head. "But Lisette is going with us, Fury."

Fury made no attempt to hide the energy in his eyes. He looked at Christie. Her attention was on Jaclyn.

"It's for her best. I've been convinced." Now she looked up at him, met his blazing heat. "She needs what only a Termite can do. This comes from Wisdom."

Joshua closed his eyes. His will fighting the order and the ways of it. The knock came, Christie letting the Termite in. He watched her sweep the room in a glance, then looked at Jaclyn dispassionately.

"Did she hurt herself?" The words were flat.

"No."

But she picked up her wrist, saw the score marks, the cutting. "She came to see Christie." Lisette met her gaze. "There was a reason for that. Did she say anything?"

"I wasn't here. Fury got to her."

"Did she say anything?" she addressed him now.

"Tigrissa. Hunt me. Playing games. I'll kill him. His fault, not God's, right." Joshua told the room. "She said that several times, that and, he branded her, and broke her, made her lust. She kept quoting Romans seven. Wretched man I am. Said, she wasn't good and asked who could rescue her," Joshua told the three women. "She repeated, it's too much and I'll kill him. With an entitlement, letting me know it was her right, not mine to take vengeance."

Ida had closed her eyes. Lisette stated the truth, "A battle is taking place. She wants vengeance. She must choose forgiveness."

"I'm sorry you had the intercept. I wish it would have been me." Christie frowned, looking him over. "She did some damage here, Fury."

"I'm okay."

"It's hard to defend yourself against that kind of onslaught when you're trying to protect you both." Ida handed him a tissue, pressed it over his forearm where she'd scratched him.

"She was very angry." He wiped his mouth next, the corner was bleeding.

"We gather that, Fury."

"Like bloodlust," he further described.

"It was bloodlust," Lisette confirmed. "Nuclear tension needing an outlet for the hate. You were smart to take her down."

He felt Christie's hand tremble, said out loud, "She'll be okay." He named a drug, it would erase the memory of this. "Give her that."

"Perhaps not," Lisette questioned. "Sometimes this is the point of breakthrough. Anger is part of healing."

"Shame is not," Fury countered. "This wasn't her and she's had enough. Please," he looked at Ida now. "She's had enough. She said it was too much."

"Trust me," Lisette said. "She's strong enough to handle what she remembers. God will work this for her good. Allow Him to heal, to turn evil's wounds to victories scars. I appreciate what you told me. It will help me, help her."

25

They took her to Heatherwood. She'd been alone for three days, this cycle slow building and brutal. A widening gap between her estrogen and progesterone causing an intensity in her anger and emotions. Ida had slowly closed the gap and leveled her off, the cycle complete.

She refused to talk to family. No one could understand a madness she was still learning had a hundred different dimensions and refracted into a hundred different emotions. The rage of revenge was new. Shame was familiar. Failure was becoming friendly. Pity was having its party. She sat in a chair in her corner room the guest of honor. She startled when the locks disengaged to her door. Someone, finally, to rescue her from herself.

"Doctor Lisette?" She sat up, every muscle going tense. Her neck complaining at once.

The Termite closed the door, used the pad to engage the locking system. "Don't get up," she insisted as she walked toward her. Her gaze scanned the room, her hand touching the footboard of the bed, the back of a chair as she passed. "It's been quite a weekend. Ready to get out of here?"

"Um." She sighed. When Lisette raised a delicate blond brow of inquiry, Jaclyn just said it, "No. I'm pitiful, having a little private party."

"Got cake? I like Red Velvet." She sat beside her, smiled.

"I'm supposed to stay away from sugar and caffeine. It stimulates my system." There was no emotion.

Lisette huffed with a lot of emotion. "There's no end to this Eros, is there? What else must you give up to heal from this devil?"

Jaclyn tensed, feeling the anger, wondering over the legitimacy and the probing question.

"I'd be one angry lady without caffeine. Caffeine blocks adenosine reception so you feel alert, injects adrenaline into the system to give you an energy boost and manipulates dopamine production to make you feel good. It's a drug. Just like Eros stimulates your lust—for power or things or even violence. Eros can give you a strong bloodlust. An echo can arrive disguised in a temper tantrum. Not everyone is asymptomatic with Eros."

"And of course, I'm not everyone."

"Not the way you were dosed," she agreed with passion. "Time release in a tattoo." She shook her head. "That snake was effectively creative. Did you ever see the tattoo?"

She nodded.

"Tell me about it?"

"It was a tiger," she described it flatly, watching Lisette.

"Did that devil show it off? Make you see his work?"

"I saw it in a mirror. I was in a bathroom . . . there were women, doing my hair and dressing me."

"Do you remembering when he put it on you?"

She shook her head. "He drugged me. I was in and out. I don't remember . . . everything."

"But you remember seeing it for the first time?"

"Yes."

"What did you do?"

"I destroyed his bathroom, sent the women running. Broke a window and escaped. I ran."

Lisette waited. Jaclyn could feel her pulse, it was painful.

"You didn't get away."

She shook her head, felt incredibly hot, very tired. "He let me go to hunt me."

"He found you. You fought him. He liked it."

Jaclyn nodded.

"Something shifted. The anger, over the tattoo, what he'd dare do, brand your body with his mark, as if he owned you and you'd never escape. There was rage. Rage and rape. But he'd dosed you with Eros now, it was in the tattoo, rushing into your blood stream, excited by your anger. A dose of lust. Physically you responded, ravaged him with the rage instead of fighting him. Violent passion and misunderstood pleasure. A climax. It would have thrilled him, to bring you to that. Incited him with lust for more and left you fighting feelings you didn't understand, feeling a horrible shame." Lisette had taken her hand, somewhere in the dialogue she'd taken her hand when the room went blurry and disappeared to the memory and her tears. "That wasn't you, that was the drug, Jaclyn, and the rage was your spirit fighting what you didn't understand. He drugged you, the pleasure a manipulated delusion. Say that truth," she commanded now.

She blinked. Saw. Realized. "He drugged me. It was Eros. A delusion."

"Yes."

"It was Eros, not me." She accepted the truth, let it flood her with light. Let the tears flow like a river to cleanse her. She wiped her eyes, took a breath.

"And he didn't brand you forever. His mark is gone, taken away, wiped clean. God's grace can turn evil's wounds to victory's scars when we allow him to heal us, to turn from bitterness and trust God, forgive. You are not his Tigrissa."

"I'm a hummingbird."

Lisette laughed. "A furious little fighter. Colorful and beautiful in its design. Yes, you are a hummingbird."

"He let me go to hunt me then? Is that what he's doing now? Hunting me?"

"Perhaps," Lisette agreed. "Perhaps you escaped the first time and he chased you. It is a game to him, I hate to tell you. What was life-changing to you is only a bit of frivolous fun in his world filled with serious evil. But, in every game there is a winner. You beat him, not many can claim that. Now the game is over. He either wants to play again or he's taken up another sport. Over time, everyone tires of even their favorite game. They look for something new. Change occurs, always."

"He didn't like losing. He'll be angry, wanting revenge."

"He is not almighty, he is a man. An evil man but only a man. And being an evil man, who did unspeakable evil things to you, we must forgive him." Lisette picked up the intercom. "Can you send us up a Red Velvet cake. Thanks." Lisette looked back at her. "When we're angry, we want to put our hands around someone's neck and shake them, choke them, or suffocate them to death. We want to cast all our frustration into the squeezing off of their rights or their life or forcing them to pay back their debt to us. In the midst of those intense and entitled feelings, God says something fantastic, He commands us to forgive.

"He commands us to take our hands off their neck and let go. We don't want to." Lisette looked into her eyes, held them unwavering as she spoke the truth, "But God says we are to allow Him the right to deal with others. He'll do a much better job than we ever could. He is Almighty. He will judge the wicked. Christ defeated evil at the cross and one day soon it will be ultimately defeated and removed from us forever." Lisette smiled. "Isn't that good news today? Ah, here's Ida and the cake." Lisette rose, rubbing her hands together. "I can smell that icing. Ah, this is going to be fabulous."

"Happy Birthday," Ida greeted her then smiled at Jaclyn.

She rose. "Is it your birthday, Doctor Lisette?"

"It is. I'm forty-four, a much better reason for a party don't you think?"

"Shall we sing?" Ida looked at Jaclyn and began.

Jaclyn added her voice, feeling oddly uncomfortable but obliged to do it.

"You're going to let me eat cake?" she asked Ida.

"It's my birthday," Lisette answered, cutting her a huge piece. "And you've had a breakthrough that's worth celebrating. Tell Ida the truth."

"He didn't break me, he drugged me. And I'm going to work to forgive . . . and leave him to God to judge."

"You must forgive him today," Lisette told her cutting the cake, and the command hung in the air like the sweet smell of the cream cheese icing.

"Forgiveness is obedience to God's command. The healing is the work. For that we have to cooperate with God through things that are difficult and be truthful with ourselves."

"Truthfully, I've lost control. Of everything. I feel powerless and now I must be humble and yield up even my anger and hate?"

"Yes." Lisette confirmed. "Viper took what wasn't his to take and gave you things you never asked for."

"Is that the definition of violate?"

"Maybe, but in Christ you're too strong to be a victim. You forgive and take away your enemy's power to substantiate the pain. You say, 'Game over. I forgive you.' Then you work through the anger and hate, you stand up." She did, pulling Jaclyn up with her as Ida took her other hand. "We gather the courage God gives us and we seek Him for the strength to take the next step toward the hope of our healing. You know courage isn't about being brave, it's about trusting God to give you the strength you need to fight in His power. Are you ready to take another step?"

"Yes." She closed her eyes and took a deep breath. On the exhale she said simply, "Game over Viper, I forgive you."

"That deserves cake," Lisette exclaimed as Ida hugged her tight.

They all sat, ate. Ida with her tea, Jaclyn with a cold glass of milk and Lisette with her dark hot coffee.

"This is good," Ida said. Smiling as Jaclyn agreed. "How do you feel?"

She nodded. Said, "Good." Kept nodding.

"Feelings are the caboose not the engine on our trains. We know the right thing, we do it and then later we begin to feel it. Sometimes much later. Time is always an element in God's design for growth or healing."

"That is wisdom," Ida nodded. Smiled. "But I meant, how do you feel physically?"

"Sorry." Lisette laughed. Blushed. "I should shut up." She ate some cake, pointed the fork at Jaclyn to answer.

"Fine. Physically, I'm feeling about sixty percent. And I like the train analogy. It helps." She was using her fork to pick up the last of the crumbs as she told them both, "Thank you."

Ida nodded. "I think we are a good team together. Perhaps we should try this way. Together."

Lisette nodded, "I like the idea. Jaclyn?"

"Yes."

"Then we'll see you this week at your appointment." Ida smiled, taking a sip of tea. "Time to go."

"You're kicking me out." She laughed.

"You're ready to leave," Ida stated seriously. "You have classes tomorrow."

"You're ride is here." Lisette announced. "Don't keep Tiki waiting. The traffic will be horrible in another hour."

She keyed the lock code then turned at the door, "Happy Birthday. Thanks for the cake."

She toasted her with a full fork. "My pleasure."

Brett slouched down in front of a vid screen, the shoulder of his throwing arm in an ice wrap, his other hand keying through the selections on the remote as he set his PDA aside. He couldn't believe she'd had another echo. He'd been worried about who she had been around when it happened, jealous, insanely jealous until she told him that this echo was different. She'd been angry. Her hormones causing rage instead of lust. By the end of the conversation he could hear the weariness in her voice, sense she'd been through an intense weekend at Heatherwood. Then he'd asked the question, had it just been about anger? Had she ultimately cycled?

There'd been a pause. She'd said softly, "Yes."

"I'm sorry, Babe." He was tender and very aroused. "Are you better now that it's over?"

She confessed she was, felt like a weight had been lifted off her shoulders. Asked him about his day. He was sweet and encouraging. Told her he missed her.

It was the truth. He missed her intensely. He would send flowers tomorrow. She said goodnight with that smooth sultry voice.

He used the remote to look at the screen selections, highlighted the title. *Eros*. He'd seen the title the first night he was here. Wondered about it for a few days, reading the recap of the movie only tempted him further. Finally he watched. He'd seen it every night since. An erotic movie about a man seducing a reluctant woman by giving her a small dose of Eros in a drink with her dinner. The starlet was a tiny buxom brunet. She had a cool demeanor when the dinner started that slowly melted down to a fervent need for the man when the drug took effect. The method was repeated over several occasions, greater doses, the sex scenes changing in intensity until the final scene when the woman dies from the extreme pleasure of the overdose and the man is left holding her limp body in his arms.

Now that he knew how it ended, he turned off the movie before the final scene and dwelt on the buildup, the transformation of the woman, the pleasure of the man.

LaRue's friend, Suzanna Santiago, had called him again. She came by for a late drink. She was tiny and buxom like the starlet from the movie. She was Cuban, her accent spicing her R's. She had a cool demeanor, but with a glass of wine she began to warm. After the first bottle she cuddled. By the second, she was making suggestions. Tonight he took her to his room. Reenacted his favorite scene from *Eros*. But she wasn't Jaclyn. And the buildup wasn't worth the hype, the pleasure very quick to leave him. The guilt a burden that confession didn't seem to cleanse.

So he closed his eyes and just daydreamed . . . about that day, when Jaclyn had been so perfect.

Jaclyn signed in to the computer in the basement, inserted her schedule and received her assignment. Pool laps and weight lifting then a ten-minute VR drill.

After the workout she donned the headgear and the sim suit. "Engage."

She found herself driving a taxi cab. Command told her an address, she used the GPS to navigate there, waited in front of the nondescript building in a pouring rain. The door opened, shut. The emerald of Christie's eyes linked with her own in the rearview mirror.

"Where to?" Jaclyn asked her

"Just drive," her aunt answered. "I'm sorry, Jaxie. I pushed too hard."

"Nothing to do with you," she told her aunt what she knew was true. "Everything to do with Eros. This time the echo made me want to kill someone, avenge myself." She watched her aunt's eyes turn troubled.

"I did that. Making you—

"No. The Viper, what he did. It's coming out. I need to work through the fact that I was raped, drugged, violated. I need the truth to set me free, Ida assures me Lisette will help us find it."

"How can I help?"

"Train me." She smiled.

"Maybe you need—

"No." She shook her head. "Train me. Be hard. If I can't take it," she shrugged, "Then I'm not up for it. You'll tell me."

"You're up for it," Christie was firm. "You're doing exceptional." She warned, "We'll be in for some trouble here. Do what I say."

There was a sudden and shocking collision, metal screaming against metal. Speed, turns, directions called out and executed. There was a gun in the glove compartment, she got it out, used it as her aunt ordered. Bullets bounced off pavement did more damage under the carriage then aimed into tires. In moments one car was taken care of, after two more blocks they'd lost a second. She told her aunt what she'd remembered, learned, feared and dreaded. She confessed she'd forgiven Viper but didn't feel like she had at all. She still hated him. Hotly. Was frustrated. Intently.

She drove through an alley, raced up a one-way street the wrong way, then forced the taxi sharply left. She watched the GPS, the traffic, the wet slippery street, navigating toward the destination, then said his name, "Joshua."

"What about him?"

"I'm embarrassed."

"Get over that. Better off mad that he scorned you."

"I need to apologize."

"You don't."

Now she looked at her aunt.

"You don't and you won't," she commanded. "Marc sent them off, so just let it blow over. It's better for both of you. He's just as embarrassed he had to take you down. He got word you're okay. Beside, you don't need the Fury right now. You need Ida and the Termite. A little Brett—

"He's gone for spring training."

"Call Jenna and have her come up. Shop and design. Create something pretty and wear it for his homecoming."

She sighed.

"That's an order by the way. It better rock the headlines, daughter. Here's my stop." She opened the door, the rain loud and angry. "I love you, Jaxie."

"Back at you."

"Keep moving forward."

She pulled off the VR headgear and found herself back in the lonely basement of the brownstone on Sullivan Street. Her lips found Joshua's cross and tags. She held them there, praying for his safety, aching with a sudden loneliness, wanting what wasn't given, her eyes burned with tender tears. She wanted to know what she'd felt for him had been real. But she'd realized feelings weren't truthful. She'd forgiven, regardless of how she felt, she had forgiven Viper, released him to God even if it didn't feel that she'd done anything. She'd obeyed what was commanded, what was right, even if she didn't feel good about it yet. But what was good?

Only God is good.

If she didn't know what was good, how could she know what was best for her?

Only God knew what was best.

With Eros and simulated situations, how could she even know what was real?

Only God knew the truth. *Forgive your enemies.*

She stood, trusted that God was working the best out in her life regardless of her feelings. She was beginning to understand His love, God's longing for her as she longed for another. She took the next step, yielded to cooperate and began another day, following orders.

26

"How is school?" Lisette asked the first question, breaking the ice with small talk.

"I have a new assignment in my legal writing class." She was holding the water bottle with both hands, uncomfortable and impatient, but knowing this was a process and every session a step toward healing that began with small talk. "I think it might be a practical tool where I can channel my anger productively. I could use International Law to cite the Viper for what he did to me in a civil case and write up the indictment for my class assignment."

"I like it," Ida said. "What have you learned so far?"

"The International Inner Port City has its own laws. They're complicated and encompass much yet stand for nothing. Plus everything about what he did is unsubstantiated. There are no witnesses, those that were there are dead or nameless or too loyal to talk. I don't know who put the Rohypnol in my drink to knock me out. I don't know who took me in Babel. I don't know what law I can cite and prove that Viper broke. It's my word against his. So it's one big puzzle to solve to find a crime he can be punished for."

Lisette questioned, “What will you do if there is no law found or enforced to bring you justice on earth?”

“Do not take revenge, my friends, but leave room for God's wrath, for it is written: "It is mine to avenge; I will repay," says the Lord. On the contrary: "If your enemy is hungry, feed him; if he is thirsty, give him something to drink. In doing this, you will heap burning coals on his head." Do not be overcome by evil, but overcome evil with good.' I won’t be overcome.” Jaclyn look at her. “I believe there is also God’s law of sowing and reaping. Viper will reap his consequences eventually. God will judge. There will be justice.”

“Great and perfect justice,” Lisette told her.

“And the way I can overcome evil is to do good. I plan to help others once law school is done.”

“I like the plan.”

“Plans for the weekend?” Lisette asked.

“My friend Brett Webb is at spring training.”

“You called him a friend.” Ida smiled.

“He is a friend.”

“Any romantic feelings?” Lisette questioned.

“There’s common affection. We’re . . . dating now, I guess. He knows my story so it makes it easier to understand the physical intimacy stuff.”

“Physical intimacy stuff?”

“He respects me. Wants a friendship. We hold hands and there’s been a kiss. It’s the way I’ve always been with guys I date. I had . . . have,” she corrected, “clear boundaries. With Brett, I’m still not sure what was real and what was just the drug. If I’m attracted to him or was just tricked into thinking I was by the echo.”

“Any ideas on that, Ida?” Lisette asked her.

“Eros intensifies attraction certainly, but at its essence is simply the physical need, the driving need, to copulate. If you were in a room with a dozen men, you would choose a preference because the drug would demand it."

"I was told I would eventually want all twelve. Be the whore of the earth Viper told me."

"No," Ida frowned. "That is a lie. You would have a preference. Eros is not indifferent."

She nodded her head, wanting to speak, feeling the ice creeping back because of Lisette and her association with *Stratia* and Joshua.

"Keep talking," Lisette encouraged.

"I'm not sure I can." She faced her.

"I'm here to help you."

"I don't want to hurt Joshua."

"Nothing you say would hurt him. This case is about you, not the Fury."

"But it involves him and you work with him, for *Stratia*."

"I work for God, Jaclyn. I love Him and because of His love for me, I want to help you and others. Regardless of what you've heard about me, I serve God with integrity and doing that requires that I want the best for others. Especially *Stratia*. Because they want what God wants."

"Okay." Jaclyn closed her eyes, nodded her head as she prayed and trusted. "I wanted Joshua when the echo happened," she confessed. "I was thinking of him, that morning, trying to find a way to him through my father. I even thought about stealing Dad's PDA and sending Joshua a deceitful message to meet me for lunch. That's not like me."

"No, it's not." Ida nodded with understanding.

"During the meeting, I remember getting angry. Joshua wasn't there. Joshua hadn't called me. I seemed to build a list of all the things Joshua didn't do and suddenly Brett was looking better and better. In fact Brett was doing all the things I was mad that Joshua wasn't doing. In the elevator, when we were crowded up against each other, Brett was all I could think about. What he could give me that Joshua refused to."

"Your levels were climbing. By lunch you were at a twenty-nine. Eros was demanding you find a mate. The physical contact caused the chemistry to adjust."

"So it could be eventually all twelve men . . . if one by one the preference was taken away and the drug was raging in me."

"The situation you encountered on the train is atypical because of the repeated dosing. Most cases of Eros consist of a single dose, like your echo, and cycle to a conclusion."

"But if that man was removed before anything physical happened then Eros is demanding I find an alternative."

"Yes. The water on boil again. Eros is demanding a physical conclusion."

"So when I sent Brett away, even my . . . father was a temptation."

"No. See this truth, Jaclyn, once you discerned the truth—this is Eros—it's deceiving me, demanding its way—you were making right choices, turning from the power of the lust. You called on your stepmother and she brought you to me, child."

"Have you ever had the urge to buy a new pair of shoes?" Lisette broke in.

"Yes." Jaclyn answered.

"Do you need a new pair of shoes?"

"No."

"But you want them?"

"Sure."

"Someone had a cute pair of heels on in a café this morning. I asked her about them. She told me the store. Then said they were on sale. The desire increased to urgency. By lunch I was making my way to the store. Searching the sale rack. I found the shoes. They were cute but uncomfortable. I tried on several others. As I turned from the mirror I realized I had an insane stack of boxes building. Then suddenly a moment of brilliance. The truth was I didn't need any of the shoes. Especially the cute, uncomfortable styles. The truth began to set me free from the urgency to covet and the greed to make a want a need. I thanked the clerk, feeling guilty I'd wasted his time, but I even got over that last nagging and nasty temptation to rationalize my sin. Repented and left.

"Next time I feel that urgency I hope to align it with the truth I know—you don't really need those shoes, Lisette. There are signals you can find in the urgency too, right Ida?"

"Yes. Absolutely. The restlessness. Headache. Building agitation. Your Spirit will grow stronger as you learn to recognize the signals, fight this drug. God's faithfulness will be a continued testimony through each experience. He will give you the power to overcome this chemical lust. I have seen this and you will experience it."

"What would happen if Joshua and Brett were suddenly in the same room and I was on Eros?"

"You would have a preference."

"So when they drew lots on the train and sent in Slim, I had already made a preference for Joshua."

"Yes." Ida nodded. "I had heard it, discerned it because of my experience with Eros, but we trusted God in his choice for you. Marc believed you would be obedient to God's choice because he knew your heart. Lisette concurred as well after speaking to your father."

"Yes, you had always been obedient to the authority in your life. I agreed that your obedience would cause a switch as you say, and believed the one chosen would be accepted by you when the time came. We were intentional with our plans and orders. You were to devise a narrative story of how you met the man chosen, to build a history. The man chosen was to slowly gain your trust, take your hand and begin to make physical contact with you. A woman connects emotionally to a man, the Eros would connect you physically through the building desire and physical contact. I trusted the plan to adjust to the divine conclusion if Fury had been removed."

Jaclyn nodded, thinking. "I wanted Joshua . . . knowing he was across the hall . . . I'm not sure I would have been obedient to your orders with Slim."

"God was in control. Made it clear who His real choice was as Slim revealed his marriage."

"But it seems I have some control," she began to pace. "I have a preference. I have a will. Eros might offer lewd suggestions, even my father, but I have the power to turn from it."

"Yes," Ida agreed.

"But at some point, when the drug reaches an optimum level my choice is to make a preference from the options available or self-destruct." She looked at Ida. "Joshua told me what happens, that Eros can kill me. My ovaries would erupt and internal bleeding would occur."

"Yes. It's similar to an ectopic pregnancy or an ovarian cyst that ruptures."

"There would be great mental anguish as well," Lisette added. "The will in a great battle against the drive of the flesh."

"Insanity."

"It is rare."

"But cases have been cited. Where?"

"In the East. When the Sheiks were first experimenting with the drug."

"They left women alone," she guessed. "And watched what happened."

"That will not happen to you," Lisette stopped her thoughts at once. "You're protected, monitored by Ida. You will not be left alone to Eros' destructive lust. You will not."

"But if I was," she looked at Ida. "How long could I stand before it killed me?"

Ida only shook her head.

"What level will my ovaries erupt? A hundred? More?" She sighed in the silence. "What level was I up to on the train when Joshua finally . . . helped me?"

“A hundred,” Ida told her. “It was the same with the echoes in Heatherwood. You were almost at a hundred when you finally took the treatment. Most women will self-treat by eighty, some strain against the drug with their wills, others accept treatment much sooner at levels as low as thirty. In all your situations, you were almost at a hundred. Above that there is severe mental distress and by one-twenty-five there will be a physical result.”

“Ovaries rupture. Game over.” Jaclyn frowned.

“You have a strong will,” Lisette countered. “And through the Spirit that power can grow stronger, maintain control until you get to Heatherwood. You are not alone,” Lisette promised her. “God will never leave you.”

Jaclyn nodded.

"Do you believe that, Jaclyn?"

"I don't understand it. How He could be there. There." She looked up, the anger hot and the shame swelling to glaze her eyes. "He was there when he raped me. The horrible first time and the times when I . . . stopped fighting. He not only saw it all, He was with me, there."

"Yes."

"And He did nothing."

"See past His sovereign permission to allow it. He is God, His ways unsearchable. Holy."

"I don't . . . understand."

"Did He do nothing?"

She blinked. Lisette and Ida waiting. She saw their compassion, the balance of love and truth here to help her. "I'll think about that."

27

"The Badger rules the states," the man across from him recited the phrase with a smile, a very cunning smile as they played a game of chess. LaRue didn't trust the Russian but he needed him. What he offered. What would slip from his lips when he had a bit of the vodka from the homeland. He filled his glass, watched an arm patterned with color move quickly to accept the offer of more drink. On his chest would be the badger, the Russian badger that ruled the United States. He was high enough to know things here and far enough removed from Russia to not know everything about LaRue.

In a card room of a yacht club LaRue toyed with him over the chessboard, countering his moves, setting himself up to play well but loose. He understood the game, the complicated hedging and profiling of an opponent's strategy. He already knew this man's moves, played into them, thinking about his next move on the greater game board. He had the pieces set now, each rook, knight, bishop. There were the pawns, his dog, Jenny Brooks, Suzanna Santiago, the erotic movie *Eros*. The diagonally moving Bishop of the Sizzle was consistently successful. The incoming Knight would be making her appearance very soon, doing her part to distract. And of course the infamous Rook of the tiny white pills of Eros's cupid. The new pill form was innovative yet subtle. Easy to slip into liquid or even cook with. The results a meager blush compared to the full onslaught of the pure liquid lust of Eros. But he only needed a blush for this game to play off his King piece Brett Webb. This game was about putting him in checkmate, once he was there, the game would be almost won. Jaclyn would trust him. And trusting him, she would be captured. A willing tiger by the tail, returned to his father with hardly a fight.

His opponent made a move, smiled and LaRue was wise enough to know others were involved in this complicated game he'd set into motion. Pendragon was lurking. The Viper watching. A Badger balancing power. A stolen Arabian filly and a certain Sheikh a wildcard. There was U.S. law and order. *Stratia's* holy war and Interpol's shifting agents. The organized crime families of America watching him. The disorganized gangs of her underworld curious. The Tiger's security force too tight. And he was virtually an unknown one-man show. A computer genius with hired help and fat pockets. His entrepreneur ideas were working splendidly in the land of opportunity. It was so easy to make money here on the internet.

"Like I told you, here, in America, the Badger will get his cut. I told him you had no colors. You were your own man with lines yet filled in." There was a laugh, a mock. "He called you a bastard. An orphaned bastard." There was a laugh. "The Viper—

"Has many sons."

"Your mother was one of his whores, eh?"

"There is little opportunity for me in Russia." He countered the move with a show of anger and impulsion.

He grunted. Nodded. Agreed. "You have been honest. Came to pay homage. The Badger is happy with the arrangement." Another smile, LaRue lost his queen.

"I'm sure he is." He studied the board, asked the important question. There was an answer. The information he needed. He made the last move. Business completed.

"Checkmate." The man smiled as he moved his Rook. "The shipments are on time?"

LaRue sighed, frowning but nodded as the fool took the clear advantage he had set up. "Customs can always be challenging."

"But the shipment will be here as agreed, eh?" He smiled at his nod. "Anything you need?"

"I will let you know." LaRue rose, leaving the obligated payment behind.

28

"Babe." Brett took her hand with a smile and a tender look as he came into her brownstone. "I've missed you." He brought her into his arms. They'd been apart for two months. The separation giving her time to heal, work, stand steadier. She felt as if she'd swept much of the chaos away. Her thinking clearer. But as he held her she realized how lonely she'd been, how much she missed his friendship. She clung tighter, breathed him in, waited, open for what God would move in her, allow to surface.

There was an indistinguishable male sound of pleasure, posturing as Brett drew her body up into his arms, perhaps feeling her willingness he kissed her, whispered, "I missed you. Really missed you." His gaze swept her face, she felt his body fit to hers. "Ah, you're beautiful. You look terrific." He smiled, standing back to view her, studying every detail.

She wore a dress, knee-skimming and snug. It was lilac, with wide cascading ruffles that shifted down her body like the petals of a delicate flower. The jacket a crocheted sweater the same color and over it a suede sweeping coat with belled sleeves and the same crocheted detailing. Her boots dyed to match came to her ankles, their zipper tassels amethyst jewels with flowers budding at the base, her tights mimicking the pattern of the crocheted sweater and died to match.

"You look like spring."

"Still too cold for sandals and showing leg in D.C.."

"Your face has color."

"I sat outside and studied today. You're already summer tan after all that time in Florida."

"You're sure you don't mind tonight? We can just go somewhere and be alone."

"No. I want to meet your friends."

There was a table full of Nationals players in a private room in a famous restaurant. They came in last, Brett presenting her. The men standing, shaking hands, meeting her as she met players, girlfriends, wives. There was a dark red wine with the rare steak, good food, lively conversation, most centered on baseball and the upcoming season. She listened, watched the bonding that had taken place during their training camp between Brett and his teammates. They shared dessert. Cheesecake and strawberries. He watched her finish the last sip of wine, apply lipstick.

"Your lips are purple." He grinned.

"Lilac," she corrected. Showed him the tube end, the name. "Lilacs in bloom. Jenna," she confessed with a shrug.

"Lilacs in bloom," he grinned against her lips, a soft kiss, eyes open. "Jenna. When can I meet her? LaRue said he'd fallen head over heels. Love at first sight."

She laughed. "He hardly ate a bite of his dinner the night they met. I knew it was serious when he ignored his wine. We drank a bottle," she confessed. "Just me and Jenna. He's got me hooked."

"Really? Little wine lush now. Up to two glasses?"

"One." She lowered her lashes. "Maybe two, if the dinner goes long."

"Then he escorted you to the spring shows in New York. I saw the paper."

"Brett Webb's Honey and her Texas designer take in the spring shows," she cited the by-line.

He drew her against his side, pressed a kiss to her ear. "Brett Webb's Honey. It's Brett Webb's Babe, don't they know."

"They need to be corrected." She smiled.

"I'll make sure of it."

"We had a great time. Jenna liked LaRue. I knew they'd click."

"Did they? Click?"

"Um. I warned her off a bit. LaRue is French, fickle. I don't want Jenna hurt."

"Of course not. I'll talk to him."

She nodded. "Please. Tell him to keep it platonic. They'll be better friends."

A teammate called his name. "You guys coming?"

"Want to go with the guys and dance at the club scene?"

"I'm tired."

"Come over for a while."

"Um."

"A while," he touched her hair. "We haven't had a chance to talk much."

"My place," she suggested.

"Your place? Really." He smiled now. "Okay then."

"Next time," he promised his teammates.

The starting catcher pointed at them. "We'll hold you to it. Great meeting you, Jaclyn."

She nodded. Exchanged a smile with his girl.

They were the last to leave. Her security joining his to lead them out.

"It's raining, Miss Cooper." Tiki had an umbrella ready. The night sky lit up with lightning and sound. Fat drops of rain falling sporadically through a cold spring night. She moved against Brett. Let him shelter her under the umbrella as they waited for their car to be pulled up with his teammates.

She was startled by the camera. Its flash an uneven beat to the natural lightning. Brett quick to defend. Deflect. The questions came. About spring training. Their night out. Names called out of famous players. Then her name was called. Who was she wearing tonight.

She didn't answer. Just smiled and let Brett throw out the sound bite. "Jenna Cooper. Lilacs in Bloom."

"Jaclyn, are you coming to opening day?"

"My Babe wouldn't miss it."

They made their escape, found a place on her back patio to watch the lightning show. The fireplace shared its warmth. Brett talked about Florida and spring training, teammates. Jaclyn about school, her brothers, family. Curled up under his arm, he told her again, "I missed you, Babe. Missed this. Being together." His ways always tender, attentive. His kiss soft against her forehead as he stroked her hair. "I was proud tonight. Proud to walk you in, to walk you out on my arm. Show you to the team, to the world. You're beautiful," he told her. "Lilacs in bloom."

She slowly smiled.

He slowly brought her closer, holding her gaze, drawing her gently with a hand to her slender waist. Her body a contrast of curves, valleys as it came into contact with him. His memories ripe. His control stellar. His kiss soft, testing. She gave, tentatively at first, then careful pecks, golden eyes, studying him beneath heavy lashes.

He remembered when she'd kissed him with eyes closed and body clinging. She'd been generous, needy, sensual. Now she was distant, demure, dependably disciplined. It was all there, still, under her calm surface. A raging river. A rushing, powerful, hungry need. Dammed up. Controlled. Waiting to be unlocked. He simply had to find the key. Love was a locksmith…

"I'm tired," she whispered, but the wine had warmed her again, made her relax and accept his affection.

"Rest here." He lifted her to his lap, cradled her head to him. "The rain is nice. Do you like the sound of water?"

"Yes."

He smiled, talking to her softly, holding her gently.

The Fury growled. It was low and unbidden but the sound came up, spoke. It told him what he wanted to deny. He bowed his head, closed his eyes so he could no longer see the security system displaying the patio of a certain brownstone on Sullivan Street—and the man who had taken his wife into his arms.

He shouldn't be watching this. There were others called to protect them. He shouldn't have clearance for her system. But he'd been given the rights. By her father.

He had rights. To his wife. He had rights… and he'd given them up. She was to have choices.

He prayed. He hadn't words so he simply praised his Father. Praised when inside something raged.

He looked again at the screen. Watched the rich and famous peacock cradle his wife then carry her into her house. He rose. Left Command to prowl. Where was the Russian…

"Brett?" she whispered as he carried her up the stairs.

"Yes."

"W-what are you doing?"

"Taking you to bed." He brushed a kiss on her forehead. "You're tired. Fell asleep in my arms." He smiled. "While I talked about my improved curve ball."

"Um. Sorry."

"Don't be. I'm tucking you in. If I can find your bedroom in this small mansion." She pointed to a door. He took her through it, turned a circle in the large room taking it all in, the desk, the sitting area and vid screen, the large bed. It was a high four poster covered in a brocade floral. He laid her down gently. She watched him unzip her boot, carefully remove it then the other one from her feet. He sat beside her on her bed. Brushed away a strand of her hair, then combed through the length of it, grazing her.

"You shouldn't be here."

"You're right." He looked around her bedroom. She saw him note her Bible, the three pictures beside it on the table. "The president? Do you know the president?"

"My family does."

He put the picture down, the only picture she had of Joshua, then he looked back at her, smiled. "I'll get a picture of us at opening day." Brett leaned over her to touch her lips, holding her gaze. "You're important to me. You can trust me. You should know that by now." He reclined over her body, his hand playing in her hair. "I'm not here to seduce you. I respect you. Who we are. Who I want us to be."

She nodded. "I know that."

"Do you know . . . how beautiful you are to me? Who you are, all that you are—confident, brilliant, healing. Do you know how beautiful that woman is to me?"

She was silent.

"Jaclyn?"

She shook her head.

He smiled. "Then I'm not doing my job, Babe." He gathered her to him, kissed her with a smile then a slow smoldering fire. "I want to love you," he whispered across her lips. There was a pause, his hazel eyes dark and searching her. "I need to leave." Another pause. She still and silent.

Finally he stood, holding her hand. "I'll call you in the morning."

She squeezed his hand. "Thank you for tonight. Dinner."

His gaze swept her. He shook his head, stepped back their fingers separated. He smiled. "Good night."

Brett thought of her. His mind full of his thoughts of her until his imagination led him down darker roads. He reran the erotic movie *Eros* through his imagination. Thought of the starlet, of the slow seduction and the tiny pills the guy had put into her drink making her prone to his pleasure.

He remembered her the first day. Elevators. Eros. Erotic. Needed that power. Craved it until he gave into it. Fed it. Simulated. Stimulated. Substituted. Engorged with the gluttony. Full.

Empty.

Guilty. Convicted. Wanting to turn, but too quickly, he was unsatisfied once again. Left empty to lust and pursue. His mind began to seek, his eyes to find, his thoughts pushed at the light, planned. What he wanted was in the shadows of memory…

As she ran five miles she thought about last night with Brett. She'd wondered over it. The subtle shift. The marked possession. The kisses. The change. Brett had been different last night. The way he looked at her, touched her. Something was different. Him? Her? It was stirring her to understand, unsettling her. He said he'd missed her but there seemed to be more. He wanted to love her. Did he mean physically? Emotionally? It made her anxious.

She spent two hours with Liu Xuing. Four hours in law classes and another three at the law library. Then stopped to speak with Ida and Lisette. She was too restless to sit. Stirring her tea, pacing, looking out the window of the office. The view of high rises, just a glimpse of the Capitol. A sliver of the dome in the near distance.

"You are restless?" Ida asked.

"Um. I've checked my levels. I'm low, a six."

Lisette stated flatly. "What is it you're stirring with that tea?"

"I don't know, I'm feeling... bothered." She looked at the reflected movement of clouds on the glass office building next door. "I've been processing all day and I still can't figure it out."

"When did *feeling bothered* start?" Lisette asked.

"Last night, maybe. I had dinner with Brett and some of his teammates. They're back from Florida— spring training." She stirred the tea, let her words just flow with her thoughts. "I wore lilac. I've never worn that color before but it feels like spring and it's still so cold here. Jenna sent the outfit. Dress, sweater, coat, boots—of course. She even sent lipstick." She smiled. Ida reflected it back. "It was a beautiful outfit. Brett liked the color. He tells me I'm beautiful. Compliments me."

"That always makes a woman feel special."

She nodded. "The dinner went well. The guys had clearly bonded during training. Inside jokes. The banter. Teasing. Like my family when we get together. I mostly listened. Brett has a good personality. The guys like him. . . he's always attentive, affectionate to me."

"Do you like that?"

"I'm affectionate. With family, friends."

"Are you comfortable with him?"

"In public. A little less one on one with the history."

"Then it's *the history* that makes you uncomfortable?"

"Maybe." She sipped her tea. "I don't know. Friendship feels comfortable." She was silent, then just said it, what she would normally keep to herself she said out loud to these women, "When he kisses me I keep my eyes open." She said it. Her teacup clinked on the china saucer. "I'm not sure why." She looked outside. There was a long period of silence. "I saw something in his eyes."

"Did it trouble you?" Lisette asked.

"It must have." She shrugged. "Maybe I'm just confused. He missed me. When he held me I realized I'd missed him too. I'd been lonely for company. My family too far away, Samuel and Jenna busy building their lives like me." There was an exhale. "Maybe I shouldn't take kissing so seriously, but it's always been serious with me. Maybe I'm not being fair with him or myself. Sometimes I think I should have closed the door after the echo. Sometimes I wish . . .

What do you want? I don't know...

Now she looked at Lisette, "Sometimes I wish I knew what God wanted me to do. When Brett was gone the chaos cleared. Now that he's back, I'm restless. Second guessing again. Decisions overwhelm me right now. I don't feel confident or trust myself, my feelings. People tell me what to do, I do it. Like a child. Maybe that's good, right, but I don't know what I want anymore."

"Rest in the knowing that God is with you, always."

"Yes, He let the horrible happen and now He's healing me."

"God let the horrible happen to a man named Joseph too. What man intended for evil God used for good to save a nation. His story is bigger than our story but our story matters very much to Him. He was with you in the horrible and He is with you in the healing and He will be with you in whatever happens today and every tomorrow. God has a purpose and plan for you, Jaclyn. Claim the promise of Proverbs, *Trust in the Lord with all your heart and lean not on your own understanding, in all your ways acknowledge Him and He will make your paths straight.*"

After the Hummingbird left her office, the Termite walked down to see the Bull.

Marc turned from his desk, she saw the irritation before he could shield it. "Hello, Lisette." She was never a welcome face in this hall of warriors. They detested her mind, her invasion into what they could fear or needed to forget. Second guessed any question she asked, pausing to answer. "Lovely weather," she tried to disarm him.

"Triples the commute," he complained.

"How is the country life?"

He smiled now. "We're adjusting."

She asked about the baby. He answered the pregnancy was going as expected. With the small talk at an end she stated her purpose, "I'd like to see Mr. Webb, can you call him in?"

"Is there something I should know?"

"Not yet. How is the Fury?"

"Just back from a mission."

"Did you send word on Jaclyn?"

He nodded.

"Have you given him opportunities to express his own anger?"

"Is he angry?"

Now she smiled.

"His simulators are to orders, you've seen the results."

"Yes. He always tests by the book." It wasn't a compliment. "Tell Mr. Webb we need to give him an update now that he's back from Florida."

"I'll get him in."

The Boys are Back.

Was the headline on the paper. Brett Webb and team mates poised under an awning of a famous steakhouse. She stood beside him in some mystic purple dress like the first flower of spring as rain poured around them. The town was intrigued with their affair. The media too easy to manipulate in a city overflowing with politicians and power. Perhaps famous was fresh, unknown remarkable. He wondered what the Russian thought. He wondered how you quenched jealousy.

There was a knock. He looked up, stood instantly, folding the paper, startled.

Jaclyn stood in his office door. She was dressed in dark gray. Boots, skirt, turtleneck, overcoat. Her hair was queued back loosely in a pony tail of long curls. A black leather messenger bag slung across her chest, hanging at her hip.

They both said, "Hey," at the same time.

"I had an appointment with the docs, then dropped by to see Christie." She pointed in the direction of her aunt's office around the corner. "She's in a meeting. You've been away."

He nodded.

"I know we've got the 'no apology clause' but I need to say I'm sorry for the echo incident in Christie's office now that you're back."

He tried to wave her off.

"No, really. It was horrible. Embarrassing. I was out of control."

"It was Eros."

"And I have to learn how to deal with it and make amends when it affects others. Please accept my apology."

"Okay," he gave her a subtle nod.

She echoed it, her gaze moved to glance around the small room. There was nothing much to see. A SEAL emblem behind the desk and a framed American flag with tattered edges on the opposite wall. His desk clear except for three files stacked and squared off with a corner.

"Your office?"

"It's small. We're not here much. How are you?"

She nodded. Her gaze wandering. There was color on her face, she'd been in the sun but her eyes were shadowed. She looked weary. He asked for courage and wisdom, dropped the paper on his chair and came around the desk. Prayed for words.

"How are you?" he asked again, quieter, closer, now seeking God's own strength to stand where He'd called him to wait with words he never knew how to say.

"You cut your hair." She glanced at him, studied, smiled. "You look like a doctor."

"Do I? Hmm. You look like a law student." He grinned. "I remember the tests." He'd taken her hand, counted her pulse.

"I, ah . . ." Her pulse jumped against his hand. The reaction as intriguing as the way she could sweep lashes over those golden eyes. "Just finished the second round." Her voice was steady, her heart beat aflutter.

"Been studying a lot?"

"Um. Honestly, I've had it up to here with ethics now that I discovered I'm a hedonist."

"No, you're not." He frowned.

"I am." There was a breath. A sudden awareness of her body as it rose and her outer coat brushed him on her exhale. He let go of her hand, pocketed his, prayed.

"Your pulse is steady, strong. Been . . . swimming?"

"Running." She brushed at a tendril of hair, pushed it back. Her knuckles healed and whole, her hands feminine, pretty, her nails polished. "I started back a few weeks ago. Keep waiting for spring to come as I trod through the slush."

They talked about the weather. He thought of her dressed in purple. Decided she looked elegant in gray. Agreed he was glad it was rain and not snow last night.

Then she asked him softly, "Can you have dinner?"

"That meeting with Christie." He checked his watch. "I have to be in it in ten minutes."

"Right." She gave a nod, backed away quickly. A smile covering up embarrassment. "Good seeing you. Thanks for understanding. About the echo. I am sorry. If I hurt you. I know. That wasn't easy. I was out of control. And you tried so hard not to hurt me." Color had risen high and hot on her face. Her words fading softer and softer, now with a swallow, silence. Then a smile strong again. "Anyway . . . God bless and keep you, Joshua."

"Jaclyn." She paused at his door. Her hand holding onto the frame. Tightly. Her brows lifted over weary eyes that were fighting emotion. "Really. I have a meeting, Baby Girl."

She pressed her lips together with the mention of that name, gave a confirming nod. "It's okay. I just needed to talk." She moved. He was faster.

He stopped her with a touch. Covered her hand with his on the metal frame, holding her at the door. "About?"

"I don't know." The gold of her eyes suddenly glistened. "That's the problem right now—I don't know anything, Joshua, except about ethics and the parts of a contract and the United States Constitution and that the International Inner Port City doesn't enforce any laws and the fact that I miss my family and I feel isolated and alone and often angry."

"You're never alone."

"Knowing God is always with me doesn't mean I'm not lonely and confused," she argued sharply then said, "Tired. Fighting depression and the anger daily. Still having nightmares." She looked away, gave a mocking laugh. "And making straight A's amidst it all. My intellect is strong but my emotions are a wreck and my will is confused. You need to go." She tried to.

He held fast. "I've got time."

"I need to go now. Really."

She lowered her hand. His followed, still covering, then holding.

"I pray for you, every day, Jaclyn. I know the healing process is painful. It takes endurance. What you're working through is difficult."

She nodded, looking down. He squeezed her hand. Suddenly she squeezed back, her whole body taking a very deep breath.

He tucked that delicate tendril of unruly hair back from her face and spoke sacred words over her. The prayer short. Complicated. "You're strong, courageous—

"Don't." She stopped him. Brushed a tear away. "I'm not those things."

"Baby girl," he denied with a growl then a grin. "You're blessed with those things—

"How can you know what I am? You've never seen me. Really. Who I was. Who I wanted to become before. You've seen me after . . . on Eros. Falling apart. Flaking out. High on Ares. Afraid. Angry. So angry it broke out against you. If you'd have seen me before. It would be different." She lifted her chin. "I was smart, pure, certain. If I'd have walked into your life then, you would have wanted me. Now . . . it's shameful."

"Jaclyn," he tried to stop her.

"I don't blame you. Really." She shook her head. Pulled away. Walked away. And he watched her go. Looked up to see Eli standing by the door.

"Another invitation?"

Joshua nodded.

"Tickets to the playoffs, I hope."

He shook his head. "Not hockey, dinner. She wanted to talk."

"Ut-oh."

"She seems weary."

"You have that effect on women, sir."

"What women?"

"Exactly my point." Eli led the way to the meeting.

29

“The son-in-law,” Jaxson showed his wife the read out, flashing a smile that winked with dimples as they sat in her home office.

“Jaxson,” Lexi warned.

“I like saying it,” he bantered back, “It’s my son-in-law. The Fury. Sounds like a linebacker from Pittsburgh.”

She swatted him. “I’m not supposed to know that privileged information, counselor.”

“We’re alone. If you’ll be quiet, I’ll put him on speaker.”

“No,” she warned. “You’ll talk to him. Privately. Respectfully.”

“I love the boy.” He answered the PDA. “This is Jaxson.”

His smile faded. Lexi took his hand.

The conversation was brief. The information critical. He hung up.

“The Russian?” she asked her husband.

“No. The daughter.” He sighed. “She stopped by his office. She said she was looking for Christie. Asked him to dinner?”

“Um.” There was a beat of silence. “That’s not like her, to ask—"

“He knows that. She asked him to the hockey game. Had him shell shocked with that and the flanking maneuver that handed those same tickets to Eli and rubbed his nose in it.”

“Yes.”

"She asked me to have him meet us for lunch. We know how that day ended. Then the anger episode."

"Is he concerned about her levels?"

"No. He said she was weary."

"She's in law school, Jaxson. Just finished a round of intense tests. In football language we're talking two-a-days in August heat."

He nodded. "He said she was depressed."

"Of course she is. She's been working through the anger. It's exhausting."

"She said she was angry, lonely, confused. She told him that."

Lexi sighed. "She's also smart. She knows he's sensitive to her, compassionate. Anger won't work. Nor does competition. Brett came back this weekend, they went out. Another picture in the paper." Lexi waved the newsprint. "Maybe she's trying to—"

"What? Play the victim." Jaxson frowned. "Jaclyn knows better and so do you."

Lexi lifted a brow. "Maybe she's trying to figure out her heart, Jaxson." Her hands lifted, palms up on either side of her body like a scale. Her left hand rose, then lowered to lift the right. "Lexi? Christie? Remember that decision? I finally had to force you to make it."

"I'm not sure I like that comparison. And you know I don't like it when you go into negotiating mode."

Now she narrowed her eyes. "I'm not sure I like the contract you and the son-in-law have come to terms on for our daughter. To give her time and choices. To keep this marriage from her. Maybe they should be together, Jaxson. Working through this together. She certainly doesn't need Brett right now."

"She needs me right now."

"Um."

"Oh, no. Don't 'um' me, counselor."

"This is an appeal, not a negotiation."

"Then speak your mind."

"I think you two might be wrong."

"He wants her to have choices. He wants her to heal."

"I believe he does. But maybe Joshua doesn't want her to choose him. Maybe Brett is his loophole out of this contracted marriage."

"No. I don't believe that. I think he believes that unless she heals independently, she'll always be co-dependent on him."

"She might become co-dependent on you."

"No, as hard as it was for me, we agreed she was to separate by time and space and go back to school. You agreed school was a familiar pattern and Georgetown was far enough away and close enough to family and Joshua."

"She might become co-dependent on Brett Webb. Are you forcing that on her?"

He was silent now, thinking.

"God made the choice for them, that's the truth of this. Joshua is eventually going to have to accept her choice. She's made it. I see it. She's longing for him, Jaxson. Longing for the union and the intimacy that she found with him. It's what you taught her about marriage. What she protected and anticipated. It's why you warned her how sacred intimacy was to be. I sense it."

"As a woman."

She nodded.

"And you're afraid she could substitute."

"It happens all the time. She's weak right now."

"Lonely," he said. "Joshua requested that I see her. The sooner the better."

"Of course. You'll go today." She touched his face. "I want you to talk to Joshua. Give him the loophole. If he wants to opt out of the marriage. Allow it."

"He won't."

"Test him and prove me wrong." She gave a nod. "If I am, then discuss the course of action. God made the choice for them. If he believes that then there's not a loophole and you need to close off the one he gave her. She's chosen. Ask him how he's proposing to begin to woo her. It needs to begin. And he couldn't have a better expert consultant on wooing or Jaclyn than you."

"That was quite the appeal." Now he stood lifting her up into his arms.

"I want to submit," she whispered, "Not manipulate or manhandle . . . or negotiate."

He smiled, touched her lips, knowing her patience with him. The kiss was soft and loving. His words certain and sure. "I need your wisdom, Alexandria. I'm thankful for your heart. You always pursue what's right, truth, never selfishness."

"Sometimes selfishness," she countered. "Sometimes I negotiate, manipulate. I'm not perfect."

"You are."

"I forced you to choose. Got impatient with Christie. Remember?"

"I remember that God made the choice for us," he reminded her, holding her gaze, adoring her. "It took Him awhile to get me ready for you. There was some refining that was necessary. I'm still amazed that He loved me so much, that He provided more than just a helpmate. A soul mate, a lover, a friend, a voice of wisdom and lately, you've been my strength."

Her hand was touching his hair, her gaze there too. "Um."

He touched her chin, waited for her gaze. "You're beautiful, Mrs. Cooper."

Now she smiled. "Are you wooing me, Mr. Cooper?"

There were dimples, a lowering of eyes, a recognized move that brought her body intimately against his. "My father told me once the wooing of a wife should never stop. I'm thankful God gave me a little bit of charm with that family secret."

"A little bit." She laughed.

"I guess it's time to share the family secret. Coach the son-in-law how to charm the daughter."

"Um." She kissed him, smiling.

"Daddy?" Jaclyn sprang up from her desk, flew into his arms.

"I thought your tests were over."

"Paper next week. I'm struggling with it. What are you doing here?"

"Do I need a reason?"

"He called you." She stepped back, frowned.

"I saw this." He held up the newspaper. Frowned. "When did you start wearing pink?"

"It's lilac."

"It looks like pink. You told me you'd never wear pink and if you did, the first time would be with me." He oinked.

She cracked a smile, sounded out the 'oh-n-ie' pig noise she used to say when she was little. "It's lilac. Purple, daddy. Dusty purple. It has some gray in it, Jenna said."

"Darling shoes, too. What did they cost me?"

"Um."

"Um-hm. Put them on. The whole get up. I want to see you in lilac. You're taking me out. I'm starving for that place with the rubbed ribs."

"Tarleton's?"

"Hurry. I'm hungry."

"Okay." But she went back into his arms. Held tight, breathing him in, clinging. "Give me fifteen."

"Fifteen," he called out with a grin, acted like he hacked his watch.

He put his hands in his pockets. She was tired. She felt thin. He would stay a few days.

She clung close to him. The conversation centered on her brothers, then spread to family news. The NFL draft was coming up. The Kentucky Derby. Opening day for baseball. Finals were almost here. Summer was discussed. She would be making up her fall semester in two summer sessions.

"Did you talk to him?" she finally asked. Her gaze was down on her plate, her fork pushing lettuce around.

"Yes, Jaclyn."

She nodded. "I asked him out to dinner." She frowned. "He turned me down. Again."

"He had a meeting. He works for a living."

"He doesn't want to see me."

"He knows what you need. Time to heal. He cares about you."

"So he called my father."

"Yes. And I'm glad he did. What did you want to talk to him about?"

She shrugged now. "I don't know," she said softly.

"Can you talk to me?"

She nodded. "Can we go home?"

They sat on the patio, she curled into his arms. They looked at the stars. Clouds moving swiftly tonight, covering stars only to reveal others. They'd been here before over the years. Her under his arm, looking up.

"Brett was here. Last night. We sat outside."

"Like this?" he grumbled.

"It was raining. I was tired. Fell asleep. He carried me upstairs. It startled me. He saw it. Smoothed it over. He promised he wasn't here to seduce me. I trust him. He promised me I could. I do, Daddy."

There was silence.

"I don't trust myself. I don't know what I feel."

"Are you attracted to him?"

"Sure, he's great. But I don't think about him like I do Joshua. So am I substituting?"

"Are you?"

"I saw Joshua. He took my pulse. When he touched me, everything inside me jumped. Did that ever happen to you?"

"Sure. A few beautiful girls made my pulse jump before Lexi."

"Rachel?" she asked about her birth mother.

"Your mother is beautiful. When we met it was fast and furious. A weekend. There was never anticipation. There was desire that was immediately satisfied. Lust."

"I'm a child of lust," she sighed.

Her father tipped her face up. "You're a miracle. Never forget that. Created for a purpose."

"And lust, what is lust—that strongest of desires? I need to understand it now that I fight Eros."

"Lust," he thought for a moment. "It's like setting a leaf on fire. It's easy to light, blazes fast, then it disintegrates. Gone. Lust doesn't last. It never satisfies."

"And love?"

"Love is a kindled fire. It's committed. Controlled. It's nurtured, needy and jealous. It takes time, energy, fuel. It blazes at times, it smolders at others. Gives light and warmth. Sometimes it burns. There can be heartache when we love. God is love, so our love is a reflection of that relationship."

"Love anticipates?" She looked at him.

"Love has a longing. It seeks, waits. You know the verse, what love is. Patient, kind."

"Yes."

"Lust is self-centered, self-serving, a sensual fixation, an obsession in the mind. It's powerful and deceptive. Temporary."

"Like Eros," she defined. "I understand that power."

Jaxson pressed a kiss to her hair. "You know the difference, Jaclyn."

"How did you decide? With Lexi and Christie, Daddy."

"God decided for us. He knew what was best."

“How did He tell you?”

“He has a way of confirming things. Opening doors, shutting others. Moving hearts and minds. He’ll give you discernment, peace. Ask and He’ll show you. Surrender to Him and He’ll be faithful to show you the way. Trust Him.”

She asked her father, "Is God always with us?"

"Jesus promised He is with us always, until the end of the age."

"So He was there?" Her voice had dropped, the question childlike yet toned with temper.

"Yes."

"Let it all happen."

Her father nodded, then said again, "Yes."

"Saw it all happen. Me with him. Viper doing those things to me. And Jesus was with me, there?"

It was like a cloud moved over her father's eyes, the blue darkened. "Yes," he answered.

Then he wiped a tear. It fell too fast for him to fight, his eyes suddenly flooded and she buried her face into the warmth of him, breathed in the smell of him as she held him and he her because she suddenly knew. She knew what her Abba Father was doing when all that was done to her. Her daddy was crying.

"God loves me and has a purpose," she said the words and believed them with more conviction. "We can trust Him," she stated the verse she had been dwelling on from Proverbs.

"Yes." Her father exhaled. His voice steady. "We can trust Him, Jaxie. Tell me about your friends here?”

“Tiki and Dena?”

“In law school.”

“Oh.” She was silent. “They already had their cliques from the fall. I was the new girl. Nowhere to fit in.”

"I don't think you're trying to fit in. You're cave dwelling. Coming and going to class. Join a study group."

"My grades are good."

"Help someone else."

"I'm not looking for dates, daddy. Life's complicated enough."

"Look for girlfriends."

"Who can understand all this?"

"All this?"

"Me. Eros echoes. Anger. Two shrinks. Security. Famous boyfriend. The Fury."

"How about darling shoes. Movies. Complaining about the weather and the ridiculous amount of work you have on legal writing."

"I'm a hedonist, by the way."

"You are not." He laughed.

"Do you know what a hedonist is?"

He tickled her now. "I know I didn't raise a hedonist. I raised a fine Christian woman."

"Um."

"No, um. That's one thing you know. There's no doubt."

They met on a golf course. Jaxson playing with a foursome of family. Senator Layne Lexington and his brother Bennett with their stepfather Curt Daniels the retired astronaut. Joshua declined to be the fifth, rode along with Jaxson in the cart. He gave a briefing on the Viper, an update on the profilers' theories and his prospective. On the third hole came the surprise attack.

"Do you love my daughter?"

"Sir?"

Jaxson got out of the cart, choosing a club he told him, "I'll give you time to think that through."

Joshua watched him walk to his ball, set up the shot, take it. It was a good one, the ball bouncing on the green. When he came back to the cart and sat down he looked at Joshua and smiled.

"Yes. I'm committed to her."

"Interesting." Jaxson drove. "The way you put that. So, it's a choice to love her."

"Love is always a choice. It's a commitment, not a feeling."

"Is it ever a feeling?" He was out of the cart again. Leaving him to think. Two-putting the hole for a par. Bennett sank a long one. There was a moan from Layne, money changing hands between brothers. The scripture weaving through his thoughts, what love was defined as by the apostle John. God's love. Sacrificial, paternal, giving. A fruit of the spirit was love in action. Obedience was love in truth. The definition given to the Corinthians listing attributes and contrasting all the things love was not.

"We can feel love, sir," he told his father-in-law.

"We certainly can." He nodded. "Deep, to our soul, when it is revealed. I love my wife. She loves me, knows me, Lexi is one with me. I couldn't keep this covenant from her, Joshua. She's known from the day we spoke."

"Yes, sir."

"She is jealous over my faithfulness to her. Have you ever felt jealous over Jaclyn? Seeing those pictures with Brett. Hearing him talk about her to you in the meetings you're forced to sit through. Knowing she's spending time with him, building a relationship with him." He stopped the cart, but this time he looked at him, waited for the response.

"Yes, sir. I've felt jealousy."

"A committed love is jealous over its object of affection."

A challenge was called out from Layne. Jaxson smiled. Whistling now as he chose his club. Accepted the bet. Prodded his cousin. They hit their tee shots. Jaxson's going the farthest. Jaxson drove on to the next tee. Taking up the rear of the cart line.

"Alexandria," he told him, "The name I call my wife when things get a little . . . serious. She disagrees with our present tactics. She believes this forced separation is wrong. She wonders if you are looking for a loophole out of this contracted marriage."

"A loophole, sir?"

"Yes, legal term. Alexandria believes you might be hoping Jaclyn will choose Brett Webb. Give you a way to opt out of your own commitment. Do you want out?"

"I am committed," he told him. "To the way of this. The waiting. She is to have choices."

"Brett Webb was not her first choice that day. You were."

"I didn't instigate this arrangement with Brett and Jaclyn. *Stratia* did."

"But you agreed."

"To the tactics. It should lure out the Viper and is ultimately for her good."

"And now Brett has become a pawn in a political game of espionage and has the potential to be an emotional substitute for what my wife tells me my daughter is longing for—the intimacy she found with you. How long should we let this *good* go on? Parade your wife on another man's arm. Confuse and tangle up her emotions. Tempt her to become co-dependent on Brett Webb. Tempt Brett to become attached to her. Deceive her for the greater good?" He was out of the cart again, letting the questions and their condemnation remain unanswered.

"I am not deceiving her selfishly but sacrificially. I think it is best for her," Joshua said at once when Jaxson came back.

"But we are deceiving her. She's married. Brett's part of a mission. She is blind to these facts."

"She can't see everything, sir. Her life is at stake, her enemy loose, a plan in action to capture him. It's a 'need to know' situation. She doesn't need to know all the facts, just the information that affects her part. I don't know all the facts, sir. I'm just told what to do, where to go. Often others have gone before me or stand behind me. See the bigger picture. Marc is networking. Wisdom overseeing. The Eagle orchestrating. God sovereign over it all." He sighed now, looking at his hands, drawing back his passion. "She needs time, sir. To heal. This mission needs time to work."

"I agree, but you have an obligation to fight for her."

"I want her to choose."

"Her stepmother believes God chose for you both. Do you?"

"God chose but there is always a moment when we agree to cooperate. Free will."

"Or the mysterious and overruling sovereignty of God has already predestined our purposes and we need to accept and cooperate with what has gone before us and stands behind us."

"I was given a choice that day. I didn't have to do it this way, make a covenant with you, accept her. But I obeyed without exception the choice of God. I'm committed to your daughter. I don't want a loophole out. But Jaclyn was never given a moment to choose me. She was victimized by Eros."

"Lexi believes she has chosen, son. She also believes she's weak, lonely, in danger of substituting her affections. She needs friends, instead she is cave dwelling and separating herself to seclusion. Her socializing is done with family or Brett Webb."

He went to the green, putted, winning the bet with his cousin. Receiving a high five from his uncle. Bennett issued a challenge.

Jaxson came back chuckling, handed him the two hundred dollar bills. "Hang on to those for me. I'm up by two. Beating Bennett at his game." He grinned at Joshua.

He was scowling at the money.

"Offended by the gambling?"

"No, sir."

Jaxson drove the cart, explained, "It's our way of competing. Even hundred is always the family wager. It's not about the money, that" he nodded at the bills, “Is just paper tally marks. The same bills have changed hands for about twenty years between the cousins. Although Ellen seems to collect a bit of a stash. In fact all the girls do. We outnumber them but they tend to outsmart us. Women have better instincts. Another reason I trust my wife with this current situation. She knows a woman’s heart.”

He was looking at the money. “This doesn’t mean much more to me than paper. Money,” he clarified. “I respect its power, see the discipline of its stewardship, and understand it is a necessary means of survival but I’m not after accumulating much of it. I’m never going to be rich or famous, sir.”

“Be thankful. Rich and famous has its limitations and temptations. There’s a great poverty in riches. A high price of fame.”

“I’m a civil servant. I’ll never be able to provide for her like Webb.”

“As Solomon said, “*If one were to give all the wealth of his house for love, it would be utterly scorned.*” You can’t buy love, Joshua. She loves you.”

He bowed his head. “That humbles me.”

“You’ve broken her heart.”

Joshua looked up, saw the compassion on Jaxson’s face. “It was for her good.”

He nodded, “Now you’ll need to mend it. Give her hope. Anticipation. It’s time for a few words. Women treasure words.”

“I can’t make promises right now. I—"

Joshua placed his hand on his shoulder. “Words, son. She’s not ready for promises. Words, that tell her there’s a bit of hope, that she needs to persevere through the healing. We’ll find the right words. We’ve got twelve more holes.”

He grinned as his cousin called out a challenge. “Send Joshua out here to hold the bets.”

“Come on. Looks like we’ve held on to Bennett’s money about as long as he’s going to let us. Some men make a hobby of accumulating paper.”

30

She'd admitted her frustration with the legal paper writing and her father had an immediate solution. Expert consultants. They had flown in this morning. Her grandmother, the honorable Judge Samantha Cooper, coming with Lexi to meet with an Interpol agent who was stationed at the International Inner Port City. Uncle Marc had staged the meeting at a four-star restaurant in a famous Washington hotel. The restaurant was empty, the famous mesquite grill heating up and preparing for the dinner hour when it would open to patrons. Jaclyn let the experts at law debate and she noted on her legal pad the building points as the conversation skipped around her and was recorded for her to analyze and site later.

The Interpol agent Ian Remmi had been stationed in the Global city for four years. He'd been an Irish intelligence agent at one time in the Queen's service, then moved into law enforcement with Interpol. He knew the art of diplomacy, had vast international experience and connections, and shocking red hair. He kept it cut short, his eyes a cool gray, his complexion ruddy. He wore a black suit, a very expensive black suit with a black shirt. Her uncle had told them it was his trademark—black on black with the red hair and the accent.

"So Babel controls the city? Why Babel?"

"Because you can land there on the roof and avoid the border stations. The small check point is known to overlook guns and visas for a price. Thus Babel became like a secret passage way. Control Babel, control the way into the city. You never know who's in charge at Babel. It changes daily, sometimes hourly as people come and go and events occur and hands are slicked with global credits. It could be the Chinese this morning, the Sheikhs at noon, the Russians at midnight. No one can claim supremacy. No one hides their identity. Black is black. White is white. But both can shift to gray. These men are both friend and foe in the same conversation, it all depends on how the current topic affects them."

"So they all know you as Interpol?"

"They know me as an overseer; they call me Red Remmi and know I wear black, keep watch for the justice of our world and sit at a certain table on the second level. Loyalties often shift, the good guys turn bad, the bad guys do good. They all lust for power there. You understand that? There, the power is shifting sand that blows from many directions and covers tracks too well. That is why so many do their darkest deeds within the tight boundaries of the IIPC, a place hardly bigger than Manhattan."

"And the Global laws?"

"The code of law from the Global Alliance of United Nations is used of course, but being a Global city and not a nation or state, it is a melting pot of mixed accountability when it comes to enforcing the law—that's the loophole. The city is 'Global' free property. No taxes but incredible rent. No property is owned of course and commerce is the government. The city is a place where the world is supposed to come together in peace and enjoy its international diversity. They don't like to advertise conflict or crime in the IIPC."

"So hear no evil, speak no evil." Lexi stated.

"What laws do they uphold within the Global boundary?" Samantha asked him.

"The Global Alliance will prosecute murder, when there are witnesses. They're extremely strict with guns. If you don't have the proper paperwork to carry a firearm in the city, you will be detained. You can't touch financials there. Money moves through that town and its banks like blood through a heart. Any currency is accepted and exchanged. Extortion is common place and overlooked unless it affects a Global force or counterbalances its power."

"Abduction?"

"It happens. The Latins take for ransom. The Russians for trafficking."

"Rape."

"The city is Vegas on steroids. You can find what you're looking for whether sex, drugs, or gambling but rape still happens everywhere."

"What kind of drugs?"

"Anything. Since most are legal there. Marijuana is as common as cigarettes," he shrugged. "And like the alcohol, drugs are sold out of vending machines."

"Eros?" Samantha said the word.

"Is an illegal."

"And the Global Alliance made a statement three years ago of outrage concerning that drug." Samantha put on her reading glasses and read from her PDA the statement. She looked up and summarized. "All nations agreed to prosecute at the fullest extent of the law for the possession, sale or production of the drug Eros and all nations includes the International Inner Port City."

"Yes, IIPC is included." He shrugged. "But the Sheikhs are there."

"They invented Eros?"

"Yes, about 25 years ago."

"Have you seen a rise in Eros use outside of their countries?"

"There's always been a discerning demand for the exclusive drug and a tight control on the supply. The Sheikhs are selfish and hypocritical. They want the drug and yet insist it is evil outside their harems. They want to be the sole supplier and have criticized the Russian strains as being rogue, impure and unpredictably dangerous if not deadly. They believe the drug is for the elite, not the common and certainly not for the advancement of prostitution. There has been a very heated moral war for about three years between the two controlling parties. Even evil has its warped ethics, ladies."

"There are not just evil men in that town, there are tourists, innocent people."

"And those people make up the background of the economy. Sometimes a person moves from the background to the foreground and innocently gets caught up in a Global drama. That's why we have such tight controls at the border going in and out of the place. Keep the gun control, demand clear Identity checks. It's not what happens inside, ladies, it's what happens when you try to arrive or leave that usually breaks the Global laws."

"So how can people get guns in or take . . . things out through such high security borders?"

"Good technology. Or slick a palm. Bribery is still at play anywhere in the world. Loyalties often shift with greed."

Jaclyn quoted him, "Black is black and white is white, but loyalties often shift, the good guys turn bad, the bad guys do good. They all lust for power there, you said?"

"Yes."

"Even Interpol?"

"We're not in the IIPC to serve justice or enforce the law; we're there to observe. We watch, we note the shift of power and the exchange of players and report back to Interpol and other agencies. That's really what Interpol does there—reconnaissance and surveillance. If we can help make a clean collar, we assist."

"Is there any law the city upholds?" Lexi asked flatly.

"The city quote-unquote, 'upholds *jus gentium* the Law of Nations'. They enforce it by deporting the accused to their country of citizenship to be prosecuted for felonies. They will gladly sit you down in their jail for ninety days but that is only to make sure misdemeanors are paid in full. Some of them are excruciatingly high for a simple misdeed."

"Like?" Jaclyn was curious now.

"Vandalism. Littering. Counting cards or cheating in the casinos. Shoplifting. And of course the privacy laws are upheld. We can thank a certain Global ruler for creating the blackout in the restrooms. If he wouldn't have been caught on tape doing what we all know he did, we'd still have access to Global restrooms. Now everyone's privacy is protected." He pointed at each of them. "A ladies bathroom can be one of the most dangerous places on the planet now. Remember that."

"Jaclyn, anything else?" her grandmother asked her.

She looked at her notes. Felt the heat of anger but didn't fear the frustration. She asked the question. "Do you know Yrasrevda, the Viper?"

"A Russian Prince. Fourth generation Vor V Zakone, *thief in law.* Family originally from the Baltic region of Old Latvia. Yes, I know who he is."

"Where have you seen him?"

"At Babel," he answered.

"Is he always with a woman?"

He shrugged, there was an edge of a smile. "He is Russian, they collect women like the Sheikhs do horses."

Now she looked up, into his brown eyes. "Did you see him with me?"

There was silence. Her gaze stayed fixed on him. She watched his gray eyes focus, his smile go flat. She could feel the energy change, from cool to very hot. Realized her uncle had told Mr. Remmi nothing of her own history or motives passed a law student that needed research.

"Last August. In Babel." Her voice was steady, almost indifferent. "I was drugged with Ares and Eros. Tattooed with a tiger. Dressed like a harlot. Chained to him. I might have sat with him on his floor, the drugs make memories a bit . . . unclear, but we played craps. I won him quite a bit of money before I escaped that night."

"You were extremely lucky." He sat back very subtly. "Very smart, brave, determined, if you escaped a man like Yrasrevda Tsilevich the Viper."

"Tsilevich? Is that his last name?"

"It is the name on all his legal paperwork, yes." There was a subtle nod. As she wrote it down he spelled it, then stated, "You won't find that on an internet search."

"Thank you for the information. I'd need his full name to make it legal."

"Legal?" His gaze stayed fast on her, she held unwavering. Smiled.

"You're not considering—"

"Like my uncle told you. I needed to interview you to cite authority. I'm a law student writing a paper."

"The first year is impossibly tedious, Ian." Lexi shifted the conversation like the professional negotiator she was.

Her grandmother followed with, "Overwhelming." Samantha sighed. "What they demand you to learn in such a short time."

"What they force you to write," Lexi shook her head. "Predictive and persuasive analysis. The legal memorandums. The motions and briefs."

"Finding the accurate citations of authority or precedents," Samantha began to list cases and motions.

"You've heard of 'legalese.' How no one can understand a lawyer's contract? We can tell you the sky is blue in a hundred thousand words, can't we?" Lexi laughed.

"But plain language can be ambiguous," Samantha defended.

"We should draft for the known, possible and reasonably," Jaclyn cited.

"Exactly." Her grandmother smiled proudly. "A lawyer in the making, Mr. Remmi. We're very proud of her. Ah, Jaxson!" Samantha beamed. "The grill must be hot. This is my son. Jaclyn's father. And a family friend, Joshua Fury."

The men stood, shook hands, chairs were rearranged as they were introduced to Ian Remmi.

"Hello, Jaclyn." Joshua greeted her as he sat purposely beside her. Wearing a dark suit and shirt, open collared and no tie, he smiled.

"Joshua," she answered, putting her pad and PDA away into her bag. Trying to be casual. Totally shaken with surprise.

"We finished early and thought we'd meet you." Her father announced before he kissed his wife.

"How was the golf game?"

"My brother-in-law beat me," he pouted.

"Your game was never golf," his mother reminded him. "Jaxson played football."

"Ah . . . right." Ian nodded. "If I remember right, you were very good at the American variety of the sport."

"He was fast and had great hands." Samantha soothed a hand on his shoulder.

"My mother gloats. Forgive her."

"That's what mothers do. Jaclyn, my beautifully brilliant daughter, shall we have the fish?" Lexi asked.

"This is a steakhouse," Jaxson announced with a growl.

All the women smiled. "I'm after the sea bass. Mother, you?"

"The tenderloin, Jaxie. Joshua, show her," Jaxson insisted. "They have a wonderful tenderloin here. Don't take the loophole and order fish."

Joshua raised the menu. Behind it he smiled, repeated as he pointed to the fish selection, "They have a wonderful tenderloin here."

"You played golf with daddy?"

"I caddied. Held the bets. It was some game. The tenderloin does look good. Side of crab?"

"Um." She looked at the menu. "You talked about me?"

"Of course. And football. The draft. Your brothers. The weather. Politics. I believe we agreed you're a remarkable woman and this restaurant has a wonderful tenderloin. The sea bass," he shrugged. "Couldn't tell you."

"Um." She looked at him, lashes narrowing. "I know what I want."

"I believe you do." There was his grin. Bold and confident as he closed the menu. "Jaclyn will have the sea bass. She knows her mind, sir. I tried to convince her to look at the other choices." He looked at Lexi. "Seems she is foolish enough to choose the fish." He shrugged. "I'll have the Porterhouse. Pittsburg, like you recommended, Sir."

"No loopholes for Mr. Fury, Darling. He's decided."

"Well." Lexi gave a nod, said no more.

"You're having the tenderloin?" Jaxson asked his wife.

"When I can have fish?" Lexi smiled.

"Mother save them."

"Three on the sea bass." Samantha smiled at him. "We do know our minds. Mr. Remmi, how about you?"

"Porterhouse," he nodded at Jaxson. "I trust a man from Texas to know his steaks."

Later they stood on the curb together as a dark limo whisk the Cooper family away. Mr. Remmi lit a cigarette. Looked at Joshua. "She was the missing American," the phrase still seemed to hold a question. He frowned. "I never would have put the two together. She should be broken and bitter not beautiful and brilliant. You found her that night."

"You thought we were impossibly too late. I told you nothing was impossible with God."

He curled a smile. "I might begin to believe you, Fury of *Stratia*." He smoked, thinking. "Her family is connected. Powerful and wealthy. Their women . . . brilliant and beautiful." He exhaled, looked at him. "I'm guessing she's still under your protection. *Stratia* watching."

"*Stratia* is always watching, just like Interpol."

"Do you know what she's up to?" He smoked, looked away. "Thinking she can use the law to prosecute a prince of Russia?"

"I was told she is writing a paper on International law."

"Is she?" His gaze returned. Through a haze of smoke, gray eyes inquired. "Warn her, them, to make sure that's all it is. She doesn't need to show up in the International Inner Port City, Fury, with a paper-thin legal threat that would be dismissed in a matter of minutes. There would be no way to protect her if she leaves America, steps into Babel."

"I'll see she's protected."

"The law could easily turn on her. She took his diamonds, the Czar's Serpent—"

"Which was stolen from the Louvre."

"It's yet to be replaced."

"I wouldn't know about that."

"She was wearing it when she escaped."

"Was she?" Fury narrowed his gaze at Remmi. "Interpol keeps tabs on diamonds but not the abducted women who wear them?"

"We saw the diamonds."

"Did you see the chains he had her in?"

"We saw the tattoo." He smoked.

"You also saw her picture." Fury had stepped closer. "*Stratia* brought it to your attention after the abduction."

"Yes. The system returned an 'unrecognizable' on her face."

"Did you look the other way?"

"No. I didn't recognize her. We didn't know yet. It was only the second time he'd brought her out. He's arrogant. It always gets the Russians in trouble with friend and foe. Law and order."

"Would you have alerted us?"

Ian dropped the cigarette, his foot rubbing it out. "The diamonds alerted us. That he would be so bold to showcase them. Her face would have popped soon after. You know that."

"I know his history is despicable with women."

"The oldest profession is one of his main businesses. The Russians make a fortune off their prostitutes. The Sheikhs pay a fortune for their harems. And here in the West, we keep sex casual and cheap."

"To some of us it's sacred."

"Yes." Remmi lifted a brow and turned a sarcastic smile. "To some of you it is. *Stratia* certainly has its place in the world and our respect, but you can't save them all, Fury. Every day there's evil, everywhere. Not just at Babel although we do seem to be the gathering place for its leaders. Even Jesus had his Judas."

"You're callous, Red."

"Realistic," he argued, then shrugged, "Weary, perhaps, but wiser to its ways. I've seen enough evil." Now he looked away and said carefully. "You aren't his only enemy. Often others do our work for us." He said a name. Sheikh Khaleel. "There is a growing enmiity between them that is coming to a boil over," there was a very pregnant pause, "a filly . . . of all things."

"The horse's name?"

"Haifa," he said in Arabic. "Sheikh Khaleel claims he stole the filly. The Viper insists he is mad, inventing the tale because his stallion lost the King's Cup. Within this public argument, there is also a private disagreement about the Russian strain of Eros. For years the Sheikhs have tersely denied the legitimate power of the Russian strain of Eros. They've made sure it was advertised as unstable and unreliable. Russian Eros like Russian roulette. That urban legend allowed the Sheikhs to hold the market. But lately we've been hearing a buzz, about the drug in tablet form, about to hit mass market.

"Cupid—a low dose pill—from the Russian chemical labs. The Sheikhs are now furious about this possible strain on the free market. They'll even argue ethics. Some call them elitists. Truthfully, it's about economics. The common strain will dilute the profit margin considerably of the elite drug not to mention the chaos it will cause morally. Lust in a pill. Our world's going crazy I tell you."

"Thanks for the intel."

Ian nodded and they parted ways.

They were barely away from the curb when the words just poured out of her. "You took him golfing, with the uncles? Talked about me, daddy?"

"We didn't talk about you—with the uncles. And we talked about a lot of other things. I like the man. He saved my daughter. I'm grateful."

"Did you buy him that suit?"

"What? No," he chuckled. "The man owns a suit, Jaxie. A good one too."

"I've never seen him in a suit. A uniform, every version now and doc scrubs, but not street clothes. I didn't know he owned street clothes."

"Jaclyn." He laughed. "He's a man, not GI Joe."

"And I'm a woman not a little girl to be talked about."

"He looked handsome," her stepmother tried to defuse the argument.

"Um." She stewed. "You could give me a heads up, daddy. Even a text would be nice—*Joshua's coming to dinner.*"

"I thought you'd like to see him. Asked him to dinner. Told him about the porterhouse."

"The porterhouse. So that's why he came to dinner?"

"I've got a beautiful daughter too."

"Beautifully brilliant," Lexi corrected him.

"I don't have to twist many arms with your beauty and good beef. Joshua was off today, had the time."

"So surprise!" She leaned toward him across the open space of the limo. "He decides he has the time, gets suited up for a four-star porterhouse. Pittsburg! But what about me. I'm sitting there without lipstick on, wearing these shoes… Don't you dare smile!" Suddenly she was close to tears.

"Jaxie—"

"Don't." She held up a hand. "Just don't. If you knew how important he is to me. . ."

It was quiet, her looking out the window, seeing her reflection—eyes annoyed, impatient—fighting frustration and an anger she was growing very tired of battling. She breathed, for several beats of heart, she just breathed. "It doesn't matter. Forgive my anger. It was good to see him. Always." The last word was a certain whisper as she looked down.

"No more surprises," he promised her.

"I should say not, Jaxson," her grandmother agreed.

She brooded. "You're *my* dad, you know."

"Don't pout." He covered her hand, squeezed it as he smiled. "You wanted to see him for dinner just the other day. I made that happen for you. And you don't need lipstick. You look beautiful."

"I'm brilliant, had my game face on with Mr. Remmi. My serious no-nonsense shoes and suit." She looked at her stepmother. "And you caught me by surprise, daddy."

"He won't do it again. Surprise you with Joshua," Lexi clarified. "That's a loophole that will no longer be executed or tolerated, Jaxson."

"I thought she'd be glad to see him."

"I'm always glad to see him. I appreciate you bringing him. Just give me a heads up, daddy. And don't pout because I'm right."

"I'm not pouting."

"You are," both she and Lexi said together and they smiled.

31

Her parents left the next day. She went to class and for the first time, she opened herself to the possibility of friends. She viewed the many faces. Asked God for direction even here. Who would He choose to be her friend. Would He help her form relationships?

She was slow to pack up. Usually she was up and out after class. The first to leave, the last to slip inside. Today, she lingered. There was a group discussing the lecture. Debating Freud's idea of good. Someone complained about the paper. It had taken their whole weekend.

"How do you find time to socialize?" A man asked her. He held up the newspaper.

The Boys are Back.

"Is that you?" A woman took the paper.

"I, ah." She scanned the group. Their gazes jumping from her to the paper.

"Do you know Brett Webb?" A guy asked.

A girl countered, "Do you date Brett Webb?"

"Wow." Another guy had taken the paper. "That is you. Can you get tickets to the opener?"

"Can you set me up with second base?" A girl cooed. "He is so delicious."

Now she blushed. Backed away. She'd been here before. Linked to the famous. Used for connections. Autographs. Tickets. She wanted a friend not a fan.

Tiki had the door. "Thanks," she said walking fast. She was embarrassed. Angry. Hurt.

"Do you want the car, Miss Cooper?"

"Yes." She nodded.

Her dad was right. She was a cave dweller. And her cave was safe. Stellar. And smelled like pasta and homemade bread. "You are home," Dena was quick at the door. Taking her bag, helping with the coat. "Miserable day, no? I was thinking where is the sun? We miss the South. I made pasta. A good soup and a sourdough."

"Yes." She smiled. "I smell it."

"Your father said you love pasta. I am sad he is gone."

"Me too."

'Tiki, are you dripping on my clean floor?"

"No, ma'am." But he stepped back to the door mat, wiping feet.

"Look here, Jaclyn. Someone sent you a breath of spring."

There were lilacs in a simple vase that she placed before her.

"Daddy." She reached for the card.

"Don't know now." Dena began to stir pots.

She opened the card.

Spring comes daughter.
Trust in Him who is faithful.
I love you. Daddy

"Daddy," she told Dena. "Tiki, please come and sit. Dena's made enough for an army and I'd love a good conversation." She invited him and began to talk about the NFL Draft as Dena served soup and crusty bread at the counter of her kitchen.

"How was your date this weekend?" LaRue asked Brett as he took a seat in his kitchen. He poured him a glass of red.

"Great."

"I saw the paper. *The Boys are Back.* She looked beyond beautiful," he praised. "Did her cousin design the outfit?"

He nodded, drank. "You two met."

"Yes." He smiled. "Jenna is . . ." There was a longing sigh. "Utterly amazing. I'm quite intrigued." He held up a hand at once, assured, "Don't worry, friend, I won't seduce her. She is Jaclyn's relation. I have my honor. Did you like my friend?"

"She definitely took the edge off."

"Good. You went to Jaclyn relaxed."

"Totally relaxed. Thanks."

"I was glad to introduce you. It is a good tactic before you see her, yes?"

"Oh yeah." Brett nodded. "What are you doing this weekend?"

"Cristina," he said her name with a smile. "I want you to meet her. She is a lobbyist for, the family, I think you would say. Against abortions, saving children, helping families to flourish and kids to find their potential. She does many things. I think the two of you have mutual interests that could help each of your careers. She has a need of your name and you told me, you're looking for ways to give it appropriately for good causes through your foundation here in the city."

"Yes."

"She is like your Jaclyn, reserved, giving me a chase, but another chance this Thursday. Shall we bring the girls together for dinner? Meet at that cozy Italian place first? Then next weekend before you have all those road games, we'll invite a few of your teammates over and we'll have a party. Give the girls safety in number."

"Sounds like a plan."

She had racked her brain for two days, listening to the interview tape with Mr. Remmi, looking at options, searching International law and past cases from the International Inner Port City for accurate citations of authority or precedents on anything she could use to build something against Yrasrevda Tsilevich the Viper. There was nothing. Nothing criminal she could prove, nothing civil she could cite him for. She was discouraged. It was fourth and long and she was out of options. The play call should be punt. Choose a backup topic and just write the paper, get it done, the clock was ticking. She stopped at a professor's office. His secretary, a Mary Greene by the name plate on her desk, was gathering her purse, she frowned, looking at the wall clock.

"Is Professor Neuville in?"

"Maybe. Depends. Do you have an appointment?"

"No, ma'am. Just a question?"

"Clarification?"

"Yes." She went with it.

"Doctor Neuville. I've got a clarification out here."

Ned Neuville came to the door. A thin man, thinning hair, a long thin nose, pants that bagged on long thin legs. His eyes were gray like his hair and they looked over the top of his reading glasses as he frowned. "I don't recognize you."

Fear made her swallow. "No, sir. I'm not in your class. Yet. Jaclyn Cooper."

"Hm." The frown went deeper. His face impossibly thinner.

"It's an international law question. For a paper—"

"How can you write what you yet know? Stick to what you do." He turned.

"Sir." She should punt. Just punt and forget this. But she pursued. "In the International Inner Port City—"

"Ee-gad, don't go there. Horrible place." He turned and scowled down his thin nose at her. "Especially for citing law or finding accurate citations for authority or precedent for International law. Do you even know what those are yet, Miss Cooper, who started a semester late against my better recommendations to the registrar when my opinion was asked over the holidays?" Gray eyes examined her over his glasses as his frown increased.

She just stood firm and looked at him. Waited.

Slowly his eyebrows lowered even more fiercely. "What's your question?"

"What's the most convicted crime in the Global city?"

He waved her off. "The law library has that answer. Use it, Miss Lazy."

"It doesn't. I've looked, searched, did my own statistics on cases over the past three years." She was pulling out her legal pad, flipping pages of arithmetic. "There is hardly anything to cite, sir. I can't find the cases."

"You won't. They evaporate mysteriously. Ee-gad!" He snapped his fingers. "I just told you it's a horrible place for citing authority or precedent, didn't I? Listen!"

"What can you prosecute successfully there?"

"I've no idea." He stared at her. "If you're going to be stubborn and still stand there with your mouth open, gawking at me, determined to write a paper on international law, then write on treaty law or law of the seas. I wouldn't go criminal or humanitarian. And leave the Global City, horrible place." He waved her off.

"I can't leave the Global City." It was said with a passionate sadness.

He turned, gray eyes looking down at her, his glasses perched on his skinny nose like a blackbird on a wire. "Stubborn," the word was almost a compliment. "Not lazy. My office." He pushed his door open. Inside there were stacks of papers and books. Dust was in the air and on the surface of almost everything. "There is no place to sit, so stand there." He pointed to one of the few spaces in the room. "You can drill me for two minutes. Go."

"If law is a system of rules usually enforced by a set of institutions then how can I write to convict in a place that won't enforce the rules?"

"Deep question for two minutes. Philosophical in nature and not what you're after. Try again. Brief."

"I need to find a rule the Global City will enforce."

"Better. Money, Miss Cooper. They like money in the Global City. Pick a misdemeanor. Since you are wearing a frown and this is clearly personal in nature, then tort law. You versus someone."

"It can't be civil, they'll expedite the case to his nation of origin and it will be dismissed."

There was almost a smile. "Then you're back to misdemeanor. He'll pay the city, not you. But he'll pay. People commit misdemeanors every day. Cite that. There should be a fair share of citations of both precedent and authority on the subject matter. Better yet, forget the international angle and just use the law you're learning about now in your current classes on your misdemeanor of choice. Back to the law library, Miss Cooper."

"But—"

"Ee-Gad! Time's up." He turned his back but said clearly. "Since you're stubborn, let it stew. The pot never comes to boil when we're watching it so deliberately. A proper misdemeanor will come to you, just watch what laws you break in a day. Now leave."

Stubbornly she went back to the library and prayed. She needed God's help, direction, wisdom and creativity. She waited expectantly for His answer, using the internet for a list of all the misdemeanor laws of the International Inner Port City. Then she looked up the fines. They were hefty. Some of them ludicrous. Vandalism, littering, petty theft, public intoxication—especially if you vandalized the street with your vomit, simple assault, disorderly conduct, trespassing, and the Global Privacy policies. She made a list of the ones she could work. He was guilty of public intoxication. Simple assault—a whole table had seen him knock her down at the craps game. Drug possession—she'd been in possession not him, but he did the tattoo, embedded the Eros. Extortion, he'd surely obtained much by threatening and forcing her and many others. She spent an hour building arguments and beginning citations but each case seemed to run out of any viable proof and disintegrate back to hear-say. She glanced at her watch and moaned. She was late.

Time got away from me at the library. Sorry. Coming now.

Brett read the text. It was uncharacteristic of her to be late but he understood her demanding school schedule, wanted to be supportive. He texted her back, found out what she wanted to order. She loved Italian food.

Brett saw LaRue come in, waved. His date was beautiful. Classy. Petite but curvy. Her hair long, swept away from a face with an exotic blend of beauty, cascading dark curls flowing down her back over a black sweater. It was cashmere over trousers. The same classic elegance Jaclyn would wear, understated over a body that wasn't. Her eyes were brown, large dark almond-shaped eyes, heavy lashed, connecting with his. He stood, took her hand, was introduced.

"Cristina Monaco."

She blushed. Took her seat. Confessed, "I've never met anyone famous before. I'm a bit star struck."

"It will wear off," he promised with a smile. "Jaclyn's running late. She wants us to order. She's having the Alfredo. No wine," he told LaRue. "She's got more studying to do."

"His girlfriend is in law school," LaRue explained. "I told Brett about your work, Cristina." He looked at his PDA, frowned. "I need to take this. Excuse me. Perhaps you could tell him darling, what you're doing in the city, with The Boys' Club."

Brett smiled at her, encouraged, "I'd love to hear about your work."

Left alone they talked of Washington's youth. Of those in need and those who had much to offer. What she was doing was truly interesting. "This is just what I've been looking for. How could I help you?"

"Really?"

His hand reached out, covered hers on the table. "Really."

They made plans to meet. Brett noticed her cross necklace. It was delicate and pretty. He asked about it.

"I'm from the Bible belt." There was a smoky laugh. Then he saw the blush, the nerves.

"I'm a Christian," he made the statement.

"So am I," she immediately relaxed. "We're few and far between here. Back home—"

"Where's home?"

"Florida." She talked about her town, her church, the small Bible college where she earned her Master's.

He listened, poured her wine.

"I don't drink."

He laughed. "Neither do I. Until LaRue. He's got me thinking wine is part of a good meal. I'm getting an education. It's about the food, the flavors. I've been trying all different kinds," he smiled. "It's been kind of fun. He likes this red. Raved about the calamari here."

They tried it together. She even took a sip of the wine. Nodded, smiled. They talked, a deep discussion about role models and publicity. What he hoped to do with his career and foundation. The decline of abortion as freezing embryos became the new way to handle unwanted pregnancies. The ethics of what to do with frozen life in storage facilities.

Jaclyn arrived, surprising him. "Ah, Babe." He rose, brushed her with a kiss. "This is Cristina."

"Hi, Christine."

"Cristina," he corrected softly.

"Everyone leaves off the a," she told them both. "It's okay. I'm used to it."

"No. I'll get it right. Cristina. That's pretty." She smiled. "Where's LaRue?" Jaclyn asked, still standing.

"He had to take a call," he told her.

"He has a shipment caught in customs. It's been a nightmare all day, he said."

"I'll get him," Jaclyn told them both. "Or find out what he wants to order on my way to the ladies room." She dropped her bag into a chair. Hugged Brett and whispered, "Thanks for understanding. I'm on a deadline."

"I'll feed you. Refuel. You'll get it done."

She pressed her cheek to his, holding tight another second, then hurried off. The place was cozy, dark, crowded for a Thursday because the food was good. She searched for LaRue, all the little places a man could stand with his PDA and do business. He wasn't out front on the sidewalk. He wasn't by the bar or in the little hall by the bathrooms. She went into the ladies room, washed her hands, freshened up. Then came out. Across from the women's restroom was the door that said, Men. She returned the smile as a man made his own exit. Then she stopped, knocked on the door, pushed it open and called out, "Any Frenchmen in here? We're ready to order."

"Lady!" It was a waiter. In his uniform of crisp white shirt and long black apron. Wearing a serious frown, he shook his finger at her. "You go in that restroom and you're breaking the law. We can fine you up to five thousand dollars. Don't you know the privacy laws?"

"Ee-gad!" She jumped up in the air and shouted. "The water boiled—privacy laws. Of course the bathroom." She kissed the waiter. "Thank you." Ran back to the table. "I have to go." She grabbed her bag. Brett standing. LaRue greeting her. Cristina confused, as they all talked at once. "I figured it out!" She kissed Brett. Surged up into his arms, jumping in place, hugging him tight. "I finally figured it out." She was already going, walking backward, explaining. "I can't stay. Eat. Have to go. Sorry. So sorry. You understand. I love you for that!" She blew him a kiss and dashed away.

The next morning she was standing at his office door. Tapping her foot, paper in hand. The document was bound formally, the light blue paper on top and underneath. Every lawyer in the family had read the original she was turning in today in her legal writing class. There had been a few edits, more legalese language added to improve the official document she would perfect. Uncle Bennett was very creative, her stepmother tightening up some slack in a few sentences. The honorable Judge Samantha Cooper had done her own research last night once she knew the direction they were headed. Together they had worked via internet on the citations, finding both precedent and authority.

She had evidence building too. It was cited in the paper for class, falsified because it was yet proven. But it would be proven. Christie had assured her last night she would have the evidence from Babel on video and audio, then she would write the final draft for her future use to cite the Viper.

"Miss Cooper. Are you still wearing yesterday's clothes? Ee-gad girl." He lifted his skinny nose into the air as he keyed open his door. He went in and shut it in her face.

She knocked.

"It's open," he called out.

She walked in. "The water boiled. I wanted to thank you for your time yesterday."

"Duly thanked. Now poof," his hand motioned in the air as if he held a wand. "Begone."

They looked at each other. She smiled.

He frowned. "You're still here. Very stubborn."

"I'm going . . . to leave this with you."

"That paper is not for my class nor is my time limitless."

"I'd like a recommendation for an International lawyer in the city who could make it official. I heard you still practice occasionally."

He lowered his head, looked over his glasses at her. "I teach."

"You can bill me for your hours."

"You couldn't afford me. No one affords my rates, I give them as I please." He turned his back.

"Pro bono, perhaps?"

"Leave me your number. I don't want you lurking around my office. Ee-gad! Be gone."

She smiled as she placed it on his secretary's desk. "It's on Misses Greene's desk, Professor Neuville."

"Close the door."

She did, holding the knob and waiting. She saw him through the foggy glass, pick up the paper and open the blue cover. Smiled. And walked away praising God.

32

"Play ball!"

It was Opening Day. Spring had finally come to D.C. The proverbial feeling of rebirth and new chances was universally felt by every team, every fan, everyone who cared to understand the spirit of what opening day was about. It arrived with pageantry, the vice president throwing out the first pitch. She stood with a sold out crowd who declared bipartisanship, cheering as one despite their personal opinions, to applaud the tradition and the effort of getting that first beloved ball over the plate.

It was official. Baseball season had begun. And she was caught up in its state of mind, welcoming this Monday as an unofficial holiday. Skipping classes and not feeling a bit guilty over it, especially when Brett was announced as the starting pitcher. Her father told her it was an honor that distinguished him as the team's best pitcher, best hope, their ace. Every fan knew, if you could win the opener, you could win the whole season. And they were in love with the man who had won them the series last October. Hopes were sky high.

She clapped as he jogged out, cheering with LaRue and Cristina. Glad to have friends here today. Smiling as Brett tipped his cap to her. Then there they were, the three of them up on the vid screen larger than life. Fans of number four.

"We're caught playing hooky," she told Cristina.

"You knew they'd get you," LaRue reminded.

"I tried to come disguised."

"With those shoes?" LaRue gave a rich laugh.

"Aren't they darling? I've been so impatient to get my feet into a pair of sandals."

"Sandals are flat, Sugar. Those are heels if I've ever seen them."

"Open toe, now for spring. No more boots, just pedicures." She winked at him. They all took a seat. Enjoyed the spring afternoon and a game of baseball. Brett pitched like the ace he was. The press got their picture in the parking lot after the game.

"Congratulations," Marc shook his hand as the three took their seats in his office.

"Great opener," Joshua seconded, always at a loss for words. Always feeling extremely awkward.

"Thanks." Brett nodded.

"Made the paper." Marc showed him the headline. "Four pitches like an ace." There was a still life of him caught at the moment of release.

"This also made the paper." Lisette placed the Globe on the desk. The shot filled most of the cover of the social tabloid. Jaclyn in jeans, a Nationals shirt and red stiletto sandals. She was pressed up into his arms, smiling as he prepared to kiss her. His hand was in a possessive and prominent position—cupping her bottom. His World Series Ring winking boldly. Her gaze was firm on Brett Webb.

"That should get his attention." A statistical profiler studied the shot. "The possession. The body positions. The ring. Did you pose for that?"

"No. I knew they were watching. Saw them standing by with the cameras ready. Thought, why not kick it up a notch? Make it count."

"What did Jaclyn think?"

"Misplaced intentions. She's tiny. She was excited. Ran into my arms. Jumped. I caught her up. It looks like more than it was."

"Always does."

"What was it?" the Termite asked.

"There was a single kiss. A lot of words. She was excited about the win. We both were."

Marc looked up from the article. "What are Marilyn jeans, Fury?"

"No idea, sir."

"Whatever they are, she had them on and they'll spread the photo around talking about the fashion trend. Wear Marilyn jeans and look what happens."

"87% chance it will bring a certain Viper out of his snake pit."

"The photo was on a tabloid TV show this morning too." Marc told them and the Profiler calculated new predictions.

"That picture goes viral, we're at 92%."

"Which is why I called us in for the meeting. Brett's agreed to get out and about this week. We'll push the media coverage. Amp it up with the exposure. Put everyone on alert. I'd like you to check in daily, Brett."

"Sure. We're having a party next week, with my neighbor and his girlfriend, we can invite some media, get a few more staged photos."

"That will work too." They asked for the date, noted it, thanked him.

"I'm glad to help. You know that. The sooner we get the Russian caught, the sooner we can get on with our lives."

Brett smiled. Lisette studied. Fury stewed.

Jaclyn studied the picture on her PDA. Her father had sent it. He should have just drawn a circle around that World Series ring and come out and said the words—what is this?

But instead, he'd sent the picture from the cover of the Globe and merely asked, "How was opening day and what are Marilyn jeans?" It was a subtle message and she frowned over it because the shot was anything but subtle.

She had no idea how they got these pictures. She'd hugged Brett after the game. Maybe she'd been a little excited, jumped a little. The heels were tricky, high, he'd steadied her. It had been totally innocent. A hug not even a kiss, with a little squeal—she frowned, remembering now—that Christie would have rebuked her as they were constantly working on turning that female sound into a growl or grunt. She deleted the message with a very good groan.

This would be everywhere, in the hands of law students, professor Neuville, family, the Fury. There was a little smile over Fury, but even that satisfaction was waning away now. Jealousy wasn't ever going to work with Joshua. If he didn't want her then why should he care if Brett's hand was cupping her rear end . . .

Her phone rang, the name startling her. Yes. The whole world had seen the photo. Her birth mother was calling. "Rachel?"

"Who is this gorgeous man with his hands all over you?" There was a laugh, husky and low. "He's totally besotted." Another laugh, now more like a Spanish serenade. "Baby, he's wonderful. You've obviously taken my advice. Are having yourself a time."

"Um." She responded, feeling the anger. She hadn't seen Rachel since she first arrived home. Her mother never calling to check on her progress, healing, plans. She didn't know she was in law school or Washington. But stick her butt in the hands of a fine looking man, and wa-lah, mommy wanted the inside scope. She listened. Rachel thought he was handsome. She liked his ad for the country's most popular soda. Had she tried the PDA he promoted. Were they living together in Georgetown? She'd not given her time to answer. She was just so glad she'd found a man who was helping her recover from her incident in Europe. They were sensual people, she'd been told not to feel guilty about her sex drive. "How's your father?" Finally the real question came.

"Fine," was her brief answer.

"I'm sure he's worked up into a lather about Brett." Another deep laugh. "Well I'm in town next week," she told her. "Bring Brett to the concert. I'd like to see you, meet him."

"I don't know. He might be playing ball but I'll check."

"Let me know. I've missed you, Jaclyn and I'd like to see you. Especially now that you look so happy, healed. I want to see you happy, baby. I really do."

"Okay," she could only answer. She thought about the stirring in her spirit to form a relationship with her mother, to know her. "I'd like to see you too."

"She's coming," Rachel Cruz told the man, her body relaxing back into his arms. "Bringing the baseball player."

"Excellent." He kissed her bare shoulder, his hand roaming her body then reaching to the bedside table. A heavy gold ring winked in the candle light as he reached for his glass of vodka with an arm covered in the pattern of ink.

Jaclyn wore a fabulous jacket. A baseball-style leather letterman with the Nationals' team emblem that Brett had given her. She had slim jeans tucked into a pair of killer boots. Brett took her hand to lift her clear of the car on the curb to the concert hall. It amazed her how they knew where to find them. The paparazzi immediately swarming the curb. Security shielding. Questions called out. She was gun shy now, they'd talked about the shot, how much they both hated it. Brett shielded her like the gentleman he really was, then surprised her with the statement.

"We'll give you a moment for pictures only if you give me some space," Brett told the group. Promises were made at once from the photographers.

He drew her to his side. Smiled now. "Want my shades, babe?" He smiled slipped them on her face. "You look cute." He laughed now, poised as they bantered.

"How can you see in these? I'm blind." She smiled at him. "No wonder you think I'm tall." She pulled them down and looked over the top of the rims at him. "I'm short."

"You're beautiful." He kissed the tip of her nose.

There was a fast staccato of cameras.

"Thanks." Brett waved, tucked her under his arm. Security led the way. At the backstage entrance door they told the man with the clipboard their names. He had arms like Popeye and a mean disposition.

"Who are they?" he nodded to the security team.

"Security," Brett answered.

"We've got plenty of security. They'll have to wait out here."

"Then tell my mother we're sorry we missed her." She stepped away and meant it.

"Jack Cooper?"

"It's Jaclyn." She was getting madder.

"Sure." He smiled. "I was supposed to be watching for you." He glanced at Brett. "The famous face distracted me. Everybody walks with muscle these days. Get too much muscle together and—"

"They're staying with us." She lifted a brow.

He opened the door. "She wants you to come to her dressing room." He called out a name. "Take them to Rachel."

"You're here!" Rachel Cruz was up, rushing to her from the makeup chair. "Look at you." Her eyes, exaggerated with stage makeup, roamed her face. "You look so good." She asked the room, "Doesn't my daughter look gorgeous?" She walked her to the crowd. "Henrietta does my hair. Joaquin my makeup. Bruce keeps me dressed. Anna keeps me organized. You know Phil, he's always kept my voice on key."

She didn't know Phil but she smiled at him.

"She looks just like you," Phil announced.

"Oh?" Rachel smiled at her, lifting dramatic brows, giving him an amused smile. "I see her father in her eyes. Her smile." Softly she told her, "I'm glad you're here. So glad." She suddenly drew her into her arms. Squeezed tight. Laughed. "Baby, you're all grown up. Are you taller than me now?"

"It's the boots," she showed her.

"Great boots," Rachel cooed then the sound shifted an octave as her gaze moved to Brett. There was the poise and the smile. A smile she was all too familiar with that her mother could produce for any handsome man. And yet today, this first time, Jaclyn had been her mother's first focus, if only for a moment.

"You're right, Jaclyn, he's much more than just a ball player. Mr. Brett Webb," she held out her hand. Brett took it politely. "I'm so glad you're in her life. The right man is critical. Right, Nicholas?"

"Absolutely," a man answered from an armchair. He was dark and elegant, wearing a suit and keeping his smile on her mother. "You could be sisters, Countessa Cruz."

"Aren't you sweet." There was a purr with a promise for the compliment. Then a man called out a countdown for her to get ready to perform and Rachel began a quick grumble of Spanish about the constant demands on her life.

"She looks just like you," Nicholas told her.

"I had her young. She finally gave me some hips." She walked away, twitching said hips "Bruce," she called the man, clapping her hands. "What are we wearing tonight?" As her wardrobe assistant began to present options, she looked over her shoulder right at Brett and told him with a wink, "Little preview of Jaclyn in twenty years." The robe fell to the floor.

"Then she strips right in front of us," Brett told Joshua.

They met at a neighborhood pub. Sat in a booth, back in the corner. His security squad a hedge that kept out unwanted interference. "Jaclyn calls her on it and her mother tells her it's show biz. There's no room or time for modesty. Then she asks Jaclyn what top she should wear." Brett shook his head. "Carries on this conversation bare chested as she dresses. It's like nothing I've ever seen. I could feel the heat coming off of Jaclyn." He looked down at his plate, ate another hot wing.

"What did you do?"

"Looked down." He looked up at Joshua. "I kept my eyes on the floor."

"All you could do."

"All night, Jaclyn can't stop apologizing. She was furious and embarrassed. I told her not to worry about it." There was silence, Brett's voice softer. "She was very worried. I forced her past it, made her cuddle to me, let me hold her. I'm careful with her. Hand on the back, hold her hand, usually let her make the moves if she wants to be closer or if she wants more. She was holding a lot in, holding onto her cross. She does that when she's upset. I could tell she was really upset."

There was silence. Joshua's emotions stirred. Envy and impatience wrestling with his duty to be here, to hear this.

"I don't always know what to do with her. What she needs. And her mother," he shook his head. "She's something else."

"How so?"

"She's sensual and she doesn't power it down like Jaclyn. She feeds it somehow, uses her beauty, body—all the assets. It's like she's seducing you. Constantly." He shook his head. "I understand how Jaxson could have lost his mind. Lady like that . . . you better run."

"Only thing to do," Joshua agreed.

"After the concert, we had dinner and it was more low-key." He sighed. "She was dressed. I can't believe she's Jaclyn's mother. Of course they look just alike. Except for the eyes."

"Did she have questions or comments?"

"She asked about baseball. My schedule, the season. Jaxson. She always asks about Jaxson, Jaclyn says. Still hung up on him, I guess."

"The press got a few pictures."

"That's what we're after, right?" Brett smiled. "She makes a guy look good."

"Did Rachel ask about Jaclyn's schedule or school?"

"Not too much."

"Was she concerned at all?"

"In our sex life,' Brett answered. "She wanted us to stay in the other bedroom in her suite. Have breakfast in the morning. She told me she was more understanding of the times than Jaxson. That she knew her daughter had needs and she was glad she'd found a man that could meet them."

"Jaclyn looked her right in the eyes and told her we were Christians and believed intimacy was for marriage." Brett looked up at Joshua. "Rachel looked at me then, into me." He shook his head. "For a moment she searched me deeper than Jaxson. I guess she couldn't believe it. Then she looked at Nicholas and said a dramatic, 'I see.'".

"Nicholas?"

"Her boyfriend." He waved his hand, searching for a word. "Latin lover, I guess."

"Nicholas? Latin?"

"European, maybe, I'm not sure."

"What's he like?"

"Dark hair. Quiet guy. Serious. Maybe her manager. He was suited up like a high money guy, European looking but his arms are covered in ink."

"Ink?" Joshua leaned forward with a sudden intensity.

"Tats. Tattoos, probably a sleeve design, it came down to his wrist, onto his hands."

"What kind of Tattoos?"

"Scrolls and lines. A pattern not pictures."

"Colors?"

"No, only black. It's strange to see since everyone wears colors now."

"Draw it." He pushed a napkin toward him and a pen. "Draw what you remember."

Brett took the pen, looked at Joshua. "I'm no artist." But he tried to reproduce it. "Like that, I think."

"What hotel?" Joshua had stood.

"What's wrong?"

"You're describing a Russian."

"Russian?"

"This pattern is an aristocratic lineage of an under prince. He hasn't earned his colors."

"Earned?" Brett shook his head, cursed. "Wait. Where are you going?"

"I've got a job to do." He had his PDA up. "I'm sending one of my own to you. He looks young but he knows what to watch for, how to protect you. His name is Seth." He pointed at him now. "Play it safe for a while."

"Jaclyn—

"We'll watch her. You take care of yourself."

"Sure. Okay." Brett put his hands in his pockets and watched the Fury rush out.

33

There was a single knock. The Fury stood in her door, his eyes charged to their full power. "I heard you're craving chocolate and never have change, ma'am." He held out a palm of credit coins and Christie stood as he nodded toward the hall. "Can I buy you something?"

They walked with purpose, she told him she was feeling fine. The baby growing too fast. "It likes almonds," she instructed, pointing at the candy bar of her choice in the machine.

"Jaclyn saw Rachel last night." He dropped the credits in, held out the candy.

"Yes." There was a hostile exhale as she tore the foil free. "I heard the wicked witch had flown into town. I'll talk to Jaxie tonight, see how it went. Chocolate?"

He shook his head no. "She's got a Russian with her."

Christie's green eyes narrowed but their power intensified as she broke off a piece and tasted.

"Nicholas is what she calls him. He's got the aristocratic lineage on his forearms. Brett saw black lines. No color."

"That's dangerous. He's out to earn it."

"Or it's a hell of a coincidence that Russian tattoos are strumming guitars with Rachel Cruz."

"There are no coincidences. Where is this Russian?"

"They'd left before I could get to the St Regis."

"I told you." Now she showed emotion. "I told you she's like a vampire. Coming. Disappearing. Perfume and poison apples. I've a sudden need to see my niece. She keeps Godiva handy."

Joshua stopped her with a hand. "I want to put a man on Rachel Cruz."

"Do you?"

"We can use the Russian for motivation."

Christie smiled now. "Absolutely." She patted his arm. "You'll talk to Marc."

He nodded.

"Send a woman. She'll seduce even the best man." She broke off another square of candy.

"Petra," he told her. "She's already dispatched to follow her."

Christie popped the chocolate into his mouth. "I like how you think, Fury." She smiled around her own bite. "Little reward for your wisdom."

"Ma'am." He gave a nod, then tried to keep up. The Peregrine was fast.

"Jaclyn," Christie called out coming in the back door. "Hi, Dena."

"Ma'am." She nodded. "How's that baby?"

"Growing." Christie rubbed her belly. "I smell something."

"Chicken dumplings. I've plenty."

"Um." Her voice lowered, her eyes traveling up the back stairs. "Keep alert."

"Yes, ma'am."

"There are young Russians in town wanting to earn their colors."

Her eyes narrowed. "Not in my house, with my girl."

Christie smiled. "My sentiments exactly." She took the stairs at a jog. "Jaxie Cooper!"

She was at her desk, ear buds in, eyes intently studying two screens. Christie plucked one of the hot pink buds out and Christian rock flared in stereo as Jaxie jumped, shrieked.

Christie hissed with crossed arms and attitude, "That's pitiful! You can't be my niece."

"I'm not on guard." She was looking around. "And I'm surrounded with protection in your house."

"Your house." She dropped her brows. "You're always on guard. And I was talking about the sound you make. It is so female and dramatic." She reproduced the shriek.

"Sorry." She bit her lip.

"I should hope so. You've got to learn to growl if you have to make noise."

"Fury growls."

"Um." She paced around the room, picked up a picture. "How was the concert?"

She looked away. "Fine."

"Rachel?"

"The usual."

"You going to make me pull teeth?"

She looked at her. "She plays me every time."

"Plays you?"

Jaclyn was up now, pacing. The story revealed. "I thought she was really glad to see me. Just me, no dad. But then I see it's about Brett. She drops her robe in front of us. Down to these ridiculous panties. Then she stands there and asks me what top she should wear. I was so humiliated, like she'd stripped me bare in front of the whole room. 'Preview of Jaclyn in twenty years.' Everyone was looking at me like I was naked. Brett was wise enough to look at the floor. I almost blew." She held up her hand. "I have enough Lexi in me to know how stupid that would have been. So I marched myself up there this morning."

"Where?"

"To the St. Regis hotel."

"Tiki with you?"

"Of course." She waved her off. "I wanted to keep him in the hall, but I was mad enough to know I needed the accountability with this bout of anger I'm trying to deal with. She was still abed," she gave the word a twist. "That's what her current boyfriend tells me." She sighed. "I sit there small talking with him—"

"Him?"

"The boyfriend. Nicholas."

"What did you talk about?"

"The weather. Law school. The food in D.C. and Brett's game. Finally, I've had enough. I just go in to her room. She had a picture of me by her bed … it just stopped me. I was so angry and that old picture stopped me. I didn't know it existed. Her, and dad holding me. The three of us, beside her bed." She brushed a tear away. "I left. Told Nicholas to tell her I was there. She looked like a child in that bed." She shook her head. "I don't know what to do with her. I never know what to do with Rachel. She's so confusing. She's my mother, but she acts like . . ."

Christie reached out, drew her close as the tears began. "I understand." She held her for a minute, knowing what it was like to have birth parents who were evil and exploited you. "I'm sorry, Jaxie."

She nodded.

"You can yell at me."

"I took an hour in the sim already."

"Feel better?"

"Sure." She was stronger. "Now I'm attacking a paper on the Third Amendment, trying to forget the whole thing."

"I'll let you get back to it. It's best to put it behind you." She stuck the ear bud in her ear, mouthed the words, "Love you."

"Love you," she repeated.

Petra told the team, “The Russian was not with her.”

“He’s not with her,” Marc repeated Petra’s statement, thinking.

“No, sir. From what I gathered, the man called Nicholas didn’t travel out of Washington with the tour.” Petra sat at attention in the conference chair. “Her group is tight lipped. They say they adore her but I sense an undercurrent. She is a diva. Difficult. Moody, to be sure. Very smart. Her people are very careful.”

“Hard to infiltrate,” Eli defined.

“Yes. They knew people at Rolling Stone. Questioned me repeatedly. Someone had checked out my press credentials.”

“The article will run next month,” Marc told her. “It will validate your cover.”

“She might consider the book idea. I saw that it interested her.”

“I don’t think it’s necessary,” Marc sighed. “The Russian is who we’re after, not Rachel Cruz.”

“Every time she shows up, something happens to Jaclyn,” Christie said coolly.

Marc gave his wife a look to leave it.

“Petra, your insight on Rachel Cruz?” Fury asked.

“She is . . . hard to tag.” Her brows had lowered, her eyes focused on the table. She shook her head. “She needs a broader look.” Now she looked up. “Her background checked. Moving about like she does, it is easy to do evil and look innocent.”

“Is she evil?” Marc asked her.

“She is a master at deception.”

Eli spoke for the first time. “What is she hiding?”

“Isn’t that the question.” Christie looked at her husband.

“And she could just be another high-maintenance diva with an entourage.”

“Or a vampire,” Christie stated.

Marc moved on. "Seth, how is Brett?"

"Rich and famous, sir."

"I think you need to stay with him until we further identify the Russian."

"Cool." He nodded. "He's got a great place and he feeds me top notch."

"How's security?"

"Tight. Focused. They're good guys. Eyes alert when we're out. Especially when the Hummingbird is with him. We all take it up a notch when she's around."

"How is their relationship," Marc looked down at his notes, "When you're around?"

He glanced at the Fury. "He's a, ah, gentleman. Sweet to her."

"And Jaclyn?"

"She," he nodded. "She's busy with school. He's busy with ball. They meet and eat on his days off. Talk during the day. He initiates it, almost always."

"Intimacy?"

"No, sir."

Marc looked up. "You've seen none?" He held up the paper. "The press sure catches them. This looks like a kiss to me."

"Yes, sir. That looks like a kiss, but I'm not out in plain sight when she's around. I was told not to let her see me."

"I know your mission. You're doing a good job," Marc stated. "And Brett's working the press angle. Keeping them in the paper." He held up a current issue of Brett at a Boy's Club function.

"That's not Jaclyn," Fury told Marc.

"Sure it is."

Seth grinned. "He's right. That's Cristina. She's a friend of his neighbor's. Is an advocate for family rights. They were doing a gig over at the Boys Club. Press thought she was the Hummingbird."

Marc studied the paper. "There's a strong resemblance."

"Maybe there's a strong resemblance between this Nicholas guy's tattoos and Russian marks," Seth threw out.

Marc nodded. "Could be. Any leads, Eli?"

"I've searched the families, sir. But the way the Russian princes populate, he could be the kid of a concubine or a whore. It's hard to trace the lineages with all their women. It's hard to know without getting a look at the ink design."

"But he has the markings."

"Like Seth said, they could be a coincidence or he could have chosen them from a catalog," Petra agreed.

"There are no coincidences," Christie was firm. "I don't like Rachel's timing nor do I like the coincidence of her showing up with a man name Nicholas, who looks European and has tattoos that look like Russian markings."

"You know the Russians, you don't wear their tats without consequences. Any tattoo artist would be a fool to put it on you without the rank required to wear it. They have their ethics, the ink artists. We all know Victor," Eli reminded them.

"What we do know is that the current probability is up to 92%. Let's stay alert," Marc told the team.

34

Jaclyn met Cristina in a chic coffee house she'd wanted to try since she moved to the city. It was the kind of place you'd meet a girlfriend. And now that she had one who'd called and asked her to coffee, she named the place. She celebrated spring and new beginnings with a joyful spirit. Wore open-toed shoes, a spring dress, an accenting celery green cardigan draped over her shoulders for her upcoming hours in the chilly law classes. Two steps behind her, Tiki and another man traveled, watched, secured. Today, even that didn't distract her a step. With Cristina the entourage didn't need an explanation. She'd already been given one and Jaclyn was learning to be comfortable with Tiki in the background of even these timeless pleasures.

She smiled when she saw Cristina come in the door. "You look fabulous. I love your handbag. Is it new?" she asked, hugging her. Feeling like a young girl again, excited to have a friend.

"I splurged. I wasn't sure about lavender."

"I love the lavender."

"I love your shoes." They chatted, the common female language, fashion. Ordered their coffees, Cristina's mocha and Jaclyn's decaf skinny latte with hazelnut.

At a table with high-backed upholstered chairs, Cristina pulled out a copy of the Globe from her new lavender handbag. "This is the reason I called you for coffee. I so hope you're not mad about this." On the cover was a photo of her and Brett with a group of boys in ball caps. The headline read, "Brett and his babe launch Boys Club season." "They thought I was you."

"Um. Wow, we do look alike." She smiled. "You're prettier. They should catch that soon. See the difference."

"I am not prettier!"

Jaclyn sipped her coffee. "I think so. The eyes," she told her. "Your whole face, the way God did the work. It's praise worthy."

"Jaclyn." Cristina blushed.

"I'm flattered, they mistook us. You're doing a great job for Brett."

"That's all it is. A job," she said it with the kind of passionate persuasion you believed. But suddenly Jaclyn began to study, a certain light illuminating. "He totally adores you. And this is," she tapped the paper. "My passion. Helping these kids. I wanted to make sure you and LaRue knew that. He told me I should call you for coffee. Tell you in person. Straighten it out."

"Oh." There was a little sliver of hurt over the motive, a sudden complexity to what should be simple. "No worries." Then a growing pain as she realized how lonely she was. How she hoped this was about something different than a face to face apology and a marketing spin on the optics of life with a famous ball player. Her smile became forced, stiff now trying to cover it up. "Really." Bigger smile. Another sip of coffee. It was an effort to find a topic suddenly. She went with something safe. "Where did you find your handbag?" Then it was the weather. Everything surface, a performance when moments ago it had been natural. There was a battle inside her, her thoughts distracting, emotions undefined but growing. Expectations had been so high and now had hit rock bottom. The landing painful and growing harder to hide. She needed to go, checking her watch she noted the time.

"I'm sorry, I need to get to class." She stood.

"I know how busy you are. Thanks for meeting me."

"Sure . . . I looked forward to it," she said truthfully, accepted her hug.

"I'll see you for dinner, tomorrow with the guys, right?"

"Can't wait."

"He really likes you, Jaclyn. You're all Brett can talk about."

"Um." She just smiled. Wished for a friend she could confide in about her ever-confusing feelings with Brett. Someone who asked her for coffee just to see her, not apologize. Was there always a motive?"

She examined her own as she slipped her sunglasses on to cover the hurt in her eyes. She walked to campus thinking about why she was dating Brett Webb. A man who really liked her. Talked about her. Wanted things from her she knew she couldn't give him. She knew he was wanting more. Knew when he kissed her. Knew how he held her. Knew by the things he said and the way he said them. She needed a friend. He wanted a lover. How would he feel when he finally found out? Like her with Cristina, wanting a friend not an apology.

It's what she told Lisette and Ida that afternoon. Asked their opinion on how to resolve it.

"Give yourself some more time," Lisette had told her firmly. "Two weeks. Spring often causes us to act rashly. We buy too many shoes. Go sleeveless before summer's heat is here." She nodded at her dress. "We see new beginnings and renewed life and think we should cut off things that are old because we're impatient to see them bloom again. Our old shoes are still good. We still need a cardigan. And certain things take longer to show themselves than others. The buttercups are blooming now but it will take a while for the day lilies of summer. Do you understand?"

Jaclyn nodded. She took the wisdom with her to dinner with the boys the next day. She'd gotten her legal writing paper back. Celebrated with Lexi and her grandmother her A. She was in a wonderful mood. Wearing old shoes from last spring—that were still darling. Her skirt was black, short and straight, a classic from her closet. The black top simple and old as well, that showcased a new necklace. It was turquoise and silver beads. A large stone cross hanging low. Joshua's cross hung long on a delicate chain against her skin, over her heart.

She came into the restaurant a little late. Found Cristina and Brett leaning toward each other, already talking at a table.

"Babe." He seemed a bit startled.

"Sorry I'm late. I was on the phone with Lexi. I got my paper back. A."

"A. Of course." He hugged her close. Cristina congratulated her.

"Thanks. Where's our favorite Frenchman?"

"Customs must have his number," Cristina told her. "They've given him trouble all day again. He's on his phone." She searched the restaurant.

"I'll find him."

She smiled as she looked, remembering her last search had solved her law paper puzzle. She stopped a waiter as he came from the kitchen. "I'm looking for a friend who stepped away to take a call—

"Blond guy with an accent?"

"Yes." She smiled.

"He's in the kitchen, cooking with the chef."

"LaRue?" she called, sticking her head into the kitchen.

"Merdi! I'm caught." He was smoking a cigarette, a skillet of sauté in his hand. A sous chef took over as he introduced her. "Jaclyn Cooper, meet a master. Chef Maurice."

He was a robust man, with a round face and thinning hair of white. He had a jolly smile and large beefy hands that took hold of hers as his gaze took her in. There was French, it had the kitchen smiling and she knew enough of the language to understand it was a flattering compliment but chauvinistic.

"He's teaching me to sauté capers."

He still had hold of her hand, his gaze all too curious. "Jacqueline is French."

"Yes, it is." She slipped her hand free. "But I'm just Jaclyn. My mother's invention. She liked the name Jack." She smiled. "That smells delicious." Nudged. "We're starving."

"Of course." He slipped an arm around her.

They came back arm in arm. "He met the chef. Was in the kitchen."

"I ordered for us. Chef's special." LaRue touched his date's shoulder as he took his seat. "I'm sorry to keep you waiting so long, Cristina." He spoke French, brought her hand to his lips. "She's marvelous company, no?" He smiled at Brett.

They ate. After dinner the chef came by the table bringing with him a dark espresso in tiny cups and a layered tiramisu dessert.

"With my compliments." He bowed.

They were quick to taste, to praise.

"For later, when you have a need." The chef laid a matchbox on the table beside LaRue, his beefy hands giving him a pat.

"I couldn't find a light," he told them, slipping the matchbox into his pocket. "I was out in the alley, swearing at the customs officer and threatening my office to get the paperwork they were demanding had the wrong digits on it. I'd had a good tantrum. Needed a cigarette to calm down and couldn't find a light." He shrugged, a soft blush on his face. "I knew the kitchen would have a fire. That's when I met the chef."

"And the rest is history," Brett said with a chuckle.

"It was delicious." Jaclyn smiled with pleasure.

"Do you just happen into this kind of luck, man?"

"Did you pick up the check?"

Brett laughed. "I believe I did."

LaRue lowered lashes and curled a grin. "A man makes his own luck." He poured out the rest of the wine and raised his glass. There was a toast, to beautiful women. A long conversation that had moved her under Brett's arm in the booth. He played with her hair, he whispered comments against her ear with soft secret kisses.

LaRue rose, lifting Cristina with him as he took her hand. "Ladies. A moment of your time. I have a new painting I'm not sure about its placement. I could use your help."

Security stepped forward as they moved to leave. Two of his men. Two of hers. Cars at the curb. "Shall we walk?" LaRue asked. "Since we're just around the corner." They had just turned in the direction when cameras caught them, couples holding hands, sharing conversation on a spring evening. Security moved in, did their jobs. The couples moved along, Brett gave a brief apology. Jaclyn wrapped Brett's hand around her waist, moved under his arm. Glad for his protection as she sensed the watching eyes of the world turn their way. She remembered Lisette's advice that certain things took longer to show themselves. Realized there was a certain level of trust she shared with him. A friendship that could possibly grow if she gave it a chance. It softened her heart, opened her curiosity, allowed for more intimacy. His eyes were pretty tonight. His body warm. He smelled clean and crisp. He was handsome, kind and always attentive to her. She liked that. Tonight she'd been a bit competitive for that attention, not wanting to share it with Cristina, who seemed to distract Brett a bit.

LaRue smoked on the way home, telling them to go ahead as he finished the French cigarette outside their building and spoke with Cristina.

Jaclyn kept him close as they entered the elevator. Watched him push the button. Knew they needed to move past the past if there was to be a future.

"Do you feel like there's always an elephant in the elevator with us?" She'd turned to him, looked up into his eyes, wrapped his arm tighter around her as the elevator shot up.

"If you kiss me," he smiled. "I'll make the beast go away."

She did, lightly, looking at him, wondering if it could happen.

He smiled, whispered on her lips. "See, no elephant. Just you and me. Beautiful you. And besotted me." He kissed her now, softly, looking back into her eyes. "See, it will be okay, Jaclyn. Given time. I know you, everything. You don't have to explain. Trust me, Babe. Relax," he asked her. "And trust me." He tightened his arms, nudged. "Relax." She tried. "Are you afraid?"

"No."

He gathered her closer. "Okay?"

"Yes."

"See, we're here." The doors opened. He walked her into the hall lobby of his floor. In the center, under the chandelier of crystals, he brought her back into his arms. "I want you to relax. Take a deep breath." She did. "Look into my eyes."

"You have pretty eyes."

"Thanks." He smiled. "Now close your eyes and kiss me. Don't think. Feel." His lips came softly, warm and undemanding, they waited. He watched. She closed her eyes, kissed him. She didn't think, she tried to feel. She tried… she felt his response. There was joy and arousal. The pure kind of pleasure when physical and emotional link together. The kiss broke slowly, their eyes open to gaze.

He was in love with her, she saw it, mourned it instantly as she suddenly realized, deeply understood that this would never be more than what it was for her now. Friendship.

"Do you dance?" she asked him, needing to move suddenly.

"Do I dance?" he mocked. They went round the square room in an easy three step as he hummed. "You're a wonderful dancer, Babe."

"I love to dance."

"Then we'll go, soon."

LaRue applauded as he arrived on the floor. "You move well together."

"Yes," Cristina agreed, holding his hand but looking at Brett.

"You better be ready to move well in a moment, Cristina." Jaclyn stepped away, grinned, dropped the jealousy in the light of the truth. "Have you met Brutus yet?"

"I have a dog," he warned her as he keyed open the door. "He is a bit enthusiastic."

"Brutus," LaRue greeted the rottweiler, taking his collar. "Sit, now. Good boy." LaRue introduced his butler, "My majordomo, Jean-Claude."

He wore jeans, a white polo stretched impossible tight over Hulkish shoulders. His biceps bulging with veins. He was bald, with tiny dark eyes and thin lips. He lifted an over large nose and said with a heavy French accent, "Good evening." He took command of the dog, an index finger tightening the choke collar as he said a soft foreign word.

Brutus at once settled into the sit. His tongue came out, his eyes excited, watching the girls pass by as LaRue led the way. "He's afraid of Jean-Claude," LaRue whispered. "We're all a bit afraid of Jean-Claude."

His butler chuckled. "You insult me when I've got your Sizzle breathing."

"Ah, this is why I pay him the big bucks, ladies. Intuition. Shall we navigate this painting around the loft. Come." He lead them.

"Wow, your place is . . . wow," Cristina said looking all around as they were led to the corner of the apartment. Propped against the wall by his bed, LaRue showed them the painting, a Genoa Radcliff in heavy oil. A face wearing a thousand conflicting feelings done in shades of blue and gray with heavy black.

"What is she thinking?" LaRue asked them all. "I just stare and wonder."

"Is it a she?" Brett asked.

"Isn't that an earring?" Cristina showed him.

"It is."

"Where?"

"There." Jaclyn showed him, drawing him near.

"Ah." His chin rested on her shoulder, his arm loose at her waist. "What is she thinking?"

"She's sad." Cristina suggested. "Perhaps mad."

"Right now, I think she is intrigued," LaRue inferred.

"Babe?" he whispered.

"I don't know. She looks like she's . . . longing for something. Confused." He felt her sigh. "Brett?"

"She is beautiful. Bored, maybe."

"Bored. I hadn't seen that." LaRue studied the painting intensely. "Yes, maybe bored. She intrigues me. I saw her and then . . . I couldn't sleep. Was at the gallery first thing in the morning. Paid full price. Just slapped it down to walk out with her wrapped in paper. Imagine, carrying her through rush hour pedestrian traffic. I couldn't get a cab." He swore. "Where shall I display her?"

"By your bed," Jaclyn suggested the place.

"I'd never sleep. Be horribly distracted."

"The bathroom?" Brett looked at another wall space in the open loft.

"Your wall space is limited in a house with no walls." She grinned.

"By your dining table?" Cristina suggested.

"Yes. By the table." They all agreed.

Jean-Claude appeared, took the painting and carried it to the place. "Your wine is poured, sir."

There was conversation. Laughter. Debate. When LaRue moved to pour her more wine she paused, "I had a glass at dinner."

"You didn't have the Sizzle. Please, half a glass." It became more. The conversation deep, sometimes light. She laughed. LaRue made them laugh. Cristina had a sharp wit to match him. They played off each other like actors in a play at times and she enjoyed it. Enjoyed watching the respectful, soft wooing carried out in front of her. LaRue was different with Cristina. Perhaps serious. Never bold like he'd been with Jenny. But Cristina wasn't Jenny. And Brett wasn't Joshua. She glanced at the painting, understood the woman, felt as if she was seeing her reflection. Suddenly wanted to be certain instead of so confused. Anger. There was a bite of it. Frustration. Impatience. She looked at Brett, leaned to his ear. "Come kiss me goodnight. I need to get going."

"Jaclyn has class in the morning and I have a game."

"I have an early meeting too," Cristina said.

"I'll have a cab sent. Jean-Claude—

"I can give Cristina a ride. If that's okay?" Jaclyn asked, deciding she should work to form this friendship and take initiative.

"Sure." It was decided.

"Good night. As always thanks for the wine."

"We'll give you a minute for that kiss. I'll see you next weekend for the party if not sooner, Jaclyn." LaRue smiled. "We'll send these National boys off to sweep Seattle."

"Looking forward to it."

They were almost to the door when Brutus shot out. Head bobbing, tongue lapping. Thoroughly excited. She was laughing until his nose went up her skirt. "Brett," she tried to push him down.

"Brutus." He grabbed his collar, dragged him back. "Babe, go. Jean-Claude!" he called out as she slipped to the lobby. Brett came out apologizing.

"Are you okay?"

"He's very naughty."

"I'm sorry, sweetheart. I won't let it happen again. I promise. No one is sticking their nose up your skirt."

"Um." She lifted a brow at his teasing.

"Um. How 'bout no one is kissing these lips, but me." Under the chandelier he took her into his arms, she closed her eyes and just gave in to the kiss. There was passion, it was there inside her, innately part of her, feared perhaps because she knew it would have a certain power. She always reined it in with a strong controlling hand but tonight she relaxed her grip.

Connected with her body, stopped thinking emotionally and tried for one last time to let this be more.

Brett responded at once. The kiss deepened, theirs bodies moved. His hand skimmed her, a passing slide up, tracing curves, resting. There was desire, a quickening lust that was purely a physical response, her mind processing it all like a computer. Each subtle detail. Like a scientist with an experiment. She was a disengaged observer. His mouth was on her neck. He said her name. Words. Praises. Promises.

When he kissed her shoulder, that certain sacred place, she could no longer be detached.

She stepped back, thinking of only Joshua. Mourning, hating, heartbroken. Knowing. Almost certain now. She knew…

"Well, good night." Cristina was telling LaRue. She smiled at them. "I escaped Brutus."

"Good for you."

They left together.

"That was some kiss."

Brett smiled, invited LaRue in for a nightcap. There were still a few arrangements left for the party next weekend. They decided to open up both apartments, put a table of food in the hall lobby. There'd be music for dancing in LaRue's apartment, soft jazz under conversation in Brett's. They both approved the caterer's suggestions.

LaRue smoked, smiled, agreed the night should be a hit.

"I like Cristina."

"Of course." LaRue smiled, a stream of smoke gave the air a masculine flavor. He tapped the matchbox from the restaurant on the counter. "She has the look of Jaclyn. Her beauty a bit more classical than exotic."

"I thought the opposite," Brett argued. "Cristina is more exotic. Jaclyn more classical."

"The eye of the beholder, I guess. They are both beautiful. Elegant. Educated. Fabulous women."

"Cristina is a Christian."

"Yes, her values are old fashion. Challenging." There was an impatient moan.

"You said you were a locksmith," Brett debated.

LaRue slowly smiled. "I said love was a locksmith."

"What's your plan? Marriage?"

"I am French. And very frustrated. Why do you think I'm smoking so much?" he chuckled and moaned.

"Give me one of those." He shook out a cigarette.

"I am a bad influence, my friend. And you are not frustrated, perhaps impatient."

Brett took the matchbox, moved to open it even as LaRue made an attempt to stop him.

"Really, no. Give me that."

It rattled like beans instead of shaking like sticks. Curious, Brett stepped back, slid it open. Inside were tiny white pills.

"I didn't go into the kitchen for matches. The chef has more than a good recipe to share."

"What are those?"

LaRue sighed. Smoked. Looked away. Brett asked again.

"They are not for you, my friend." He held his hand out. "They only work on females."

"Is this Eros?"

"They call it Cupid. The lowest dose of Eros available. Soft, safe, beautiful lust. I am French."

"You're not giving this to Cristina." He fisted the matchbox.

LaRue sighed, smoked. "I told you about the Sizzle. It's history. A hot summer, a rare blend of grapes. Have you noticed her, when she drinks a glass? She warms to you."

"Have you drugged the wine?"

"It doesn't affect men. And the wine is already drugged, the grapes were sprayed with a chemical." He smoked. "It very modestly raises the levels of LH in a woman. Much more subtle than Eros. Similar to a single pill of Cupid. She has been molested, my friend. You are helping her to heal. The wine is not evil in that process. I saw the kiss. The passion tonight, no? Brutus smelled her lust. Came running to stick his nose up her skirt."

"Do you have a command for that?" Brett scowled.

"He has a heightened sense of smell—her pheromones indicated to his nose the availability of the female for breeding. Simply put, Jaclyn was turned on. The smell turns Brutus on." He smoked. "She wanted you on a physical level. Eventually in most women that desire transfers totally to the emotional level. The Sizzle is helping you to that end. It is a good sign of progress, having Brutus nose up her skirt, yes?"

Brett didn't answer. A battle raged. A matchbox in his hands. "She was given Eros when he raped her. She's had echoes." He looked at LaRue. "She checks her levels daily, uses her PDA. She can't have Eros."

"That is Cupid. The Sizzle has the same potency. It hasn't harmed her."

"I want her to heal, marry me."

"Of course. Seduce her until you are both mad, then elope and have her. Old as time, no." He exhaled a sweet stream of smoke then grinned. "Did you touch her?"

"Are we in high school?" Brett narrowed his eyes.

LaRue blushed, smiled, smoked. "I am French."

"That excuse is getting old."

Brett's phone rang. Twice before he took his narrowed eyes off LaRue and answered. "Yeah, Babe. You home okay?"

"What! Where are you? I'm coming." He looked at LaRue. "The girls were in a car accident. They can't find Cristina."

35

Fury got the call and broke out into the night. Command was in his ear, a chatter of voices and information. They had eyes above the intersection. The smoke was clearing. A car had caught on fire. Traffic was backed up for blocks. He raced in between cars on his motorcycle, came as close as he could get before he parked and went in on foot, running. Street lights were out for blocks on the north side of the street. Chaos building. People standing outside vehicles, sirens calling, horns impatient, headlights making shadows. Smoke was in the air. His team calling in. The Kid was opposite him coming from the East. Eli said he was on scene, searching. Pax ten minutes out. Petra was even now teaming up with their police liaisons on scene. Command called out coordinates again. ETA was two minutes at the pace he was moving. He sprinted.

Police had a barricade of vehicles. There were two ambulances parked with red lights sweeping to a cadence. Firemen were spraying off the smoking car. It was hers.

Fury walked the perimeter, studying the scene. Seven cars were involved. The first a white tiny two-door coupe, the rear end pushed clear to the front seat, the blue sedan the next in the chain, squeezed at each end. Then came the three blacks. Her Range Rover both sandwiched and squeezed, air bags filling the interior, the structure twisted and bent. It had been struck on the passenger front door by a larger SUV with doors left open and hood sprung up. A parked black luxury model had been caught up in the accident and pushed onto the far sidewalk. Behind the three were two trailing vehicles. A hefty Hummer, turned at an angle still spewing fluids out that firemen were covering in foam and a last sedan, silver and expensive.

He searched for her, for Tiki and her men. Looking for the men in black. For EMTs. A policeman stopped his progress. "This is as far as you go."

"My . . . wife was in the accident. Where would they take her?"

"Around the corner, sir." He pointed, a hand on his shoulder, a gentle guidance to the left.

Someone was crying on a stretcher. Her pelvis crushed. EMTs working to stabilize.

"He just stopped for no reason," a young man was telling an officer. His face was bleeding, his neck already isolated with a collar. "Why did he stop? In mid-block. He just stopped for no reason."

"Can you describe the car?"

"Silver. I think. Maryland plates. Maybe. He stopped for no reason. Everything happened. Bam. Bam. Bam. When we came to a stop, the road was wide open. But I swear he was there. In front of me. He was there. He just stopped for no reason. In the middle of the block. Locked it up."

Joshua walked on, scanning faces. Then he ran.

"Joshua?" she said his name, holding a cold pack to her head and gripping a thermal blanket around her shoulders, she said his name with confusion.

"Are you okay?" He took her face in his hands. His gaze gripping hers. "Are you okay?"

She was nodding. Her eyes wide, confused. "You're here."

"You're safe." He was holding her. Tight. Against his body. Speaking words over her.

"Tiki's right here." Joshua glanced at him, at both men standing over her as he held her.

"The air bags launched. It was like being in a bounce house."

"I've never seen so many air bags," Dave her driver said. "Engineering at its finest. The car is amazing."

"What's this?" He lifted the cold pack, saw the swelling, the cut on her eye brow bone.

"I banged my head against something. When everything happened. Will it need stitches?"

Her voice was childlike. He touched her hair, stroked it back. "A little derma glue. So you won't scar."

"Will you do it?"

"We'll take care of you. You'll be fine."

"You're here." Her teeth were rattling. She was in shock. Cold. She got cold easily. He held the cold pack, tugged the silver blanket closed. "I'm safe?" she repeated, her mind engaging suddenly. "It was an accident. Right?" She blinked. "Eli?"

He crouched beside them. "Hey, Miss Cooper. You okay?"

"Yes." She glanced back at Joshua, took his hand now. "I'm okay. Right?"

"Just a bump on the head," Joshua assured.

"We're missing Miss Monaco." Tiki told them. "She was in the car with Miss Cooper. Back seat, passenger side. Everything happened in slow motion and then it rushed too fast. I was disoriented for a moment, punctured the air bags and looked back. Jaclyn was there, but Cristina was gone. Her door was open and she was gone. The vehicle was smoking. Smoke was everywhere. We got out, got clear."

"We can't find Cristina. She looks like me. She's wearing black too, just like me but slacks with a sweater and jacket. I had on the skirt. This was an accident, right?"

"We don't know yet."

She gripped his hand tighter. "That's why you're here? You don't think it's an accident?"

"You're safe," he promised her.

"Where's Cristina? They think she's me. You have to find her."

"We don't know that yet," Joshua soothed her.

"You have to find her. She looks like me. She's tiny, long hair." She began to fight to rise, her voice elevated and demanding as she stood up. "Tiki help me."

"Jaclyn," Joshua brought her close, spoke firmly. "Let us handle this. I want you safe. Tiki could be hurt. So could you and Dave. Internal injuries. You need to stay calm."

"Okay." Her lip was quivering, her body leaning into his embrace. "Seth?" she said his name as he came up to Eli. "Seth is here," she told him, holding onto him. "Please find her. She's so sweet. She lobbies for family rights. She's a Christian. She's wearing a pretty cross. Silver with black scrolls. It's hanging here." She touched her turquoise cross, showed his men. "Smaller than mine, but right here in the open neck of her sweater. She looks like me. Prettier. She's prettier."

"We'll find her. I'm going to take you to *Stratia*, have them check you over. You'll be safe there."

"Don't leave me." Now she whimpered, holding him tight. "Please, Joshua."

"Jaclyn!" Brett Webb shouted her name, coming to them through the maze of cars, workers and wounded at a frantic run.

He felt her hands grip into him, her body cling. Her words strained as she told Brett, "I'm okay. We're okay."

Joshua stepped away.

Tiki stepping up. Coming in between. "Your father, Miss Cooper."

She took the PDA as Brett took her hand. "Daddy? I'm okay. Yes, I'm sure. Brett's here. And Joshua." She looked at him. "I'm safe, Daddy."

f

LaRue watched Brett take the Tiger from another man's arms. She was clearly reluctant to go. The man an obvious intimate and too obviously militia to risk an introduction. He shrunk back, stepped to the side, observed. His mind racing. The information limiting. Cristina was missing. He glanced over at the wreck, at the Range Rover strategically pinned by a larger SUV.

They would have caused a stall from the front, after the light turned green. Got the traffic moving only to pile it up then cut her vehicle off. Pin it to the parked car. Before the airbags finished firing, they would have snatched her out, thinking they had the Tiger, realizing too late it was Cristina.

He played like a media reporter. Gathered information. Walked the street, north then south, asking questions, then all the side streets east and west looking for answers before he made his way home. He found her cross necklace draped over his doorknob, beside the pendant on the delicate chain was another. Larger. Gaudy. A Pendragon cast in gold.

He carefully eased the door open. Brutus at once at attention. Jean-Claude calling him. LaRue said a word, the dog immediately at his feet. Eyes alert. Mouth firm. Waiting obediently.

His majordomo standing still now, looking at the dog. Ten paces back. Looking at LaRue.

"This was left on my door knob."

"I heard nothing." There was fear.

"And the dog?"

"He waits for you there, at the door. He stood once."

"When?"

"Thirty minutes ago, maybe. When you leave him on command, I can't come near him. You know that. He'd kill me."

"Yes. He alone is loyal."

"I am loyal," he proclaimed.

"Loyalty is earned."

"Let me earn it. I will kill for you. Tell me what to do."

"My brother took Cristina. Left this as proof." He tossed him the necklace as he walked. The dog at his side. Jean-Claude giving both a wide berth to pass.

"Pendragon. He is English. Stuffy with it. Stupid." He smiled. "He took the wrong girl."

"Maybe." LaRue glanced at the painting, cursed. "He is also Russian, my rival. No doubt raping her now because she was mine and she is not the Tiger."

"I am sorry."

"She means nothing but a means to an end. Now she is a problem." He picked up his PDA, thumbed through a list of contacts. Made a call, gave instructions and offered a price. "In fifteen minutes then, sweetheart." He told Jean-Claude, "The girl, from the Bronx, in the whore house at Annapolis."

"Yes."

"We'll pick her up. Use her to solve our problem. Blame the whole thing on the Badger. Use the trouble I've kept brewing in customs over his shipment." With a snarl he broke the chain of the necklace, took off his brother's pendant. "It will all work into a fine knot that will hold us for a few days. I only need a few more days." He suddenly smiled at the pendant. "And this might come in very handy later." He slipped it into his pocket. "He is stupid." He walked, ordered the dog to the door. "You will listen and back up my story. Earn your loyalty. I will walk the dog and set up the first bit of evidence. Come when I call."

Later, they drove into the night, dropped off the women LaRue had called to his curb with her pockets now a bit richer. As the city passed, LaRue plotted through the next moves. His Knight had been taken. In the real chess game, his opponent had attacked. The clock was ticking now. He must reevaluate the game board. Move quickly. Aggressively. Very carefully. He was making a bold move. There would be questions. He had answers in place, people in place. A legitimate business, enemies and problems that would eventually be blamed. His cover was based on truth. If he was exposed, truth would ironically clear him. No matter the turn of events, he would have the Tiger. He smiled, tasting success. Victory was so close now. In a few days he would earn what he lusted for.

Power.

"Did you find her?" Jaclyn stood up from the hospital bed she refused to lie down on. She'd leaned against it, waiting. For over an hour, waiting and praying. Now Joshua was here, with Eli and Seth.

"No."

"They took her."

"We don't know that."

"They thought she was me."

"We don't know that." He glanced at Brett.

"Mr. Webb, if you don't mind, could you help us out a minute. Answer some questions?" Eli asked.

"Sure. Of course. I'll be back, Babe."

The room rang with sudden silence when he left.

Emotion rose in her, higher, demanding to be expressed. Joshua stopped her saying, "How's your head?" He lifted her face, brushed her hair back.

"They put the derma glue on." She sniffed.

"Duchovny does good work."

"He knew better than to bandage it. Said, you'd want to see the work."

He made a sound. "It's fine work. It won't scar."

"I don't care about that."

Another sound, the doctor "um" as he examined. "Feeling okay?"

"No concussion. I'm worried about Cristina." His gaze came to hers. "I won't cry." She moved into his arms, held tight. He accepted her, his arms a certain haven. She sighed deeply after a few moments, his smell a comfort. "Joshua." She said his name with a longing she couldn't hide as she clung. Here, like this, with him. There was no confusion about what she wanted, it overpowered every sense. Eros had preferences and so it seemed did her heart. "I'm so glad you're here." She clung all the tighter to him. "It could have been me. He could have me again."

He stepped back, his eyes a sharp blue, his tone no nonsense now. "God is at work, Jaclyn. Trust him."

She held on to his arms. "I want you."

"I'm not sovereign. God is. He will protect you."

"I know He will." She looked up at him. "I know what I want. When will you trust me?"

"Fury. We found her!" Seth was at the door, smiling. "Brett just got a phone call."

Brett was on his phone, nodding, a hand raking through his hair. He smiled at Jaclyn, reached for her hand. "Can I talk to her? Sure, sure." He tucked her close, moved her hair away to look at her injury. "They must have hit heads. Jaclyn's got a puffy eyebrow." He chuckled. "Well, yeah, you'd think those eyebrows would be good for something as thick as they are. There's some people here that need to . . . sure . . . okay," he looked up at the men. "Can you call back? We've been worried. I understand. We're just glad she's okay."

They sat in a meeting, going over every detail again. Marc paced with the report, briefing the details to the team. "Webb and the neighbor take the girls out. Not the first time. Earlier in the week Cristina worked a philanthropy project with Brett. The press gets her by mistake in a shot for the Globe, thinking its Jaclyn at the Boys' Club event." The shot was flashed on screen for them to see and he stated the obvious, "There is a strong resemblance between the two women."

The recent cover of the Globe came up next with the headline *Double Play*. "In yesterday's paper, Brett is seen holding Jaclyn's hand with Cristina on his other side. His free hand at her lower back, escorting Cristina it would seem, but she was holding what we know is the neighbor's hand. They cut the guy off for their own spin. Now they know there's two girls and so do the Russians.

"Our assumption is the Russians set up the accident, used a stolen SUV to nail the Hummingbird's car, trapping her security in the front seat. They snatch and grab the wrong girl. When they realized it, they dumped her off. Disoriented and frightened, she wanders back to the apartment building. LaRue finds her as he's walking his dog. Security in the building verify a woman in black on the curb. LaRue takes his girlfriend immediately to a minor medical facility two blocks away. The fast food-type joint diagnoses the concussion, treats and releases her." Medical records were flashed up next. "Clearly shaken, Cristina asked LaRue to take her to a friend's house. The next morning, Misses Monaco comes and takes her daughter home to Florida to recuperate. LaRue provides private transport."

"But no one's seen the girl."

"The neighbor, his driver. Her girlfriend. Hospital staff. LaRue has her necklace. It was broken during the incident. He promised to have it fixed for her. It was a family heirloom. Jaclyn verifies this. Remembers talking about it on the ride home. Cristina had the necklace on in the car."

"How do we know this French guy isn't part of this?" Eli crossed his arms.

"He was with Mr. Webb when the accident happened. Got stopped at the barricade when they came on site and they were separated. He's cooperated fully. Been questioned extensively, along with his driver. Same story. Same timeline, events. Small discrepancy on calling the mom. Driver says LaRue tried to get Cristina to come to his house, but she wanted her mother. LaRue claims he had her call her mother, never mentions the offer to come home with him."

"Did she call her employer?" Christie asked the next question.

"Yes. The next day. She's taking a week off. Says her face is bruised, her body sore."

"Did she contact Mr. Webb?" Lisette asked the question.

"Brett's left several messages on her phone. Doesn't realize yet that we have it."

"The messages?"

"He's very worried. Wants her to call him back."

"Double play?" Christie looked at the picture. "Did they finally get something right?"

"There's guilt and responsibility. I'm not sure what's motivating it," Lisette answered.

"Assuming this string of coincidences is all true, where are we?"

The profiler had statistics. Listed off estimated assumption percentages for different variables.

"Those are numbers," Christie stated. "These people aren't statistically practical."

"Lisette?" Marc turned to her.

"Processing," she answered. "The Fury is quiet."

"Processing," he replied flatly.

"You're in good company, Wisdom is also processing."

Joshua stood twenty rows back, and on the right, Jaclyn and Brett were seated on the left of the large church. At the benediction, he watched the man lean down to Jaclyn, his hand at her lower back, his words produced a nod from her. No doubt Brett Webb knew just what to do when she got upset and tears filled her eyes. She leaned into him and he consoled her, drawing her closer still.

In this sacred place, something about the posture quickened something hot in him. He felt it rise, spur the energy, reveal more than jealousy in him now. His prayers had intensified since he'd met with Jaxson, refused the loophole, recommitted. He'd asked for direction, clear direction. He knew she still needed time. And he knew she needed words. But for the life of him, he didn't have pretty words. He had her father's words, his suggestion. And maybe it would have to do, at the right time. His eyes stayed open during the prayer, open and on his wife. He was impatient, he told his God. If she was to choose, then let the choice be made and may God's will be done. He was yielded to it.

He nodded at a man and made his exit before the Amen sounded. He slipped sunglasses on and took the stairs at a jog, his pace matching his impatience as he found open sidewalk to stride. He questioned the insanity of this whole out of the ordinary mission. How one little woman could affect so much of the known universe, the big of it and the small of it. Global powers of nations. Single thoughts of men.

"Look what Eve did? And the daughters of Eve are doing?" he muttered to his Lord. "Why in the world did you create her?" The answer was immediate.

Man was incomplete. Unless God had intervened in his own life, he would have been incomplete for a lifetime, single and satisfied to glorify His God as the Fury. His life perhaps short, his purpose great. And if he reached old age, then perhaps he would be restless in the incompleteness as he was ever so often when he had time to rest.

Man needed a helpmate. Unless God had chosen her, he would not have realized he needed help. Needed that evaluation that intimacy could accomplish. Needed the compliment of beauty, emotion, softness in a world strict with masculine simpleness. Needed that voice that asked, "hold me," that hand that says, "take mine."

Man was commanded to be fruitful and multiply. Well, he'd multiplied alright. Seven embryos locked in ice somewhere. How could he raise seven sons? That was a football team. Wouldn't his father-in-law love that. But perhaps a wife enabled a man's soil to be more fertile for the purposes of God as well, perhaps marriage would produce in him a hundredfold when left alone he could only be fruitful for thirtyfold.

"I will be patient. Trust your time. Trust your ways . . . all of them. May your will be done."

36

LaRue keyed the door, cracked it open and paused. Brutus wasn't at his post. His balance shifted, his hand drawing out his weapon. The elevator had already started back down. He glanced at the stairs. Too far. Move forward. His palm carefully eased the door to swing open. If he would meet an enemy he would do it with courage. He walked in. At once he saw the man. Jean-Claude sitting opposite the stranger bound with duct tape. The dog was on the ground.

"Did you kill my dog?"

He shook his head. "I had to de-armed him with a tranq. He's trained to kill."

"Yes." He cocked the gun. "Why should I not kill you?"

"Because you don't know who I am." The man rose, moved to Jean-Claude ripped off the tape from his mouth. "He is big for a Frenchman."

"We are not all small, gay, chefs." Jean-Claude cursed him with furious beady eyes.

"True. Perhaps you have something to do." He cut the tape from his hands. "Somewhere to go?" He looked at LaRue as he helped the big man to rise. "An errand to run for your boss."

LaRue nodded to the door. "Get the mail." Jean-Claude obeyed at once and left.

The stranger moved to his kitchen, uncorked a bottle of wine and poured. "You have good taste. I like the picture." He lifted his glass toward the painting. "You can kill me later if you wish, or have a drink and listen to what I have to say."

"A name."

He shook his head, stated, "This plan will not go well for you." He drank. "Your brother is reckless with his greed for power. You've worked very hard, been patient, calculating, wise. Impressive really, the contrast. But they've been waiting, baiting the trap. Why do you think they send her out with the pitcher? Lure you and others to him with all that press?" He sighed. "The Americans are predictable, they're anticipating you now. Their technology is cutting edge, their intel," he shrugged. "Sometimes good, sometimes not. But their law," he frowned, "Their justice system will have no mercy. If you break their law, you will pay. Your father knows this." He drank. "He understands limitations. He sends others to pay because he will not be caught in the trap of law and condemned by its order."

"My brother is subtle and smart. He sent you." He raised the gun. "Show me your colors, preacher."

"I am not Russian. And you are French."

"I am . . . impatient. Undress to the waist."

He took off the black suit coat, the black shirt, the tie. His skin was a rash of ruddy freckles and had no marks, but one. A small tattoo on his right bicep. A meaningless symbol of a Celtic cross of never ending knots. "I have no colors. Like you. Though you are marked. The minute the Americans see them, they will know who you are. Roll your sleeves up and let them see, confuse them with a twist. They will be coming to arrest you for the girl."

"They can arrest me for nothing."

"Cristina is not at her mother's."

"Oh?"

"In days they will know."

"In days I'll be gone."

"To Russia? What is there for you? You've already made a mark here." He drank. "Look outside the box, see your true opportunities. Let your brother come and do his best, take the girl. He will be caught. Often it is others who take care of our enemies. Cannibalism is a tactic."

"My brother sent you." He raised the gun again. "He sent you to deceive me, preacher."

"Your mother sent me."

"My mother is dead."

"Yes, eight years gone now." He drank. "But I made her a promise. I'll fulfill it." He set the goblet down empty. "You don't need colors. Another man's marks. You have lived too long under that tyranny. Stop lusting for a power that will leave you empty or soon dead. You are nothing to him but a pawn. Let him be nothing to you." Now he smiled. "Then you have found a greater power with your indifference. Freedom."

"Who were you to her?" His voice was flat and dry.

He called him a name, a name only his mother whispered to him when he was small.

"Your name?"

"Preacher works." He held his gaze. "I loved her. She tolerated me."

"And you promised her what?"

"More than I should have. Your house was bugged." He set a handful of devices on his bar.

"By who?"

"Not my problem to solve. They're going to come at you from every angle. Expect the Americans to know everything." He was putting his shirt back on, buttoning it up.

"They've already questioned me."

"They already know the answers, most of them. Use the story until you have to change it, then I'd use the Badger, blame him. He's easy to aggravate. Impatient with his shipments in customs, right? Make sure they sit, then shift. Let him come for you as well. Be not black or white but gray. And gray has many shades." He suggested, smiled. "I'm preaching again."

"And I've done well enough so far on my own."

"So far." He tightened the knot on his tie. "Your man would have died for you. Continue to discern what makes a man loyal and use it to form a network. You need to grow. Diversify. Employ more than muscle." He tapped his head. "You are not an island. Nor can you afford to be short sighted." He began to walk to the door.

"Your name." The demand was impatient.

"You will learn it eventually. And the fact that a chameleon is cleaver to camouflage itself in whatever surrounding it finds. Be clever, my friend. Let the Pendragon be caught." His Irish eyes held a merry light. His smile cocked and callous. "You. Like a cunning little lizard, shall escape."

"Jaclyn, come in," Lisette called to her from the door.

She'd had to wait, in an anteroom, but it had given her time to read Professor Neuville's finalized legal document from her paper. She had three hard copies. One for her, one for the accused and the final for the International Inner Port City. Another electronic copy had been downloaded to her PDA then sent to Lexi, Bennett and her Grandmother. Christie had already responded with the evidence, she was waiting on Interpol to get her the video from the night at Babel. Once she had the evidence, she could serve the indictment.

She stood, folding the paper lengthwise to stick in her coat pocket, and walked into her office. "Thanks for seeing me on short notice."

"I'm sorry Ida couldn't meet with us."

"It's okay," Jaclyn went in, stood by a chair, waited for the door to close.

"I love your jacket." The small talk began. She was used to it. Understood its purpose. The therapeutic warm-up you did just like when you exercised. "You look great."

"Jenna has a way of doing that for me. She's here. Brought this outfit along with her Texas charm."

It was a little black dress that laced up the center front, tying in a tiny tidy satin bow at her neckline. The overcoat was satin, black, trench coat style. The black heels lacing up her arch to tie off at her ankle with another bow.

"And some other ideas." She used her PDA to show her a few designs. "She likes details and themes. What do you think of this?"

There was a brilliant hummingbird sketched over a distinct pattern, a very distinct and familiar pattern.

"I, ah," Lisette looked up, for the first time Jaclyn saw an unguarded concern then quick recovery.

"You recognize it."

"The Hummingbird, your code name."

"Um." She looked at her. "The pattern."

"Yes."

"I love it." Jaclyn looked at it again, then up at Lisette. "The pattern."

Now Lisette sat. "The name fits you. You are like that furious little bird, Jaclyn."

She smiled at the description, the combination.

"The pattern however, is sacred. Like all tattoos of loyalty it is not to be copied but is given."

Jaclyn sat down, startled. "Oh, I didn't know."

"Of course not." She crossed her legs, cocked her head subtly to the side. "Perhaps one day it will be given. Now, what's in your pocket?"

"Oh. Professor Neuville polished my paper, made it legal. I'm just waiting on the evidence."

"Will you indict him?"

"I'm praying about that. My parents asked me to work with Marc and Christie, to trust their judgment. It was the process," she confirmed. "God taught me the law can work to bring about justice."

"It's why he gave man government. Romans 13."

Jaclyn nodded. "Another step forward I think, so I should expect two steps back. I'm afraid right now, Lisette," she confessed. "Wondering what Viper is doing. After the accident. I keep thinking what if it was me. Where would I be? What would he do to me? How would I handle it? I don't want to ever go back, be with him."

"Of course not." She leaned forward. "But God is with you, always, sovereign over every situation, and if it happened, God would supply what you needed. His Spirit gives a measure of grace for every situation we are in and He's promised not to give us more than we can handle or ever leave us. He's promised that. Grace empowers us to endure suffering and bring Him glory even if it's in a martyr's death."

She nodded. Agreed. "Fury told me once, we're immortal until our work here is done."

"Yes. Our faith fights our fears, empowers us with courage. Don't rehearse the past or imagine the future. Stay in the moment. Abide in His love, today. Tomorrow has enough worries of its own. Have you taken to heart a Word or promise from God for this?"

"Help me, God."

"Works in a jam." Lisette gave a rare grin. "But you are not yet in a jam, and when fear comes we must use the Word to cast it back. *Stratia* begins a mission with a Psalm of ascent, the hundred and twenty-fourth.

"If the LORD had not been on our side — let Israel say — if the LORD had not been on our side when men attacked us, when their anger flared against us, they would have swallowed us alive; the flood would have engulfed us, the torrent would have swept over us, the raging waters would have swept us away. Praise be to the LORD, who has not let us be torn by their teeth. We have escaped like a bird out of the fowler's snare; the snare

has been broken, and we have escaped. Our help is in the name of the LORD, the Maker of heaven and earth.

"If the Lord is on our side, who then can be against us?" She rose. "Be strong and courageous, Jaclyn, by engaging God's Word to strengthen your faith."

She took a deep breath, exhaled, re-centered and said, "Okay." Stood. "My cousins are here, Jenna and Samuel, I left them with Christie. Would you like to come meet Jenna?"

"I'd love to."

Together they went to Christie's office, it was a long walk, down elevators and over glides. As they entered the operations unit, she noticed heads turning then ducking as they saw Lisette. People seemed to scramble, as if an incoming typhoon was about to hit shore. In Christie's office there was laughter. She was ending a story about her sons, rubbing her belly, "What in the world will I do with three of those knuckleheads?"

"Four," Jaclyn corrected. "You have to include Uncle Marc in the knucklehead count."

"Of course." Christie stood, her gaze on the Termite.

"Jenna, this is Lisette." Jaclyn made the introductions. There was small talk. "I told her about you but I wanted her to meet you in person. She's going to design something for you."

"For me?" Lisette stepped back.

"From me." Jaclyn smiled as her hand touched her back. "A late birthday gift, we'll call it."

"A challenge, I'd call it." Christie muttered.

Jenna asked a few questions, her gaze circling Lisette, her green eyes studying.

"How does it feel?" Christie asked her. "To be scrutinized."

"Aunt Christie, I don't scrutinize. I study. Do you like certain colors?" Jenna asked.

"I'll let the expert decide. I've simple tastes."

"Hardly. She wears browns and blues a lot. I'd put her in chartreuse." Christie pretended to read a report.

"Christie, be nice," Jenna scolded, sketching. "Do you have signs or symbols you like? I'm fascinated with embroidery right now. Weaving cloth."

"She's a Termite."

Jenna narrowed her eyes at her aunt.

"Really. That's what we call the psych squad, destructive insects. Termites, ticks, leeches."

"For your information," Jenna rose and smiled, closing her sketch book, "Insects are some of the most incredible creatures God designed. Do you have any idea how genius the silk worm is?"

"I've never thought of it."

Lisette told Christie, "Termites can fell a redwood tree."

"Exactly my point."

"Or clean up something rotten and make a garden grow from its ashes," Jaclyn added softly. "Everything has it purpose."

"Yes, it does. Like the hummingbird."

Jenna smiled. "Did you show her the—

"Ah, is that the photo from the cover of the Globe?" Lisette moved to Christie's desk, picked up a photograph, showed Jaclyn. "Have you seen this?"

It was the recent cover shot from the Globe. LaRue holding Cristina's hand. Brett holding hers. They'd made it look like Brett was with both girls when they'd cropped it for the tabloid. Here it looked like he was closer to Cristina. His hand at her back. Her and LaRue at arm's length of the couple in the center. Brett's gaze was caught on Cristina, that smile on his face.

"You can have the picture," Christie told her.

"Is that Cristina?" Jenna asked.

"Um." She looked up at her cousin. "Don't tell me I hear envy in your tone?"

"Um."

"Jenna?" Jaclyn narrowed her eyes, curled the photo and put it with the legal document in her interior pocket.

"LaRue understands me."

"Oh, please, you're not hard to understand." Her eyes gave her a once over. "And LaRue is French and fussy. Fickle to be sure and hardly a—

"He's not fussy."

"We'll see what Samuel thinks."

"I love brothers," Christie grinned. "They do come in handy. Where is the Chevaux heir?"

"Playing commando down the hall with Joshua."

"I do love my cousins." Jaclyn smiled at the women, taking Jenna's hand.

"I'll send you some ideas," Jenna told Lisette.

"See you at the party," Christie reminded. "We'll see what Uncle Marc thinks of the Frenchman."

"Great," Jenna mumbled. "Thanks a lot."

Jaclyn linked their arms. "I don't want you hurt, and I'm afraid LaRue will seduce you or worse, break your heart." She looked around, lowered her voice, "About the hummingbird. I can't have it."

"What?"

She explained, "It's a sacred symbol."

"The hummingbird."

"No, the design under it. It's a mark of loyalty and can't be copied."

"Ut-oh." Jenna's green eyes went wide before she laughed.

"It's not funny. I can't believe I let you do that. If anyone sees it, I'm in big trouble."

"Then you'll have to keep your jacket on." She patted between her shoulder blades where she'd embroidered the design into her dress. "Too bad, too, it was quite a silent statement. Now you might just have to step up to the plate and tell him."

"Um, you're mixing metaphors."

"No, I was talking about Brett." Jenna gave a nod. "The way you've got your walk on," she bumped her hip. "I know who you're really after. It's time to pull the pitcher. I don't think Joshua Fury has the patience for baseball."

"Um. He's very patient. Excruciatingly patient."

"There you go, your lashes just went low." Jenna laughed, called out. "Brother, where art thou?"

"In here," Samuel called back.

They stopped at the door. Eli and Joshua standing. Samuel leaning on the desk, arms crossed. Smile wide. "Ladies."

"Scoundrel. You've been talking about us," Jenna stated.

"Of course. Strategizing my best defense."

"For what?"

"Beating back the brutes at this party tonight."

"I've got bigger muscles hired for that."

"Tiki doesn't interfere with your personal life or he'd have sent that pitcher packing months ago."

"Um. Fury believes Brett's proven himself." She picked up the photo from his desk. The same picture that Christie had. "This seems to be making the rounds."

"Is that Cristina? She's pretty. Looks like you."

"Prettier."

Samuel took the photo. "You girls are so competitive."

"I thought that was gracious." Jenna narrowed her eyes at her brother.

"Is there a problem with this picture?" Jaclyn asked.

"We needed a recent shot of Cristina," Eli answered.

"Are you the strong silent type today?" Jaclyn finally looked at Joshua.

There was a slow grin.

"Going to check the eyebrow? It's healing."

"With so much eyebrow there, it's hard to tell, cuz."

"Samuel." Jenna smacked him. "I swear you are rude."

Samuel stood, tucking his sister under his arm. "Better let these men get back to work and earn their living."

"He knows so much about that." Jenna rolled her eyes.

"I know it takes three herds of registered Angus just to keep you in shoes."

"Don't start with the shoes."

"Darling by the way, cuz."

Jaclyn posed her feet. "Do you think?"

"I think Jenna needs to find something else to do with her time. Those bows are trouble."

"What! Oh, please, brother. You don't know what you're saying."

"I like the bows," Jaclyn stated.

"Knots are better. Bows just make a man's imagination tug on the ends."

"James Samuel," Jenna smacked him again.

"It's true. Fury—

"Don't turn to me with that." He stacked his arms.

"Do you like the bows?" Jaclyn asked him, lashes low, brows lifted and feathered high.

He struggled, Eli jumping in at once. "You always look nice. Yes, ma'am. Top notch. Nice. And you too, Miss Cooper."

"Are you coming tonight, Eli?" Jenna lowered her own lashes, smiled.

Samuel suddenly stepped in. "Don't start with that, Jenna. She's trouble. More than you can handle, Eli. Out, girls! Hit the hall. That's right swing those hips and do that walk thing. Flash the eyes and lower the lashes. Give the little wave and the Cooper smile. I've seen it all before and the after-effects. Heaven help them." He waved to the men. Escorted the ladies away.

"I wanted to talk to him," Jaclyn whispered.

"He has no idea what to say to you. You've got that effect on him, make him tongue-tied, he said."

"He said that?"

"Interesting." The girls exchanged a look.

"What else did he say?"

"Nothing I'm repeating."

The conversation carried through traffic, the banter heating up, Samuel muttering to himself, texting and ignoring them when they drifted into purely female topics. He pretended not to have patience for it, but in truth he was totally in his element.

"Now look," Jaclyn took charge in the elevator. "I've got things to do up here. I don't want trouble from you." She gave Samuel a look then shifted to Jenna. "Or you. Tiki takes care of me." She gave him a smile. Tiki gave a nod. They'd had a conversation since the accident, a tightening up of their own basic practices. He texted her and she gave a numerical response. One to five based on how she was feeling. A one was a call to come. A five stand down. Between them Tiki gauged her instinctual awareness. Two be near. Three be close. Four just watch. They were both happy with the system. "There will be a bunch of people here, good food, music. And with Cristina recuperating and *Stratia* up in arms that there's a possible coup in the works, the night already has me stressed. I've got to hostess for Brett."

"I'll help." Jenna promised.

"Um. Here we are. Oh, this elevator makes me crazy." It surged to a stop then drifted down a degree of a drop. The doors opened. The hall lobby already set up, apartment B and C's doors were open. "LaRue has a new painting, he'll want to show it to you, Jenna. Brett?" she called out.

Music was already playing and LaRue already drinking. He greeted her with a glass of wine, his sleeves rolled up. Dark scrolling tattoos marking both forearms, curling to an end at his wrists. "My Cherie Amour," he kissed Jenna's hand, held it regally as he smiled into her eyes then brought her close so they could look Jaclyn's outfit over. "Stellar. Simple. Love the satin. Do turn around."

Jaclyn obliged him.

"You are brilliant, Jenna. I adore a woman wrapped up with a bow."

Samuel cleared his throat. "My brother," Jenna introduced him. "James Samuel."

"Call him Cletus." Jaclyn winked. "I didn't know you had tattoos, LaRue."

"Ah, the ink." He drank, blushed. "A mistake of youth, but none the less, I do." He called for Jean-Claude, "We have a coat."

"Ah, no. I'll keep the coat. I'm cold. What have you done with Brutus?"

"He is on the roof." Jean-Claude looked relieved.

"And happy to be there in his little crate with his juicy bone. You are safe. Come and see if you approve." They went in apartment C.

"There's my Babe." Brett came to them smiling. "Is this Jenna? You are incredible," he praised. Added more to it and the group weighed in. Everyone except Samuel.

There was a handshake. A pause. Then Brett smiled again. "We're glad you could make it. Did you tell her the news, LaRue?"

"Cristina has agreed to come tonight. Flying in and then I've a helicopter that will deliver her to the roof. She's a bit reluctant, says her face is still swollen." He drank. "Perhaps if you agreed to meet her there, stay close as she re-enters social life, she'll feel more confident."

"Sure. A helicopter?"

"There's a helipad on the roof. LaRue uses it all the time."

"Sometimes." He shrugged. "The traffic can snarl."

"These are for you," Brett handed her a huge vase of red roses mixed with sprigs of greenery and soft spring flowers.

"Brett, these are beautiful. Thank you."

"There's another vase for Jenna." Brett smiled at her. "Jaclyn always looks incredible and you've had a lot to do with that. And then a third for Cristina. Where should we put them?"

"Ah, it begins." LaRue winked. "Shall we let the girls work? Drink, Cletus?"

It was a rush of activity, somewhere in the midst of it LaRue had put a goblet in her hand. Samuel had lit up a cigar, on the roof she was told, with Brutus and Jean-Claude. It was the best place for him until the party started. Players were arriving from the team with dates and friends. People stirring already. Music playing. She'd been caught up in conversation with the catcher. Talking about Brett's sinker, when he came up behind her, filled her glass, kissed her neck, excused them both and guided her into his kitchen. "I've got this bottle stashed over here, just for you."

"I'll share."

"No. Not this. The Sizzle is for us. To us." He toasted her, drank. Kissed her. Moved closer. Kissed her deeper. "Thanks for helping pull this off."

"Sure." She nodded, took a small sip, pulled back. There was conversation on all sides of them. The kitchen busy, this corner quiet.

"I've been thinking about you a lot this week. After the accident, I, ah," he shook his head. She saw the emotion, watched him fight it. "You need to know something. I'm in love with you. Don't say anything." He touched her lips. "This is too soon, I know it. But I need you to know. Since the first time we talked, before we ever met, I felt something for you. It's grown." There was a little box in his hands. "You're not ready for what I want to give you, but maybe this can be a stepping stone." He opened it. There was a cross, jeweled with diamonds. He lifted it out, set the heavy piece around her neck. Took off the other cross, the simple cross on black beads with the tiny tags behind it. She watched him set it aside on the counter and came out of her shock.

"Brett." She shook her head. Anxious, suddenly intensely restless.

"You need to know how I feel."

"So do you," the words were soft, achingly soft. She cleared her throat. Covered Joshua's cross on the counter to fist it up into her hand, holding it dearly. "I need a friend, not a lover. I tried—"

"I know." He moved closer. "I know you're trying. I understand what you've been through. How hard this must be to trust me, yourself, your body. In time it will be natural. I feel you warming up to me, the passion—"

"You're a handsome man. So attentive to me, of course there could be passion, easily," she told him. "But Brett, emotionally, I can't connect." She held tighter to Joshua's cross. "I'm in love with someone else," she finally said it. And with the statement she took the cross off, placed it back in the box and into his hands. "And I'm almost certain someone else is in love with you." She pulled the paper out of her coat pocket, showed him the picture of the three of them.

"No." He shook his head. Began to rationalize.

"It's okay. It happens, sometimes without our permission, it just happens. Cristina is a wonderful girl and the picture tells the story. LaRue and I are at arm's length, you're leaning toward each other."

"It's the angle. You know how they make these pictures look like something else."

"Maybe. You might not have realized yet because I've been in the way, distracting you from it. If it's the truth, I'd be very happy for you both. Really." She put Joshua's cross back on. "I love you, as a friend, and once I knew my own heart and began to see hers, I knew I needed to tell you."

"Who gave you that cross? When you're upset you touch it and I've never seen you without it."

"Joshua."

"The Fury?" he stepped back, a look of confusion crossing his face, his gaze glancing across the room. "It's him then? You're in love with him."

"It's hopeless."

"I know the feeling," he told her.

"So the three of us, we're going to be a sad little triangle of hopeless disappointment."

"I guess so."

"Brett Webb. Be honest. She's perfect for you." She touched his chest. He covered her hand.

"If you'd give me one night, you'd see I'd be perfect for you."

"I gave you a night. A deceptive night of Eros and it deceived you, destroyed anything we could have been romantically. Eros has a preference, Brett. When it's given to a woman. She'll choose, seek her preference."

"You chose me."

"I'd tried all day to get to Joshua, I substituted and when I was with you, I was thinking about him, how angry I was at him. When I realized it was back, that Eros was driving me, I went to Heatherwood and cycled there. It's a horrible drug, Brett. Lust on steroids. It's deceptive, destructive. It's not how two people should ever share intimacy. Love is. Love can take you places Eros never will. Lust is smoke and mirrors. A flash fire. Love last past the climaxing moment. Love never ends. Right?"

There was a strange look on his face. Of pain and guilt. Remorse, maybe as he nodded. "Jaclyn, I, ah," he spilled her wine glass. She turned to get a towel, then jumped when something crashed. The bottle of the priceless Sizzle shattered in a puddle of red wine on the floor.

"Okay, cuz?"

"Yes." She looked at Samuel across the kitchen. At Tiki across the room. "I'm fine. Just an accident."

A caterer moved in at once. "Mr. Webb, let me, sir."

"Don't cut yourself, Brett." Jaclyn took his arm. "Those hands are pretty important to the city of D.C., Ace."

Stepping aside, he took her into his arms, held her desperately tight, whispered, "I'm sorry. You're right. I've been . . . " He just shook his head, held her tighter, said her name. "Forgive me, Jaclyn. I do love you. I love you," he repeated the confession.

She held him tight, understanding, totally understanding what it feels like when your heart breaks.

37

Marc had arrived with a series of questions to draw out the truth from the Frenchman. He'd had the photograph in his pocket that showed the tail of the tattoo that was the beginning and the end of a historic legacy that had nothing to do with the French. But the man had surprised him, shaking his hand with his sleeves rolled up and the truth in plain view.

"You're Russian," Marc had announced.

He swore in French, narrowed his eyes as he stepped back. A hand whipped at a sleeve, then the other. "How would you know that?"

"What are you doing here, LaRue Tsilevich?"

"That is not my last name. He might be my father but I am bastard born and far removed from him for years. Who are you?"

"Someone who knows you are dangerous."

"I have no colors."

"Worse, you're out to earn them."

"I don't need his colors, nor want them."

"Why are you here? Here, living beside Brett Webb?"

"He moved beside me."

"What a coincidence. One in a line of several." Marc moved very close to him. "Be very, very careful, Mr. Tsilevich."

"I am not Russian," he reminded him. "I am French and very certain that you have miscalculated my loyalties and intentions."

"We'll see," he told him. "And we do see, everything."

Fury frowned as he listened to the conversation. LaRue was either very stupid or extremely clever. Being young with no history to examine, it was hard to read him. Joshua stayed in the background, planted himself in a corner of the hall lobby by the stairs. It was the only way to get off the floor, beside the elevator. His team on ear buds. Command calling out the hour and clearing every party guest who came in the door with face recognition software. The space was full of music, light spicy jazz and famous people with their buzz of conversation. Jaclyn tied the whole thing together with a pretty little bow. Flitting around with bows on her shoes, a goblet of red wine in her hand, totally in her element playing hostess. A natural conversationalist. He knew they wouldn't try anything here. It would be a snatch and grab. At school or on the street. In transit somewhere or in a crowd. Not here, with no way in and no way out. Which is why it very well could be here, now. He'd do it here… He considered how, as he watched the colorful crowd of people, listened to the various conversations coming through his earbud, and saw the Hummingbird darting in and out.

It was awkward, but she swore she wouldn't let it be. Jaclyn stayed beside him, tender now that the truth was told. More natural than perhaps she'd ever been with Brett because she could finally be herself. Christie came up to her and said they were going to be leaving soon. She stepped aside, asked, "Have you heard back from Mr. Remmi on the evidence?"

"He said he's working on it."

"Do you think he really is, Marc?" she asked her uncle.

"I think if anyone can get video from Babel, Red Remmi can, Jaxie."

"But you don't agree with the indictment, even if I have the evidence."

"It might be useful, played the right way. I'd like you to let us help you know when that time is."

"Okay." She nodded.

Her uncle kissed her. "It was a great party. The team's going to follow you home. Christie's tired."

She nodded. Smiled as Brett said his goodbyes as well. The elevator shut and they stood there for a moment, by the door of apartment C with Joshua Fury opposite them in the corner. He stood alone, looking like security.

"You can talk to him," Brett told her.

"He's not here to talk." She took his arm. "Have you seen Jenna?"

"Not in a while. Where's LaRue?"

They found him in his apartment. Jenna under his arm, the two staring at the portrait, LaRue drinking wine, flirting ridiculously. As they walked to them, Jaclyn stated quietly, "He can flirt all he wants but if he moves into seduction mode—"

"He won't. He's promised me."

"LaRue, showing off your new love?"

"She means the painting," Brett cleared.

"Jenna believes the woman is watching the rain fall."

"Um." Jaclyn took another look. "Perhaps she's looking at her reflection," Jaclyn pondered anew. 'Trying to decide who she is."

LaRue looked at her. She smiled. There was that moment of connection between two people and she realized she wasn't alone in her search. "I like that." He toasted her. Looked at Brett. "You've an incredible woman there."

"We broke up tonight," he told them. "She's in love with someone else. Thinks I'm in love with Cristina. I'm not." He pocketed his hands, looking at LaRue. "You are."

"I'm not," he answered. "I'm very fond of her, but I'm French and smart enough to understand I'm addicted to the conquest. Be warned," he told Jenna now. Blushed with his smile. "I'm fond of you too, and others. A bout of honesty there, sweetheart." He drank.

The gauche silence relieved by the ringing of his phone.

"Not again." Jenna stepped back, filled in. "They've been hounding him. Some testy customer, making threats."

"No, it's my pilot," he told them. "She's due to land." He smiled.

Now Brett stepped back. "Then you should go, the two of you, greet her."

Jaclyn reached for him. "Brett, you'll come."

"No." He sidestepped, smiled. "I'll stay down here with Jenna. We'll watch over the party. Go on now. She needs you and LaRue. She's nervous. You'll reassure her."

"Brett."

"Go on, Babe." He stepped back further. Firm.

LaRue took her hand. "Shall we?"

They opened the door and Brutus lunged toward them. LaRue gave a command. Like a switch it turned the dog off. He sat, alert, eyes focused only on his master. "Ah, here's my boy." LaRue gave Brutus a smile, a firm stroke as Jean-Claude held him on a leash. "How was his walk?"

"Good, sir. We went down the stairs a few floors then caught the lift."

LaRue smiled, ushered her forward. "It's a bit windy up here. Good thing you have your jacket, warm enough?"

She nodded.

"Mind if I smoke?"

"No, go ahead. Pretty night." She turned to the north, looked up into the sky, named a constellation. She strolled along the roof, they talked of the stars, she told him her father had a telescope when she was young, taught her about the night sky.

"It's windy. There's no railing. Don't get too close to the edge." His hand reached for her, coming from behind. A hand. The white cuff. A dark tattoo, curling over his wrist bone, like a coiling reptile tongue. It struck a chord. A memory. A hand, marked with color, sliding over her body, slithering to private places. She shivered. Terrified then fortified as she prayed. Stepped back, stood under his arm. He was a friend.

She was alone.

"Where's the helicopter?" She glanced at the door, where Jean-Claude stood with a very obedient and alert Brutus.

He was a friend. She was alone. On a roof. Trapped.

In her coat pocket she fingered her PDA now, a simple keystroke would send a message to Tiki. She pushed the three. She needed him to be near. She should never be alone. Especially right now. On a roof. Trapped. Stupid. She looked at the door. Really stupid, Jaxie.

"I hear it. Listen."

She did. The sweeping high pitch, the thud, thud, thud of power.

"It's coming."

Brett was coming his way. Alone. His hazel eyes were green, troubled.

"What's wrong?" Joshua asked him.

His gaze changed, became competitive, focused, that flat steel color he'd seen when the man pitched the change up and struck a batter out.

"We'll talk about it later. All the things you didn't tell me. Like her loving you." He swore. "Me loving her. And Cristina loving me. Who knows what LaRue's been doing." He yanked the door open for the stairs.

"Where are you going?"

"To meet Jaclyn and LaRue."

"Where?"

"Upstairs."

"They didn't go upstairs. I've been standing here all night. She's in LaRue's apartment."

"You must have missed her," he said with an edge of contempt. "They're on the roof. Cristina's coming in on a helicopter." He pulled the door open.

"No." Fury put his hand on the man. "I wouldn't miss her. She didn't go up these stairs."

Tiki came to them. "Where's Jaclyn? She paged me. Wants me. I lost her in LaRue's apartment."

"Find the Hummingbird. Now." Fury sent out the command to every alert ear. "Get me all access modes to the roof. We just went green," he gave the high alert. "Tell Marc. It's the roof."

Brett jerked away, went through the door with confidence. Up the stairs at a sprint. Tiki and Fury came behind him. He could hear the helicopter. Knew.

"Get me wings on the roof to chase," he was calling out orders. "Brett, get back." He pulled out a weapon. Tiki's already out. Brett charged ahead, her name echoing in the stairwell in his reckless wake. Without thought or skill, Brett was first through the door, unarmed. The high pitch whine of the copter already accelerating. Bullets coming at them from an automatic. Fury took Brett down, Tiki fired beside them from the roof floor.

"Don't!" Fury growled. "You'll kill her if they crash."

Brett pushed him off with stellar strength as he found his feet and sprinted toward the helicopter.

"Lord, protect him," Fury prayed aloud as he chased low, sweeping wide, giving orders, insight, firing only to create a cover for Brett's impotence.

From the new angle he saw a fight. One man swinging at another. LaRue's fancy shirt optic white in the night, billowing in the air blast, his opponent in black sending him down with a final blow. Then the man in black jumped into the copter and with a blast it hovered off the roof.

Below it was a body.

The urge to sprint was only overruled by staunch training. It was inbred in him but barely overruling his emotions. Like Brett, he had a sudden single focus. Jaclyn.

As the helicopter launched into flight the blast sent Brett to his face. The Fury struggling to stay on his own feet. Now he ran, calling out tail numbers. Repeating the sequence, giving the direction of flight as he received ETA on his own ride to chase. On the ground there was a Rottweiler, the big Frenchman and LaRue. Brett was holding a woman.

"It's Cristina," he declared.

"They took Jaclyn," she told them, clinging to Brett. "Drugged me. More," her words were muffled against Brett as he held her. Joshua checked the large Frenchman, calling for medical help. He'd been shot, lung and leg, so had the dog. It whined softly, looking at him, showing teeth and growling even in its disability.

LaRue gave a word, stirring to consciousness, looking at the dog, his man, cursing as men came running through two doors onto the roof.

"There were stairs in his apartment," Seth told him. "They must have come up that way."

"We did," LaRue moaned. Cursed. In a rapid string of French, he struggled to rise. "Russian bastards! They took a million for her ransom. Now they've taken Jaclyn. Shot Jean-Claude. My dog."

"Ransom? Who?"

"The Badger. Kozlov." He was up, wiping his mouth, looking at Joshua. "He's had her. I've been in a standoff with the Russians over a certain shipment caught in customs. They were using Cristina as leverage. I lied to you, but I knew where she was, how to get her back. If I got you involved, they would have killed her."

There was silence, the team knowing better than to speak. They let LaRue use his PDA. His words were Russian now, curt, threatening words, that made a demand to speak to Kozlov the Badger. Command was interpreting them, Eli standing close now, as commanded, the wounded being treated.

The dog growled again. LaRue gave a command, curt and clear. The dog closed its eyes.

Joshua turned as Brett picked up Cristina. The resemblance in this light was startling. Her voice different. "He let me go."

"Yes," Brett told her. "You're safe now."

"They took Jaclyn." She began to cry. "They drugged me . . . more."

There was pain in Brett's eyes, tenderness as he kept her close, said soft assuring words.

"I found this." Seth was holding Jaclyn's PDA. Joshua took it. Tiki was troubled.

Too many people needing too much. He began to give orders. Divide the tasks. Put people into action. He took Cristina's blood to test it before he sent them down to Brett's apartment through LaRue's stair access. Tiki was to end the party, by whatever means necessary. His team was to stand by and be ready.

"Find her," Brett ordered.

Joshua nodded. "Take care of Cristina. *Stratia* will tell you how." He watched him take her away. Heard the beating of wings. LaRue was still on his phone.

"End your call," Fury told him. "You're coming with me."

The chaos was common, he commanded through it. Was used to the surge of adrenaline. Even the unknown twist of LaRue and the Badger. What was new and uncharted was his emotions. He was worried. Anxiety at a level he'd only experience with his brother when Caleb had been MIA. He pushed the dread aside, refused it. This would not end like that. He prayed, as he dressed. As his team geared up on a copter moving like a cutter on the high seas. As a Frenchman spoke Russian, loud and sharp into his phone. As Command told him the Hummingbird was moving across the Atlantic Ocean.

"She's not with the Badger." He finally spoke to LaRue. "She's in flight across the ocean, headed to the International Inner Port City."

"Did you sell her?" he screamed into the PDA in perfect English. Cursed in French. Threatened in Russian. "To some Sheikh at Babel!"

"End the call," Fury commanded. "We're about to unload. Get on a jet."

He took him by the arm, escorted him into a jet. Marc was waiting. Mad as the Bull he was named after. His nostrils flared. He pointed to a seat. The interrogation began.

Brett had laid Cristina down on LaRue's massive bed after they came through the stairwell door from the roof into his neighbor's home. The apartment private now. Tiki already moving people to the elevators. There was apparently a gas leak. Everyone was cooperating. The hour was late.

"Do you need some water?"

She shook her head. She hadn't stopped crying or clinging to his hand. They'd told him she was in shock. *Stratia* was sending a medical team to help.

"Do you need anything?"

She'd come back into his arms, clinging tight, sobbing now. He held her. Until she stopped, he held her. Her breath was gentle, slow. Her head resting against his chest. He thought she might sleep, but she whispered his name.

He looked at her. Her brown eyes wide and frightened. "They drugged me… more."

"I'm so sorry," he told her.

She curled into him. Restless. Clinging. "Hold me. Please."

"LaRue went with . . . the police."

She nodded. "I want you," she explained. "He's fine, fun, but I need you. You're who I need right now. I want you, okay?"

"I'm here."

"He raped me." Tears filled her eyes and his.

"We'll get you help."

"He gave me a drug. A horrible drug. It made me…" she shook her head. "I'm sorry." She'd curled into his lap, the whole of her needing to be held.

He felt the vibration of the text message, instinct knowing what he'd be told. He read the confirming words, his arm keeping her close then placed his PDA beside them on the bed. There was a moment of temptation. A quick plot and plan. A fantasy. But now he saw the final scene, the death scene, what Eros did eventually. How lust killed. Lust had killed anything he could have had with Jaclyn. It was waiting to attack anything he could hope for with Cristina.

He confessed his lust, knew what love was supposed to do. Knew what love never did. Knew that love's patience would ultimately bring the greatest blessing. Knew that God, who was love, would enable him now to do what was right.

There was a prayer, the confession quick, the repentance true, the request fortifying, then the truth in love was delivered. "He gave you Eros. You're cycling now, Cristina."

"Cycling. Eros?"

He explained all he knew then told her about Jaclyn. What she had been through. How they were involved in her story. "There's a place I'm going to take you to. They know what to do."

"No, don't leave me."

"You need Heatherwood, not me."

"I want you."

"Eros wants me."

"No. I want you. Since we met. I'm sorry." She began to cry. "I'm so sorry. I shouldn't have told you that. Lord, I'm a mess." She'd reached for her neck. "They took my cross."

"Here." He took the box from his pocket. Didn't question it. "I have one. I bought it for Jaclyn, but it wasn't meant to be hers. She said we were better as friends." He slipped it on her neck. "We broke up. She's in love with someone else." He smiled. "She thinks you and I should date."

"She does?" She touched the cross, looking at him, then shook her head.

"She knew too. She said if she wasn't distracting me, I would have figured it out. We'll wait until you're better, see, okay?"

"I want you now."

"I know."

"You could help me. Here, in this beautiful bed." She was drawing him closer. "Make it better. Make what he did go away."

"There's another way to help you, now. It's not here." He shook his head. Believed and trusted. "I don't want lust now, I want the real thing, love and it will have to wait for you to get better. And you will, but not this way."

She looked at him, her hand still on the cross, then her gaze. "This is beautiful, Brett." She shook her head.

"She helped us," he told her. "Jaclyn would want you to have that. To pray for her now, like she did for you."

"Those men," she shook her head. "Those awful men. Pendragon they call him. He has her. They'll—"

"There's help on the way. They know where they took her. And it's time to take you to Heatherwood. Get you help." He picked her up, knowing what he needed to do. Who to find. He asked Jenna to help. Tiki would drive them. Samuel was pacing, worried, needing something to do as well. As they waited for the elevator, Brett asked the group, "Mind if I pray?"

They bowed together and did.

38

Jaclyn knew. Without opening her eyes, she knew. Orientation came slowly, and because she had been practicing the exercise for months every time she woke up, she put it into action and controlled her consciousness. She could hear the jet. Sense the speed. She'd be somewhere over the Atlantic. Her left hand was chained, she felt the cuff. Fought the fear of it quickly. Temper came. A nice hot temper even as she prayed. She heard their conversation, the words Russian, the voices unfamiliar.

But his tattoo, on his wrist, snaking out from the edge of his sleeve—those marks she remembered. And his eyes. Common brown eyes in a familiar face. Her right hand reached out and slapped him brutally with the outrage.

"Harry Olstrom," she said his name with marked contempt.

"Now love, is that any way to treat an old friend." His accent was British. As charming as it had been the night he'd drugged her drink at Babel.

She slapped him again. Harder, reaching across the space of the quad seating arrangement letting her anger surge with her outrage as she yanked her chains to reach him.

There was laughter. Russian words delivered in a tone of mocking banter.

Harry's eyes narrowed on her, his gaze boring into her own, his smile gone. He didn't retaliate, and that answered her question. He couldn't touch her. But he called her a disrespectful name.

"She is a tiger, Pendragon," an older man corrected as he drank his vodka and ran his gaze over her body as he gave her a smile.

"A tiger," then he added the degrading name again.

She slapped him again. Harder. This time he came out of his seat, gave her a knee to the stomach. There was a burst of pain. She growled when only months ago she would have squealed. Let the energy roll through her when before she would have held tightly to it. Feared not, his hotly breathed threats hissed at her, nor did she fight when her free hand was chained to the armrest. Her mind was focused on the Psalm of ascent, the battle call to war. Her spirit gearing up to engage in a battle he knew nothing of as he said the word again, against her ear. As he talked about her body, slowly untied the bow, unraveled the lacing of the ribbon down the front placket until the dress gaped and her body was revealed to her navel.

He couldn't touch her but he could taunt her. And Harry Olstrom did, using imaginative threats and predictions about the Viper's intentions. She didn't look away, she didn't listen, she prayed. She was strong, courageous, faithful, beloved by God. She stared her enemy in the eye and prayed the words of David,

I call on you, O God, for you will answer me; give ear to me and hear my prayer. Show the wonder of your great love, you who save by your right hand those who take refuge in you from their foes.

Keep me as the apple of your eye; hide me in the shadow of your wings from the wicked who assail me, from my mortal enemies who surround me.

Rise up, O LORD, confront them, bring them down; rescue me from the wicked by your sword. O LORD, by your hand save me from such men, from men of this world whose reward is in this life.

If I perish, I perish . . . but I will not be afraid. Lord, give me the grace I need to suffer well.

Lisette awoke to the shrill call, sending a fat cat to the floor with a feline protest as she searched for her PDA. She blacked out the vid, her voice answering, "Yes. Yes," as she pushed back a fall of pale hair from her eyes. "When?" she looked at the clock, seeing the hour, predicting their location. "Tell the Peregrine I'm coming in." She was out of bed. "I don't care what she wants." Grabbing clothes. "Tell her I am duly alerted and now on my way." She began to dress, as her hands trembled and dread coursed through her body, she did the only thing she could do at this moment to help free a snared Hummingbird. The Termite prayed.

Fury watched, as Marc interrogated the Frenchman. He was adamant about his story. It had started with a late shipment, a customs hold. An impatient Russian client. LaRue claimed he'd told the man to forget the deal. Transferred back his deposit, but he declined the offer. Demanded his goods and wanted them immediately. The standoff had been going on for almost a week when they had grabbed Cristina. Demanded not only the goods but also a million in ransom for the girl.

He'd told them about the con to lead the authorities astray, to make them think he'd found Cristina to protect her. About his lies that covered up the truth that the Russian Badger had kidnapped her, to protect himself as well.

Then Marc pulled out the dossier on LaRue. "I don't believe in coincidences," Marc informed him. "And there are far too many in this case. You might have a French name and a French mama, but I know *thief in law* when I see it, and you have been marked. You are out to earn your colors."

"No," he denounced firmly. "I hate these marks."

"But they come in very handy sometimes. Open many ABepb," he translated the Russian. "Doors."

"I speak the language."

"You wanted your colors. Wanted your name. Especially since your half-brother found loyalty. You were patient, smart, savvy. Worked systematically and began to be very successful at your side import business cover. But after all that hard work, all the effort, you got outsmarted by an older half-brother and he stole the girl. Punched you in the nose, shot your man, your dog and left you for us to prosecute. Now you've paid the Badger a million dollars to cover up a botched attempt—whose botch, doesn't really matter now, except to the girl. Cristina was innocent. A pawn in a high-stakes game of sibling rivalry—raped by your half-brother, discarded at your feet as he took what you worked for. The Tigrissa. He has the Tiger and he will earn the reward. Am I right, LaRue?"

"No," he denied again. Said no more.

"I've been on to you from the beginning. I laid the trap, a trail of breadcrumbs and I watched very carefully after the first foot who followed it. I knew the moment you bought the apartment next to Mr. Webb."

"I was there before him."

"It does look that way on paper, but you were there after him. I have good IT people."

"I came for business."

"Yes. And you've done it with a lot of people, including Russians. I know what you're really importing. I know who your contact is with the Badger, where you met to do business, what game you played while you talked. I know your strategy, a remarkable con on the chess board that allows your competitor to fall into your trap, win without knowing you orchestrated your own loss. I know the hypocrisy, who you are under the masks you've worn. I warned you. I know who you are."

"You believe what you want to believe. There is no proof to this madness. I am fond of Jaclyn. I would never do this thing you say."

Marc closed the file. He leaned forward and the brogue of the Scotsman singed the words now with his anger. “Ye are French, fickle. Aye?” He smiled. “Ye hav done er’athing as I’ve told ye. Ye came to tak’ a tiger, to earn yer colors and ye’eve failed, ye hav. Yer brother beat ye square, will be rewarded and now yer sin, it is a comin’ through this verra door, it is to master ye as well.”

For the first time the Frenchman smiled. “Yes, it looks that way, doesn’t it?”

Fury knew, as Marc did, looks could be very deceiving.

Harry gave Jaclyn a menacing look as he leaned in close and spat, “Slap me again, sis, and I’ll send an order back to the states to have your famous boyfriend killed. Slowly. Understand me?”

“Um.” Her gazed stayed fixed to his, like it had been for the last half hour, fixed, unafraid.

“You misbehave at all and I’ll start a list. Hunt down your family. You have a very pretty mother. She wears good shoes. Did she teach you that?”

She would say nothing more. There would be no negotiating with Harry Olstrom. She just held his gaze, unswervingly, even as he pulled a pressure syringe out and prepared to give her a dose of something. There was fear over what it could be. Dread that she could lose control. She funneled both into a focused anger. She would allow anger, prayed for strength. She would need to be wise.

He smiled now, coming close, flicking open her coat, sliding her dress up her thigh to expose skin. “Cristina. She looks a lot like you. Softer. You’ve got these,” he grinned, positioned the syringe, shot her high in the thigh with a burst of power, “Muscles, love.”

She’d flinched. He smiled, the same troubling triumphant smile of the Viper. “I bet that hurts like a bloody…ut-ut, now love.” His hand slapped the painful spot, banded around her thigh to stop her kick. “I see your intentions. I will kill the pitcher.” He squeezed her leg, patted the muscle.

"Now, since you're so naughty, spread your legs." He moved her feet wide. "Pretty panties." He sat back, studied her exposed body. "Very pretty. Cristina looked like you, a little prettier maybe, but she was soft. Cried a lot. Until I gave her the Eros." He grinned. "Then she was wild. Wonderful drug, Eros. Don't you think? It binds you forever to the man who mated you. Did you know that? That your first preference will always be for the Viper?" He checked his watch. "Cristina will be wanting me about now. Madly. And in a few more hours, you will be mad for someone as well, Tigressa."

She said nothing. Just stared at him as the drug began to move into her system. Calculating the time if it was Eros. She might have eight hours. It took two to get across the pond in the faster jets. At least an hour for the drug to begin to cause effects. Depending on the dose… he could have maxed her out. Intramuscular injections would quicken faster. She wasn't a virgin to the drug either. The echo effect would engage. Her levels could shoot up, be out of control, up to a hundred, in no time ...

He chuckled. Instantly her eyes blinked. She'd lost her focus. Feared. Her gaze narrowed, fixed again to his common brown eyes.

No matter the dose, she would want Joshua. Her preference would only be for Joshua. Anyone else would only make her mad, extremely mad. If he wanted a tiger, he was getting ready to get one.

The plane descended. Slowed. A surge of thrusts as it began to hover. Harry stood. "Now. You're going to do what I say or people you care about are going to wish you did." He undid her seatbelt, then the first cuff, removed the second and left it on the seat. "Stand up."

She did, pulling down her dress, adjusting her coat. Harry's hands began to weave the satin ribbon back through the eyelets, leaving it loose, exposing her skin, until he stopped short and tied the bow at her cleavage. He smiled. "Perfect." Laughed. "He's going to love you in this. Wrapped up with a bow like a gift ought to be."

There was Russian. The taunting and mocking of lewd male joking as Harry cuffed her to his waist band.

"After you." He followed. At the door of the hover jet he told her to duck, then with an arm wrapped around her, escorted her from the helipad. At once men were standing at their station to greet them in bright red coats. An incoming border patrol stationed on the roof of Babel with a check point. A man in a red trench coat welcomed their party to the International Inner Port City, asked to see identification. Checking it as he looked at each face. His skin was very black. His eyes white. His smile bright. His English accented but very clear.

Harry handed him their ID's. Global bills folded inside hers.

"Pendragon," he nodded as the scanner cleared him. "How is Latvia?"

"Good."

"I don't show that the Tigrissa ever left the International Inner Port City last fall. How then is she returning today?"

"Oh?" At once more money was on the ID. "Check again. She was in a hurry last time she departed. Perhaps the scanner missed her."

"Ah, no-no. Here she is. Yes." He smiled wide, pocketed the bribe. "Here she is. Welcome back, Mademoiselle."

Red Remmi was sitting at his table on the second floor when he got the call. He rose, went to the railing as he heard the Herald blow his horn, announce her name very loudly, "The Viper's Tigrissa."

It was a grand entrance that caught the attention of the powerful who made it their business to watch all those who entered Babel. The woman stood, with chin lifted and posture proud. Those hot gold eyes full of the kind of fury you expect to see in a man. Around her was the kind of entourage you expect to see for a queen. And beside her, smiling oh, so boldly was the Pendragon.

Red, too smiled, stepping back. He made the phone call not because it was his job, but because he had the means to subtly shift the power. "It's Red," he announced, "The Pendragon just brought the Tigrissa into Babel." He pocketed his phone, glanced up to the fourth floor. Saw Sheikh Khaleel also at the railing. Their gazes connected, held for only an instant, before the Sheikh turned away and Red went back to the recon work of observing.

For a moment it overwhelmed her, the sounds of the many languages, the clutter of faces, the syncing of gazes. The evil here, battling itself for control, like a mighty game of king of the hill. Lust was hot, it came in scorching male glances. Was displayed by too many women, dressed in too little, showing too much. Their fragrance overpowering her senses. She could hear the ice, rattling in empty glasses, diluting resolves and expounding expressions. She could sense the anger of enemies. Hate, such a powerful bitter poison, fueling the undercurrent energy of this place. She could feel her blood, the restless surging of it already. Her body racing, yanking at the reins to break free of her will, her spirit. She could taste her own lust, a growing fear, she swallowed it back, prayed now fervently, prayed, expected the measure of grace to come, any time now, it would come. She couldn't trust herself. She would trust in the name of the Lord her God.

Red couldn't hear the words he said but he saw their effect. Jaclyn slapped the Pendragon. There was an eruption of laughter then an eerie silence as everyone but the Tiger looked at the Viper.

Red moved closer, heard Jaclyn tell the boy, "Forgive me, Eros makes me edgy." She'd rolled her r's and held out the last e sound dramatically. Latin. So very Latin, that for a moment he swore she was another. He blinked. Time warping back. To Sainte Maria, the Spanish woman who escaped the Adder right before he died and his son took power, took Felicia. He thought of her. For only a moment he thought of LaRue's mother as he watched the girl's golden gaze slowly move to the Viper with heated hate. She lifted her chin and Pendragon back handed her, brutally.

All of Babel in a collective gasping, "Ah." The sound a babbling of curious awe and very little outrage. The people here entitled to find entertainment. Red looked up at the fourth floor, the Sheikh had narrowed his gaze, then given an order with a very subtle lifting of his right hand.

Now, Red smiled.

Jaclyn wiped her mouth. She'd been surprised, but her training had honed her reflexes, her body automatically moving and taking energy instead of blocking it. She'd stayed on her feet when he struck her, looking past his violence to its source. He was showing off for Viper.

She called him by name. "Yrasrevda Tsilevich, you are the devil's own."

"I warned you." He walked to the right, taking her in. "I clearly told you, not to take long, Tigrissa." He circled around to the left. "I've never known a woman to stay in the restroom for nine months. Did you deliver my bastard there?" He smiled, tilted his head, asked, "Will you not slap me too if I come in range?"

"You know I will."

"Yes." He said the word with confidence. "I know you will." He came close now, his gaze a study of her as Pendragon roughly gathered her hands, wrenching them behind her back. "I have motivated you to train. You are stronger." He smiled. "I like that. What you've done, because of me." He took a breath, bowed out his chest, his tattoo playing within the open neck of his shirt. "You think you escaped but you were not free of me. You can never be free of me."

Freedom isn't the absence of something it is the presence of someone. The words came to her as she felt the binding hold of her enemy's power to immobilize her. She swept the circle of strong men, saw beyond them to the captivated audience who would stand by and do nothing, entertained by the evil and titillated by its power. Where the spirit of the Lord is there is freedom. She knew the truth, Jesus with her always. Free, she faced the very devil.

He'd come close now, his gaze traveling down her dress. "The memories, they come to you unbidden. The echoes that drive you, drain you. The fear that will not let you rest. The fury because I took what can never be returned. Do you want to kill me for what I did?" he asked her, touching the bow, tugging slowly on the ends of the satin.

"I could care less about you."

"You've been taught how to kill, no? How do you fantasize about killing me?" She felt her dress give, the tension ease down the center as it opened.

"I've forgiven you, Viper. Left you for God to judge. You have no power over me." The statement was flat and emotionless. Her sigh, one of boredom.

He gave her a look, right before he laughed, a look of rage. "Oh, but I do." He lowered his voice, had the crowd leaning in. "Power to untie your dress, to take whatever I want. Before this crowd, before the hour is over you will take my hand, willingly." His voice was confident and loud. "You will beg for what only I can give you. Beg, like you did before. Break, beneath me from the pleasure. The tattoo might be gone, but I marked you forever. You lust for me, even now."

"No," she shook her head. Her gaze fixed on him, her smile confident. "You have no power over me because I chose to release you to God. I'm not like you, lusting after absolute power, needing to control.

"When you couldn't break me physically, you used a chemical. Made me into a puppet. You know the problem with puppets? They're not real. The lust wasn't real, the pleasure wasn't real, the power wasn't real. You were deceived." She stepped toward him now. "That's why God gave man free will. He did not make us puppets to control us. Then man's love, obedience, worship would be counterfeit. God gave us free will to choose

Him. And when we do, when we choose to accept His salvation, choose to love, obey, worship our Creator, it is real and it is very powerful."

"Your God is impotent."

"My God is sovereign. God does not use His sovereignty to supersede man's choices, to stop your wickedness or mine like a great puppet master, he lets you chose, lets the choices play out to their end where every man is finally judged and God's sovereign rule is also seen and finally judged by us for what it is, good. God makes all things work together for good for those who love and trust Him. That promise will prove true. My God is omnipotent."

"Your God?" He asked the crowd. "Where is this God? Let him show himself to us," he demanded. Turned in a circle, waited for dramatic effect. He looked at her, shrugged his shoulders. "Your God can not help you here. I get to make my choice and He is powerless to stop my free will." He smiled, his hand closed over her neck, the grip caused a surge of her blood. A reminder of the Eros let loose in her body. "And you, are mine."

"Jac-lyn Mar-ie Coop-er." Her name was called out in distinct syllables from a man in a group of white robed Sheikhs. The five men had the same red and white patterned head dresses, the same fat black coils that sat like crowns on their heads. The same elegant robes, the edges embroidered with gold.

At once all the Russian spectators seemed to come to arms. The balconies of Babel filled with the nations. The Chinese and Columbians. The Koreans and South Africans. There were the platinum blond Swedes and the bright red-headed Highlanders, the dark almond eyes of the Jordanians and the dark skin of the Kenyans. The tension rose to a pounding level of anticipation in the center hall of Babel. The wind of power blowing across the sand, stirring in an unseen direction.

"The daughter of John Jax-son Coop-er, the owner of the CX ranch of Texas," he announced.

“Yes.” She met the dark eyes of the Sheikh, saw at once his power and took advantage of his surprise arrival to tug her wrists free of Pendragon with a basic self-defense move. She bowed her head in respect as her hand tugged the satin ties, gathered back her dress, secured the ribbon in a tight firm yank.

“Your father has come.” His hand lifted, presented another group. “And we are to talk of,” his gaze shifted, his eyes like piercing arrows as they looked at the Viper. “Horses.”

She was surprised. To see her father here, standing with a group of business men she did not recognize. Behind the suits were several men in the battle gear of *Stratia*.

“Jaclyn,” he said her name in a way that bore no emotion. It was the tone he used when he was very serious but incredibly controlled. He had his game face on. The face he’d worn when he played football against his staunchest rival. The anger he showed when he was out to win. He was dressed in a very dark suit, the shirt white optic in contrast, the tie blood red. His gold watch, a family heirloom from his grandfather, lay heavy across his wrist. One of his three Super Bowl rings was worn on his right hand from the game he considered his best and had won him the MVP award. He didn’t wear it very often. She realized he had not come in haste, but prepared.

“Daddy.”

Jaxson pointed to her left, a silent order to step aside as he stepped forward, looked the Viper in the eyes and stated in his best Texas accent, “And this Russian must be the horse thief.”

39

Jaxson was set to kill the snake. He had a loaded gun and every intention of taking his life and paying the price for the privilege. He'd been secretly set to do it. Plotted and planned, maneuvered and manipulated his way into this moment. Agreeing to the plan of *Stratia*, to his part in it even as he incorporated his own revenge. Now here he was. Finally the moment he'd waited nine months for and he wasn't afraid.

He was ashamed. Ashamed that his daughter would be the one to teach him the truth of his rebellion. Again.

Jaclyn Marie Cooper. With her golden eyes and his dimpled smile. She'd stood in front of him at two and changed his life forever. Taught him over and over the truth of love and the power of God as she grew. Now she stood in front of him a woman, forgiving her enemy and renouncing his power over her. She had pursued forgiveness. And as she had healed, he had secretly pursued vengeance, positioning himself for this opportunity to take it. With a deep breath he repented, prayed. Received a powerful provision of peace with the grace to overcome the temptation as he took his hand off the weapon.

Immediately his enemy attacked as he repented. The Viper taking possession of his daughter with a molesting touch. "Is this the man you would cry for, Tigrissa? Daddy? Are you the one to give her such spirit?" he questioned with disbelief. "She is no horse." He laughed. "You raised a tiger, and I thoroughly enjoyed her."

Joshua felt the energy rise up in him in a righteous fury with those words. He had stood in the background, but now he stepped forward. Faced evil. He was called to confront it, fight it. He was anointed and he would be empowered. He would protect. And right now the person to protect was Jaxson Cooper. His father-in-law had a lust in his eyes, a lust to kill. Joshua moved against the temptation at once in the name of his Lord.

"Say nothing," the Fury spoke boldly. "He is not worth answering." He set his feet and crossed his arms. His uniform was battle gear, but he'd removed the jacket, chosen the short sleeve shirt. His tattoo clearly shown. His eyes hot with the energy, his spirit totally controlled, the calm a power in itself. The deceptive eye of the storm.

"What's this?" The Viper cocked his head, looked at Joshua. "Does your servant give you orders, Tex? Does a boy tell a man what to do?" He raised a taunting brow at Jaxson. Waited. "Is this not the man that rode your filly all the way home, Mr. Cooper. Yet, he cannot even buy the grain it takes to feed her." He shook his head, laughed, then looked Joshua in the eye. "You have no place here, Fury of *Stratia*. You are a servant."

Joshua slowly grinned. Perhaps finally realizing as the Spirit made every piece fall into place the impossible truth. "Thank you." He smiled very subtly. "That is the highest compliment you could give me. I am a servant." His eyes lit with fire, the energy humming from the Holy Spirit within him. "A servant of the Most High God. And you are a serpent, ripe for judgment."

"Who is your God to judge me?" he scoffed. "Where is He? Will He come down and face me?" He looked up and around.

Jaclyn stepped up, looking at her Uncle. He nodded and from her pocket she pulled a blue document. Joshua watched her smile, watched his wife turn and ask her enemy, "Are you Yrasrevda Tsilevich originally of Latvia, now a prince of Russia and its new Czar?"

The Viper curled a cunning smile. "Yes, I am the Czar of Russia."

Jaclyn placed the document in his hand. "You have been officially served."

"Served?" Yrasrevda looked at the paper he now held. He laughed, mocking her, yet immediately the red coated soldiers of the IIPC had closed ranks around them. His hand went into the air, his heavy ring flashing in the lights. Fingers snapping an order. At once two men came in a hurry. He handed off the paper. Said two words in Russian.

"Let me translate for you, please. Since the law is a language you haven't been taught. You have no prudence, Viper. You are a huge Hedonist." She told him without emotion.

"And that is a crime?"

"On the night in question, you broke the International laws of privacy twice by entering a woman's restroom here in Babel. Once, while I was inside. You and one of your men, now deceased, came into the restroom, took my dress and drugged me with Ares."

"None of that can be proven," he scoffed. "There is no video record of what goes on in a restroom."

"That is hearsay," one of his men argued.

A man handed her a computer screen, she held up the thin tablet before him and played the video image. There you are, Yrasrevda Tsilevich, going into the women's restroom and here you come leaving it with my hideous dress."

"So fine me."

"Oh, they will," Jaclyn nodded. "The first time the misdemeanor will cost you a hundred thousand a person for you, Yrasrevda Tsilevich and the deceased Mr. Borg."

"Write them a check," he ordered a man. Smiled at her. "That is less than you won me at the craps table, Tigrissa."

"Um." She shrugged, showed the next image. "Exactly seventeen minutes later, you broke the law again. You and an army of your men—one, two, three, four, five, oh my! It's hard to count how many of you have raced through the door of the women's restroom. Looking for something, or someone." She looked at him. "Fourteen men in a women's restroom. That cost you seven hundred thousand Global credits for those men. And because it was your second time to break the privacy law, two hundred thousand for you. Paid of course, to the International Inner Port City. I believe that is an even million, Mr. Tsilevich, in fines for your... law breaking. Did we win that much at the craps table?"

He laughed. Looked at her father, "She is a cunning little—"

"The funds are due today. If you cannot transfer the fine for these progressive misdemeanors, you can serve out the time in jail." She said flatly.

"I will not go to that sewer of a jail." He told her frankly, "I have the funds." His gaze suddenly went very dark. "And you are playing a very dangerous game."

Then the herald blew his horn again.

"The Pendragon's Filly," was suddenly and loudly announced from the grand entry door of Babel with the piercing shriek of trumpets. "Her Royal Highness Sheikha Haifa bint Khaeel bin Kalfin Al-Thani."

Everyone turned to look. Most, clearly startled. No proper Princess of the House of Saud came into Babel, nor displayed her hair, in all its long glorious magnificence, in public. Her name might have been known, linked for years with stunning beauty, but her face would not be recognized. A high born daughter of a Sheikh clearly kept protected for her husband alone. Here and now the tall, stunning woman was seen by all. Draped in gold, the fabric fine and iridescent, the style classic. And beside her was

LaRue. He brought her forward, her dark eyes clearly drugged, now terrified. Her gait was fragile, her steps slow in the narrow skirt, her hand holding tightly to LaRue's arm as he protectively walked her into the crowded area. Her eyes were cast down, her head bowed. Behind her came Petra and a team from *Stratia*.

"Brother," LaRue greeted Harry. "I found the," he looked at the Sheikh, at Jaxson, then back at his brother and shrugged, "*Filly* you've talked so much about. The filly of our father's rival. That has given you such a fine race. No one has seemed to know where she was—lost for months. But alas, here she is—found, in your stable of all places when I went to find Mr. Cooper's daughter."

"She is not mine," Pendragon declared at once.

"Oh?" He lifted a pendant. A gaudy gold Pendragon that was strung around the woman's neck. "Is this not yours?"

LaRue looked at his brother, watched Harry glance at their father.

"You have quite an appetite for . . . horses, Harry. You came to the states. Caused a vehicular accident and took what you thought was Mr. Cooper's *filly* from me. But, alas, the bays were well matched and when you rode her you realized she was not Mr. Cooper's *filly* but Mr. Monoca's *filly* with Spanish blood. So you left her on my roof, taking," he nodded at Jaxson, "Mr. Cooper's *filly* to bring to your father. Now I find the Sheikh Khaeel bin Kalfin Al-Thani's *filly* tied securely to your own bed." He held up one of her hands, the wrist wearing a jeweled handcuff.

"No." Again Harry glanced at his father, proclaimed, "She is not mine."

"No, she was not." The Sheikh moved to his daughter. Broke the chain from her neck. Held the pendant in his hand. "But now you are my son-in-law, Pendragon. By holy law. You are her husband and will come with me to my house, to pay the wages of her bride price."

"No!"

He stepped back but a crowd of white robed men had already circled around them.

"She is not mine!"

The Sheikh raised his hand, held the Pendragon's pendant. "Is this not yours? Your sign. Or is she marked somewhere else with another unholy brand?" His nostrils flared above a thick dark mustache.

"Father?" Harry looked at the Viper but met only silence. "She is fast. Passionate. Tell him. She was not mine alone but," he gulped now, fear made him pale, pride made him exclaim, "It has taken many riders to quench her demands. She was not mine alone but many had her."

The Viper shrugged and said without emotion, "But she can have only one husband, per her father's holy law. I have many sons." He turned away from Harry as several robed men took hold of him.

"Father!—"

"You must pay the fines that are due. Abide by the code of . . . International law. You do not bring accusations into my house," Viper calmly made the proclamation.

"Adieu, Harry," LaRue called out. "Their holy laws state that they cut off a thief's hands for stealing, what must they do for rape, eh?"

Harry cursed him, charging, issuing threats of revenge, then insisting as the Sheikhs took him in hand, "She is not mine. I never touched her. She is my brother's. His! LaRue brought her here." Two men took him away, his shrieks now curses.

"Your daughter," LaRue presented her to Sheikh Khaeel bin Kalfin Al-Thani.

"Is dead to me," the Sheikh stated flatly, never looking at the girl as he turned away and left, his men following, their robes billowing out, the edges dripping gold, their walk proud and slow. As they lost sight of them, Harry's disturbance mysteriously was hushed into silence.

Jaclyn looked at the beautiful girl. Shocked to silence as was everyone else. Unsure what to do. It was her father that moved. Spoke softly to the woman, nodded at Petra. Gave LaRue a look then called her name. "Jaclyn, it's time for us to go."

The Viper held up a hand. The room suddenly coming to the balls of their feet. "We abide by international law here. And clearly," he looked at Jaclyn now, smiled so slowly, "Your privacy was breached, Tigrissa."

"It is Jaclyn Marie Cooper. And I am not a tiger nor a filly."

"But you are a jewel thief." He moved to her, his hold like iron now. "You stole the Czar's Serpent."

"Um. I don't recall that. I was drugged, heavily in your presence."

"Where are my diamonds?"

"Your diamonds? I believe a certain museum in Paris claims the rights to them."

"They are mine."

"Mine. Mine. Mine," she mocked him. "You sound like a two-year-old, you hissing snake."

He hoisted her up off her feet, demanded now very softly. "You had them on in the video, when you walked into the restroom. They were gone from your neck in the trash room. Now, where are they?"

"Um."

"You are not leaving until I have the Czar's Serpent. And these fine men in red coats will detain you here with me until I do."

"No, they will read me my rights and deport me back to my country of origin. America. I'm afraid jewel heisting is grand larceny which is a felony, Viper. Under International Inner Port City laws, felonies are not prosecuted, indicted, nor detained here. You better know the laws if you're going to use them against me. Have I broken any misdemeanors?"

"Jaclyn." Her father once again called her. She stepped back, *Stratia* stepping up now as many Russians came to arms.

"How are you feeling?" Viper asked her in a low voice. "Stepping away from me? Is your blood surging? Your feet restless. Spots hot and burning on your sensitive flesh? There is an ache, that awful ache unquenched and driving you. Ah, look, my Arabian filly is feeling it. See how she looks at me."

Jaxson stepped in front of the princess.

"LaRue, bring me the daughter who has no father." He swept the crowd. "LaRue!" Russian words biting out orders as everyone looked for him. But LaRue had slipped away.

Jaclyn tried to, at once Viper clenched a tight fist around her wrist. Tugged her around. Brought her back to his chest to face him. A secure hold, an intimate hold that fit her lusting body to him as his men surrounded them and the two sides began to argue.

"You mean nothing to me now." His gaze was hard, his hold violent. "One of so many. But I, am the only one who had you first. You are mine. Did they tell you? That your preference will always be for me, first. Not Fury. Or that ball player. Me."

There was a knife, a wicked thin blade that tapered to a sharp point and paralyzed her. In a move he sliced through the quick knot that had once been a pretty bow, her dress giving way opening again as the slick satin quickly uncoiled through the eyelets down the front. Then with a move he'd sliced open her bra, proclaimed, "You will stand here naked and they can do nothing. If you know the law then you know this. Even *Stratia* must work covertly in Babel. And if even one of them pulls a firearm, they will be arrested by these men in red." His voice purred with a haunting hiss of vodka. The scent bringing with it a hundred horrible memories. "Look at your father, how he suffers. Wants to kill me. Perhaps he will pull the first gun. Or Fury, the servant, will he die for you, kill for you and rot in prison for his principles? Come with me, now, come and protect them." He looked at her with that titanic power. "You alone have the power to save them and I alone have all that you lust for. Yes," he purred, moved her closer. "Only you can save them."

She'd stopped praying. Been listening. To his lies. Letting fear persuade her to his temptation by looking at the knife. Like Eve, looking at the fruit.

Seeing. Thinking. Doubting. Hadn't she learned. It's not what I see. It's what I know. I know how to fight.

"If the LORD had not been on our side — let Israel say — if the LORD had not been on our side when men attacked us . . .

She used the Word and her body just moved. Used its training. Leverage. Skill and surprise. She was out of his grip. Breaking free of his ranks. Clutching her dress as her forearm dripped from a long, deep wound.

There was a growl. The Fury going nuclear with that zealous heat. She could feel it. Held up her hand, begged the Lord to protect him, her father, not daring to even give them a glance as she defused the situation the only way she could, announced. "He wants his diamonds back."

The room fell silent. Her blood dropped, like fat wet tears onto the black marble floor from the screaming cut.

She repeated, "He wants his diamonds back." She began to walk, hoping he would following. Leading him now. From the protection of her Father, Stratia, the crowd of onlookers. None too steady. Her arm bleeding. Screaming now. The blood like a river through her binding fingers. Holding her dress, the wound. Praying. Going through the door of the women's restroom and taking a paper towel, holding it to her forearm. Waiting. For what seemed like forever. As she prayed out the battle cry of God's word.

Finally. The door opened. She smiled, secretly, looking down as he came in so confidently with his army of Russian men.

"Tigrissa," he growled with bitter control as if he announced victory.

She turned around and stood against his fury. "Yrasrevda Tsilevich of Latvia, you are now under arrest." From behind them came a unit of men dressed in red coats with weapons drawn. Among them was Ian Remmi all in black and wearing a frown.

"You have broken the Global privacy law two times already. Paid fines. But still you don't learn, Viper. That is why on the third violation there is not just a fine. There is a nice sit in jail. Ninety days. If you behave. And these men of yours." She dramatically counted them, "They will be fined, either for a first violation or," she pointed at two of them. "A second. That will add up. Too bad you killed poor Borg and Czenky the Bear of Moscow. They could have kept you company in the International Inner Port City jail." She scrunched up her nose. "I've heard it has a stinky nickname, the Sewer. Apparently the place has quite a horrible odor and you most certainly will sit there. No one on earth gets away with breaking the privacy laws. Not a president or a prince or the new Czar of Russia. You will serve your time. Excuse me." She walked away as a man began to read him his rights. Then ran, into her father's arms as she squealed with joy. "I did it!"

"You're hurt. What did he do?"

"They're arresting him." She didn't care. Smiled as they heard the uproar.

"Let me see." It was the Fury who took her arm.

"I'm okay." She was giddy. Silly with it. Smiling. Feeling the drug. The desire flare as Joshua touched her and she told him how she'd slipped free of Viper, but caught the point of the blade. "I don't like knives but I trusted the training. It worked."

There was a low growl.

Her father's concerned words.

"It's a deep cut, if we don't get it closed it will scar."

She didn't listen, just curled into Joshua, wanting him. Just him. Alone. Now. She whimpered. She took his hand, kissed the scar on his palm that he bore for her, because of her. Jaclyn smiled up at him. "I don't care about the scar." She quoted his words now, "I'll wear the scar and remember the victory. It was a mighty one for me. I needed to do this. Know I could do this. See that the law has a certain order and power. Evil's wounds become victory's scars. I'll heal."

Fury told her, "We need to go. Get you out of here."

"I can't miss this." She looked toward the bathroom. "Seeing him led away in handcuffs."

"Don't give him an opportunity," Joshua counseled, looking at Jaxson.

Her father agreed, "We should go."

But they brought him out. With his hands behind his back in handcuffs, the tattoo on his chest alive with color, the symbols slithering in the open neck. He was calling orders at once in Russian. Then his dark gaze penetrated her. "This isn't over," he hissed. "You silly Spanish whore. You daughter of a cunning witch. I had forgotten you existed but now I will never forget. Your mother and father will mourn and you shall rot in a place worse than a sewer, you shall find yourself in my pit." His gaze swept them all as he announced his intentions, then came back to Jaclyn. "We are not done, Tigrissa. We will never be done. You shall live in fear of me the rest of your very short life."

"Take him away," Ian Remmi ordered, looking at Marc he nodded toward the elevator. "Your ride is on the roof."

"Harry Olstrom gave me Eros," she told them as Fury bound her wound. "Almost two hours ago. I don't have my PDA. Don't know my levels."

"Here." Her father handed his PDA to her as they entered the elevator.

She took her blood, punched the cube into his PDA as Marc said, "Hand me that gun, Jaxson."

Her father looked at him. Marc's hand was out. "I don't want problems for you at the check point. The gun. I imagine it's a high quality graphite that will move untraceably through any scanner, but nonetheless, I'll take it."

"You're disarming me?"

They squared off. "I am."

"That gun's expensive, brother."

"Not as expensive as what it would cost me to raise up another, Fury. He'd have stepped in front of you. Taken the bullet meant for your enemy to protect you."

They both looked at Joshua, then Jaxson told him. "Once Jaclyn forgave him, how could I stand and take revenge?" He took the pistol from the holster, handed it to his brother-in-law.

"How long have you been wearing that?"

"A while. Now it's no longer an issue."

Marc handed it to Eli. "Hold that for Mr. Cooper."

"Yes, sir." His gaze ran over the gun.

"And Jaclyn, we don't stand by for evil. They'll take any and every opportunity to spread their lies. Once our job is done, we move out. I should have moved you. Forgive me," Marc told her. "We don't respond to their words, but we do respect their power, be alert."

They took the elevator up to the roof. A team in black was waiting. The area secure. Marc talked to the border patrol unit, cleared them all at the check point. A helicopter was already firing up, the blades slowly wiping the air into a whistling wind.

Joshua took the PDA from her, read it. "You're at a sixty-four." He showed her the read out. "The Sheikh's daughter is in the forties."

She looked at her watch. "I can make it to Heatherwood. I have time."

"Ida sent this." He handed her a hard stainless brief case. "In case you can't. The girl might need your help. I'm sending Petra, two other female agents. You'll take the hover transport. We'll flank you, follow. If you need anything—"

She hugged him tight. Held him close. She could smell his scent, feel his strength. Then she heard his prayer, the sacred words. She couldn't pull away, but he helped her. Commanded her, "Go, Jaclyn. They're waiting."

"You'll be okay," her father told her. "I'm proud of you, Jaxie."

40

Three men waited in the small private area of Heatherwood. It had been three long days. Lexi had told them she was coming out today. She and Cristina. Haifa would take longer. The Ares was still demanding. The detox could be several weeks. The emotional healing longer. The echoes assumed.

Brett paced the room. He had said little but his body language told much. He was anxious.

The Fury leaned against a wall, his arms crossed, his face blank. The eye of the storm, he wore jeans, flip flops and an old black motorcycle T-shirt. Wouldn't his daughter be amazed the man owned jeans . . .

Jaxson grinned, looked down at the ground, received the light thought in the midst of so much serious considerations. He prayed, knowing it was time, said, "Why don't you boys take a seat?"

They did, at opposite ends of the couch.

"Cristina's going to be released today?"

Brett nodded. "She told me this morning. I've been keeping up with her through text messages."

"You're her donor," Jaxson said. "My nephew told me. That's honorable of you, Brett."

Now he looked at Fury. “Cletus told me you’re Jaclyn’s donor.”

Fury gave a single silent nod.

“That you had to . . . help her when she escaped. There was no hospital or center like this. Why didn’t you tell me?”

“Not all information needs to be made known.”

“Apparently not.” He rose again, paced. “You played me. Knowing how she felt about you.”

“No. I took orders. Obeyed them, sacrificially, because I knew it was best for her.”

“They used me.”

“*Stratia* used an opportunity,” Jaxson took over. “They offered you a part in helping her. You agreed to be an asset.”

“I was a means to an end.”

“No one knew the end, but I trusted the means. *Stratia’s* wisdom in making them all effective to protect my daughter.”

“I fell in love with her,” Brett stated with honest emotion. “You can’t be close to Jaclyn and not fall in love with her.” There was a stare, his gaze holding on Joshua, then slowly, finally moving to Jaxson in the silence. “You have a special daughter.”

“Yes.”

There was more silence. For several beats the three of them lost to their own thoughts. With his gaze on the floor now Brett said softly, “She thinks she distracted me from Cristina. Believes there could be something between us. That made me angry . . . at first. But these last three days . . .” He shook his head. “Before I volunteered to be her donor, they told me she could get pregnant. I knew then, that Jaclyn might be right. That I might care for her because I didn’t question it. I didn’t want her donor to be a stranger. I wanted it to be me.” He looked at Jaxson. “And if she’s pregnant, we’ll marry.”

“You’re a good man,” Jaxson said at once. “Forgive me if I misled you, Brett, but God seems to have a plan in all this. We can trust him.”

Brett nodded and there was silence again. A long space of it.

"Are you in love with her?" Brett asked the Fury.

"You can't be close to Jaclyn and not fall in love with her," Joshua answered him with his own words.

"You should tell her."

"Right now she needs her father—"

"He should tell her," Brett told Jaxson. "It would make a difference, sir."

He looked down at the text message on his phone. "He has a few things he'll have to tell her today. She's coming with Lexi now."

Joshua closed his eyes, prayed. Brett stood.

Jaclyn smiled, drawing strength from Lexi. Glad to have her stepmother beside her to greet the welcoming party. Her father held her, gave her a kiss, stroked her cheek. "How do you feel?"

"Stronger. Better," she told the room. "Glad it's over. Brett." She went to him next, held him close, hugging him hard. "How is Cristina?"

"Healing." He nodded, stepping back from her. "She's coming out today too. I'm taking her home to get some things, then down to Florida to her mother's. She's going to stay there for a while."

"How are you?"

"Fine." He nodded again. "Glad it's over." He repeated her words. "Glad you're okay. I heard you were an ace over there. Read him the law, tripped him up, then locked him up."

"Yes." She tucked an errant curl back into her ponytail. "God was the ace. He helped me."

"You're going to be a brilliant lawyer, just like your stepmom."

"I'm pretty proud." Lexi beamed.

"Now that she's over being left out," Jaxson tucked Lexi close. "She was pretty angry that we left her at home."

"Um." She gave him a look. "I like to see my children's accomplishments."

"I'm proud of you," there was a pause where Brett almost said Babe, filled in with, "Jaclyn."

"Thanks." She hugged him again. Tight. Whispered, "My friends call me, Jaxie. And I want us to be friends. Take care of Cristina. You know how. I'll be praying for you both. Here, anytime you need me. Okay?"

"Thanks, Jaxie."

They both pulled away, nodded. Smiled.

Then she looked at Joshua. Standing with hands in the pockets of a faded pair of jeans. A black T-shirt that advertised for Harley Davidson in San Diego stretched tight across his chest. Flip flops on his feet. There was emotion, it just sprang up from some deep well in her. She couldn't say what she wanted to say, so she simply told him, "Thanks again, Joshua."

"It's a nice day for a walk," Jaxson said looking at Joshua. She watched them silently communicate. Knew there had been a previous discussion. Felt an unreasonable surge of jealousy that she couldn't quite identify. It was then that her father slipped his hand into hers, squeezed. "I know you're ready for some fresh air and there's some things you two need to talk about." He looked at Joshua and told them both, "Go on," as he led her forward a step then let go.

They walked in silence. Anxiety rose as Joshua said nothing. Simply led them on a walk across a street, to a park. His strides were slow. The pace easy through a winding trail canopied with trees. A space between them. She looked straight ahead. Found it harder to breathe. To wait. Wondering about the things her father thought they needed to talk about. Finally she said, "What is it?" as she forced them to stop. She looked at him. His gaze was guarded, his eyes that fierce blue, the lashes thick.

"How are you?"

"I'm okay," she answered. "Good, I guess, now that it's finished."

"I never wanted you to endure that again."

"It's done." She saw his concern, exhaled, assured him, "I'm fine."

"You pushed yourself too far. You were almost a hundred when you hit Heatherwood."

"I made it."

"You fight it. You don't have to."

"I hate Eros. What it does. I won't give in without a fight."

"I understand." There was a nod. "It's hard to be the one watching, waiting. Worried."

"You shouldn't be worrying."

"I work it out in prayer."

"How was my dad?"

"He was proud of you. We all were."

"LaRue? What happened to him?"

"He's disappeared for a while but Marc will find him. In the end, he did the right thing."

She nodded. Troubled. "I thought he was our friend."

"Maybe your friendship helped him do what was right. God used it. Rescued Haifa."

"Brett? How's he been with all this? Have you talked?"

There was a beat of silence then he told her, "He's been helping us, Jaclyn."

"Helping us?"

"*Stratia*."

"Helping *Stratia*? With?"

"Viper."

"How?"

"We asked him to—"

"Date me?" She stepped back.

He stepped forward now. "He came on board. After you met. We talked—"

"When?"

"After you met."

Her brows were low, her gaze fixed. "After the Eros night. You talked to him. Explain how that went."

"Your father rode back to New York with him. Then your Uncle Marc met him at the airport. They had a discussion. Days later another. I was included."

"And you decided he was a good man. *Stratia* material. Sign him on as an asset and gave him an assignment. Date the Hummingbird and keep her out of trouble."

"No, it wasn't like that."

"Just say what it was like then, Fury."

"It was about the First Amendment. Someone took your picture and we couldn't stop them from publishing it. The first picture put you at risk. Forced us to go on the offensive to determine Viper's reaction and intentions. Brett agreed to the security risks. To follow your uncle's plan. To check in with me. To talk with your father. To take you places where the press could get more pictures. No one could guarantee you would agree to see him. Date him. Stay out of trouble or keep him from falling in love with you."

"Um." She was silent for about a second then erupted. "Does he know about us? What you did for me? Or did you keep him in the dark about that assignment just like you've kept me in the dark about his."

"I never told him about us but Cletus did recently, when they took Cristina to Heatherwood."

"He thinks he's in love with me, Joshua."

"Yes."

"I hurt him."

"You were used by God to train him. You were part of God's plan. He'll help Cristina now. You both will. Can you see that this is bigger than just you, me, Brett? When we put the focus on ourselves we're always short-sighted to see God's greater plan. One affects many."

She sat on a bench in the sun, looking out across a small pond. There was silence, in her mind the great promise, that all things work together for good, reminded her of God's faithfulness to those called to His purposes. Suddenly she saw past her limitations, herself, or her limited understanding to the breadth of the horizon. God, present in every detail of her life, could be trusted. "Brett was part of God's plan for me."

"Yes, I believe that," Joshua agreed, sitting beside her. "He was worthy of you. To tend to you, steady you on your feet, give you confidence." He leaned forward, looked across the water. "I'm not good at this, Jaclyn. I'm hard and serious. When you cry, it makes me nervous. I don't have the words to say."

"Maybe you need to be trained."

He glanced at her. She was smiling. Slowly he gave a small grin.

"I'm a good trainer. Patient. Cooperative. Forgiving."

"You're strong, courageous, faithful, beloved by God."

"Those are beautiful words. You do have words to say, you just need some. . . courage maybe to speak them."

He took a piece of paper from his pocket. "You said something that bothered me the afternoon you asked me to go to dinner." He looked at her. "I really did have a meeting, Baby Girl."

"I know."

"But you said I'd never seen you, who you were and if I had, it would be different. It bothered me, those words. So I wrote down some things I wanted to tell you." He opened the paper. Handed it to her.

She glanced at the writing, then handed it back to him. "You should read it to me."

She saw the look, a terrified embarrassment. "I wrote them for you to read."

"And I will, but first tell me." She directed him, "Just read it, Joshua."

There was silence. Then he cleared his voice, spoke, "I want you to know the truth. I've seen you, Jaclyn. Standing in your freedom before we left the train. You stared out the window and I watched you praise our God after He'd delivered you from the Eros.

"I've seen you, Jaclyn. I've seen you dine with my men, bless them with Grace and toast their courage. I've seen you run to your father. Meet Denise and Nathan. Fight for our children.

"I've seen you, Jaclyn. Dressed up in beauty. Naked, cold, sick with vulnerability. Resurrected from a fever, laughing with your family, using the law to find justice. I see God's Spirit working in you and it is beautiful.

"You are still smart, pure, certain. You are strong, courageous, faithful, beloved… by God. He longs for you. Abide in Him. Be, until you become who He's called you to become.

"When I look at you, I see her already."

He looked at her with those electric blue eyes framed by the softness of those thick, long lashes and held out the paper. Nodded.

She took the letter. Tears were in her eyes but she blinked and read it three times. Heart beating. Soul stirring. Longing.

"Thank you. This means," she couldn't finish. Wiped her eyes. "Thank you."

He stood, drew her up beside him by the hand. "We should go back."

She kept hold of his hand and squeezed. "I… can't go back. Back," she explained. "And if I could, I wouldn't want to. You were right, God allowed the horrible to happen, was with me every moment of it. It wasn't His ideal will, He loves me and it hurt Him as I was hurt by Viper's evil choices, but God permitted it because He had a greater plan at work. I forgave Viper and it freed me from the bitterness and anger to begin to accept the good God is working out—it's mysterious and supernatural and full of love and power—for me. God really loves me," she said with very strong conviction. "And I am becoming who God called me to be. I could never be that person, fulfill my purpose if I went back to who I used to be—that innocent, naïve young daughter of my father whose faith was superficial."

There was a grin, that subtle lift at the corner of his mouth. "You'll always be a daddy's girl, Baby Girl."

"But I'm also strong, courageous, faithful and beloved. I'll be able to help Cristina and Haifa. Others as He calls me to. God is going to use me, even as he heals me."

"Yes." Fury softly ran the pad of his thumb over the long healing scar on her forearm. "He's healing you."

"I don't know the complete plan but pieces are falling into place. There's things I'm certain of—I know my heart, Joshua."

"You need time to sort things out," he interrupted.

"Things are sorted out," she tried to tell him but he was speaking over her.

"You've got law school. Healing to do. Time to mend." He looked toward the horizon.

She whispered with a plead, "Please don't be against me anymore."

There was a glaring silence. She could hear her heart, the yearning and the hurting.

"I'm for you, Jaclyn," he stated, looking at her, assuring her, searching her eyes and then blinking. With a tender firmness he told her, "Always, for you. I want God's will for you. It's bigger than you, me or us. And it will be accomplished, Jaclyn, in His time."

With that statement he led her forward, holding her hand then tucking it to his arm and drawing her closer still as he looked ahead.

Softer he said, "Let me lead, Jaclyn. Let me pace us. Trust me… to discern the timing. Wait with me… as you heal and God works. Uses you to help others. Trust God." He said a word. In Hebrew.

She looked at him, but he looked ahead, nodded to the corner where her father stood with Lexi. "Your father's waiting. He knows what's best for you right now. Loves you. Respect his wisdom. I'm trusting him, to direct your healing as I wait." He touched the cross she wore. "Brett's right," Joshua said softly. "A man can't be close to you and not fall in love."

Suddenly his arm came around her, his face leaned down to her, his voice soft and clear speaking the sacred words she didn't understand over her like a blessing. For only a moment she saw his blazing eyes then his lips touched her face, there by her ear, a light caress, a parting kiss. The first kiss. So unexpected it happened before she even understood it occurred.

Then the Fury of *Stratia* handed her to her father and walked away toward tomorrow with his promise echoing in her heart.

ABOUT THE AUTHOR

I believe words are powerful. Writing is a great privilege and carries a responsibility with its creative expression. I pray for inspiration and the right amount of balance in creating deep and compelling characters in a story world that is authentic and yet hopeful. My books are founded on relationships—spiritual, friendships, and family and forged through the real and raw stories that take place as sinners are saved by grace and sanctified through the Word of truth.

My characters are connected from one book to the next. Ones you love will show up again in another story and like old friends, I hope you're glad to see them. Ones you don't like might catch you judging them. Every good story needs an antagonist and we've all been that from time to time. We need grace for the proud and the hurting. I hope you're open to changing your opinion of some of my 'bad guys' as they are transformed. We should never assume the arm of the Lord is too short to save any character. After all, we were all at one time that "character".

Reviewers agree that my stories are raw, real, sometimes intense and might not be for readers who are looking for the classic "sweet" Christian story where characters do everything right and the story world is heavenly. Unapologetically I was not called to write that way. My style is to write it real—meaning closer to real life, exploring issues of universal importance in a God honoring way by telling the truth in love—so that story may be a tool to inspire spiritual transformation, discover the love of God and His grace & peace in Jesus Christ. My characters will never be perfect but they will proclaim to you the love, grace and mercy of a perfect God.

J.L. Kelly is an American speaker, Bible teacher & author of Christian novels that combine compelling story worlds with unforgettable characters in tremendously moving novels. Her writing is dedicated to the Lord Jesus Christ in thanksgiving for the many relationships that have inspired, redeemed, sustained, challenged, encouraged and transformed the life God has invited her to humbly fulfill for His glory.

J.L.Kelly books include-The Glory series: *The Psalm of the Offended, The Stripped, The Choice.* The new FURY Series. *The Secret*, book one of The Honor series. And also, *Pregnancy the Miracle Journey* a nonfiction devotional journal.

For more information visit author's website: www.JLKellybooks.com

Keep up with J.L. Kelly by subscribing to her blog: www.4JLKelly.com

About FURY book Three EFFECT

Jaclyn Cooper knows Viper's revenge is coming, the question is how will it arrive and what is her enemy planning. Her life is full of hope and new friendships. Even Joshua Fury seems to be opening up to her finally yet she is secretly shadowed with a fear even her growing faith can't shake loose. As the world becomes more global Jaclyn worries that everything is about to change. Two worlds are colliding and she's in the epicenter.

EFFECT is the parable of the coppiced tree.

The story of the death of our self and the new life found abiding in the love relationship with Christ as we deny that we have the capability to do anything good of ourselves. Sometimes when God shines His light on the truth it's hard to look, much less see. But what is always found is that we are in dire straits, a world of hurt. Left to our self, we are dead. Enslaved to selfishness and a prisoner of worry we are only as strong as our self-sufficiency can exert control. Desperate, we seek a rescuer outside our own strength to save us and rescued by Christ we then must by faith subject our self to God's resources and rule as we obey His Spirit where it calls us.

Effect is the story of how self-dies and Christ fills us to overflow in abundant life.

Book Three of the FURY Series is about the power of influence and the motives of the heart. It is the journey from surviving and striving to thriving and abiding.

Effect is the vision of the furious love of God so often misunderstood as it is seen in the pruning shears in the Father's hand that purge away everything but that which brings glory to Him and abundant life to us.

Read FURY book three Effect:

http://www.amazon.com/J.L.-Kelly/e/B00D9887C8

J.L. KELLY
FURY
BOOK THREE EFFECT

Books by J.L. Kelly

Don't miss the story of Jaclyn Cooper's family in the Glory Series—
The Psalm of the Offended, The Stripped and The Choice.

The Psalm of the Offended is the story of Cheyenne Cooper. Born to sing, her anointed gift of songwriting takes her farther than she ever imagined into the music world. But Cheyenne never wanted fame or fortune, just the love of one man. Yet her anointed purpose keeps putting more people, places, and problems between the love she longs for and the life God has ordained her to live. She can't silence the music and she can't stop the furious pursuing love of God from transforming her through its song. Her epic story spans glorious mountaintops and the dark valleys of the soul that will change your thinking forever.

In a world entitled to blessings and unconvinced by religion, **The Psalm of the Offended** is a raw wrestling match of spiritual reality in a tremendously moving story.

For anyone searching for the answer to why,

For anyone hurt by the tragic happenings of life and aching for healing,

For anyone stirred to finally move towards forgiveness and acceptance,

For anyone who loves music and is interested in the creative process behind the melody, **The Psalm of the Offended** is a fresh and original perspective on suffering and surrender.

This parable is a must read for anyone who has been offended by the all-powerful sovereign supremacy of God.

Could the answer to "why?" be Hallelujah?

Broken whys turn to whispered hallelujahs

as we learn to open clenched fists and lift empty surrendered hands.

This is both the posture and the praise of surrender-JLK

The Stripped is the story of Beau Cooper. Born to lead, the heir to the Chevaux ranch is patient and good. Beau does what's right in a manner that tends to bring out the absolute worst in a few very remarkable sinners. He's blessed and people envy his success. They seem to be hoping he will fail and that adds even more performance pressure to succeed. So what is a good man supposed to do when God ushers in a beautiful woman his exact opposite. Seductive with resourceful survival skills, his new neighbor is hiding something as she tries to keep things skin deep. And Beau has never been more aware that God is calling him to seek what is behind her bravado and toughness and his own judgmental attitude.

In a world of the haves and have-nots, the good boys and bad girls,

The Stripped is a layer by layer uncovering of the universal depraved soul at the heart of us all who long for redemption.

For the abused who wonder if God really sees them,

For the faithful who grow weary of doing good,

For the self-sufficient who long to trade performance for intimacy,

The Stripped is an honest unveiling of the revelation of God's justification; His gracious exchange with sinners. Their sin for His holiness. His strength for our weakness. His peace for our conflicts

A parable of how God removes our self-dependency and teaches us to abide and trust in Christ alone. Because when pride works too hard to cover everything up, God will allow us to be stripped naked and humbled. But even in our nakedness, Love makes us beautiful.

Love never looks back, instead in each moment,

it bears all things, believes all things,

hopes all things, endures all things ~JLK

The prequel to the FURY Series

The Choice is the story of prodigal son Jaxson Cooper. Born to overcome, some people grow up hungry, with an appetite that feasts too early and gives in too easily to desire even knowing the Truth. Like the mighty men of old, Jaxson battles for modern victories on a football field. A conqueror, he pursues the quest for praise, the delights of trophies, and the indulgence of pleasures. He's deceived, and too soon his desire has given birth to consequences that change his life. The Prodigal returns home to his faith a single father with new choices before him.

In a world desensitized to sin and compromising the truth about love, **The Choice** is the lesson that we choose our own way until our choices determine for us.

For anyone born with a carnal appetite who feasted too early,

For anyone who needs to believe that with second chances time tells new tales,

For anyone ready to learn that the short cut to blessing is obedience,

The Choice is the dilemma of letting go of the past and reaching forward to the future as we stand in the present crucial moment.

A parable of how the lover of our souls who established freewill also works his sovereignty to perfection for our best as we are called to trust Him.

The future is in your choices.

It's time to believe and so become

What He says that we already are~JLK

To Purchase The Choice

http://www.amazon.com/Choice-Glory-Book-3-ebook/dp/B00GQBX2QG

Book One in The Honor Series.

The Secret is the story of Jillian Montague. She's Irish and an actress and she's fallen for the Dake Family in a way she never expected. Intuitive, Jillian's learning their secrets; those sacred things people keep from knowledge or view of others, sometimes even themselves. Quarterback, Jude Dake has shared a confidence. Dr. Ellen Dake's mystery is about to be solved. Stephanie Dake and her sisters divulge their spiritual secret and Jillian realizes that handsome smile isn't the only secret-weapon John Dake's handed down to his boys. Jillian's learned sports broadcaster Dylan Dake's infamous destruction has left a trail of heartbreak and coach Dwight Dake's search for success has found her out.

Jillian's a witness to the conflict of how holding onto secrets forms a triangle—involving one and excluding another—that precariously separates and distinguishes friends. In the end the secrets they try to keep divide and breakup the very relationships they long to protect. And the most dangerous secrets of all are the ones you hide from even yourself. But God, always sees into the darkest depths of the heart and everything secret will be revealed in His timing so that we can be forgiven and free, redeemed and reconciled.

For anyone with a secret they've hidden away under shame.

For anyone who longs to have the courage to be more than their secret.

For the one who knows a secret has divided a relationship or stolen their joy.

For all of us who long to know the secret of living a life of faith.

The Secret is a story of spiritual discovery. There is a secret to faith, of love and finding hope.

The parable of a woman with a secret will remind us how you can think you really know someone but everyone has secrets. The dark are covered up. The holy are beyond understanding. And the lesson of our secrets is this; we all think we keep secrets; actually they keep us. God longs for us to be free.

To Purchase The Secret
http://www.amazon.com/dp/B00QN0PYIE

www.ingramcontent.com/pod-product-compliance
Lightning Source LLC
Chambersburg PA
CBHW072332020726
47506CB00004B/862

* 9 7 8 0 9 8 9 7 7 4 5 4 3 *